SPEED RUN

SPEED RUN

PURIFIER ▪ BOOK 3

Curator Omega

Podium

Cover design by Podium Publishing

ISBN: 978-1-0394-2502-6

Published in 2023 by Podium Publishing, ULC
www.podiumaudio.com

Had enough of the tale, passerby? Has your mind been crushed to a pulp by the deluge of horrors waiting just beyond this mundane dimension?

No?

How curious. You must be rather brave . . . That, or well versed in the multiverse's menagerie of strange occurrences. If I'm not mistaken, you've just finished the second volume of Dak Korasa's tale. Even an interdimensional being such as myself struggles to recall the myriad twists, turns, and reversals present within those pages, so let me grace you with a brief summary that will serve you in your crusade to finish the story.

At the start of the second volume, Dak and his companion—the cobalt seer Akasha—had just reached a planet of robotic monks to begin the former's mind training. You see, Akasha, in her prescient wisdom, knew Dak would not be able to withstand the treachery and reality-tainting efforts of the Unmade. Not with his ordinary, flippant mind, that is.

This being the case, Dak bonded with the inhabitants of the monastery and dutifully followed their prescribed course of study. During his stay, he learned about concepts such as Wayfarers, Wellsprings, other universes, and the vast reservoir of power that is sentience. However, he also acquired bits of other, less inspiring knowledge. One such bit was the revelation that the Unmade had been subtly influencing the course of events in the monastery's region of space for a long, long while. Another was, naturally, the fact that Scryer Narbu—head of the monastic order and pseudo–father figure to Dak—had been manipulating fate just as drastically as Chanzig.

Ah, and of course, we cannot forget the most disturbing twist. In the final confrontation between Dak, the Unmade, and Narbu, it emerged that Akasha herself had once been the Unmade's mother. Or rather, her past incarnation had served as a mother to the past incarnation of the Unmade. Whatever the case, this did little to boost Dak's spirit.

In the end, Dak was forced to slay Scryer Narbu and dismantle his scheme to absorb countless sentient minds into an enlightened collective organism. A victory . . . but perhaps in name only. When the dust settled, Dak's problems had in no way improved or been resolved. His only rewards for stopping Narbu's abomination were life-threatening injuries, an unconscious Akasha, and a pursuing Hegemony battle unit.

On the brink of death and trapped in a maze of tunnels, Dak found himself ready to surrender the hard task of living. His hand was stayed, however, by a mysterious arrival: a fellow Purifier arriving aboard a ship with stealth cloaking. The newcomer's initial words were friendly, even jovial, yet all but the most foolish of beasts know that appearances can be deceiving . . .

Particularly when the name of such a newcomer relates to being duplicitous.

Let's not get ahead of ourselves, however, or risk spoiling your reading pleasure. The third volume of this tale is less mysterious than the first, and certainly less convoluted than the second, but this is not to imply you'll be drifting off midsentence. In fact, if I may be so bold, the third volume is my favorite. Not just of the collection, but of all texts related to the phenomenon of the Purifiers. It is a masterpiece of the absurd, a crowning and apt destination on this winding road of madness . . .

In short, it is a treat to behold and ponder. So read, wanderer, and read with great diligence. Once you've reached the final word, you will never again view this universe as you once did.

As always, I remain in observation, in service, in the warp and weft of reality's fabric. Such is my existence as Curator Omega.

SPEED
RUN

1

It's a curious thing, spending time in close proximity with someone who wants to either help you . . . or brutally murder you. Some of you with truly horrendous ex-romantic partners might intimately grasp this phenomenon. As your brain works in overdrive, frantically trying to suss out which intention the stranger holds, you find that your body becomes incapable of fully adopting a comfortable stance. You're too alarmed to set your elbows down on the table or lean back, yet you're also too nervous about potentially offending your savior to let your hand stray toward your sidearm.

In short, you are trapped. Even more so in a situation like mine.

See, I'd spent the last five minutes in a pressurized can with a woman who could undoubtedly kill me with her eyes. Her aura alone—which, in light of the monks' training, felt overwhelming yet cryptic—confirmed my worst fears about her power levels.

There was nothing *outwardly* terrifying about her. She had a reasonably approachable face, and, despite her covering of high-end body armor and the selection of polished, top-of-the-line weapons magnetically attached to shelves all around us, she seemed like decent company.

I tried to take some comfort from her easy smile and the way she leaned back on her L-shaped satin couch, but I just couldn't make it all the way. I still wasn't sure whether to interpret her silence as an instance of giving me space or letting me sweat. In either case, she definitely had the predatory stare down to a T. I felt like a cornered mouse, withering under her gaze.

Perhaps I should've been more grateful. She had, after all, just delivered me from a terrible fate. If left to my own devices in those tunnels, I'd have been captured and tortured before too long. Akasha, too. Her little pickup run in this ship had just bought me another serving of freedom. At the same time, however, I'd been dicked around a *lot*. It didn't take an overactive imagination to consider the possibility of her turning me over to the Hegemony or otherwise murdering me in some sadistic ritual. Purifiers, after all, aren't often known for being benevolent.

At a bare minimum, I took some comfort from the sight of Akasha lying on a nearby futon. Her breathing had stabilized, and despite her worrying lack of consciousness, she seemed closer to the recovery side of the spectrum than the brain-death side.

"Wife?" the mysterious Purifier asked, evidently having caught on to my concern.

I shook my head. "Colleague, you might say."

"Ah. Like, a colleague you have sex with?"

"We're platonic."

"That's what they all say." She shrugged, grinning ear to ear. "What's your name, by the way? I'm Rogaji."

I just blinked at her, momentarily unsure if I was in reality or another dream realm conjured up by the Unmade. In just five minutes, this damn Purifier had ambushed me with a stealth ship, taken Akasha and me aboard, sat me down in the living quarters, and struck up a casual conversation. All while presumably dodging Hegemony sensors that could detect a gnat two millimeters out of place, no less.

"Dak," I said at length, still examining her face for any hint of deception. If one was there, I couldn't spot it. "You mind telling me what the hell is going on?"

She smirked. "Judging by what I saw on the way in, it might be best for you to give your side of things first."

"Which begs the question of how you even knew to be here."

"'Begging the question' is a logical fallacy, so it's not quite being used correctly here," she said, raising a scholar's finger that soon crumpled and returned to her lap. "Sorry. Old habits. The corruption of phrases is just one of my pet peeves."

"Well, that's one way to dodge a question."

Rogaji didn't seem too ruffled about that. Her easygoing manner probably came from the fact that she was entirely in control here. Most top-notch ships had fail-safe features linked to the owner's pulse. The minute their heart stopped beating, just about anything could happen. The ship might depressurize, hard-seal its doors, fill the corridors with lethal fumes, or deliver any number of other, more inventive responses to punish those still alive. Even if Rogaji didn't have that feature active, she was still packing a chok'tal. Still capable of drawing on the Unmade's seemingly limitless geyser of power.

In that moment, it also struck me that this was my *first* encounter with a living Purifier. Modri didn't count, seeing as he was just a disembodied consciousness in my skull. No, this was a real, flesh-and-blood specimen that clearly wasn't starving for Kill Points. How did I know that last tidbit? I didn't, but it was a damn good hunch. Imagine the KP for taking down a fellow Purifier. Unless killing Purifiers was considered cannibalism, and thus worthless . . .

I didn't know and certainly wouldn't test that theory by provoking a reaction from my host. Not until I was out of her ship and on neutral ground, anyway.

"I doubt my explanation would make much sense to you—at this moment in time, anyhow," Rogaji said. "I'll explain everything when we get back to the compound."

I quirked a brow. "Compound?"

She must've picked up on the obvious jolt in my voice, because she was quick to clarify by saying, "Relax. Not a Hegemony compound. It's mine!"

"Too soon to know if that makes it any better."

"My, my. Aren't you a cynical one? If any other Purifier had found you and your 'platonic friend' on the verge of death, they'd have skinned you alive and eaten your chok'tal for the KP. Me? I'm offering you a hot meal, a shower, and a massage clinic."

Admittedly, all that did sound nice—even if I'd been offered two of the three by the same monastery that had just been eradicated—but my mind snagged on a detail many would've considered less important.

"Did you just say *eat*? As in, Purifiers physically *eat* others' chok'tal?"

Rogaji blinked at me as though I were a chattering kid. "Yes?"

"Have . . . you done that?"

"A few times. They're not so easy on the stomach, but the boost is worth it."

It took all my self-control to force a neutral, almost approving expression. At least she'd just answered my unspoken question about Purifier-on-Purifier violence. Answered it without missing a beat, no less. The woman was just casually sitting here, describing the acts of cannibalism she'd performed on those who were just like me—if not in personality, then certainly in biology. That was enough to trigger my paranoia. How many other Purifiers had been given last-minute, seemingly miraculous rescues in this stealth ship? Better yet, how many of them had ended up on her evening banquet table?

"That's rather uncharitable," Rogaji said while I was midthought, jarring me. I looked up at her, startled, but she just smiled. "You're probably wondering what rank I've reached. I'll tell you that later, but for now . . . just know that I can do many, many things considered impossible by humanoids."

The intensity of her gaze, paired with a smooth, sultry grin, filled in the blanks left by her words. She could read minds. In fact, she'd probably been reading mine since I first stepped aboard, if not earlier. I suddenly wished I'd undergone more mind training in Narbu's halls.

"Don't worry," she said, winking. "I won't hold your thoughts against you. I'm sure you learned a bit about their nature on that planet. You know, how they come and go without your consent . . . sort of like emotions, huh?"

"What *else* can you do?" I asked bitterly.

"Oh, not much. Nothing you need to know about just yet."

"Sure about that? Because I'd sure like to know if you can make my heart explode in my chest."

She giggled at that. "Only made that happen once, and I think it was a fluke . . . "

The sincerity in her voice didn't do much to assure me such a "fluke" might not happen again. More uncomfortable than ever, I glanced over at Akasha. She was still out like a light, churning occasionally in the grips of some tortured dream. Until she woke up (if she ever did), I was on my own.

"All right, look," I said, opting for the direct approach in light of Rogaji's mind reading, "I just need a cursory explanation of how you found us. I'm okay with some suspense. I'm okay with trusting you until we reach your compound. Not that I have a choice, but still . . . The point is, I'd really, *really* like to hear why you saved our asses."

Rogaji seemed to consider my words, though I could tell her reception carried none of the urgency I'd tried to instill. The way she looked about the room, lifting and furrowing brows, suggested she barely saw me as living, let alone an equal. Perhaps in her mind, Akasha and I were just dream characters. Insects.

"Okay," she said at last, giving a shrug that conveyed an air of *Why the hell not?* "While you were down on that monk planet, you probably found some type of fungus, right?"

"'Fungus' is a bit of an understatement."

"Precisely so." She held up a finger and smiled. "That fungus, new friend Dak, developed quite a reputation in the local galactic clusters. One world, a shipping hub, became a sort of unofficial black market for it. Imagine that . . . a whole orbital zone full of pilots tripping so hard they can't even find the comms panels."

"You mean, there's *more* of it around the 'verse? Shit."

"Hold on, now," Rogaji said firmly. "Let's not get ahead of ourselves. You asked how I got here, and I've barely had time to lay out the opening steps."

I gave a mock flourish, as though requesting a royal court petitioner to get on with it.

"Thank you kindly," she said, smirking with equal flippancy. "Now, before . . . all *this* . . . I was working the circuits as a competitive simmer."

Despite my best efforts to stay restrained until she'd finished, I couldn't stop a slow trickle of disgust from migrating across my face. Simulation gamers, known colloquially as simmers, were the exact sort of people I'd blamed for the chok'tal's existence. People so addicted to the cutting edge of stimulation, winning, and "fun" that they were willing to create the Unmade's style of blood sports.

That being said, simming on a pro level wasn't a mindless waste of time. Not entirely, anyway. There were some massive prizes for winning these tournaments. Some paid out tried-and-true bux, while others sent ancient data packets or virtual relics to the winner's cache. In any event, one could become very wealthy very quickly if they survived the pain. *Real* pain.

You might assume that simulated competitions didn't involve that. Who would be stupid enough to program pain and death into a data-driven program designed for amusement? I don't know, but I *do* know that the vast majority of competitive sims featured real death, suffering, and agony. Come to think of it, there was a lot I didn't understand about sims. My best reference information came from memories of Dak Korasa's former colleagues.

About three-quarters of all known sims (particularly the high-end experiences) were alien creations, their makers and rewards unknown to all but the dead stranded within them. A good number of these were, in fact, crypts instead of games, intended to serve as fatal gauntlets for the humanoids bold (or stupid) enough to jack in and probe the virtual waters for alien treasure. Others were of a more enigmatic design, their purpose beyond our conception, and tended to wind up in Hegemony labs or third-party excavation bays for impossible analysis.

Anyway, all this is a long and detailed way to explain that I had a passing understanding of sims—and I didn't like them one bit. Competitive simmers themselves had a reputation of being brash, arrogant, cybernetically mutated freaks that cared for little beyond winning and telling fellow simmers how they would violate their mothers.

Rogaji didn't seem to fit that description, but then again, it was impossible to say how she might've looked in the peak of her career. Her rank alone probably meant she'd mastered the art of bodily manipulation. How extensively she'd mastered it, though, was the question. Was she just warping her DNA, or was she projecting an illusion through my mind? Was she an old man wearing a young woman's skin?

Rogaji seemed to detect every flicker in that train of thought. Her smile deepened, and she let out a long, wistful sigh. "I was the good kind of simmer, Dak. I wasn't there to kill or to get rich . . . I was there to *win*."

"What does that have to do with fungus?"

"*Well*, since you're asking so patiently . . . I ended up at that shipping hub between matches. I like to have a little fun in my downtime, so I hit the bars there. Took a few tabs, a few strips of amp-dust, a few downers, a rounder . . . "

"Faster, please."

Rogaji gave a mock scowl. "I took everything in sight, but I still wasn't done getting loaded. I hit the underbar. You know, like a bar, but a seedier bar. There were a few weirdos in there, and one of 'em had the fungus we've been discussing. They wanted a *ridiculous* price for this sludge they'd cooked up and loaded into a vial, but I figured, what the hell? Being scammed is just part of the fun in hubs like that."

Her mention of *sludge* sent goose bumps up and down my arms. She was clearly referring to the same "sacrament" Narbu had cooked up for decades.

"So, I fork over the bux, get my vial of fungus juice, and head back to my quarters to do a little prebed tripping. Drank it on the way." She shook her head, eyes staring into the carpet near me as though in a trance. "Never in my *life* has something hit that hard. Woof. It plowed right into me, had me on my back faster than an investment analyst."

I just perched my chin on my palm and blinked.

"This'll sound crazy," Rogaji said, evidently not knowing how much craziness I'd just experienced, "but I saw *time*."

"You saw . . . time."

"Yeah! It looked like a giant, spinning torus made of light and energy. Sort of like a cosmic doughnut, I guess. But, yeah . . . next thing I know, I'm flying *through* the cosmic doughnut. I'm seeing the past, the present, the future, the timelines that run through and around all of it . . . " She let out another shaky, awe-stricken breath. "What I'm trying to say, Dak, is that the cosmic doughnut showed me the entire course of my life. Sure, it was a little spotty in places, but I got the gist. The second I came down from the trip, I pulled up my memory implant and double-encoded everything to make sure it was saved."

Not for the first time in recent days, I was taken aback. Up until now, I'd assumed the fungus granted people either visions of the Absolute or replays of past victims. But this . . . this was new. Perhaps in hindsight, I should've seen Narbu's prophetic obsession as a clue that the fungus divined the future.

"What exactly did you see?" I asked.

"Everything," she explained. "The upcoming match results, the plays I needed to make, the venues that hadn't even been built yet . . . I saw the whole shebang. The most important thing I saw, of course, was the chok'tal. I saw the *exact* spot on the *exact* planet where it was buried."

"Hold on. Are you telling me that *you* went after the chok'tal?"

"Naturally!"

I opened and closed my mouth several times, starved of any coherent thoughts. Eventually, I gathered my wits enough to ask, "*Why?*"

"Because I'm a simmer, Dak," she said easily. "I like to *win*. This chok'tal is the ultimate game."

"It's *not* a game."

"And how do you know that?"

"Because I've met the one who made it."

Rogaji grinned. "Huh. Me, too. We'll have to compare notes."

Confident that this verbal sparring wouldn't lead anywhere beneficial—as I said, simmers are a different breed—I returned to more mundane questions about her future-seeing experience.

"So . . . did you see me?"

Rogaji nodded and picked at her nails. "Sure did. Well . . . sort of. That's the reason I'm here. Or should I say, the reason *you're* here."

"I'm not following."

"Everything up to here and now was perfectly clear. But after this, it starts to get a little . . . muddy. Hazy, you might say. I think that has something to do with you, and I'd like to sort it out together."

"What do you mean by *hazy*? Can you see anything in the future?"

"Nope."

This, at least, caught my attention enough to entertain the idea that Rogaji *wasn't* a roaming psychopath who liked to capture and eat fellow Purifiers. In fact, her reasoning was very logical—find the one humanoid who's interrupting your future vision, and get some answers from them. Simple. Easy. The only problem on her end was that I, her wonder boy, wasn't nearly as simple or easy to figure out. Between Chanzig's birth manipulation, the Unmade's general mucking about with the universe, and Narbu's attempts to "fix" things, I wasn't sure there was even a sense of order or causality to untangle. Perhaps the universal timeline—insofar as it involved me, that is—was bonked beyond hope.

"What was the last thing you saw?" I asked.

"This," she said, indicating the living module around us. "You, me, here . . . talking about this."

"Not worried I might kill you?"

She snorted at that. Actually *snorted*. "Hardly."

"Fair enough," I said, trying not to let her very realistic take on the situation bruise my pride. "That means you have no idea what happened down on that planet, right?"

Her eyes jumped wider. "Oh, that reminds me! I *did* see one last thing before it went dark . . . Something related to that planet, no less."

"Well?"

Rather than answering directly, she stood and beckoned me to follow. I did as requested. She led me into a small, burned plastic–smelling module that felt more like an oven than a habitable station. Crisscrossed wires and soldered-on patches of circuitry hung from the ceiling like a drunk spider's web, and every wall shone with flickering vidscreens displaying core readouts and turbine speeds.

"This is the operational heart of the ship?" I asked, ducking beneath a dangling plug that intermittently gave off sparks.

"Yeah," Rogaji said, entirely too proud. "Had a few of my guys get it up and running. Neat, right?"

I mumbled in the affirmative, though I was certain she'd read my true thoughts already.

"So, when I saw this planet in my visions, I knew it had to be something big," she explained while pecking at a pair of consoles. "I started researching it. Y'know, privately contracting mineral analyses and whatnot. Did you know there's about sixteen tons of palladium buried under the northern crust?"

"Fascinating, but I'm not sure what.it has to do with me."

"Patience, Dak. Patience."

She pulled up a live feed of the ship's rear cameras, displaying a wide, mostly empty image of space. Far in the distance, though, was a small blot that I faintly recognized as the monks' planet. Before I could question her point, she flicked a few dials and threw the image into sharp magnification. Now the entirety of the planet was in frame, occupying the entire screen. You still couldn't see much in the way of detail, unless you counted the basic terrain colors and atmospheric movements, but it was a marked improvement. For better or worse, it also revealed the handful of Hegemony ships lingering in orbit.

"Remember how I said that black-market hub station had a ton of the fungus?" she asked.

I nodded.

"Well, there's a reason it hasn't spread much farther than a few stations. It's too dangerous."

"What, for your brain?"

Rogaji fixed me with a grim look—one that looked even more severe in the module's pale lighting. "Dangerous for everything. The fungus itself is inert, but the moment it makes contact with a few very obscure fission processes, it turns into a high explosive."

"What?"

"Yeah, pretty insane, huh? Gram for gram, that stuff has about a quarter of a hydrogen charge's power."

I stared at the vidscreens in horror. "The head monk covered the entire planet in a megacolony of that fungus."

"Oh, I know. Only problem is, the Hegemony doesn't. Which is why they're about to pound the surface with a casual opening volley of ionized bunker-buster rounds."

Rogaji then pointed to the screen, but she was about a half second too late in her prescience. Her finger was still in motion when the planet's entire surface began to ripple with overlapping waves.

Shock waves, I realized. The swift, all-consuming blasts tore across the surface in twos and threes, sometimes feeding one another to produce gargantuan waves that circled back to mop up whatever had survived the initial blast.

Midway through the apocalyptic show, Rogaji broke the silence with a long, shrill blow on some type of party horn. She then pulled a handful of confetti from her armor and tossed it all over us, her smile utterly manic in the screen's light.

I just glanced at her, lost for words.

"This is the moment where I stop seeing the future!" she shouted. "Don't you get it? It's marvelous! No predestination . . . no need to follow the course of destiny! I am *free*! Everything is so out of control. So beautifully, absurdly out of control!"

All I could manage was a tight swallow and a nod.

"Did you, uh, have a good bond with those monks?" Rogaji asked, her glee fading by degrees as she caught on to my true reaction.

"Not with most, no," I said quietly. "And the ones I liked are dead."

"Well, if they weren't before, they are now." She sputtered a quiet laugh, then cleared her throat. "I mean . . . sorry about that. It was predestined, you know. Not much to be done about planetary extinctions when the Hegemony is involved."

Much as I tried, I couldn't tear my eyes away from the planet's slow, silent blackening. In a matter of seconds, one stupid miscalculation had wiped out millions of lives. Worse yet, it had erased the last vestiges of the monks' teachings. Countless millennia of wisdom and progress . . . gone. The logical half of my brain knew I ought to be relieved about, if not celebrating, the fact that Narbu's schemes and tainted knowledge couldn't leak into the 'verse any longer. But the other half, the illogical and optimistic one, took a punch to the gut. The monks' leader had fallen to defilement, but that didn't mean anything else on that planet deserved annihilation. Nor did it mean the tomes they'd compiled and stored in the repositories were worthless.

My only solace lay in the fact that the Hegemony wouldn't get their hands on that information. I had no clue what they were planning, apart from hunting Purifiers, but restricting the enemy's access to information is never a bad thing.

Worrying I might go legitimately insane if I kept debating the pros and cons of an entire planet's obliteration, I wrangled my mind back to greener pastures.

"Where's this compound of yours?"

Rogaji flashed me a thin smile. "You know that permawar world? The one where your ship crashed?"

"Uh, yeah? How did *you* know about that?"

"It's my property."

2

About ten minutes later, it became clear that Rogaji wasn't joking. My first indication that she was telling the truth came in the form of the ship's speed. We hadn't gone into a faster-than-light pinch despite being clear of any gravitational obstacles, instead opting to cross the vacuum using the vessel's standard engines. In plain terms, this meant our destination was local, not cross-galactic.

What really sold her wild claim, however, was the story of how she'd acquired the planet. It was about as ludicrous as you'd expect.

Apparently, Rogaji had racked up somewhere in the neighborhood of 4.2 trillion bux from her career as a simmer. On the off chance your currency is different or operates with altered value, let me offer a point of reference. One trillion bux, in most parts of the 'verse, was enough to purchase an orbital station capable of holding five flagships. Two trillion, and you could literally buy a species on the distant edges of the Nogo Zone.

It was a staggering amount of money, but it made sense when I considered the unintended effects of knowing the future. Rogaji had seen every match, every planet, every step on her long and predestined journey. No wonder she'd crushed the competition and quickly risen to her galaxy's place of prominence as the highest-earning simmer. The most curious aspect of her success had to do with the legality. Most future-seeing species were banned from competitions and financial positions, and with good reason. It seemed that Rogaji's magic bullet lay in her birth as a pure-blooded human. Had she been any other species, even one with 99-plus percent humanoid DNA, she'd have been discovered and executed on sight.

Anyway, to make a long story short, she'd emerged from her career with a shitload of money and the ability to perceive the future. In that future vision, not coincidentally, she'd purchased a property deed long assumed to be lost or destroyed: that of the permawar world. The way she explained it, even *she* didn't know the full purpose behind owning the planet. That hadn't stopped her from "miraculously" tracking down the owner—a fifth-generation krill farmer who'd won the planet from a dice game—and paying him just shy of 3.5 billion bux for the deed.

According to her, the farmer hadn't had any qualms about getting rid of the planet; in fact, he'd wanted to do so for some time. The reason for this was simple: he didn't know what the hell to do with it. The planet's entire surface was, as I'd been told, a scorched and vicious wasteland populated by swarms of machines designed to kill. Bit of a problem for any up-and-coming real estate developers with ambitions of building a resort world there.

All this information left me more confused than ever. Rogaji seemed to think this planet was the greatest purchase ever, but . . . why? You couldn't use it for anything except a training course to practice dodging bullets and nuclear warheads. Hell, I wasn't even sure she'd visited this place.

None of this seemed to dampen the woman's spirits, though. At the one-hour mark since we'd started flying, she led me to the cockpit. There, she urged me to sit in a hovering bucket chair covered in red satin. By Halcius, was it comfortable—though I suppose I shouldn't have been surprised. The entire cockpit was luxurious in design, from the majestic, sloping viewpanes to the wood-lacquered panels to the tribal artifacts tastefully arranged on bronze plinths. It was more a showroom than a pilot's command center.

Rogaji slid into the main seat, palming a few armchair buttons to begin peeling back the viewpanes' protective armor. While she waited, she pulled a lever embedded in the floor. Not three seconds later, a tray descended from the ceiling to reveal two extra-full, extra-bubbly glasses of champagne. She gulped half of hers in a single swig, then angled the glass to cheers—before I'd even touched mine.

"Is this really the time to be drinking?" I asked.

"Oh, lighten up," she said, rolling her eyes in exasperation. "Champagne isn't *drinking.*"

"False."

"Agree to disagree." She shook her glass to remind me she was still waiting for that cheers, at which point I relented and exchanged a clink. "There. Don't you feel better already?"

I took a tiny sip and was disappointed to discover how good it was. "I'll feel a lot better if we survive this landing."

"Why wouldn't we survive?"

"Oh, I dunno . . . because it's a planet full of automated death?"

"What's your point? Plenty of penal colonies use wild animals in moats. The guards aren't afraid they're going to get eaten, are they?"

"They do *not* use wild animals in moats."

Rogaji scoffed. "Says who?"

"Lasers are more efficient than wild animals."

"Oh, yeah? Have you ever been to a penal colony?"

"No?"

"Just what I thought," she said with a self-satisfied smirk.

"Wait—you've done time at one?"

"Of course not. I made over four trillion bux. You think rich little *me* would ever spend a day behind bars?"

"Touché," I said, scrunching up my face. "It's good that the money kept you humble."

"It is, isn't it?"

I just shook my head and returned to nursing the champagne.

As the viewpanes finished up their retraction cycle, I puzzled over when to tell Rogaji about my encounters with the Unmade. Although she'd *said* she had experience with him, I doubted it was to the same extent. She almost certainly hadn't seen him literally give birth to himself out of Akasha's body. So, one half of my fear was that she wasn't ready for the depravity our foe could dish out. The other half, in contrast, was just the opposite. What if she *had* seen him, in all his wicked, defiled glory, and started to admire him? Emulate him, even? Of course, there was also the worst-case scenario . . . that Rogaji was an active agent of the Unmade.

This last possibility gave me the heebie-jeebies. There was a reckless, indifferent side to Rogaji—one that didn't seem to distinguish between victory and slaughter. In her simmer mind, for all I knew, humanoids might've been just as inconsequential as virtual avatars. It wasn't a stretch to imagine that the Unmade had seen this quality, amplifying and encouraging it for some nefarious purpose beyond my understanding.

It was also possible that the Unmade was using her in a way neither of us understood. Our last encounter had cemented the theory that the Unmade didn't want to kill me—he wanted to torment me. To make me draw upon my inner wrath and disdain. This was, in many ways, far more frightening than knowing he wanted to rip me apart. Mostly because it cast doubt on any and all hope of ever escaping his clutches.

Given the Unmade's unthinkably vast timeline for universal manipulation, was it really so absurd to think that *he* was the one who'd granted Rogaji her future visions? If that was true, it also meant he'd engineered the steps along the way. He'd sent her to rescue me, to bring me to this planet, to put me right back in the crosshairs.

Once more, I felt myself wandering toward the cliff of insanity. I turned back to the taste of champagne and the emerging view to avoid losing my mind.

As I should've expected, the ugly sphere of the permawar world lay before us. It was a jagged, crusty thing, almost like a glass marble that had been repeatedly hammered until it fractured from top to bottom. Those fracture lines, though, had nothing to do with damage; they were enormous trenches and defensive lines the warring machines had carved into the surface. The fact that they were even visible at this range—several hundred thousand kilometers away—spoke volumes as to the width of those formations.

"Home sweet home," Rogaji said.

I set my glass down, transfixed by the constant flutter of small lights all over the planet—nukes, I guessed. "Where's your compound?"

She glanced my way, smiled lightly, and pointed downward.

"Underground?" I asked.

"Bingo. Only way to safeguard against the fallout."

"Did you tunnel it all out?"

"Of course not," she said, chuckling. "The farmer who sold me this planet had no idea there was a network belowground. I doubt he'd have given it up so readily if he did."

"A few trillion bux is an easy selling point."

"Perhaps . . . but I got the better deal." Her smile broadened to off-putting, maniacal levels. "This place used to be some kind of advanced research center for a megacorporation, from what I've gathered. They were interested in the site due to the ambient conditions."

"Meaning?"

"Oh, don't tell me the monks skimped on explaining this corner of the 'verse."

I caught her meaning. "You're talking about the quantum weirdness, right? The fact that this region has an unstable relationship with time and space?"

"That about sums it up." She nodded once, satisfied, then pointed back out the viewpane. "If you ask me, they were trying to crack the code so they could manipulate it under controlled circumstances. This area is the 'verse's best-kept secret."

"Hard to keep a secret for long in this world."

Rogaji assented by way of a vicious *humph*. Still, she seemed to pick up on my unspoken question, which was how this place had faded to obscurity (if not nonexistence) despite the presence of a planet-wide corporate base. "A few years after the research installation went live, it started . . . going wrong. Weird signals over the networks, cross-dimensional traffic, occasional bouts of madness and mutiny . . . Wasn't long the researchers went fully off the rails and weaponized the planet's security forces to fight one another, thus creating the permawar."

"Oh. It was one of *those* stations."

"Sadly, yes. Well, sad for them. Wonderful for us."

"I guess. I just . . . don't get it. Whatever you paid for this place, that corporation must've paid twice as much to even lay the cornerstones. It's not cheap to hide this kind of site from the Hegemony's intelligence networks."

"What can I say? When classified research goes terribly wrong, you never hear about it. They just bury it. *Or* nuke it from orbit. Which, by the way, they attempted to do. Those machines have some very sophisticated technology for grabbing hold of enemy weapons and pointing them back at the sender."

I just cringed, feeling unexpectedly sorry for the poor bastards who'd tried to launch that first surface-clearing volley. "Right, so, everybody went insane and died."

"That's the short version, yes."

"Why haven't you gone off the deep end, then?"

The grin she gave me was enough to momentarily question if she already had.

"I fixed the problem," she said after a moment. "And it was a *big* problem."

"Don't keep me in suspense."

"Oh, I will. Just for a few minutes, though. I'm fairly proud of the surprises I've prepared for you."

I rubbed the bridge of my nose, silently willing the permawar world beneath us to vanish into thin air. I'd had more than enough surprises over the last week and change. The prospect of being surprised by Rogaji, who was now able to experience the thrill of spontaneous decision-making once again, did not excite me.

Still, she was in her own world as we approached. She kept refilling and draining her champagne glass, humming little ditties to herself as though we were some old nautical vessel preparing to mosey into port after a long voyage.

I used this precious opportunity to check my Status Display. I knew I was more than set on time, seeing as I'd triggered a rank-up shortly before Rogaji's arrival, but I'd learned from personal experience that planning time was never to be wasted. Too often, I'd been forced to make split-second choices or stupidly allocate points just to survive a rank. (Just look at my most recent upgrade purchase, Photosynthesis). Now that I had a little breathing room, I could get some perspective on my trajectory and figure out a medium- to long-term plan for the coming days.

STATUS DISPLAY
PURIFIER RANK: 13
RANK-UP NOT AVAILABLE (1,638,400 KP required)

Kill Points: 0
Genofacturing Points: 3,334,240

Rank Points: 0

Rank Time: 19 Hours, 41 Minutes, 38 Seconds
Storehouse Time: 25 Hours, 18 Minutes, 41 Seconds

Anima: 360%
Dominion: 0/5

The million-and-a-half KP requirement for the next rank was still daunting, but it also put a vein of curiosity in my thinking. If Rogaji really had ascended to some untold peak of power, yet had also stabilized her situation enough to be this relaxed around a potential foe, it meant she probably had a reliable and bountiful source of KP on tap. I'd need to ask her about that. Of course, given her history as a simmer, it was highly possible that she'd managed to find and exploit a loophole in the chok'tal's reward circuit. I myself had already found quite a few, though I had no way to extract value from them—certainly not in any repeatable, controlled manner.

For starters, the chok'tal didn't deal well with distance or poor visibility. In dense fog or a pitch-black room, the chok'tal assigned terribly skewed KP values. To give you an example, imagine duking it out with a soldier carrying some flesh-melting weapon. If the chok'tal couldn't see or otherwise discern that flesh-melting weapon, it didn't count it toward the reward total. Conversely, the chok'tal *upped* its rewards the moment conditions cleared and the new threats became perceptible.

This might be a bad case in point, seeing as my chok'tal had never artificially *inflated* the reward, only dropped or miscalculated it. Still, it suggested a degree of subjectivity in the chok'tal's consciousness. If it could make mistakes in awarding higher KP totals, why couldn't it make mistakes with overassigning them?

A similar hiccup affected the chok'tal's ability to decide what was or wasn't a valid threat. Theoretically, an enemy could conceal their weapons so well that the chok'tal didn't even see them as a problem. Outward power, range, and some unknown comparison of my weapons and the enemy's all factored into the equation, but without the ability to crack open the chok'tal's coding and understand its metafunction, there was no way to predictably say what would or wouldn't happen in a given situation. So much of it seemed to be decided on a whim.

Perhaps Rogaji, in all her simmer glory, *had* cracked the code. Perhaps she'd developed strategies to take those vulnerabilities, flip them on their head, and use them to award herself multitudes more KP than she actually deserved.

There was a dark side to that possibility, though. Rogaji's reaction to the sudden extermination of a planet had been confetti and a party horn. Granted, she'd known about that event for a long, long while and had probably been reacting more to her own renewal of freedom than mass death, but still . . . it hinted at desensitization to violence. It wasn't a huge leap to consider whether she'd been using nuclear weapons to eradicate entire fleets or worlds for bucketfuls of KP.

And yes, yes, before you say anything—I can already hear the barrage of complaints—I'm aware that I am no poster child for resisting desensitization. A few weeks prior, I'd never even handled a gun, let alone taken life. Now I was able to put bullets in deserving skulls without batting an eyelash.

Even with this small wrinkle of irony, I doubt it was hypocritical or alarmist to be concerned about the details of how Rogaji had ascended so high. While I hadn't asked her for her true rank, I suspected it was at *least* three times as high as my own. Assuming the chok'tal's KP-doubling rank-up requirements continued indefinitely, she had to be regularly chowing down on billions (or even trillions) of points just to survive. This realization was grim enough to make me hope she'd figured out a loophole instead of going about things the old-fashioned way.

Now, enough of that doom and gloom. It was time to plan, not clutter my brain with a new assortment of fears. Fears such as Rogaji's real reason for airlifting Akasha and me. The jury was still out on the true value of that last-minute rescue, but one thing had become clear since I came aboard: assuming Rogaji was decent and *not* planning to skin and eat me, I could finally go on the offensive.

Up until Akasha brought me to the monk planet, I'd been running blind and tossing Rank Points into anything that could give my ass one more day of life. I'd also been genofacturing the items recommended by Modri as opposed to exploring the options on my own time. Hell, even on the monk planet, I'd been subjected to Narbu's manipulation and "direction," which had removed any need to think or plan ahead. To make it pithy, I'd been running around like a decapitated bird, driven solely by primal terror and hatred.

No longer, though. Now I had options. Shelter, access to information, a potential combat buddy. A strong-as-hell combat buddy, no less. With all these resources combined, I stood my best chance of taking this fight to the Unmade and halting the Glorious Game in its tracks.

The question, of course, was how to do that. Even if Rogaji had managed to construct and use one of the gateways needed to reach the Unmade's dimension, it didn't mean she had any secret tips for overcoming the bastard. Not that I needed to get that far ahead of myself. There was still the question of Akasha and when—indeed, *if*—she would ever come back to full consciousness. And if she did, what the hell would I even say? *Oh, good morning, Akasha! By the way, you're also the Unmade's reincarnated mother and played host to his disgusting avatar!*

I tried to put that out of my head. It was a bridge better crossed when I came to it. For now, I still had to cobble together a rough plan for taking on the Unmade. With luck, Rogaji would already have one, but I didn't want to bank on that. Despite my exceedingly young "real" age, I'd already learned ten times over not to trust anyone except myself.

The way I saw it, there were two main routes. The first was to build a gateway, go through it, and hack my way to the Unmade, at which point I would curb-stomp him to oblivion. The second was to cut off *all* access to his dimension. It wouldn't kill him, let alone stop him from mucking about in the multiverse, but it *would* lock him out of our world for the foreseeable future. Doing the latter, though, required a lot of Purifier killing and gateway hunting—neither of which I had any expertise in doing.

Then there was the big, *big* problem looming behind the Unmade and my plans to dispatch him. That problem was my personal fate. Let me explain. On the surface, it seems intuitive and even inspired by sim games—kill the big bad guy, remove his curse. But how the hell could I know if that would work here? The Unmade didn't seem like the type of being that would just undo his damage as a reward for victory. In fact, he was just the opposite. I had a grim feeling that killing the Unmade without entertaining his scheme would lead to a rash of incurable chok'tal madness. The only reason I still had hope was because I hadn't fully figured out the link between the Unmade and his creations, and I didn't *want* to. If I'd somehow learned, with full certainty, that nothing and nobody could remove the chok'tal from my body, suicide would've been my first pick . . . rebirth be damned.

Suddenly, something intruded on the mental space that housed the Status Display. Not quite a wave, but more than a ripple. It took me far longer than it should have to realize it was the dull, distant throb of something trying to wake me in the real world.

I snapped myself out of the Status Display to find Rogaji straining toward me, tongue between glossy lips, nudging me with her elbow and wearing a wicked grin.

"The hell's the matter with you?" I growled.

She leaned back and tucked one knee up on her chair, feigning offense. "My, my . . . and here I was, thinking training with those monks would've taught you better manners."

"I spent *two days* there."

"Then they must've failed spectacularly with you, given your downgrade. I've heard you can't even fly off Halcium Alpha or Beta unless you've passed an eighteen-hour-long decorum exam." She looked me up and down. "That's where you're from, no? Your eyes say it all. Your . . . *prominent* features as well."

I grunted. "Prominent? Could you be any more ambiguous?"

"Many think the Hegemony's citizens are the highest expression of beauty in the cosmos," Rogaji said as she swished her third or fourth glass of champagne about, threatening to soak me in delicious synthetic grape fluid. Her eyes fluttered in some imitation of a coy princess, and she pulled on a sweet and innocent voice to complete the mockery. "Ah, yes, the true and chosen heirs of the universe . . . a people whose very genes are ordained by the great and powerful Lord Halcius, in all his shimmering, shining, erect—"

"All right, spare me the lecture," I cut in. "I've got Hegemony DNA, sure, but not in the way you're probably thinking."

"Oh. Love child of some legislator? Some sort of borderline-extinct alien with a fetish for scraping humanoid DNA and using it to mold your appearance at will?"

I scrunched up my face. "Option C."

"This ought to be good . . . when I get a chance to hear it." She winked, then used her champagne glass to gesture toward the main viewpane. "We're here."

For the first time since exiting the Status Display, I turned my gaze ahead. The change in scenery was almost enough to make me vomit; my meat-sack brain simply couldn't handle how drastically the outer world had shifted.

Beyond the viewpane was the pitted, blistering terrain of the permawar world. Specifically, the terrain of the starlit side. It looked to be about sunset in this region. We were just beginning to break atmosphere, as indicated by the orange tracers zinging over the hull and the crackle of emergent sound.

Then again, maybe *atmosphere* wasn't the proper term. There were no clouds to speak of, only a thin, dragging smog that masked the entire surface, aside from a few shadows of movement that suggested the presence of hulking war machines. On top of that, we were only a few kilometers up. The first layers of atmosphere should've been breached a long while ago.

"It's thinning," Rogaji said, probably in response to reading my mind. "Too many thermobaric warheads, particle splitters, nano-cannibalizing pulses. Not a problem for the machines, though. They only care about how much territory they control and how many foes remain. Atmospheres are a luxury that matter to creatures with respiration."

Nodding absently, I surveyed the ongoing war below . . . though I doubt *war* will really convey what I saw. As a caveat, I myself have never been in a war, but I learned enough about them through my work with Chanzig's employees. According to my sources, most humanoid wars are long, boring affairs—years and years of tedium, the bulk of it spent smoking or drinking or just shit-talking in bunkers while waiting for an enemy drone to blow you to smithereens. Due to survival instincts and general human apathy, soldiers are more than okay with hunkering down or marching at a snail's pace to satisfy their commanders' orders, but not so enthusiastic about storming an enemy hill position or flying in the vanguard of a combat squadron. On top of all that wrinkle, humanoid wars also rely on humanoid brains, which means bureaucracy. Supply requests, movement orders, communications hiccups, internal squabbling . . . Put it all together, and you get wars that are 99 percent waiting, 1 percent actual mayhem.

In contrast, a machine army had none of these problems. Their blind, efficient algorithm ensured they could make, deploy, and destroy troops in thousands of combat zones at once—but so did the enemy's. The result was nonstop, widespread, all-out carnage. A permawar.

Auto-targeted aerial batteries filled the skies with thousands of neon beams and black flak puffs, each one of them determined to take down the flocks of roaming aircraft engaged in their own ultra-fast dogfights. Colossal self-propelled artillery prowled the wastelands on rusted, spiderlike legs, lobbing nuclear shells at enemy factories that had only been constructed minutes prior. Every so often, hundred-meter-tall flares of fire and irradiated sparks came bursting up from boreholes in the earth, suggesting the conflict was taking place at all possible elevations—including underground.

All in all, it looked like a madman's military simulation cranked up to eleven. It was a pure stalemate and apparently had been for hundreds of years. Unstoppable force, meet immovable object. A strange, hollow feeling moved through my chest when I realized this war would last infinitely longer than any humanoid in existence.

"Quite the spectacle, isn't it?" Rogaji said. "Same thing, day in and day out, but it's still fun to place little bets on which side will take which zone on a given week."

"What exactly are they fighting over? Like, what's the victory condition?"

"You're presuming there is one," she said with a dark laugh. "There are no true leaders in this war. It's just data bouncing off itself. Not even sentient. I doubt the two factions know how to end this fight, even if they wanted to. All because of a workplace conflict."

"An entire planet going insane is a little more extreme than that."

She shrugged. "A matter of perspective. I've never found the direct cause of either side arming the security systems, but I'm not sure it matters anymore. There's no kill switch. They made sure of that."

"Maybe they wanted to keep people away."

"Hmm?"

I looked at her intently. "Turn the planet into a shithole with nukes flying everywhere, and nobody's going to come poking through the rubble."

She grinned. "What a coincidence. That's the same reason it seemed so appealing to me."

The stealth ship glided down over an ocean of viscous, burning fluid, then banked a hard left to thread its way through a canyon that had been blasted to charcoal. About halfway down this crispy divide, the ship made another hard pivot to head down a long, rectangular tunnel lined with LED squares. Every so often, the ship slowed using its anterior thrusters, giving the tunnel's various gates just long enough to flash green and peel back before jolting onward. Although we didn't have access to the rear cams, I guessed each of these "security checkpoints" locked back in place once we'd made entry. Not the most sophisticated system, but it had clearly been working for Rogaji.

After almost two minutes of gate-hopping, I turned to her. "How deep is this thing?"

"Deep enough." She pointed to the tunnel walls, highlighting their sudden shift in angle. Whereas our previous course had been purely horizontal, it was now rather slanted. "The compound's about twelve kilometers under the surface. Used to be twelve and a half, but the machines somehow gave the entire surface a haircut with their last major scuffle."

"And they've never come looking for you?"

"Between the cloaking tech and our own . . . shall we say, *homegrown* solutions . . . we've been more or less invisible to them. All our grid activity is self-contained, and we're good about dissipating any thermal buildup in the compound."

I nodded, rather impressed with the steps she'd taken—even if most or all of them had been preordained by the fungus. "If I didn't know better, I'd have guessed you were an engineer, not a simmer."

"I'm whatever money can buy. My team includes engineers, weapons operators, pilots . . . "

"You sure you're not building an army down here?"

"Who said I wasn't?" She flashed me a devilish grin that did nothing to dissolve my suspicions.

Another gate slid back—the final one, I assumed, based on the presence of *three* flashing green strips—and suddenly we were hovering through a massive, cavernous hangar. Well, more than cavernous; it was a literal cavern. Every surface aside from the concrete-plated floor was rough-hewn, volcanic rock illuminated by scores of lighting strips.

Banks of floodlights had been bolted to the ceiling, bathing the ships below in pale beams that revealed the true extent of gas and dust in the air. The vehicle collection was impressive, if a touch concerning. Rogaji had acquired everything from high-end cruising barges to alien gunships to mining rigs that weren't even on the market yet. The fact that she didn't brag about this hardware, let alone glance down at it as we passed overhead, suggested these weren't even her prize pieces.

"Now, then," she began, unbuckling her seat fastener even as our ship eased down into its neon landing spot, "you'll probably receive a lot of questions from the others. They're quite curious. Answer in whatever manner makes you feel comfortable, and don't be afraid to bark at them if they keep pressing you."

I grimaced and undid my own fastener, trying to prevent Rogaji from peering into my mind and seeing how much I *despised* first impressions. I'd always hated them—even Mr. Korasa and Modri, my de facto "parents," shared that quirk—but the last few days had turned my hatred into revulsion. Every newcomer I met seemed to harbor some dark secret, some hidden desire to murder me. I was out of patience when it came to new people.

"Do you have a medical center?" I asked as I followed Rogaji back into the living module.

She glanced up at me while packing assorted gadgets into a rucksack. "Medical *center*? Dak, I have a full team of experts and fabriques on hand. They can treat about 87.2 percent of all known species."

Mentally, I whistled at that. Even the best hospitals in "nice" sectors could only deal with half the patients that came slithering through their airlocks—namely, those with enough humanoid DNA to respond to standard treatments. Fortunately, Akasha was quite humanoid. Hopefully humanoid enough to benefit from Rogaji and her team's expertise.

Almost as though reading my mind (maybe she did?), Rogaji nodded toward Akasha. "Can you carry her? It'd take ten minutes for a hover-stretcher, and I'm a little knackered today."

"Yeah," I said, narrowing my eyes. "Sure."

I didn't narrow my eyes because of the request itself, but because Rogaji's explanation was bizarre. Here she was, a Purifier with an aura so dense I could almost grab it, asking battle-weary and starving *me* to carry a woman off the ship. This was either a calculated power play . . . or hinting at something amiss. At the time, I thought it was the former.

Oh, if only.

Five minutes later, we came marching down the exit ramp like a pair of pack mules. Rogaji had two or three large bags slung over her shoulders, while I hefted Akasha and an additional bag. Waiting for us at the end of the berth was a welcoming committee, of sorts. Stagnant vapors and poor lighting obscured any details, but their silhouettes painted them as tried-and-true humans—a rare comfort, after dealing with various abominations and interdimensional beasts for so long.

"Welcome to the compound," a familiar female voice called out as we approached. It belonged to *someone* I knew, but I couldn't place it.

I squinted as we walked, trying to suss out their identity. Liura? No, definitely not. One of Chanzig's concubines? Unlikely. A politician I'd heard talking on the vidscreens at some backwater bar? Maybe.

All the guesswork proved useless, however, when the speaker shook their glowstick to life and lifted it to head height.

It was Rogaji.

Freezing midstep, I looked over at the woman beside me. *Also* Rogaji. This version, however, wasn't bulked up by all the armor. New Rogaji was instead wearing a formfitting black dress with a plunging neckline. In spite of everything going on, the outfit managed to induce drooling in my cross-wired brain. Until I shook myself back to common sense, that is.

I opened my mouth to ask what the hell was going on, but I never got the chance. The Rogaji beside me let out a bloodcurdling scream and collapsed to her knees, sending bags spilling everywhere. She then began clawing at her own face and pulling viciously at her own eyelids, nose, and ears. Scratch by scratch, more blood and bits of tissue spattered the concrete.

"Help her!" I shouted, unable to do anything except waffle about with Akasha slung over my shoulder.

"Don't let it upset you," the glowstick-holding Rogaji said with a casual, dismissive wave. "Everything has its expiration date, Dak."

I hesitated for a moment, helplessly turning from New Rogaji to Dying Rogaji, trying to figure out why *nobody* seemed alarmed in the slightest by this act of sudden disintegration. Just as I was about to lose the last of my sanity, New Rogaji stepped forward and cleared her throat.

"Dak, really?" she said. "You haven't figured it out yet?"

"Figured out *what*!?"

"Oh, you precious, stupid man. Did you honestly think someone of my stature would go on that kind of rescue mission with my *real* body?"

Half baffled, half horrified, I turn back to Dying Rogaji, who was now Dead Rogaji. The last dregs of her skin, organs, and other assorted components were oozing out of her suit, forming an absolutely putrid puddle of reddish-green slop. Even her skull had started to melt.

"If you're . . . you," I said, watching New Rogaji carefully, "then who is *this*?"

New Rogaji laughed. "The fifth pseudoclone this month." Sensing my still-very-present confusion, she clarified, "One of my upgrades, Dak. Makes a sturdy, remote-controllable copy of myself for up to six hours. Not the best range limitations, I grant you, but sufficient to nab you and get you back here. And that's what matters!"

"Oh," I said, totally unsure of what anybody normal was supposed to say in this situation. "So you're *not* dead."

"No, of course not. We're talking, aren't we?"

"Yeah . . . " I pointed to the growing slop of Rogaji's clone. "But she—"

"Was a temporary tool!" Rogaji cut in, sighing. "Come, Dak. It's quite clear you'll need extra time to acclimate around here."

3

If there was a personality difference between the cloned version of Rogaji and the real deal, I couldn't detect it. Which made sense, I supposed, seeing as Rogaji had been using remote control to converse with me from the start. I did have a few burning questions related to the transfer of information speed between her clone and real body—most FTL transmissions were handled by a *very* complicated system, not neural connections—but I decided to set those on the back burner until we'd hashed out more immediate matters.

One of those immediate matters, of course, was figuring out what the ever-living hell Rogaji planned to do with an underground compound, an empire's worth of funding, and a cohort of seemingly well-adjusted contractors. It seemed prudent to understand whether she wanted to stop the Unmade . . . or take over his job.

This being the case, I readily agreed to Rogaji's offer of dinner and a drink—after ensuring Akasha had been off-loaded to the compound's medical facility and scheduled for a battery of tests, that is. Hungry or not, I hadn't forgotten about my companion's dire situation. My desire to get some answers on that front was outmatched only by my need to grasp Rogaji's big-picture plan. Both situations were important and concerned the fates of innocent people, but one of them also involved a madwoman with her finger on several proverbial big red buttons.

"Here we are," Rogaji said at the end of yet another long chrome hallway, ushering me through a doorway labeled Fine Dining.

I eyed the sign warily but entered nevertheless. To the room's credit, it was, indeed, a fine-dining environment. Oh, who am I kidding? It was four times as nice as any restaurant I'd ever visited. Low, moody lighting. Soft twelve-string jazz piping in through ceiling speakers. Immaculate basalt tables and booths of quilted black satin. In another life, Rogaji surely excelled as an interior designer for those with too much money and too little taste.

"Where do I sit?" I asked, feeling woefully underdressed despite the absurdity of it all.

Rogaji shrugged. "Anywhere you like. The servers have feet, you know. Well . . . most of them."

After a few seconds of indecision, I slid into a booth on the far side of the room. Rogaji stood in place until I was fully seated, then gave a huff of approval and joined me.

Between her black dress, the luxurious atmosphere, and the artificial candlelight painting her face, Rogaji looked every bit like my date. Maybe that's what this was—an elaborate and roundabout scheme to bring me here on a romantic date. It sounded ridiculous, even to me, but I'd seen wealthy people do far more twisted things. All that money really screws with your sense of normal entertainment.

"This . . . isn't a date, is it?" I asked, leaning over and speaking softly even though nobody else was around to hear it.

She smiled and handed me one of the menu tablets docked on the tabletop. "If it were, I'd already have your clothes off."

"I don't think that's called a date."

"Yes, well, we all have our private definitions of words." She gave a satisfied pip, seemingly to herself, then began perusing the menu. "Oh, look at that. A dry-aged gaffin steak, complete with a cilantro-vinegar reduction. Doesn't that just sound delightful?"

I cleared my throat and lowered the menu. "If it's all the same to you, I'd like to talk. You know . . . about everything."

"Be my guest, Dak."

"I— No, I meant I'd like answers. From you."

"I'd need questions to give you answers."

It took every bit of self-discipline to bury the growl in my throat. "All right, fine. For starters, you can tell me what you plan to do with this compound. What's your strategy for the Unmade?"

"The whom?"

"The Unmade. That's the real name of the son of a bitch behind the Glorious Game."

"*Ohhh*, you're referring to Endgame."

I scrunched my brow.

"That's *my* name for him," Rogaji explained. "Every sim has a final dungeon, objective, or boss that's required to fully complete the experience.

In the biz, it's called endgame content. This, erm, Unmade of yours . . . is the endgame boss."

"Don't you think it's a bit weird, still thinking of this as a game?"

She studied me over the rim of her tablet. "Why?"

"Because it involves *real* bullets, *real* killing, *real* death."

"And? Most sims worth their salt have neurofeedback, too."

I sighed. "Okay, but the difference is that you're choosing to enter those." Even as I spoke, I saw the complaint forming on her lips. I raised a finger for patience. "Yes, yes, I'm aware *you* wanted to play. Most of us didn't, though. And the people who get butchered by Purifiers certainly don't. What I'm saying is, in this fucker's game, there's no divide between the virtual and the real."

Rogaji just shrugged. "Life itself is a game, Dak, and consciousness is just data. What's got your knickers so twisted up about *this* game?"

Try as I might, I couldn't assemble a single thought capable of getting through to her. She'd made it patently clear that she didn't want to beat this "game" out of fear or survival drives. Trying to further use emotion-based, human logic on her would only result in me slamming my head against the table until I turned my brain to gelatin. It wasn't just because she was stubborn, either. No, it was because she'd already wandered so far beyond the pale of normalcy that my words were like gibberish to her. That, or the buzzing of an insect. I'd probably have had a better shot at convincing a cannibal to give up his diet for health reasons.

Put bluntly, it was a lost cause. Thus, I steered the conversation away from her weird adulation of the Unmade and toward the original point: her intention in this game.

"What's it all about?" I asked. "If you're not trying to get this chok'tal out of you, why keep playing?"

"When did I say I wanted the chok'tal?"

"You didn't, but I'm getting that impression. All I've sensed is how much you enjoy the game."

Rogaji set her tablet down and laced her fingers on the tabletop. "Well, you're correct. I *do* enjoy this game. In fact, I *love* this game. It's got all the thrills and twists of ordinary, organic survival, just . . . dialed up a few notches. It's funny, really. Until the chok'tal bonded with me, I didn't realize just how lacking the sims were. Reality has much better graphics."

I couldn't tell if she was being ironic or not, but by this point, I'd come to take her words at face value. The fact that she hadn't addressed her clone's brutal death-by-acid experience since we left the hangar was a good reminder of where her head was at.

"So . . . are you just gonna keep playing forever?" I prodded.

"With the same rules? Of course not." She looked at me like a brain-damaged patient who'd forgotten ordinary social etiquette. "The aim of the game is simple, Dak. Kill the 'Unmade' and run things in their stead. You know, transition from a survival sim to a management or dungeon-building version."

"Please tell me you're kidding."

"Not in the slightest—and yes, I've already figured out what you're surely about to tell me. Namely, that there's no true victory condition in the game, and that it was created as some kind of sadistic ritual for an eldritch being who feeds on suffering."

My lips hung open for a few seconds. "That . . . about sums it up."

"As I suspected." She raised a brow at some menu item, then glanced up. "For what it's worth, I'm not the crazed, one-note simmer you might take me to be. The fungus and its predestination ensured I walked into this finale with everything I needed."

"Such as?"

"Information. Tens of thousands of archive entries, each of them from different worlds or eras or species, all describing contact with Purifiers. That's the one thing we humanoids possess that sets us above the Unmade, you see: our ability to coordinate through knowledge. Just wait until you see my collection. It's remarkable, the sheer amount of data that's been recorded and curated in isolated communities across this galactic cluster. All they needed was one bright mind to put it all together and see the common threads."

Although my latest experience with esoteric archives had been colored by paranoia and madness, Rogaji's words gave me a spurt of hope. She certainly seemed more forthcoming with what she had to share. At the very least, it would provide a more complete context for my next encounter with the Unmade. If I was truly lucky, there might even be something related to his original birth among Akasha's people.

"If killing the Unmade is what you're after, I'm at your service," I said. "But I'm not so sure about this whole ambition to run the game afterward."

"Let's process one issue at a time."

I shrugged. "Fair enough. It does raise a question, though."

"Ask away."

"If you've got all this money . . . all these crew members . . . all this knowledge . . . all this goddamn *power* . . . what do you need me for?"

"Oh, would you prefer I send you back to that planet's radioactive ground zero?"

I flinched at that. "No, no, no. I'm just . . . curious."

"Relax," she said, giggling. "I'm being playful, Dak. It's a fair question, and a very astute one. In truth, I'm not entirely certain what I need from you. All I know is that I *do* need something from you. The fungus was quite clear on that point."

"With all due respect, I'm not sure it's a good idea to continue believing the fungus is entirely benevolent. If you consumed some of the corrupted strain—"

That got her attention. "Corrupted strain?"

"Oh, right. You don't know the whole thing about the monks."

"Don't keep me in suspense."

I let out a long, pained breath and slumped back. "None of *that* tale is going to make any sense until I fill you in on my life story. Buckle up. It's pretty short."

And so, for the next forty-three minutes and change, I regaled Rogaji with the complete tale of my existence while nibbling on the bread and tapenade provided by a robotic waiter. I covered every base, from my creation in Chanzig's lab to the fight on the fungal mountaintop, even tossing in secondary descriptions of things such as the monastery's teachings and my acquisition of Morphic Imprints.

The *one* thing I left out—and also prayed she couldn't see in my mind—was the convoluted explanation of the Unmade's birth. Naturally, this also meant I didn't leak any information about Akasha's past-life experiences, nor the childbearing contained therein. Rogaji was still a wild card, and as such, I didn't feel comfortable entrusting her with a devastating secret. Particularly when Akasha herself didn't know that secret yet.

Once I'd finished, indicated by meshing my hands atop the cloth napkin in my lap, Rogaji spent about a minute nodding and studying me.

"Quite the string of events," she said at last. "*Exactly* what I was hoping for."

"Which part?"

Just as she was preparing to answer, our waiter—an oblong hunk of plastic, rubber tubing, and chrome wheels—came zipping up to the table, each tentacle arm hoisting a steaming dish. Without so much as acknowledgment of our existence, let alone a friendly remark, the machine efficiently deposited our food and sped back toward its home: a short, stout porthole in the kitchen's retaining wall.

Rogaji leaned over and took a generous whiff of her entrée, which looked to be a fillet of some large, fatty red fish. "Oh, by the Burnished Heavens, what an aroma."

I used a fork to poke at my own selection: a risotto that involved far too many unidentified sprouts for my taste. Consciously or not, the monks had caused me to become a casual vegetarian . . . but they couldn't do anything to undo my recent, horrible experiences with flora.

"What's it smell like?" I asked her, intrigued by how intrigued *she* was with her dish.

"I haven't a clue," she said with another orgasmic inhale. "I just know it smells . . . rancid."

"Then why keep sniffing it?"

"Because I've never ordered this. It's *new*. Exciting. Even the miserable experiences are euphoric when you view them in the proper light."

"Oh, right. I guess food isn't as flashy when you've already experienced yourself tasting the future."

She waggled a spoon at me, indicating I was right on the money. "Us humanoids don't really appreciate the value of ignorance. When you know what's around the corner, sure, you might survive longer than your average peasant . . . but you won't enjoy the journey. There's no tension when you know the end of each chapter. What we really crave isn't the cake, or the sex, or the drug—it's the feeling of utter surprise when we bump into the fresh and unknown."

I nodded and sipped at my wine, inwardly thinking how much I would kill to have some, or even *any*, sense of the future that awaited me. "Circle back to what you were saying about me. Something about how I'm 'what you hoped for,' or whatever it was."

"Ah, yes." She dabbed at her lip with a napkin. "You see, Dak, I've come to understand why the Unmade has never been conquered. Each Purifier who attempts to battle him is, invariably, slogging through a dimension of the creature's own making. The odds are stacked against them."

"Right . . . ?"

"My precognizant visions suggested that you'd have some 'balancing' ability to help even the playing field," she went on. "In a purely physical fight, I could turn the Unmade to a fine powder in seconds, but we both know that's not quite possible. What I need is somebody who's well versed in the strange side of things."

"How strange are we talking?"

Rogaji cut off, chewed, and swallowed a large hunk of fish, then fixed me with a hard gaze. "It just so happens that I've come to learn about a device capable of fusing the material and the . . . immaterial. Not permanently, granted, but long enough to cross the divide and accomplish the mission."

That reminded me of a different line of questioning. "Back on Chanzig's world, I found some kind of gateway he'd recovered from the Unmade's planet. Is that what you're talking about?"

"A gateway?" Rogaji nearly spit out her wine in laughter. "Dak, please. That's amateur-level thinking. I've been able to make a gateway since Rank 30."

"*Thirty?*" I blurted out.

"The problem isn't forming or accessing the gateway—it's making it to the finish line. I may be wrong, but I believe his dimension is an asymptote. One can come closer, closer, and closer to winning but never truly reach the end point. A bit of a living mirage, if you will."

"And what makes you think that?"

Rogaji polished off her wine, then grunted. "I've made it to 99.998 percent . . . twelve times. The gateway's default save point is still set to 90 percent."

"Maybe it's just a little—"

"Farther?" She smirked. "I've killed sixteen thousand enemies in the Unmade's dimension, Dak. I've traveled the equivalent of fifty thousand kilometers. The nearer one gets to the Unmade's sanctum, the more the world warps. Entire legions might appear just behind you, for example, or the sky might split open to spill lava across the landscape. The Unmade seems capable of altering his dimension's time, space, and energy on a whim."

"That lines up with what I've seen," I said with no shortage of disappointment. "He told me that time moves infinitely slower in his world. Seems like it might be the opposite of a black hole. No matter how far you get, you never enter it."

"Precisely my takeaway," she said, waggling her brow as though impressed.

"So, if your device isn't one of those gateways, what is it?"

"I've no idea."

I let out a breath I hadn't realized I was holding. My one seemingly miraculous shot at turning the Unmade's game on its head, and it was a bust.

"Don't turn so glum on me," Rogaji said. "I'm certain the answer to our problem is lurking somewhere in your precious little noggin."

"You don't plan to cut it out of me, right?"

"Be serious, Dak. There are at *least* five courses of action to attempt before we consider invasive measures." I waited for her to crack a smile or walk back that remark, but those never happened. "What matters is that I *know* there's a solution."

"Just because we know something theoretically exists doesn't mean—"

She shook her head, halting me. "You misunderstand. I may not know what the device is, but I know precisely what it's designed to do."

"I'm all ears."

"We need, in essence, a wormhole. A stable, artificial wormhole capable of cross-dimensional translocation. It's the only way to overcome his perceptive advantage."

I scratched my chin. "Okay, repeat that . . . only slower, and at a three-year-old's level."

"Very well," she said, bristling. "What . . . we . . . need . . . is something capable of launching us directly from our physical universe into the very heart of the Unmade's sanctum. It's the only method swift enough to prevent him from deploying countermeasures or altering spacetime in advance." She took a long pause, considering that. "Well, he *may* still be able to alter spacetime, but I doubt it. Everything is relative, and his sanctum—the belly of the beast—is the center of relativity for his domain. He can't alter that battlefield without weakening himself."

"Bit of an assumption, no? He *is* the dimension. It's all under his thumb."

"My findings challenge that interpretation." I gave her a curious look, but she waved it off. "Later, Dak. You've only just arrived. For the time being, I'd prefer you view this compound as your private training site. Unlimited food, world-class showers, and no local threats to speak of."

"About that last part . . . I know you've probably reached the level of a minor deity, but plebs like me *need* threats to survive. Kill Points and all."

Rogaji laughed. "We share that particular need, Dak. It's part of the Purifier territory."

"But if there aren't any threats here . . . ?"

"Correct. No *threats*. I said nothing about a source of Kill Points."

This was intriguing enough to make me pause in my wine sipping. With those few words, she'd more or less confirmed my suspicion that there *was* a workaround for the system.

"Tell me about it," I said, leaning forward in anticipation.

She slid back. "Why do that when I could just show you instead?"

"You mean, it's . . . here? In the compound?"

"Of course. Everything's here." She picked up her wineglass and swirled it. "I believe it's time for your grand tour."

"By all means, lead on."

In response, she jerked the glass toward me. Pungent wine splattered all over my chest and lap.

"The fuck was that for?" I asked, more out of shock than outrage.

She neatly mopped up the rim of the empty glass and set it down. "Oh, no idea. It just seemed so *deliciously* spontaneous. So out of character!"

I sighed and dabbed at my soaked robes. This was going to be a long, long day.

4

Midway through Rogaji's grand tour, I came to the conclusion that this was closer to a small city than a compound. We'd spent two hours navigating a maze of industrial lifts, conveyors, catwalks, and hallways, yet we still hadn't seen more than a handful of storage warehouses and assorted quality-of-life modules.

Her labor force largely consisted of humanoid-shaped fabriques, all of them faceless and whirring as they shuffled around us. There were a few flesh-and-blood workers, too, but they tended to stay out of the way and avert their eyes whenever we passed. They'd probably learned those behaviors from watching Rogaji "deal with" another laborer who hadn't been so cautious.

In any case, the compound's general ambience didn't do much to inspire socializing. Rogaji had clearly gone to great lengths to beautify the modules—scouring off rust patches, repainting faded lines, so on and so forth—but there's only so much lipstick one can apply to a hog. Carpeting and a few potted, artificial plants do *not* a comfortable living environment make.

The core of the problem was that this compound had been designed for engineers, researchers, and corporate overlords with little to no concern for aesthetic matters. The ceilings were too tall, the air was too drafty (and chlorine-smelling), and the corridors were too wide. Then there were the ravages of time. Everywhere I looked, a floor panel or two showed signs of buckling—the result of tectonic stress, I supposed. Several modules had even been sealed or intentionally collapsed due to "irreparable structural flaws."

To squeeze it into a nutshell, Rogaji plainly saw this compound as a home, if not an impressive spot for entertaining guests. I didn't share that sentiment. Not at all. Luckily, she provided such an enthusiastic and incessant narration of the compound that she didn't seem to notice this.

"And *this* is the Meat Wing," she announced at an intersection, gesturing to a pressurized aperture door that was only remarkable due to its missing placard.

"Meat Wing?" I repeated. "Some kind of freezer unit?"

She gave me a thin smile. "It's our colloquial term for the area that concerns humanoids. Well, technically *all* organic life—I'm a nondiscriminatory employer—but we haven't had any alien applicants in a while. Hard to find good help in my line of work."

"What do you mean by 'concerns humanoids'?"

"Sleeping quarters, training gauntlets, fitness modules, hydroponics, vehicle bays for the jobs too complex for my fabriques . . . "

"But not your fine-dining joint?"

"Of course not," she said with genuine alarm. "That's for *me* and only me."

"Oh. That sounds a little . . . lonely."

"Far from it, Dak. My fabriques are often permitted to stand on the sidelines and watch me consume food. It's a real treat for them."

My lips quirked up at the joke, but Rogaji's didn't. Then I realized it wasn't a joke.

Rogaji palmed the biometric pad to the left of the door, and the aperture unsealed with a shrill hiss to reveal some kind of recreation room. Lining the walls were the same pinup posters, buzzing neon signs, and dartboards you'd expect to find in a bar. That comparison was further cemented by the presence of a thick, reddish smoke haze and thumping electronica tunes.

Gathered inside was a hodgepodge trio of human males, all sprawled out on grease-stained sofas with dozens of tiny burn marks—the same kind left by amp-sticks, it seemed. The reason I say "males" here, as opposed to "men," is simple: one of them appeared no older than fifteen. Even so, that outlier fit right in. The whole lot of them were weary, rough-and-tumble-looking sorts who'd surely earned their downtime here.

"Hello, boys," Rogaji said, crossing the room like a princess arriving at her coronation ceremony.

She looked terribly out of place here, between her poise and general attire, but the rec room's inhabitants barely lifted a brow. Their nonreaction was surprising, given the trepidation and overall dread I'd seen in the other humans here. Then I understood: *this* was her crew. The others had to be temp workers . . . or maybe even clones she'd snagged off the black market. Thinking more on it, the latter seemed more likely. Rogaji didn't strike me as the sort to leave loose ends flopping about—especially when it came to loose ends that knew the location and inner workings of her supersecret base.

"Everyone, this is Dak," she said, pointing to me as though I were a new pet. "Dak, this is everyone."

I raised a limp hand that none of them cared to notice. "Hi, everyone."

Rogaji frowned upon witnessing the cold reception. "Ahem. Shall you offer your own introductions like polite humans, or will I have to do it for you?"

"You do it," they all said in a whiny, half-hearted chorus.

"And so I will." Rogaji shook her head like a disapproving mother, then pointed out the man sitting farthest to the left—a large, stout specimen that looked to have some beast DNA spliced into him. "This is Frownmaker, head of compound security."

Frownmaker's only response was to fix me with a glowing, hollow stare, courtesy of his midgrade retinal implants. He had a bushy, straw-colored beard, a thick brow, hands studded with tungsten rods, and more scars than smooth skin. All this was suitably wrapped up in an—I shit you not—armored trench coat, complete with crisscrossing bandoliers that held bullets thick enough to belong in the magazine of an antiair cannon.

Faced with this demon of a man, I went with a strategy commonly reserved for rabid animals: glancing away and pretending he wasn't there. It seemed to work. Despite his brief and stomach-lurching growl, he soon lost interest in me and returned to huffing down his amp-stick.

"Next," Rogaji said, her eyes tracking to the duo sitting nearby, "are Toast and Jar, our mechanics. They fix the training module, mostly."

I glanced at her. "Please tell me these aren't real names."

"Oh, but they are." She nodded back toward them. "Toast is the tall one, and Jar is the hairy one."

The description was vague, but when I looked at them in earnest, I found it fairly practical. On the left-hand side, tinkering with a small, grenade-like device using a pair of pliers, was a tall and thin man caked in motor oil. Not one, not two, but *three* amp-sticks dangled from his tattooed lips. His patchy hair, patchy shirt, and patchy pants—which might've once been khaki but were now better described as "every-colored" due to various industrial fluids—painted him as the spirit of mechanical work incarnate. Given the obsessively focused look on his sooty, severe face, I doubted he even noticed me.

Beside him was the one known as Jar—the fifteen-year-old, by the way—who was mostly distinguished by an outfit that had half the holes and twice the gadgets. His massive, floppy cotton swab of hair nearly obscured a pair of polished welding goggles. He was currently reclining, head and tongue lolling about in ecstasy. Probably enjoying some dopamine rush created by the pucker pads attached to his temples.

"Nice to . . . meet . . . you all," I said, earning me exactly as much attention as I'd expected. None, that is.

Rogaji gently nudged me onward, leading me to the hallway at the far end of the room. Along the way, she said, "Don't mind them. They've forgotten their people skills from working here too long."

"It's fine," I said honestly, knowing I was just as burned out on introductions and idle chatter. "So, did they sign a lifetime contract or something?"

"Yeah. Something like that."

Her tone convinced me to set aside whatever follow-up questions I'd prepared. Instead, I followed her down the maze of hallways, wrinkling my nose each time we passed through a new miasma zone. Some segments smelled like rancid cooking oil, while others reminded me of coolant vats or wet dogs. Meat Wing indeed.

"You mentioned this area's for jobs that are too complex for the fabriques," I said as we turned a corner and came within sight of the next module. "Toast and, uh, Jar are your go-to mechanics?"

She glanced sidelong. "Yes. Why?"

"They just seem a little . . . eccentric."

"Everyone here is. I offered them enough money to retire five times over, but at the cost of losing forty years of their life and all memories of the experience. You can imagine what sorts of men might jump at that chance."

"You're going to blank their memories when they get out?"

"Well, of course. It's how I ensure a tight-lipped operation." She grimaced upon catching my expression. "Oh, no, no, no, Dak. They all know the conditions, and they agreed readily. I would never do such a thing to you without your consent."

"To be fair, I wouldn't have any way of knowing if you did. Memory erasure and all that."

She rubbed her chin in thought. "What an excellent point."

At that moment, I resolved to stop giving Rogaji advice on how to fuck with my mind.

We entered a large, dim space illuminated mainly by the overlapping beams of ceiling-mounted floodlights. The deafening chorus of hydraulic lifts and angle grinders hit me in an instant. All that racket seemed to originate from the very center of the room, where a small and weathered gunship wobbled on its network of tethering chains. A thin, silhouetted body scrambled over the hull, tackling tiny repair jobs and applying finishing touches with a handheld laser.

"Bit loud, isn't it?" I asked Rogaji.

She squinted and signaled that she couldn't hear me.

"Bit *loud*!" I repeated, shouting this time.

That did the trick. Rogaji pantomimed a great *ahh* of understanding, then snapped her fingers—and deleted almost all sound. The shift was drastic enough to make me question whether I'd gone deaf. Where I'd once heard whining and cranking and banging, I now heard only the soft rasp of Rogaji's footsteps on the concrete floor.

"It's Local Insulation," she said by way of explanation. "Some variant of the Silence upgrade, I suppose. Quite handy at higher ranks."

"How far does the bubble extend?"

She shrugged, then winked. "Test it yourself."

Figuring there was little harm in trying, I turned and moved away from Rogaji's side. At about twenty meters away—much farther than I'd anticipated—the full din of the hangar returned with a vengeance. Startled, I leaped back into Rogaji's sphere of influence and returned to her side as she approached the vessel's underbelly.

"Dak, I'd like you to meet the team responsible for all our off-compound missions," she said. "They've been with me for a number of years, and they've been rather instrumental in my coming as far as I have."

Rogaji's eyes flashed white, befuddling me for a moment—until I realized it was her way of pinging the workers atop the ship.

This was confirmed when a small, wiry boy came swinging over the side of the ship on his harness, all the while groaning, "I'm here, Miss, I'm here . . . "

Floodlights revealed the boy's face as he landed. They *also* revealed that he couldn't have been older than thirteen or so. He had small, dark eyes, a splotchy jumpsuit, and buzzed-down hair with far too many nicks and burns to put me at ease.

"Dak, this is Nugget," Rogaji said. "Nugget, this is Dak."

Nugget's eyes lit up. "Dak, Miss? *Purifier* Dak?"

"The very same," she said with a smile.

For some reason, that irked me. If this little pipsqueak knew who and what I was, it meant the laborers back in the rec room had also known—and still hadn't found me impressive (or frightening) enough to pop out a brief greeting. The pricks.

Nugget rushed forward with a bulky glove extended, beaming up at me. "Nice to meet you, sir, Mr. Dak, sir, Purifier, sir."

"Dak is just fine," I said with an awkward grin and a weak shake. My hand came away with a thick film of grease.

Rogaji fixed Nugget with a strange, unreadable expression, then made a shooing motion. He nodded hurriedly and yanked himself back up on the tether line, returning to work without missing a beat.

"Very polite, that one, but not the sharpest butter knife in the drawer," Rogaji murmured.

I leaned closer to her. "You said these guys have all been with you for years."

"Correct."

"Isn't he a little . . . young . . . to be taking on lifetime contracts involving memory loss?"

She snorted. "Lifetime? Dak, Dak, Dak. You must think bigger. That young man is going to leave here with enough bux to purchase ten sets of new bodies. He'll live five thousand years, provided he doesn't have another accident in a pressure bay . . . "

"But he won't have any memories when he comes out."

"I'm well aware." She grinned at me. "Memories are overrated, Dak. Better to live in a haze of spontaneity and ignorance."

Realizing just who I was talking to, I opted to nod politely and let her continue the tour.

She moved to the nearby ramp—a rusted, flaky length of metal grating—and pounded on its railing several times. This caused quite the clamor, which was soon revealed to be her intention. Long before the railings had stopped creaking, two figures came hurrying out of the ship and down the ramp.

The first was a full-grown man wearing a tricorne and a long, luxurious coat that probably had been cut from an aquatic beast, judging by its slick, oily texture. Beneath the tricorne's shadow were sunken eyes, both dilated to shit from one narcotic or another. Then there was his crooked smile—which unironically displayed signs of predator DNA—and his patchy beard, complete with clumps of follicles that had been scorched or dissolved. On top of all that, he had the stumbling gait of a bar patron who'd never been cut off . . . and a pair of scaly, albino boots with ears still attached to them.

"Dak," Rogaji said, clearly brimming with pride, "this is Krezz Holmes, pilot extraordinaire and all-around savant. A man of exceptional judgment—by humanoid standards."

His only response was to shoot me a finger-gun gesture and sip on a flask he'd seemingly drawn from thin air.

I didn't trust this guy enough to offer me directions, let alone fly a ship.

Following in his wake was a smaller, yet no less curious man. Boy? I couldn't tell. Rogaji's disregard for child-labor regulations had skewed my perspective beyond repair. At the very least, he seemed a year or two older than Nugget, though younger than Jar.

Every one of his features—coppery skin, shaved hair, dark, guarded eyes, and a thin frame—spoke of a childhood steeped in hard work and blood, but his clothing said just the opposite. He wore a freshly ironed, open-chested blazer, tailored pants, and needle-pointed shoes, all of which sparkled with gold fabric and embedded rubies. Picture, if you will, an exotic animal–smuggling sultan who'd been afflicted with the curse of reverse aging.

His face, too, was marked by all-too-adult wisdom—although wisdom might imply something kinder and more agreeable than what I actually saw. There was real cunning in his eyes. A keen, predatory ambition that seemed to frame me as a pawn on a gameboard. The wolfish curl at the edge of his lips vindicated my interpretation.

"Dak, meet Bodhi," Rogaji continued.

Unlike the pilot, Bodhi stepped forward and offered a well-manicured hand that gleamed with pricy bracelets. "Pleasure to meet you, Purifier. I'm Bodhi Drezek, and this here is my humble vessel."

Holmes smacked him upside the head. "You little shit. It's *my* vessel. You're just the hired help."

"Possession is eight-fifteenths of the law!" he pointed out, grinning like a weasel.

That earned him another smack.

"Pleasure," I said weakly.

I didn't feel comfortable asking this in front of these . . . gentlemen . . . but I questioned what Rogaji really needed these people for. She was, for all intents and purposes, a wandering power plant who could snap people out of existence on a whim. And even if they did play some vital role in her plans, was this *really* the best she could wrangle up with more money than an extinct civilization? Hard to find good help, I supposed.

"Excellent," Rogaji said with a ceremonial clap. "Now that introductions are done, I can show you the pride and joy of my compound."

Bodhi wiggled a brow. "I thought *I* was your pride and joy."

Rogaji seemed briefly charmed, but that ended when Holmes once again gave Bodhi a thwack.

"I didn't even do anything that time," Bodhi snapped.

"You keep opening your mouth," Holmes growled at his young assistant. "What'd I tell you about that?"

"At least my breath doesn't smell like the inside of a fecal incubator."

"Yeah, you just bought yourself another stint in the maintenance crawl space."

"But . . . uh . . . it's still flooded with radiation."

"I'm aware," Holmes said, hooking his arm around Bodhi's scrawny neck and dragging him back up the ramp. "Very, very aware . . . "

Once they were out of earshot, I glanced at Rogaji and asked, "Is he gonna be okay? Does he need help?"

"The one thing that boy has never needed is help," Rogaji said with a chuckle. "Come with me, Dak. The anticipation is gnawing at me."

I followed her through the hangar, frowning. "Anticipation? But you already know what you're going to show me."

"Obviously. It's anticipation over your reaction!"

Again, I was well past the point of enjoying surprises, but I decided it best to hold my tongue and let Rogaji finish her tour. The sooner she finished showing me the compound, the sooner I could shift to formulating and carrying out a plan to kill the Unmade. Before I even reached those steps, however, I wanted to see Akasha awake, moving, and just as sharp as before. Rogaji hadn't given me any cause to fear her, but she also hadn't provided any guarantees that she would use her wealth and resources to fix Akasha after I served my purpose.

This all spiraled through my mind as Rogaji took us down a network of corridors and yet another lift. When we stepped out into the new sublevel, my nose prickled from the aftereffects of chemical sprays. It wasn't all bad, though. This area's smaller dimensions—narrower hallways, lower ceilings, thinner doors—and generally clinical aesthetic made me feel more at home than anything I'd seen topside. Hell, even the lighting was only at about 40 percent—a change that felt like a Jacuzzi for my eyeballs.

"Secret level to a secret base?" I asked.

She unsealed the next door and ushered me through, smiling softly. "Something like that. The compound's redesign architect suggested we place the sensitive equipment deep, deep under the surface. The machines aren't above tossing EMPs at one another."

I nodded, somewhat surprised at how logical the reasoning was. "Where's the architect now?"

"Dead."

I stopped in place. "Dead?"

"Well, yes? He attempted to sell this compound's schematics to a half dozen bidders. It's a good thing I found out when I did. A few minutes later and I would've vaporized his brainstem *after* he transferred the data."

"Oh . . . "

"I'm kidding, Dak."

I let out a sigh of relief.

"I didn't vaporize his brainstem," she continued, working the next door's controls. "I tortured him for sixteen days straight, at which point his pathetic little heart gave out."

"As any reasonable person would do," I said flatly.

If she picked up on the sarcasm, she didn't show it. "Exactly! The others were a bit miffed, seeing as the architect was their best card player . . . but at least it made an example."

When the door slid open, I found myself expecting more doors, another hallway, or the next grid of interlocking lasers. What I got instead, however, was . . . bizarre. It appeared, on first glance, to be a larger variant of the hangar we'd seen in the upper levels. Obviously an enclosed space, despite its vastness, and lined with hundreds of small, inactive ceiling lights. There was just enough ambient illumination to make out the rim of a massive wall standing about fifty meters ahead. Some type of labyrinth?

"It's not a labyrinth, if that's what you're thinking," Rogaji said. She tossed me a thin smile. "Sorry. It was quite loud, even for you."

"Then what is it?"

She led me toward the wall, prompting rows of ceiling lights to trigger as we wandered beneath their sensors. "This, Dak, is how I've reached my current rank."

"Which is?"

"I'll save the surprise for later."

"It can't be *that* high, can it? You don't have any, uh . . . stored energy on your body."

"Fat?" she said, smiling. "Don't get the wrong idea, Dak. The chok'tal will *always* require energy from the body. Difference is, mine is also drawing from implants. Miniature fission cells, to be precise."

"You implanted fission cells . . . in your body?"

"They're biological in nature."

"Fission . . . cells . . . "

She shrugged. "We can talk about getting you some internal upgrades later. For now, though, let's stick to the module. Just to ensure you're proud of me, I ought to mention that I didn't inherit it. This beauty was a custom design."

"No offense, but it's hard to be proud when I don't know what it does."

"Have you ever heard of a training loop?"

"Yeah, sure," I said, leaning back on residual memories from my genetic donors. "They're sims, right? Meant to train soldiers, pilots, that sort of thing?"

Rogaji nodded. "In some contexts, yes. More generally, however, training loops are intended to be hand-holding experiences that help one master a particular skill. Most high-level sims feature one when you first jack in. The sim's idea of fairness."

"Okay, right . . . but what's that got to do with this? Is it a gigantic sim arena?"

"Arena, yes. Sim, no."

I scratched my head as I continued to follow. "I'm confused. If it's a real, physical environment that's forgiving to the 'player,' it sounds fine for actual training . . . and not so useful for Kill Points. On the flip side, if it's filled with actual opponents, I don't think I'd call that training. Just more combat."

"Precisely," she explained. "This is the best of both worlds, Dak. I call it . . . the Godmaker."

"Quite a name."

Coming to a stop, she let out a sharp breath. "All right, fine, I've always called it the training circuit. But now that I have a fellow Purifier to experience its power, Godmaker it shall be."

"It works for me." I folded my arms and studied the towering walls. "Still, you haven't actually said *how* it functions. Am I able to go in there, start up the program, and chow down on rank after rank without doing any work?"

"It's not technically a program, but rather an exploit," she said, beckoning me to approach a small lift that had been slotted into the base of the wall. Once we'd stepped inside, she continued, "If you play a sim long enough, you begin to understand the glitches in the system. At its core, all sims are really an elaborate set of checks, balances, and authentications. That means, in practice, that there are virtually infinite places for a sim's integrity to break down and introduce . . . alterations."

"Okay, I'm following."

Rogaji shut the lift doors, then glanced my way as we began slowly ascending. "The chok'tal, for all its complexity, is no different than the AI constructs running a recreational sim. And that means it can be exploited."

"That's exactly what I've been thinking," I said with a spurt of genuine excitement. Finally, somebody speaking my language (and on my level). "So, how do you break it?"

She sighed, plainly loading up a long and stale explanation. "Essentially, every chok'tal has a four-stage loop: homeostasis, detection, engagement, and return to baseline. Homeostasis is self-explanatory—the chok'tal runs its normal functions to keep you both alive. Detection is when the chok'tal becomes aware of a possible threat in your environment. Under the surface, it toggles on a series of perceptual feedback systems to pick out and begin assigning Kill Point values to any target deemed a threat. Then there's engagement, which is also quite straightforward. Chok'tal goes into kill mode, shuts down its conscious functions, and tracks enemies using the HUD. That phase ends with the last stage—return to baseline. Here, the chok'tal switches consciousness back on, wipes the threat-detection activity, and assigns the Kill Points."

Despite knowing all this on an intuitive level, the ease and confidence with which Rogaji spoke left me slightly droopy-lipped. It was clear she'd analyzed the chok'tal with the analytical precision of an AI technician, right down to her labeling of the stages and the interactions between them. The question of how she'd learned all this with objective certainty arose in my mind, but at that moment, I was more interested in the solution than the way in which she'd arrived at her conclusions.

"The thing is," Rogaji continued, not noticing my mental tangent, "there's a flaw in the system between stages two and three. Have you ever been engaged in an encounter, only to have the chok'tal alter the Kill Point values?"

I nodded. "A few times."

"Let me guess . . . you found some larger subsection of a beast, or gained better visual clarity?"

"Nailed it."

"What I'll also guess, Dak, is that the chok'tal has never *reduced* the Kill Point total. Only increased it."

Again, I nodded. A flicker of curiosity stirred at her implications.

"In brief, the chok'tal wasn't engineered to reverse its judgments about threats in combat," Rogaji went on. "In order to assign Kill Points, the chok'tal draws from a sort of decentralized information bank that compares perceptual information to your current capabilities."

I gave her a blank stare.

"All right, let's try again," she said, groaning. "The chok'tal is connected to some sort of server that isn't in our universe. Probably the Unmade, if what you've told me is accurate. Whatever the case, every chok'tal is determining what is and isn't a threat based on past experiences from other Purifiers. That means it ranks some threats higher than is realistic, and some lower. It all depends on what the algorithm says."

"A little technical, but okay. I *think* I've got it."

She blinked at me for a moment, probably waiting for me to raise an issue, then proceeded. "If the chok'tal starts noticing sounds, sights, smells, feelings, or mental impressions that correspond to a high-level threat, it will increase its Kill Point values . . . even if the stimuli that triggered that Kill Point increase are no longer present."

A light bulb flicked on in my skull. "So what you're saying is . . . if the chok'tal experiences something scary, even for a moment, it raises its KP award . . . but if that scary thing goes away, the Purifier keeps the new KP total."

"You're smarter than I first assumed, Dak."

"Thank . . . you?"

"Quite welcome."

The doors slid open to reveal some kind of fishbowl-shaped control room with hundreds of vidscreens and blinking lights. Server stacks hummed along the walls, filling the room with a dry, blistering heat that tickled my eyeballs.

"The heart of the machine," I commented.

Rogaji gave a hum of assent and led me to the far end of the room, which featured a long console and more buttons than I could count. It also featured a swiveling, quilted chair that overlooked the entire facility below. The view was equal parts mesmerizing and panoramic; a seemingly endless expanse of robotic arms, patchwork-style floor textures that ranged from soil to brackish water to moss, and ominous-looking trapdoors. If I hadn't known better, I'd have assumed it was a revolutionary theater innovation that allowed the director to swap sets on the fly.

"Damn," I said, whistling through my teeth. "How big is it?"

"End to end, about sixteen kilometers square," she said casually. "Don't worry, though. When you're actually inside it, you won't be moving very much. The program tends to bring threats to *you*."

"So, it's like an arena sim? Waves of enemies attacking your position?"

She looked me up and down with a playful eye. "You know more about sims than you've let on, don't you?"

"Mr. Korasa was a casual player. You can thank him for giving me some background."

"Understood." She returned her gaze to the sprawl below. "To answer your question, no, it's not an arena sim. Quite frankly, I'm not certain what it is. The fungus showed me the design, and I built it."

"So, when you said this was *your* machine . . . "

"I didn't say I was the architect."

"Fair enough." I folded my arms, pondering the strange sight. "Do I get to try it out?"

"Soon," she said with a grin. "Once you get inside it, you won't want to come out. Better for us to finish the tour while I still have your undivided attention, then let you loose in there."

"How much more could this base possibly have?"

"Oh, not much more. Just one thing, to be precise." She backed away from the console, savoring my expression of utter confusion. "I save the best for last."

5

My mind wandered as Rogaji led me down a fresh set of corridors and lifts. She'd already shown me a five-star compound, a full complement of *eccentric* staff members, and a training facility that probably cost a good fraction of the Hegemony's entire military budget. What more was there to see?

Knowing her penchant for "fun," there was a good chance she'd lead me to a spiffy hotel room or a high-end starship just to see my reaction. Either of those sounded good, considering the alternatives. And what were those alternatives? Oh, just off the top of my head . . . A man-eating plant the size of a factory. A sentient machine that had evolved to digest fingernails. A tribe of nonspacefaring humanoids she'd shrunk down and trapped inside a treadmill generator.

The possibilities were endless, and that wasn't good when it came to Rogaji.

Hence my questions.

"You're sure it isn't a man-eating plant?" I asked—again.

"I'm sure."

"What about a miniature black hole?"

"I got rid of mine a while ago."

I groaned. "Could you just give me a *hint*?"

"I'm getting the sense that you don't share my affection for the uncertain, Dak."

"Not anymore."

She palmed another door open and smiled at me. "How much do you know about the field of aberrant consciousness?"

"Huh?"

"Right. I'll take it that means 'very little.'" She led me into what seemed to be a well-worn bunkroom, turning her nose up at the scattered piles of holographic nudie cards and half-empty narcotics inhalers like a displeased mother. "Aberrant consciousness is a broad thing, but in brief, it refers to consciousness that has been knocked out of its standard 'orbit' through things like drugs, rituals, spacetime rifts, quantum—"

"Okay, I've got it," I said, sidling past a literal heap of used underwear to follow Rogaji into an adjoining room. "What's the relevance?"

"The relevance? Dak, please. Your wife is quite plainly experiencing a bout of aberrant consciousness."

"First off, not my wife. Second, I'm well aware, but I don't get why you're giving me the textbook definition of this stuff. Where's it going?"

She sighed. "As you might imagine, I became rather interested in the subject following my brush with the fungus."

"Don't you mean the fungus became interested? You know, predestination and all that."

"An interest *arose*," she said flatly, silencing my nitpicking. "Whatever the case, I thought it might be prudent to enlist the aid of specialists who were trained in aberrant consciousness. Individuals who can deal with problems beyond the physical plane."

"What, by lighting a few candles and saying some magic words?"

She stopped, spun, and fixed me with a stern gaze. "Sometimes."

I put both hands up, signaling surrender until she decided she'd put enough respect (read: fear) in my heart. Then she moved along without missing a beat.

"So, just to clarify," I said after a few moments, "is this 'specialist' for Akasha?"

"It's for whoever needs it. If they can work their magic on her, then yes. Though I suspect they'll be far more interested in you."

"Me? Why would I need someone poking around my consciousness?"

Rogaji glanced back and cocked a brow. "Isn't that how you spent your last few days?"

"Yes, and I'm done with that phase of my life."

"We'll see if the expert agrees."

Before I could slip in another rebuttal, Rogaji unsealed a door at the end of a dark, narrow hallway and stepped inside. Curiously enough, not a speck of light came pouring out through the doorway.

What *did* come pouring out, though, was a brass-knuckle sucker punch of aromatics and pungent, earthy reagents. Notes of pepper, citrus, sulfur—all of it came rushing out like a boiling miasma. This was my first indication that Rogaji might've hired a crackpot more interested in sampling her exotic ingredients than putting them to medicinal use.

After another long moment of wondering what the hell I was doing here, I followed her into the shadows.

The moment I crossed the threshold, I sensed a faint, almost whispered presence animating the air. In some ways, it was reminiscent of a watered-down version of Rogaji's aura. Much as I wanted to dial in on the phenomenon, it was a useless effort in the wake of that damned odor bomb.

"You feel it, don't you?"

Seeing as my eyes were still adjusting to the gloom, I flinched at the new voice. It was that of a man—deep, raspy, colored by a weird regional twang I'd never encountered.

Blink by blink, the room sharpened from sheer darkness to a dim, candlelit hovel. The low ceilings and pitted walls made me wonder if this had once been a maintenance closet. In any event, it sure as hell wasn't any longer. The walls, ceilings, and even mold-crusted floor were covered in thousands of intricate sigils and interlocking motifs. The way the light glinted across the designs suggested they'd been carved out with a knife.

Rogaji stood over the lone section of floor that was covered not in etchings, but tapestries and frilly pillows. Strewn across the fabric were prayer beads, half-assembled hookahs, small vials, the bones of animals I couldn't even imagine, and other "mystical" knickknacks.

"Well, do you?"

This time, I managed to spot the man when he spoke. Barely. You see, he wasn't a human—and in most jurisdictions, probably not even a humanoid.

He was just over a meter tall, swaddled in glimmering robes the color of lapis lazuli. Beneath his oversize hood was dark, sandpaper-like skin and a wide yet lipless mouth. There were no eyes to speak of, and his only analogues for ears or a nose were the rows of tiny, fluttering holes that ran across the middle of his face. One of his hands—thick, brutish things somewhere between pincers and paws—clutched a gnarled staff with dried organs hanging from it. As my eyes adjusted more, I noted dozens of slimy "limbs" creeping about beneath him.

"Feel what?" I asked, largely still in shock over the being's strange physiology.

"Don't play dumb, boy," he growled. "The resonance in the air. You tasted it from the moment you entered."

I just blinked at him, wondering if he could see the gesture.

"I'm unsure about this one, Madam Ro," the thing growled. "He is not forthcoming. He hides. He obscures."

"Play nice," she said in a warning tone. "Dak, I'd like to introduce you to Izamem Hukish, former seer and resident acass. And Izamem . . . this is Dak. Though you knew that."

I narrowed my eyes at her. "Acass?"

"It's an acronym. Afflicted consciousness and altered state specialist. He came highly recommended by his peers."

Izamem yipped like an angered pup. "I am *still* a seer. Do not besmirch my good name and work by invoking your corporate jargon."

"Yes, yes, Izamem. You're a fantastic seer." She leaned over to me with wide eyes, then whispered, "He's a staunch anticapitalist. Then again, he still signed on for my generous salary . . . "

"I did *not*," Izamem huffed. "I came here to do my work."

"Yes, you did," Rogaji said, patting the little seer's head—much to his displeasure. "Right now, Izamem, your *work* is this man and his acquaintance. So I suggest you take a few of your sedating roots, take a deep breath, and cooperate. Dak is very important to me."

Izamem's only reply was a deep harrumph and an eyeless glare in my direction.

After a few seconds of that awkward silence, Rogaji stepped back and clapped her hands. "Well, gentlemen, I believe it's time I allow you to get familiar with one another. All I ask is that there's no bloodshed."

Again, Izamem harrumphed.

Rogaji sidled past me and headed for the door, pausing just long enough to slip me, "He's a charmer, isn't he?"

Then she was gone, and it was me and the grumpy seer.

"You felt it," he said with no preamble.

I sighed. "Look, I don't know—"

He used his disgusting claw-hand-nub to indicate a small, faintly glowing crystal on the ground beside him. "It was felt."

Frowning, I took a few reluctant steps closer to Izamem and squatted down before the crystal. Just as the seer had said, I *did* feel it. There was a subtle current flowing off its surface, rippling out into the air like echoes from a cave. I moved my hand around its edges, marveling at the way the energy circled my skin and raised the little hairs on my arm.

"What is it?" I asked.

Izamem grunted. "My people used these crystals to determine who had crossed the Flesh Plane."

"The *huh*?"

"The Flesh Plane. This plane. This lifeless, empty, horrid plane you call reality."

Despite the fact that I'd been cloned against my will, I still found myself slightly offended by Izamem's dismissive perception of the physical universe. Sure, most of it was full of death, plagues, barbarism, liars, and sycophants, but there were *some* redeeming qualities. I just couldn't think of them at that moment.

"What did you mean by 'crossed' the Flesh Plane?" I asked.

"You've gone beyond it," Izamem whispered. "You have felt the winds of the other planes."

I glanced at the crystal, wondering if it (or the seer himself) was truly capable of discerning where my mind had gone. Even I didn't feel capable of doing that.

My cross-dimensional experiences with the monks had been interesting, if not a window into madness, but I still found it difficult to believe they'd left any lasting marks on my being. Keep in mind that almost every aspect of my consciousness—from Modri's stone-cold tactical approach to Korasa's skeptical analysis—had conditioned me to view physical reality as primary, if not all-encompassing. The notion that there were infinite dimensions of mind, or energy, or whatever the hell else was truly world-shattering . . . and it would take time to become my default mode of perception. Even at that moment, withering under Izamem's critical gaze, I didn't feel like half my encounters were even real. Things like the Accretion and the junnara-gol still felt like vivid hallucinations rather than actual beings I'd slain.

"I take it you've crossed the planes yourself," I said.

Izamem let out a barking laugh. "My people are born beyond the Flesh Plane. If I didn't have such a . . . keen interest in your dimension, I would not be here."

"You picked one hell of a place to explore in the Flesh Plane."

"This is but one stop among thousands," he said quietly. "Once my work here is finished, I will shuffle along. No sense in clinging to anything in this fragile world."

His words reminded me of Rogaji's remarks. "What did she mean when she said I'm your work?"

"You and your *acquaintance* are my work."

"Right, fine. But what does that entail? No offense to you, but I think I've gotten more than a crash course in the mind from those monks."

"The Order of the Radiant Throne," Izamem said with a thick coat of venom.

"I take it you aren't old pals."

"Far from it. Those mechanized bastards are an affront to the disciplines my people have spent centuries cultivating, exploring, mastering. They can tell you as much about the mind as a wild beast can tell you about table manners."

Again, I felt a surge of vicarious offense. "They taught me how to cross your precious planes. So far, all you've done is show me a vibrating crystal and pout."

That got a genuine laugh out of the crotchety seer. "Even a withered tree can provide shade, I suppose . . . "

"Besides, you don't have to worry about them anymore."

"Ah. I take it their fate has come to pass. Eradication in the fires of ambition . . . "

"Yeah, that," I said, scratching my head awkwardly. "Did Rogaji tell you about it?"

He shook his head. "There was no need. I saw it myself, boy."

"What . . . else did you see?"

"Surely as much as you." The seer's mouth extended into a long, flat line punctuated by serrated teeth. His imitation of a human smile, it seemed. "Keep your wits. I won't be telling Madam Ro anything you haven't already."

"Thanks, I guess." I glanced around, noting several lockers that had been converted into ad hoc bookshelves. "So, if you aren't teaching me the ropes of plane-crossing, what's your role?"

"To make you better with ropes."

"How specific."

Izamem nodded slowly. "Madam Ro is kind, and often amusing, but she's got no clue what she's meddling with."

"You're talking about the Unmade, right?"

"Such an uninspired, loutish name," he growled. "My people know him as the Endless Mouth of the Void. Even as he corrupts the Flesh Plane, he moves in silence across the higher realms. Feeding, feeding, feeding."

Daunting as it was to hear, this at least confirmed what the monks had told me about the Unmade. He really *was* a multidimensional threat. It had been easy enough to disregard this unfortunate factoid while under

Narbu's tutelage, considering how hyperbolic their texts were, but now that it had been explained by two independent sources . . .

"Do you think she's right?" I asked. "You think I'll be able to create some kind of rift that can cut straight through to his world?"

With a sigh, Izamem turned to crushing bundles of herbs and seeds with his pestle. "You are a key ingredient to the process, but to answer you with the point of the blade . . . no. You will not open a rift. Madam Ro misunderstands your destiny."

I didn't know whether to be elated or disappointed by that. "Does that mean you know how to do this? You have the solution?"

"When did I say that?"

"You just said—"

"Knowing where *not* to look is as critical as knowing where to look," he said. "Your mind is an enigma, boy. A strange, dark, squirming thing. It's no riddle why those monks took such an interest in you."

"And yet it's not enough to flip the tables on the Unmade."

"You are too obsessed with words. Listen closely. You are a *key ingredient*, boy. Not the catalyst, but the path, the method, the roots. You see? You cannot do it, nor can it be done without you."

I settled down on the tapestry and let out a long breath. "Sorry. I've just heard a lot of prophecies in the last few days. Hard to know which ones are legit."

"Forget prophecies," Izamem said, grunting. "Fickle, deceptive little things. I am speaking only of capability. What you do with my words and instruction is your business, and yours alone. Remember . . . my people can roam the infinite planes. Yours cannot."

"Just tell me what the hell you need from me. You're not going to teach me to open a rift, so what's the course of study?"

"Impatient, impatient. Good to know."

"I *swear* to Hal—"

"No need to invoke that hideous deity here." Izamem cackled. "There are two priorities, boy. The first is shoring up your mind. Hardening it. Madam Ro may be powerful, but her foe will surely devour her when she sets foot in his realm. She will need the aid of a Purifier who can turn the tides and reshape reality."

Just like the monks had told me, then. A realm was nothing but a combination of the minds that inhabited it. External reflections of internal states, so to speak. It made sense that Izamem expected *me*, not Rogaji, to be the realm's sanity anchor.

"And the second priority?" I pressed.

"To awaken the dreamer."

"Out with it."

"The Cobalt Seer," Izamem whispered. "Heir to the sins of the Unmade's empire."

I tried to stare at him, but there were no eyes to focus on. "She might come out of it on her own."

"Who told you that? The monks?"

"Medical deduction."

Izamem just chuckled and kept grinding his mixture. "This is no *medical* matter, boy. Stop thinking with the logic of the Flesh Plane. Your seer is not in this world, nor in any other. She resides in the space between worlds."

"What?"

"Is your skull soft and rotten, like a plum?" He leaned forward and tapped my forehead with his walking stick. "If you wish to bring her back to her flesh, you will need my help."

"Seriously? We're not even going to attempt medical intervention? I don't think so."

"Do as you wish," Izamem said with a flippant wave. "She is not my seer, nor the object of my affection."

"Now you're just reading too deeply into things."

"Am I?" He offered another wide, haunting grin. "If you insist on working in the realm of flesh, her mindstream will drift farther and farther from the body. This is not an accident, boy. It was the order's intention. They knew she would be sealed in a place beyond all hope."

"You're wrong," I snapped. "They wouldn't have done that to her."

"And yet . . . they were quite happy to send her to her death." He paused and angled his chin up, seemingly studying my reaction. Even without eyes, I'm sure he sensed my tacit agreement with his words. "Once the order had you, she was a pile of meat. Scraps. They just needed a method that would keep her from being reborn."

I sat there for a time, weighing his words, his unspoken intentions. It was obvious he didn't want to do any further harm to her—otherwise, why not let her stew in unconsciousness?—but it was less clear what the solution might be. Izamem's coy nature made it difficult to discern how much he really knew about her condition. How much he really knew about the secrets locked in her head, to be precise.

Don't get me wrong—on the inside, under my layered mesh of cynicism, I was scared shitless about Akasha. Pain and adrenaline had worked in a pinch, keeping the worst of my fears out of sight, but they were only temporary fixes. Fixes that were about to end, no less, given my transition to a state of relative peace.

Still, I couldn't help but worry about the repercussions of all this. There was no user guide to working with the strange and the immaterial. Even if Izamem *could* free Akasha from her mental prison, how could he ensure he wouldn't also free less desirable things—namely, her Accretion? The way Narbu had described it, her Accretion was still very much active, partially repressing her past-life memories and partially acting as a warden to prevent her from accessing said memories. Whatever freedom Akasha gained might also apply to the Accretion.

"Can I do something for her?" I asked.

Izamem considered the question for a long while. "You won't just do *something*; you'll do everything. Much safer than me."

"How convenient."

"You think I fear the death of this decaying meat, boy? No. I am speaking out of practicality. You share a karmic link with her, and that will be sufficient."

"If you say so. What's the protocol?"

"Whatever works," Izamem said, laughing. "The swifter you do your work, the swifter the Cobalt Seer will awaken."

I sighed. "If I didn't know any better, I'd say you were just waiting for the medical teams to do their work and bring her out of a coma. Nice way to take credit."

"How good that you know better, then. Otherwise, you would be tossing her corpse into the incinerator."

After a long and bizarre face-off, which mainly featured me glaring into the seer's wrinkled forehead skin, I stood and brushed myself off. I'd had about enough of this asshole. Then again, maybe what I needed was an asshole of a teacher. Narbu and the others had been exceedingly kind, for the most part—up until they revealed a betrayal of untold magnitudes.

"That's right," Izamem said, unprompted.

I paused while heading for the doorway. "Huh?"

"Nothing, boy. Just try to think a little quieter."

When I finally gathered my wits and stepped into the corridor, Rogaji leaped out from behind a retaining wall like a large cat waiting in ambush. With a devilish grin, she asked, "So? Did you figure it out?"

Too exhausted to be startled or even pause, I just kept walking. "You don't really expect results that fast, do you?"

She jogged to my side. "High expectations are what make me successful."

"Maybe so, but your seer's nowhere close to having the answers you want. Right now, his main priority is getting Akasha out of a coma. And I can't say I disagree."

"I'd think nothing less of a devoted husband."

"I'm not—" I gritted my teeth. "For the last time, we are not a couple. Why is that so hard for you people to understand?"

Rogaji seemed taken aback. "Well, it's just . . . a handsome, relatively young human man, and a beautiful, relatively ancient alien woman. Everyone has their preference, but I suspect you're a heterosexual. Just your . . . musk. Or is it called an aura?"

"None of your business, one way or the other," I said sharply. "You brought me here to figure out the Unmade's weakness, and that's what I plan to do. If you want to gossip, I'm sure that Bodhi kid would be more than enthused by the offer."

"My, my—you've grown testy." She tossed me another cheeky grin. "What's the matter? Ready to see your accommodations and take a long nap?"

In truth, there *was* a reason for my grouchiness. I had about a thousand, between all the bullshit I'd endured as of late, but one in particular stood out like a gangrenous thumb. That reason was Narbu. Yes, he was dead and probably rotting in some hell dimension, but he hadn't left my life in the slightest. Izamem's words had only cemented my theory that Narbu had deeply, irreparably harmed Akasha for purely selfish reasons.

On the surface, and certainly at that moment, sealing her mind away had made sense from a practical point of view. The Unmade had just used her as a portal into our world, and there was no telling what she might've done upon realizing the truth of her past lives. Taking it a step farther, there was definitely no telling what the Unmade might've done with that information. His powers and schemes were alien enough to confound even Wayfarers.

Yet here and now, far from the chaos of the Throne of Radiance, I found myself viewing Narbu from a fresh perspective. He'd spent millennia building an order based on protecting and enlightening all sentient beings, only to decide that *some* beings were deserving of abject misery if it meant aiding the greater good.

Akasha was one such casualty. He'd cast her into a deep, dark pit he'd surely never foreseen her escaping. That was bad enough, but it became horrendous when I realized how much Akasha had sacrificed for him and his blind quest. Even before this life, she'd been his empress—and a damned good one, from the sounds of it. And for all that, her only reward had been a murdered child and madness.

All that pain, all that fear, and nothing to do with it except shove it into the same landfill where she probably now resided. How much of that suffering could one being's mind really handle, though? How high could you stack the agony until it came spilling out in a flood?

This line of thought probably explains why, in the course of chewing over Rogaji's question, I felt a pang of urgency.

"Take me to the Godmaker," I said. "It's time to speed-run this game."

6

In between her bouts of plugging data into the control room's console, Rogaji sized me up with critical stares. She'd given me ten or twelve reasons why this plan was ill-advised, but I was beyond the point of caution. This was the safest I'd been in a number of days, and if her machine was the wondrous contraption she claimed it to be, there was nothing to worry about.

She didn't seem to agree. "You're *sure* you'd prefer this over a massage, ten cycles of dopamine stimulation, and a twelve-hour sleep marathon with a late wake-up?"

I nodded and kept examining the small city below, transfixed by the sheer volume of movement as the mechanized components warmed up. "I guess you sold this Godmaker a little too well."

"It's not a walk in the park with a full stomach, Dak."

"I'll handle it."

"Not to mention your internal damage, which is still only about three-fifths healed."

A jolt of pain in my spleen reminded me of that fact. Still, I shook away her concerns. "Just give me a straight answer. Will it kill me or not?"

"No," she said in a drawn-out manner, "but it's not just your body I'm considering."

"Well?"

"The Godmaker tends to produce . . . unpleasant stimulation for the mind."

I leaned against the console, intrigued. "Why? Do I have to connect my neural network to the program's?"

"No, no," she said, waving away the idea as though it were ridiculous. "As I've explained, the Godmaker utilizes zero elements of virtual reality. It's closer to augmented reality, but even then, I would hesitate to call it an exact fit. Everything you see, hear, feel, smell, or taste represents a physical presence that's been generated by the machinery."

"So why worry about my mind?"

Rogaji let out an irritated sigh and stepped back. "The Godmaker, as you've surely guessed, is highly experimental in its nature. So experimental, in fact, that I don't know how or why it renders what it does. That being said, it's rather obvious that it exerts a mental strain."

"Has it caused any injuries?"

"Physically? No." She looked away, suddenly uncertain. "Before Toast and Jar signed on to my crew, I had a pair of mechanics that decided to do a touch of unsupervised testing with the machine. Nobody's quite certain what happened, but when we found them, they were incapable of forming conscious thoughts. Completely vegetative."

"Maybe it was because they went in there as a duo."

"That could explain part of it, yes. My theory, however, is less charitable to those two. I believe their minds weren't strong enough to endure the experience. Something broke them."

I glanced back out at the Godmaker, pondering Rogaji's words of caution. Maybe she was right to be concerned. Even so, I was more concerned about the consequences of wasting time while the Unmade prepared his grand finale. If my mind could handle the junnara-gol, it could surely handle the Godmaker.

"I assume there's some kind of warning system," I said at last. "You know, a way to alert you if things get too hairy."

She nodded, but not before swallowing around a lump in her throat. "I don't typically enlist anyone's aid to supervise—you'll quickly understand why that would be fruitless—but you'll be fitted with a remote device that automatically shuts down the system, in the event of unforeseen consequences."

Her plain discomfort undid whatever security she'd hoped to provide with the explanation.

"But?" I prodded.

"*But*, there's an additional element that complicates things. You recall our discussion of the Unmade's ability to alter spacetime, no?"

I nodded.

"My repeated encounters with his dimension produced some insights in that domain," she continued. "At least, the fungus certainly gained insights."

"I'm not following you."

"The Godmaker seems to have incorporated some of our shared enemy's qualities." Moving closer, Rogaji pointed out a small section of the mechanical jungle below. "There. You see the cogs working?" When I nodded, she said, "In reality, they aren't moving that quickly. The apparent increase in speed is caused by a distortion in spacetime."

I stared at her, bug-eyed. "You built a singularity?"

"No! Well, I don't think so."

"If you're able to speed up or slow down the rate of time, I'd say you did."

Rogaji gave the cogs a helpless look. "Whatever the mechanism of action, the effects are the same. While in the Godmaker, time moves significantly faster."

"Oh." I began putting the pieces together, and I didn't like how they looked. "You're saying that if I need to shut the system down, it might take ten seconds from up here, but an hour from my reference point."

"Precisely, although the divergence isn't so severe. Time within the Godmaker appears to move at approximately one hundred times the speed of standard reality. A full—and *safe*—emergency shutdown requires twelve seconds, which means—"

"Twenty minutes of hell."

Rogaji pulled on a thin, nervous smile. "The silver lining, Dak, is that the chok'tal's internal clock continues to move at the standard rate. Twenty-two hours per rank isn't much, but twenty-two hundred . . . "

"That's only if I stay inside it the entire time."

"Correct." She smiled down at her creation, the lights of the console giving her eyes a manic sheen. "For what it's worth—and I don't recommend this by any means—I've spent upward of three weeks at a time inside those walls."

I smirked. "Must've been some serious crunch time."

"No, not quite," she whispered, her eyes losing their excitement and gaining something more . . . reverent. "You won't understand until you set foot inside the Godmaker, Dak, but it's an experience unlike anything else. A window into worlds you couldn't envision in the deepest of sleep."

Now, this . . . this threw me for a loop. Up until now, I wasn't certain I'd seen so much as a smidgen of gravity from Rogaji. Between her absurd level of power and staggering wealth, she didn't have much to contend with, let alone take seriously. For some reason, however, the Godmaker broke through that illusion. There was something worth respecting in its domain—especially for a relative insect like myself.

"You're certain you want to do this?" Rogaji asked, snapping me out of my thoughts.

"I think so."

"Good, because I saved your skin and brought you here to perform this explicit task, and I would *hate* to kill you without getting a decent return on my investment."

She smiled at me, unblinking, for a good five seconds, then pounded a large blue button on the console. A moment later, another set of elevator doors—this one located on the Godmaker side of the room—slid open and bathed us in halogen light.

"Good luck," Rogaji said with a hint of unease. "Go slowly, Dak, and don't hesitate to pull the plug if you feel overwhelmed. We have all the time in the 'verse to do this right."

I stepped inside the lift. "Just have some pureed vegetables ready in case my mind doesn't come back with me."

"Oh, such a natural comedian!" The doors began to shut, but just before they came together, Rogaji zipped forward with a speed that was quite literally too fast for my brain to process. She wedged her hands in the doors and eased them open. "I seem to have, ah, forgotten to equip you with the emergency button."

I blinked at her. "Could I have it?"

She used her same zip power to reach a nearby lab table, then zipped back with a lanyard-looking device. The whole affair took less than a second. Without preamble, she slipped it over my right wrist and tucked it into my sleeve.

"Needs your fingerprint to activate," she explained. "Hold it for three seconds. Remember, it'll take twenty minutes for that signal to reach the shutdown receiver."

"What happens if it breaks?"

She laughed, but only for a quarter of a second. "Don't break it."

"Yeah, but if I—"

"Don't. Break it." She pulled on another pageant smile. "Got it?"

"Got it."

The elevator prepared to descend yet again, at which point Rogaji added, "By the way, Dak—if you *do* fry your brain on this first session, I won't puree any vegetables. Just you."

My unmentionables clenched as hard as the sealing doors.

As I settled into yet another long, frustrating ride, I wondered what I was in for. Well, that and why Rogaji hadn't installed faster motors in her lift systems. Everything about the Godmaker screamed *danger*, but it was impossible to prepare for that without knowing the source. Specifically, the source of insanity her two former employees had encountered.

It wasn't unheard-of for people to jack into a sim and have their minds deconstructed neuron by neuron at the hands of a rogue AI construct, but I doubted that was the case here. For one thing, it wasn't virtual, so there was no direct interfacing between organic and machine intelligence. Second, even the brightest bulbs in the 'verse have no way of creating a construct out of thin air. To the best of my knowledge, any extant constructs were made millions of years ago by extinct species. And just for your information, any construct with actual sentience might as well be considered a god. All this combined meant it was very, very unlikely the facility was run by an AI.

The next culprit was signal overload. There are plenty of stories involving explorers, tinkerers, or other down-and-dirty types being exposed to signals that wreaked havoc on their precious internal systems. If you believe the legends, some of those signals come from planes or universes or domains or whatever the hell else beyond our perception. Humanoids aren't the weakest breed among the stars, but they're also far from immune to the infinite threats they might encounter.

One of Korasa's "borrowed" memories even reminded me of an incident in which a human archaeologist received a full blast from an abandoned alien logic core. Despite the core running at 6 or 7 percent capacity, it had been strong enough to scramble his DNA and turn his amino acids to sludge.

This fear didn't affect me much, though, as I suspected Purifiers were far more robust than members of their unmodified host species. Even if lethal signals *were* oozing out of the machinery, I'd probably have a few minutes to hit the kill switch and let the chok'tal do its healing.

The last possibility—by far the worst—was that the machine broke people the old-fashioned way: through fear. According to Rogaji, the Godmaker worked by rendering situations and enemies that posed an apparent threat to the chok'tal. It didn't take an overactive imagination to envision a scenario where the Godmaker continuously churned out monstrosities that were *just enough* to break the victim's contact with reality. Purifier or not, the mind could only take so much.

In any event, it was clear that I needed to keep my wits about me and avoid getting lost in the mechanical menagerie. Simmers were infamous for a phenomenon known as waffling—which might sound fine, even delicious, if you're not familiar with it. To make a long story short, waffling is what happens when simmers don't spend enough time decompressing between sessions, leading to breaks with consensus reality and firmly held convictions that they're permanently trapped in a sim. More clinically, this is known as SIDP (simulation-induced derealization and psychosis). Don't worry about the acronym, though. "Waffling" sums it up.

When the elevator doors slid open, I stepped into a dark, black-paneled room best described as an antechamber with a tall ceiling. Gravel crunched beneath my boots, and the air thrummed as though populated by thousands of invisible insects. There were no exits, corridors, or windows to speak of.

I spun in place, trying in vain to locate some type of switch or panel, only to find that the elevator doors had already closed.

"Hello?" I called.

Nothing.

By this point, my panic was starting to creep up. Intrusive thoughts scurried around inside my skull. *What if she just put me inside a personal zoo? What if the machine's broken, and I can't get out? What if time's already dilated, and I've been here for years without knowing it?*

Just as I began descending into paranoia land, a glowing green cylinder appeared in the center of the room. Its glow was so eerie that I couldn't tell whether it was digital or physical. I squinted at it for a moment, then approached. The nearer I drew, the taller and more vivid the green bar became. Some kind of visual display of the Godmaker booting up, perhaps?

Three feet from the green bar, it expanded to reach the ceiling some twenty or thirty meters overhead. The thrumming intensified. I lifted my hand toward the neon glow, equal parts curious and concerned, trying to—

In a blinding, deafening flash, the cylinder *exploded*. Well, not exploded, per se—my body was spared from a hail of radioactive shrapnel—but near enough to loosen my bowels. It certainly disintegrated into a wash of white light and clear, high ringing, momentarily erasing all sensory perception and memory of having a body. A few days back, this would've traumatized me for life. But given how many times I'd been jarred in and out of this skin-bag by various rituals, it didn't take more than a few seconds to settle back into a place of crisp, neutral awareness. I drifted around in that timeless, dimensionless space for a good while, eventually becoming so relaxed that I regarded the situation with boredom.

At some point, though, everything shifted. The spotless white of eternity was replaced by darkness, then faint shapes swimming in and out of perception. Silence trickled into sound. My body felt as though it had regained its weight and shape.

Before my mind could grasp at anything, much less understand what was going on, I found myself standing on a dusty, moonlit road that stretched across hills in the distance. The air was warm and oddly sweet—probably a result of the meter-tall wildflowers crowding the fields all around me.

"Beja, are you well?" a woman asked. "Does the wind trouble you?"

I instinctively turned toward her voice. Instead of one woman, however, I encountered several dozen figures lined up in parallel columns, all of them draped in elaborate regalia that glinted under the starlight. Most were shrouded under gold fabric and clusters of precious gems, staring at me through narrow slits in their masks. All except one.

The woman who'd called out was sitting atop a high, flowery palanquin, her body covered in so much amethyst and jade that she resembled a living mosaic. She was humanoid, no doubt about that, but her elongated limbs and craning neck marked her as distinctly alien. Upon squinting, I also noted that her arms and legs were quadruple-jointed . . . and curved much like a canine's. Nonhuman confirmed.

The servants carrying her palanquin grunted and shifted as she leaned forward, exposing long, scythe-shaped bone protrusions on their shoulder blades.

I stood there, totally frozen, for no less than ten seconds. What the living hell *was* this? Everything around me was so real, so tactile, that I wondered if I'd fallen into a dream or a deep coma while entering the Godmaker. In fact, only two things kept me tethered to reality: my still-human clothing and body, and my memories of Rogaji explaining the machine's inner workings.

This isn't real, Dak, I assured myself. *It's just an illusion. A very sophisticated illusion.*

Still, this pep talk didn't hold up very well when I analyzed the environment once again. It looked damn *real*. Whether or not it was a projection, the horizon's infinite collage of spires, mountains, forests, hovering ships, and crackling lightning clouds had all the fidelity of waking life. Everything did. Even the silent crowd gathered before me looked and felt authentic enough to induce some mild social anxiety.

"Beja," the woman said again, firmer this time, "what is the matter?"

Obvious though it might seem to you, it took me those extra few seconds to realize *I* was the one known as Beja. I blinked at her, trying to figure out the appropriate response, then decided to just play along. No sense triggering a catastrophic glitch in my first few minutes of Godmaker training.

"Uh, nothing," I said, adopting a suitably regal voice. "I just . . . thought I saw something."

The woman slid back into her throne. "You're certain?"

"Pretty certain. I think."

"Very well. We mustn't be late for the festival." She dipped a clawed finger into the goblet resting beside her, then flicked some sort of liquid onto the palanquin bearers. "Onward, beloved ones. Let the beja set our pace."

I turned back to face the empty road, puzzled. *Beja* wasn't a name, it seemed, but rather a title. Some sort of rank.

This might seem like a small thing, but it's not. The fact that the Godmaker had assigned me a temporary identity—in a fully-fledged and realized society, no less—indicated there was a whole lot more data running behind the scenes than Rogaji suspected. Unless this was a scripted event, which I doubted, there was an entire universe running in here. Billions upon billions of interactions that came together to form hierarchies, economies, cultures, religions. To the best of my knowledge, only full-blooded AI constructs had the kind of logic nets capable of rendering something like this for a sim's inhabitants. Even then, those constructs usually harnessed the powers of multiple stars to simply get their world up and running. In short, this whole scenario was fascinating . . . but also terrifying.

On a lesser scale, it also spawned a barrage of questions: If I had an established role here, what was my damn name? Did these simulated people know I was human? Could they distinguish themselves from me? Were they conscious? Was the Godmaker's world different for every user?

Each line of inquiry left me more frazzled, more unsure of my environment and how "real" it all was. No wonder a few of Rogaji's test subjects had lost their marbles in here.

To quell the anxiety, I let my hand wander down to my belt. The Sparkseed-infused hammer I'd received at the mountaintop battle—which still felt like a fever dream, mind you—hung heavily from a loop on my left side. Silly as it might sound, its presence was an anchor to me. A totem, if you go by the old simmer terminology. As long as it was there, cold and solid under my touch, I had a point of reference for this mirage.

I wasn't quite sure what to do, but seeing as the enormous procession behind me had started stamping forward, it felt appropriate to follow suit. From what I'd gathered based on surface details, I was the vanguard of this formation. Some kind of scout or spearhead intended to locate threats. As such, I headed down the road.

There was just one problem with this approach—namely, that I had no idea what to look for. Our destination seemed clear enough, given the expansive city on the horizon, but it wasn't so easy to identify possible threats. I had no context for this world or its behaviors. For all I knew, garden-variety herbivores might be considered lethal foes to these people. Likewise, there was a risk of me stabbing a vicious-looking creature that was actually revered as a god. The joys of relativism.

As I walked onward, accompanied by the low *pwoom* of marching drums and the pounding of countless feet, I turned my attention to the surroundings in hopes of analyzing the Godmaker's magic tricks. Every so often, the distant skies blurred as though struggling to render a cloud or patch of darkness. This didn't happen to similarly busy textures such as the dirt near my feet, however, which suggested that visual fidelity broke down at long range. This was a given in virtual universes, due to how the system conserved energy by only giving detail to objects in focus, but the reasoning broke down in an entirely physical system.

My best guess was that the Godmaker used a system of small, dynamic projectors capable of painting the surrounding walls with textures that mimicked various distances. In other words, nothing was *really* out there—it was just an illusion of scale.

This didn't explain nearby objects, however. If Rogaji was telling the truth, or at least speaking accurately, the system was rendering living creatures in real time . . . possibly using organic materials. A disturbing possibility on several levels. For starters, it meant she had access to a matter-configuration setup. Quantum teleportation, in other words. The system had to be rearranging molecules, quarks, and even chemical bonds on the fly to assemble and disassemble things. Not so bad, on the surface, but it gets icky when you start to consider the fates of these fake people.

Let me give an example. Pretend someone teleports "you" across a starship. This is done by ripping your fundamental particles apart, then reassembling them in the delivery area. For all intents and purposes, the "original you" is killed by this process. The "new you" is just a clone that happens to have your memories. Not so different from my own birth.

Now take that example and apply it to the Godmaker. If the machine was constructing and deconstructing living creatures at high speed, it meant it was essentially giving birth—and then murdering—every creature I encountered.

Deeper than even that, it implied one of three possibilities. The first, and least upsetting, was that the Godmaker was creating living beings without consciousness. Maybe not even a brain. The second was that they *did* have consciousness but were somehow blocked from realizing the horrible truth of their existence. The third, and most upsetting, was that these beings *were* conscious, *weren't* blocked from realizing the truth, and might someday stumble across it firsthand—assuming Rogaji or one of the other Godmaker testers hadn't already revealed it to them before killing them.

If the third option was on the money, I'd need to talk with Rogaji. These people might not *know* they'd been assembled in a vacuum, much less what was awaiting them when I moved too far away or exited the Godmaker, but it didn't mean they were any less conscious than me. They just had abysmally short life spans.

The minutes ticked by, with me awkwardly leading a mystery convoy and the azure reeds along the road whispering their strange songs. Every so often, we passed groups of locals that were quick to set down their baskets and kneel before us. What really struck me, though, wasn't their deference; it was their bodies.

Everyone in the procession behind me was cloaked from head to toe, but these locals were practically naked. Their only bodily coverings were loose, off-white strips of cloth they'd tied around their hips or chests. This left plenty of skin exposed, though it wasn't exactly skin. Instead, it was some kind of short, thick fur that had the colors and striations of orangey citrine, with crystalline studs cropping up all over. Same proportions as the royal caravan members, same multi-jointed limbs, same protruding shoulder blades.

The locals also offered me a glimpse of their species' facial features. Unlike your standard human, these beings had four tiny nostrils running up the center of their face, as well as black striping that seemed too randomized to be a cosmetic addition. Their mouths were practically beaks, given how far they protruded. And their eyes . . . Well, those threw me for a loop.

They had two jet-black eyes, roughly in the same place as a humanoid, but there was *also* a third eye perched just above their nostrils. This eye was nothing but white sclera, yet somehow blended so well with their "skin" that I almost missed it. Its presence was further obscured by the sizable number of locals wearing blindfolds or facial veils.

Wait . . . blindfolds.

The minute I made the connection, a chill wormed up and down my spine. What were the odds that these people, in a facsimile universe seemingly pulling from my own mind—Rogaji's words, not mine—would have the same type of blindfold Akasha wore? Sure, it was higher up on their heads and didn't obscure the two "normal" eyes, but the connection was undeniable. Whether it was a product of my subconscious or something more, I couldn't yet say. For now, it was just another quirk worth discussing with Rogaji.

Suddenly, the tall reeds along both sides of the road began to rustle. It wasn't the same rustle as earlier, where the foliage had been stirred by wind or small herbivores. This was more akin to a hurricane . . . but without any hint of a breeze.

Almost on instinct, I spun around and raised a closed fist. The procession, to my surprise, immediately halted. Shrill whistles went up from their ranks, and a few seconds later, warriors in robes and bulky lamellar armor went rushing to the sides of the road. There, they interlocked their body-height shields to form an impenetrable wall around the palanquin. Teams of warriors with pole-mounted shields hurried to action throughout the crowds, raising and angling their equipment to assemble a tightly packed dome that vaguely resembled a turtle's shell.

Within a few breaths, the palanquin had gone from an open target to a mobile fortress. Everywhere I looked, pole arms protruded through slots in the shields. Nothing but air was getting through that formation.

My eyes lingered on the tips of those pole arms. They didn't end in a single point, much less a spearhead or axe blade. Instead, they featured crescent-shaped prongs that resembled . . . beast-catchers? To the best of my knowledge, those things were meant for nonlethal crowd control and usually relied on magnetic clamps. These prongs were nothing but bare metal and velvet pads.

Midway through assessing the tactic, however, a familiar itch cropped up in my brain. I didn't need to question its source or purpose. Instead, I spun on my heel and thrust my hand toward a random point in space— which didn't turn out to be so random.

A thin, dark shape came screaming out of the reeds just ahead of me. It was fast as hell, but I was ready. I snatched the projectile as it passed, clamping down on it as though it were a fish leaping out of a stream. The damn thing's momentum whipped me around. Once I'd stabilized, I got a good look at what I was holding: a heavy wooden spear packing an obsidian tip.

That seemed to do the trick. My HUD bloomed, framing a patch of reeds that had already drawn my eye due to the silhouettes moving around in them.

Road Ambusher (HUMANOID)
CALCULATING . . .
Estimated Kill Points: 3,500

Despite the general clamor coming from the procession behind me, all I felt was disappointment. Here I was, training in Rogaji's miracle machine to reach Rank Infinity, and the best I could get was thirty-five hundred goddamn Kill Points. Talk about overselling an experience.

I sighed and drew my hammer, preparing to delete that underpowered blot from existence. Before I could take more than a step toward the enemy, however, the rustling resumed. Then it got louder. And louder. And louder.

Without so much as a battle cry, hundreds upon hundreds of murky forms came spilling from the reeds like overgrown locusts.

For what seemed like the first time ever, my HUD couldn't keep up with the shifting data. All I saw, aside from the encounter's shift to a Slaughter Event, was the mounting Kill Point total. First a few thousand, then over a hundred thousand, then two . . .

I squeezed the grip of my hammer and grinned.

Now *this* would be a proper fight.

7

Even as I rushed the oncoming horde, I could hardly make out the bastards in their ranks. There were so many bodies that my visual field resembled a mosaic of blue squares. It was worse than useless; it was actively hampering my capabilities.

This being the case, I tried something I'd never thought of, let alone had a reason to try: mentally toggling the HUD's enemy frames *off*. Amazingly, the chok'tal played along. Every square vanished in tandem, leaving behind a churning, howling mass of enemies with bloodshed on their minds. This happened just in time, too—within seconds, the living wave was within spitting distance.

Rather than seeing individuals, I saw motion. Hundreds of objects in motion. Raggedy robes, spears, swords, clusters of bones and dried organs, flailing beads, garish, hollow-eyed masks . . . It was as though they'd birthed themselves straight from the surrounding mud.

I had no idea who or what these humanoids were, but their hideous shrieking told me all I needed to know. That, combined with the fact that they weren't real people, gave me the green light to rearrange their faces.

The first of the ambushers came barreling toward me in a tangle of muddy hair, sharpened, gnashing teeth, and clinking femurs, their already-bloody mace circling the air in preparation. They never got the chance to strike. After flicking on Overclock and Indomitable, I drew my arm across my chest and delivered a backhanded swing to the attacker's temple. *Kwok.* The body pitched forward and slid through the dirt, completely limp apart from a few postmortem twitches.

There wasn't a dull moment to admire my work, though. Even as I prepared for another swing, the horde surged forth and tried to encircle me. My sensory field was reduced to darkness, screeching, septic odors, and flashing metal. That wouldn't do.

I sprang back, narrowly dodging a tusk-helmeted ambusher keen on sealing off my retreat. He thrust his spear at my chest, but I was faster. I batted the crooked wooden haft aside and slammed the hammer's head straight into his third eye. He let out a wild screech and dropped to his knees, gushing dark fluids. I just had to finish him—

Wheech! A black arrowhead careened past my cheek, missing my eye by less than a centimeter. This was followed up by a handful of sword slashes, a sling's stone, and more shivs than I could count, all forcing me back a step or two at a time. Soon enough, I lost sight of the spearman I'd whacked. The ambushers flowed around them and continued to nip at me.

Despite having me against the proverbial wall, the bastards didn't get greedy. They crept up as a ragged yet dense mass, relying on their blades and bloody grins to keep me at bay. Up close—and able to smell them in their entirety—I became more convinced than ever that these were demons. Their mud-smeared faces and tumorous growths suggested they felt closer to maggots than sentient beings.

I kept backing up, ceding more and more territory, trying in vain to locate openings or weak spots before their ranks reformed. Then it hit me . . . *Why the fuck am I playing this so cautious?*

The revelation almost made me chuckle, in spite of the horde before me. My all-too-real reaction was a testament to Rogaji's machine. In that moment, I stopped viewing them as a genuine threat. Instead, I perceived them as flickering bits of meat that had been assembled in a glorified warehouse.

"Well, Ro, you call it a Godmaker," I whispered under my breath. "Let's see how accurate that is."

I rested my hammer on my right shoulder and gave the crowd a taunting, *come 'n' get it* gesture, pulling on a vicious smile for maximum effect.

Strangely enough, this had a real reaction on my foes. They ceased their constant advance and began exchanging glances, perplexed by my sudden shift in mood. Those glances soon turned to murmurs, then a kind of muted rage that was quickly redirected back to me.

One of the foremost ambushers, a tall and lanky specimen carrying rusted daggers, bellowed a challenge that rattled in my chest.

In response, I leveled the hammer's head straight at him. "Thank you for volunteering."

The ambusher shifted side to side warily, perhaps trying to gauge my angle of attack. The problem for him was that I didn't need one.

I triggered Telekinesis, reforging the impressive bond I'd made with the hammer while fighting on the mountaintop. In just tenths of a second, I felt every vibrating quark that comprised its form. Every atomic bond. Every mote and droplet of pain woven into the Sparkseed.

When the dagger wielder crept forward, wildly slashing in some kind of ritual display, I let go of the hammer and settled both hands at my side.

The weapon kept floating without so much as a wobble.

All at once, the ambushers stilled. My new nemesis with the blades shrank back, probing the air with his weapons in search of . . . magic? That's no joke. There was an earnest, haunted look in the eyes of that man and everyone around him. They shivered and whimpered as I rotated the hammer in midair, their eyes wide, fingers tensing and twitching. I could only imagine how they'd look if and when I brought out a high-powered flak rifle.

Then, like the first crack in a failing dam, the son of a bitch with the shivs leaped toward me with a bestial cry. The tips of both blades were primed to skewer my eyeballs.

With one mental push, however, my hammer jolted forth and caught the ambusher square in the sternum. Both shivs skittered to the dirt. Bone cracked and scraped. The man's huge, wiry body folded over the hammer, giving me enough time to angle the hammer and drive it straight down into the dust—along with the man's spine. I winced as the hammer pinned him there, gradually driving him toward the center of this illusionary planet as though he were a nail going into wood. For long, agonizing seconds, the bones of his rib cage squirmed beneath his robes. He clawed and kicked at the telekinetic weapon, but it was no use.

Through it all, I just stood there, watching in a trance. It felt as though I didn't inhabit my body. As though I were just a stranger observing someone else's memories.

This pseudospell was broken at the same moment as the man's ribs, however. With that low, sickening crack, I felt a surge of vomit in my gut. It was too much. Too cruel. Snapping myself back to attention, I hardened the telekinetic link and drove the hammer directly into the underside of the man's chin. It rammed straight through. The resulting cloud of pink mist settled into a cone of blood, bone, and stringy bits forking away from the man's neck stump.

I stared at the mess with a grimace. At least it had been quick.

The mass of ambushers didn't seem to agree. Primitive, guttural screams and wailing cries filled the night. They scurried back with plain fear, not even bothering to shower me with a parting volley of some kind. The most composed of the bunch managed to keep their spears leveled in my general direction, even if that did require hunkering down behind burned leather shields.

Then a curious whispering crept into the silence—not from the ambushers, but from behind me. From the procession.

I peered over my shoulder. The formation was still in place, all shields and steadfast pole arms, but the sound was most certainly coming from within it. They were repeating something. Chanting it. I strained to hear their words, but it wasn't long before the voices rose to an ear-aching shout punctuated by stomping.

"Beja! Beja! Beja!"

Apparently, I was some kind of badass to these people. What *was* this machine? A power-fantasy simulator? An ego trip with a heavy dose of violence?

Despite these questions and the constant clamor of the *beja* chant, I was lucid enough to catch the squelch of heavy footsteps moving through muck. Glancing back revealed that the ambusher horde had split roughly down the middle, making way for a figure nearly twice their height—and width. Its entire body glistened with scar tissue in the starlight. All except its head, that is, which was sealed in a crude, permanent helmet with three eyeholes and a thin slit for a mouth. The damn thing even had zigzag welding marks on both sides. It only got worse from there.

Each of the lumbering brute's hands were the size of my torso; it dragged them in its wake, leaving trails of trampled reeds. On top of that, it had the same wonky limbs and shoulder protrusions as the locals we'd passed, but their versions were dialed up about ten notches. The shoulder protrusions, for example, were closer to enormous, scythe-like blades that flexed of their own accord. Even its movements were closer to that of a canine than that of the "normal" species here. It had a cagey, predatory gait, balancing itself on . . . a tail. A long, thrashing tail that carved up the mud with its bony outer shell.

The ambushers had varying reactions to this newcomer. Most cowered and retreated farther into the reeds, while others edged closer to it or even pressed their faces into the dirt at its arrival. A skittish few tossed beads or dried entrails at it.

When the brute reached the edge of the embankment and deftly scrambled up to face me, one of the ambushers tried his luck at touching the thing's tail. The response was a blind yet stunningly accurate swipe from the left shoulder blade. The offending ambusher seized up, then collapsed where they stood. Their severed head rolled down into the swamps, where it quickly became the reward for a wrestling match among the victim's comrades. The brute, meanwhile, carried on without so much as a peek at its kill.

Another pulse of Telekinesis tossed the Sparkseed hammer back into my grip. I let it hang by my side as the creature lumbered closer and closer.

At five paces away, my foe reared back on its scar-covered legs, screeched toward the heavens, and extended its shoulder-scythes to form a grisly plume. That was enough to get my HUD's attention.

[NEW COMBATANT DETECTED]
Defiled Champion of the Western Horde (HUMANOID)
CALCULATING . . .
Estimated Kill Points: 206,500

The Kill Points were nothing to write home about, but the same couldn't be said of the chok'tal's assigned name. Given how I viewed and thought of my enemy, I'd been almost certain the name would register as some variant of "brute." My chok'tal was either reaching into my subconscious or had access to information I did not. Either way, something was up.

I cocked the hammer back, ready to strike, but the champion didn't waste any time. Its right-hand scythe came darting toward me without a lick of warning. The impossibly sharp point swelled in size as it approached my eyeball, and yet . . . it didn't hit.

For a solid three seconds I just stood there, half flinching, half confused. The scythe's tip continued to approach, but with each millimeter, its speed decreased. The same was true of the world itself. Everything from the wind to the wild, pumping fists of the ambushers slowed exponentially. The only thing *not* affected by the slowdown was my own body. Of course, this also meant sounds were slowed. Not altered in pitch, just . . . slowed.

Given the near standstill to which everything had come, I decided to play around a bit. I waved a hand, dragged a boot through the dirt, even yawned. None of it caused the scythe's tip to accelerate. Before long, the tip came within three centimeters of my cornea—and hung there. Sure, it was still *technically* moving, but I only knew that due to my Telekinesis ability sensing the quantum flux. For all intents and purposes, I was an asymptote, no different than how Rogaji had described the Unmade. I had a feeling that the tip wouldn't ever reach me, even if given a hundred years.

A wiser man might've shifted out of the way or even counterattacked at this point, but I was amused. This was truly novel tech. I used the opportunity to dial up my Telekinesis skill and probe my surroundings. Sure enough, the quantum activity underlying the champion's physical form had continued to decelerate.

I moved my awareness into the mesh, swimming around and analyzing the strange, frothing energy. Insights blossomed in my head, though most were too nuanced and esoteric to present themselves as words in my mind, let alone words that a reader like you could grasp. All you need to know is that I began to understand the bonds between the dancing quarks and other subatomic particles. I intuitively sensed how they arose, interacted, and dissipated.

While doing this, a prior idea returned to me. Back then, I'd theorized that the divide between organic and inorganic matter was largely conceptual. The same quarks that comprised my body also formed things like walls, rocks, and rubber. The only difference, when you got right down to it, was the complexity of those structures. Organic (read: living) matter was orders of magnitude more intricate than inorganic matter. Probably something to do with consciousness, if Narbu's words held any weight.

If I kept examining this superslow layout of energy, I might be able to pinpoint the exact functioning of organic matter. And if I could do that, there was nothing standing between me and manipulating that organic matter via Telekinesis. Exploding heads, anyone?

That would have to come later, though. The longer I spent perusing the quantum world, the less anchored I felt to my body. Maybe my mind was overtaxed, or maybe the time-dilation system wasn't without consequences. Either way, I felt it best to recall my awareness and deal with the monstrosity about to skewer my eyeball.

I drew the hammer over my shoulder, slid along the brute's left, and delivered a backhanded blow with the force of an imploding star. Close enough to it, anyway. It turns out that when you're able to move hundreds of thousands of times faster than the objects around you, it doesn't take much effort to utterly demolish things. Force is, after all, mass times acceleration. And this was a ludicrous amount of acceleration.

Between Overclock, the Sparkseed hammer's vicious head, and a slight boost from Telekinesis, the hammer tore through the champion's helmet—and face—as though they were wet paper. Then, before I even knew what had happened, time snapped back to normal.

Chunks of pulverized flesh and smoldering metal sprayed across the reeds. The champion's upper body snapped skyward, spasmed, and sank with a foul, slurping *kwok* sound. Unlike the other simulated foes I'd taken down, however, it didn't die. Not immediately, anyway.

To my horror, the thing kept clawing madly at the dirt, shuddering and letting out gurgling howls from a throat that was no longer intact. Half of its head, skull and nervous system and all, was exposed to the wind like a vivisection display. Jets of thick, bubbling blood pumped up through the shredded arteries.

Wild cheers rose from behind me. I spun around to find that the royal procession had dissolved its fortresslike formation, leaving the guards free to drum their pole arms against their shields in haunting unison.

The champion thrashed on the dirt before me, desperately stabbing at pebbles and reeds with its shoulder-scythes. Its remaining eye snapped about in panic. Intelligent panic. When I lifted the hammer to my palm and strode over to the champion, that same eye fixed on me.

Cold roots spread through my chest. Cold, aching roots. They cut up my spine in a rush of dread, then cut through my thoughts, stilling me where I stood. It was like an intravenous shot of mercy. There wasn't a drop of bloodshed left in me—only regret. This wasn't right. None of this was right. It was the same slash of hesitancy and weakness that had come over me while slaying the corrupted tortoise. Against all logic, this creature felt like kin to me.

Even so, what could I do? It was already dying. Better to put it out of its misery and reap the Kill Points. Besides, it was simulated—though it sure as hell didn't feel like it.

Yet as I raised my bloody hammer, the guards behind me resumed a familiar chant.

"Beja! Beja! Beja!"

That damn chant tickled something deep in my brain.

"Beja!"

I knew it from somewhere. Someplace.

"Beja!"

I could almost *taste* the memory, the dark spot it illuminated . . .

"Beja!"

All at once, the experience flipped from a magic show to a nightmare. Everything around me felt simultaneously unreal and too real. The faces, the blood, the night sky—it was a puppet show animated by nobody and nothing, put on for my hideous amusement. I staggered backward, fumbling to hold my hammer at my waist while I jammed down on the emergency shutdown's button. After a few seconds of dizziness and shaky breathing, I heard a confirmatory *bleep*.

Then nothing. It took a moment for the relevant memory to bubble up through my maelstrom of thoughts. *Twenty minutes. Twelve seconds in the real world, twenty minutes in here.*

Shit.

Out of nowhere, almost as though signaled by some inaudible whistle, the hordes of ambushers arranged along the road and reeds went into a fleeing frenzy. They scattered away from me, dispersing into the reeds like a startled flock. Within seconds, nothing remained except the corpses, the overlapping prints in the muck, and the trampled foliage.

Throughout the disordered retreat, the formation at my back continued their grim chant.

"Beja! Beja! Beja!"

My HUD spat out a perfunctory end-of-encounter message.

ENCOUNTER INCOMPLETE
Kills: 3
Kill Points Awarded: 246,720

Almost a quarter of a million KP. Great. But at that moment, I wanted nothing more than to be ejected from this place. The odors of pungent alien blood and piss were overwhelming. I craned my neck skyward, then to the horizon, trying in vain to distract myself and wait out the emergency shutdown's timer.

While glancing about, however, my gaze landed on the tremendous city in the distance. Much like the chanting, there was something familiar yet guarded about it. The longer I stared, examining the jagged silhouettes of towers and crenellations and floating platforms, the quieter my mind became. My mind gradually shed its disgust in favor of the city's majesty. Well, maybe *majesty* was the wrong word. Its allure, perhaps. Try as I might, I couldn't tear my eyes away. It seemed to exist in a haze of bittersweet nostalgia.

One building in particular continued to hold my focus, much like a singularity fighting to gobble up everything in range. Coincidental or not, it was also the largest building in the skyline: a tall, ziggurat-style rise covered in vertical streaks of bold, black paint that ran down its sides like reversed sunbeams.

I've seen it before. It wasn't a theory, but pure knowing. An assertion. *I've been there.*

The certainty of those thoughts jarred me yet did little to distract me. My attention traced the monolith, and bit by bit, the structure became more detailed. More *real.* Blurry spots resolved into sharp, stunning patches of architecture. Elaborate carvings in the shapes of birds and fish appeared along its sides. For perhaps the first time in the Godmaker, I witnessed the "creation" of this world firsthand.

But even when I perceived the building as it were only a few meters away, the details didn't stop coming. Rather, the details of my immediate surroundings began to *lose* clarity. My peripheral vision soured into a dark, blotted ring, excluding everything but the building.

By this point, I couldn't do a thing—even move a muscle. I found myself totally transfixed, somewhere between this body and the infinite "space" all around me, no longer able to cobble together the millions of sensations that formed a clear mental picture of my physical form. In fact, it wasn't long before all physical input quieted to a distant hum. Nothing remained in my consciousness aside from the building. Against all odds, it grew larger, and larger, and larger . . .

Then, in a trick of perception I can only liken to suddenly seeing *through* a window as opposed to staring at a reflection, my ordinary mind and body reemerged—but the environment didn't.

Whereas I'd previously been located on a starlit dirt road, I was now standing in a vast, obsidian chamber illuminated by braziers and sconces arranged along the walls. The same part of my mind that had recognized the city and the word *beja*—that haunting, assured part—wasn't rattled by the scenery shift in the slightest.

In fact, it now filled me with more certainty than ever before. This wasn't a new place. It was an old place. A place so old it had been burned from my mind. Yet even as I turned about, inspecting the chamber's assortment of rectangular contemplation pools, well-oiled furs, and golden furniture, I had no clue how or why I'd ever forgotten it. All I knew was that this recognition nullified the remnants of my fear. That, and the fact that I was standing inside the massive ziggurat I'd seen moments before.

Odd as it was, I felt as though I was precisely where I ought to be. And I hadn't felt that way in a long, long while.

"Beja, what are you doing?"

I snapped toward the voice—only to find the woman who'd been perched atop the royal palanquin. She leaned against a thick column covered in hieroglyphs, a gem-encrusted golden goblet in each hand.

Her outfit, for the most part, hadn't changed—she was still covered in a mesh of overlapping necklaces, bracelets, and sashes—but she'd at least removed the heaviest of her gem-laden pieces. The chamber's flickering blue flames also revealed her face in its entirety. Though she bore a superficial resemblance to the laborers we'd passed on the road, her face was decidedly more . . . refined. Beautiful, even. A strange thing to say about an alien, seeing as I had no real context for what passed as beauty, but I felt it all the same. Even her numerous eyes had the sheen of unsullied quartz.

She also stood and moved with the lithe precision of a noble. Each movement of her limbs, no matter how subtle, carried the weight of royal authority. Simulated or not, the woman put a genuine shudder of fear in me. Once again, though, there was also a shadow of something less distinct. Something that called to me through the veil of ignorance and patchy memories.

"I'm . . . thinking," I said finally.

"You seem unwell this evening," she replied, moving closer to offer me a goblet. Up close, I realized we were roughly the same height. "Perhaps I should call for the oracles."

For reasons I didn't fully grasp, the idea sounded horrid. I took the goblet from her with an appreciative half bow and shook my head. "No, no. I'm fine. Very fine."

"You're certain? It was a long campaign."

"It—"

She evidently wasn't done speaking, because she carried on as though I'd never said a word. "I know the other cities are likely fine, with or without the consecration rituals, but it's my duty to perform them. It . . . gladdens the heart. It lends courage to the people."

I just nodded. What the hell could I say to that?

"With any luck, this war will end soon enough," she said quietly. "Then you'll get the rest you deserve."

"I'm rested. Really."

She surveyed me for a while, then gestured for me to walk with her. When I followed, she led me between the rows of pools and flower-filled shrines. "You fought admirably on the road."

"Just, uh . . . doing my job."

She hummed in approval, though it seemed she had plenty more to say.

Then again, so did I. Mostly in the realm of questions. Based on my rough estimate, I still had another fifteen minutes or so until the shutdown procedure yanked me out of the Godmaker. Seeing as I would *hopefully* spend those minutes here, in relative safety and with a goblet of sickeningly sweet wine in hand, I saw no reason to squander my time.

No matter what Rogaji had explained about the nature of this simulation, there was more to it than met the eye. Somehow, some way, this machine was pulling from my own mind. If that was the case, it also meant this experience was a dialed-up lucid dream. A physical arena to explore, confront, and analyze my subconscious and all the secrets it held.

Going by that line of logic, the "people" within this experience were shards of my own mind projected outward. Various facets, perhaps? Hard to say, and it was too early to speculate. Still, there was a nonzero chance that this woman—indeed, that everyone I met—might hold clues to figuring out my maelstrom of a mind. If there was any stability to the sessions in the Godmaker, such as a linear progression of events and continuing characters, I'd need to deepen my connection to this place and its inhabitants.

Hence, I'd use my remaining minutes as a time to gather info. With any luck, if and when I returned to the Godmaker, I'd have better bearings. At minimum, I might know where to look for higher-level foes.

"Why did they attack us there?" I asked her.

She gave me a curious look, all three eyes narrowing in unison. "Is this rhetorical, Beja?"

"No," I said with another sip of the wine—and another grimace. It tasted like rotten berries and straw. "I just like to be certain, I guess. It's good to be clear about why you're killing things."

To my surprise, she smiled at that. At least, I took it to be a smile. It was a bit hard to tell given the difference between my fleshy mouth and her beak mouth.

"It's always wise to know why we do what we do," she said. "Their incursions have become bolder and bolder, it seems. They must've been fed information regarding our route. A matter for the inquisitors, I'm sure . . ."

"But why?"

She stopped walking and studied me. "Why what, Beja?"

"Why are they attacking us? You? The city?"

"Perhaps you ought to lie down. You don't seem like yourself."

Inwardly, I smirked at that. For a simulation, she was on the money. It seemed I'd have to get a little experimental with my approach if I wanted to learn more.

"Well, about that," I said at length. "I think I've been, uh . . . cursed. Yes. Cursed."

Her eyes flew open in shock. "The work of the cultists. I knew their marks were present on the road. I'll summon the oracles at once."

"It's fine," I said, raising a hand to keep her from bolting off that instant. "I just . . . need a refresher, of sorts. If you can fill in the gaps, I'm sure my mind will recover easily."

After a long period of blinking, cocking her head to the side, and generally waiting for me to alter my course of "treatment," she nodded. "If you wish, Beja. What shall I tell you?"

"Your name, for starters."

She whispered something under her breath. The small, feather-like protrusions across her bare arms and legs rippled in agitation. "Surely their foul magics have not corrupted the memories we share."

"Of course not. Just . . . a little bit."

"Do not worry," she said softly, setting her goblet down and approaching me with both hands out. She rested her palms on the sides of my head and met my gaze directly. "You are mine, Beja, and I am yours. Our minds are interwoven."

Well, this . . . this added a new layer to the dynamic. There was more than just employer-employee concern in her eyes. More than even the concern of a trusted confidante. Unless I was terribly mistaken, or my intuition was somehow thrown off by our difference in species . . . this woman was *into* me.

"I am the Empress Jalisa Multheri Nodran, Third of the Blessed Name, Priestess of the Nine Realms, Radiant Guardian of Oracles and Sages." She gave another, softer smile. "Do you remember yourself, Beja?"

I struggled to consume her word salad but didn't let that show. "Yeah, I think I've got myself down pretty well. Beja."

"Yes. Good, my dear. Very good."

As she examined me, her alien face somehow registering as soft and inviting, I put together a few moving pieces. If *she* was the empress, and we were in some sort of relationship, did that make me . . . the *emperor*? No, that couldn't be. No sane empire would march around with its leader exposed and left to handle the worst of the enemy forces.

Then again, maybe I was overthinking all this. This wasn't a real world, after all. Not in the same way as the physical universe beyond the God-maker. In this world, up could be down, right could be left, and black could be white—and I'd have no choice but to accept that as normal. Given that, was it really so impossible that I was an emperor *and* warrior with the boring name-slash-title of beja?

Time to find out.

"What is a beja?"

Again, the woman—Empress Jalisa, I should say—looked at me as though I'd started eating food via my rectum. "My dear, what have they done to your mind?"

"Just humor me. Your words are already helping more than you know."

She frowned. "I really think we ought to summon the oracles. This . . . degradation of your mind . . . It's overwhelming. They've deprived you of even the simplest of knowledge."

"No, uh . . . Empress. That won't be necessary."

"You're certain?"

"I am."

The empress looked away, sighing. "Very well. Perhaps receiving the customary rewards will revive your mind."

"Customary rewards?"

"Yes, dear." She placed her hands on my cheeks once again and smiled, then began reciting words with the cadence of an ancient prayer. "The beja is the protector of the throne and its people. The starved animal with an insatiable appetite. The one awash in blood, purified through pleasure."

Before I could ask what the hell any of that meant, she took my hand and began tugging me down the lane of pools. She had a remarkably strong grip. Before long, I realized where she was taking me: an elegant, eight-post bed in the center of the chamber, sitting high atop pyramidal steps and draped in fabric that sparkled like mica.

Was she about to . . . deflower me?

"Whoa, whoa," I said, trying in vain to slow my steps. It was fruitless against Jalisa's power. "Are you sure I'm allowed to—I mean, *we're* allowed to—"

"Hush, my dear," she whispered. "Let my touch guide you back to sanity."

As we neared the bed, I glanced back in search of any entrances or exits, trying to figure out where and what this structure was. I never got the chance to locate what I sought. While looking about, I caught the faintest reflection of a creature in the rectangular pool near my feet.

Only it wasn't a creature—it was *me*.

To my horror, I looked nothing like a human. Hell, I didn't even look like Jalisa or the laborers of her species. But I *did* have a point of reference. A solid, tangible point. One I'd killed just minutes prior.

The pool's dark, placid surface presented me as something disturbingly similar to the brute from the road. The contrast between how I perceived myself and how I *actually* looked in this world was enough to take my breath away, and not at all in the good sense. In fact, the only difference between "me" and my victim was the degree of mutilation.

The brute I'd slain had been covered in scars, burns, and other injuries, while I had only a network of light scarring. Then there was my head—instead of being encased in a brutal proto-helmet, I had a functional (and jewel-encrusted) face that roughly lined up with the brute's features. Finally, I realized with *some* relief, I didn't look nearly as monstrous as my dead counterpart. If I wasn't mistaken, there was something distinctly . . . human . . . about my own appearance. Almost as though the barbaric traits had been shaved down, softened, muted. Not enough to dispel the similarities between the two of us, but enough to prevent me from fainting.

What in the Halcius-lovin' fuck am I?

The answer didn't come. At that very instant, the world began rippling away from me, distorting and breaking into pixel-like fragments that shrank and bubbled until they were nothing but empty space. Every sensory field became a psychedelic whirl. Akasha, the chamber, the pools—all of it broke down into a flurry of light and dancing particles. In less than a full second, however, the storm was over. In its place was the same dark, featureless chamber that had thrust me into the facsimile universe. The same faintly glowing column.

I was *out*. Back in reality.

Even as I stood there, struggling to catch my breath, to deal with my galloping heartbeat, a burst of static came through hidden overhead intercoms.

"You hear me?" It was Rogaji's voice, no doubt about it.

I mindlessly patted my whole body down to ensure nothing of me had been left in there. Everything was intact, yet it didn't seem that way. Some intuitive sliver of my mind held the conviction that I was still inside the Godmaker, still gripping Jalisa's hand. Hell, the taste of that devilish wine lingered on my tongue like echoes of a forgotten dream.

"*Helloooo,*" Rogaji called, more aggravated this time.

"Yes," I said in response, more to shut her up than anything else. "I can hear you."

"Why'd you pull the plug?"

Swallowing a lump in my throat, I said, "I've had enough for today."

"Enough?" She snickered. "Dak, you were in there for less than a minute."

8

Once I'd mentally recovered enough to take the elevator back to the control room, I made a beeline for the nearest chair and slumped down in exhaustion. My mind whirled as I sat there, eyes shut, trying to hold on to the experience like the dregs of a fading dream. The only thing keeping me tethered was the constant pressure of massaging my temples.

Well, that and the fruity cocktail Rogaji used to nudge my shoulder.

I glared at the icy highball glass, then up at Rogaji, but she didn't seem to take the hint.

"Go on, drink it," she said, gently sloshing the bright-green drink about until I snatched it from her in frustration.

"Not the time," I explained.

Despite my best intentions, however, I *was* thirsty. The Godmaker had taken more out of me than I'd anticipated. This being the case, I swallowed my pride—and then swallowed a glug of Rogaji's cocktail. It was pretty damn good. Sweet, tart, with a vaguely chemical edge that I might've mistaken for sedatives, had anybody else prepared the drink. There wasn't much room to worry about being drugged when I knew how easily she could kill me.

"There you go," she said, plopping down into a chair across from me.

"I'm not in much of a partying mood, you know."

"Most first-timers aren't. They usually come back up looking like you."

"What, about to go insane?"

She smiled. "Precisely. Which is why I added some mild sedatives to your drink."

I spat a mouthful of the concoction all across her floor. "You *what*?"

"I also suspected you'd stop drinking when I told you that, which is why I added about fifty times the normal dose. You've already swallowed enough to put a grayclaw on its ass."

Assuming she was telling the truth—and unfortunately, I had no reason to believe she wasn't—there was little point in blowing a gasket now. I eased back into my chair and set the highball glass on a nearby console. With any luck, the sedative would do its job and bring me back to a place of relative sanity.

"What would've happened if I drank the whole thing?" I asked.

Rogaji studied me for a second, then scrunched her brow in consideration. "Huh. I hadn't thought of that. You probably would've had a seizure and died."

I rolled my eyes—an action that seemed significantly harder than usual, though it may have just been my hypochondria reacting to my unwanted drugging. "What the hell did I experience in there?"

"You tell me."

"Tell . . . you? You were the one in the control room."

"Correct," she said pleasantly. "And *yet*, the control room's only job is to oversee the functioning of the equipment. It doesn't dictate or record anything that occurs inside the Godmaker."

"Why the hell not?"

"Dak, Dak, Dak." She shook her head and gave me a sweet, if patronizing, smile. "You're still under the illusion that I had any conscious role in creating this machine. There was never an option to add or remove features. I built what the blueprints revealed and nothing more."

"You're saying you couldn't have even mounted a camera in there."

"Could I have? Possibly. Would I? Never."

"But *why*?"

"The Godmaker is a marvel," she explained. "Others might feel brave enough to tinker with its design, but I am not. Besides . . . it's not as though a camera would capture anything of value. Things move too quickly. Though I'm far from a technological savant, I know enough to understand why it would be a flawed endeavor. There's too much data loss from the time dilation. To you and me, anything recorded in there would be a meaningless blur. If that."

"So you didn't see a single thing I experienced."

"Not one." She delicately folded one leg over the other. "By all means, describe it to me."

"Can't you just pluck it out of my head?"

"No. The Godmaker's experiences are . . . peculiar like that." She grinned. "So, go on. Don't leave me in suspense."

She seemed earnest, if a little too eager, and I found myself resenting the fact that the sedatives hadn't already kicked in and dragged me to unconsciousness. Vivid memories of my short stint inside the Godmaker whirled about in a frenzy, yet reaching for any one in particular—even trying to put it all in chronological order—brought me to the very edge of fatigue. I was in no mood, let alone shape, to deliver the account to Rogaji.

"What have you seen when you go in there?" I asked.

The sudden shift caught her off guard. "In terms of . . . ?"

"I don't know. The scenery, the enemies, the things people said to you."

"Well, Dak, they aren't *really* people, so—"

"Humor me."

The last vestiges of amusement trickled off her face. "What are you driving at?"

"You told me it would be something like a simulated combat environment," I said at length. "It . . . wasn't that. Not entirely, anyway. It felt like its own world. It had history, culture, personalities. You really think the Godmaker would invent all that just to set a backdrop for combat?"

She leaned closer. "I *also* said the Godmaker is unlike anything you've experienced. Now you're beginning to understand my relationship with it."

"So, you've seen this stuff, too? What did it look like?"

Rogaji mulled it over for a moment, clearly trying to choose her words with care. "It's different with each session—most of the time. Sometimes the landscape is black and blistered, and at other times it's marshy, or pitch-black, or underwater . . . "

"Any reeds? Marching caravans?"

She cocked a brow. "No, I can't say I've seen those. More to your earlier point, however, I *have* experienced sessions in which there's a running storyline. Some sort of impetus to go forth and slay the enemy." After a moment's pause, she shrugged—seemingly to herself. "The equivalent of a quest description, if I had to guess."

The way she described the system made sense, though it was a bit sparse on the technical side. She didn't *really* know how or why any of the content was generated, only that it served a purpose if viewed from a pragmatic angle. That much, at least, I could verify—the Godmaker had taken several minutes to set up my initial encounter on the road. But that still didn't explain the phenomena that bothered me deep down.

For starters, there had *clearly* been some sort of overlap with my mind and its contents. On top of that, or perhaps because of it, the whole thing had been colored by a disturbing sense of déjà vu. A cold and imprecise certainty that it was more reality than fantasy. Almost like my own memories.

Rogaji touched my knee, breaking my temporary stupor. When I met her eyes, she was smiling at me with equal doses of pity and interest. A concerned therapist. "Dak, what *exactly* did you see?"

"I . . . " I stopped myself, unsure how to convey any of this without sounding completely off the deep end. "It felt like I'd been there. Like the people *knew* me."

"As I said, the Godmaker's mental toll is—"

I raised a hand to stop her. "No, not like that. It felt like it constructed an entire universe out of my mind, only . . . "

"Only?"

"Have you ever felt like something was familiar, even though you hadn't seen it before?"

"Bear in mind that you're speaking to someone who lived through a preordained future."

I nodded stiffly, acknowledging her point. "I think the Godmaker is tapping into some part of my mind that I don't understand. A part that's hidden."

"Ah, how fascinating. A sort of subconscious study. Perhaps you're more sensitive to the effect, given your time with the monks."

"That's what I thought at first," I said distantly, my attention anchored to the floor panels, "but it wasn't like that. I know what lucid dreaming is. I know how it feels. This . . . In there . . . It was all too *real.* There was actual structure to the experience."

"Absolutely. That's where the magic comes from. It doesn't feel like a training sim at all, does it?"

I took a deep breath and let my head droop to the back of the chair. The sedatives were starting to kick in, if the heaviness throughout my body was any indication. A welcome reprieve.

"You just need a night of solid rest, a nutritious breakfast, and maybe an upper or two," Rogaji said, patting my knee like a doting mother. "You haven't had a wink of sleep since your brush with the monks, have you?"

Against my instinctive judgments, I nodded. "Maybe you're right. There's . . . been a lot lately."

"Never underestimate the power of the mind, especially when paired with new technology and sleep deprivation."

I grumbled in assent.

"Let me show you your quarters," she said as she stood. "Once you're properly rested, I can show you my personal armory—including all the Polyps I've found. Might make your voyages a touch easier to stomach."

Seeing no point in arguing, I slid forward in the chair. Tried to, anyhow. I'd evidently slurped down far more of the sedative glob than I originally suspected, because damn near three-quarters of the muscle fibers in my legs refused to respond. I rolled my helpless gaze toward Rogaji.

"Oh, you poor thing," she said with a sigh, hauling me up and supporting me without any visible effort. "Nothing a thousand-thread-count bedsheet and a nightcap won't fix."

To Rogaji's credit, she didn't abuse her privilege as a temporary nurse. In fact, she handled me quite gingerly, forgoing any opportunities to use me as her personal rag doll. Granted, she *had* been the cause of my drugging, but still.

As she ferried me back through the network of lifts and corridors, I ran through the experience in hopes of gaining personal clarity. It wasn't easy to do, given the near-lethal concentration of sedatives in my bloodstream, but at least I had some distance from the Godmaker. Far as I could tell, there really was some mumbo-jumbo going on with the machine and its ability to read the user's mind. It wasn't a bold assumption, but rather a starting point. A starting point that only generated further questions.

For instance, what was the deal with those blindfolds? Or better yet, with the third eyes? The only being I'd encountered with that kind of physiology was Akasha, and although she had been on my mind rather intensely, it didn't explain why the Godmaker had drawn so heavily from her features.

And what about the shift in locations? Had I triggered that by staring at the city, or had the Godmaker decided to shuttle me along? Had it even been a choice? Had the machine influenced me to make me *believe* I was teleporting myself?

By this point in my internal discussion, we'd already reached my quarters. If it sounds like I was thinking slowly, it's because I was. Thoughts seemed to arise at one-tenth their normal speed, and those that did come up were often so nonsensical I lost my mental footing and had to loop back to the prior sentence. Faintly, somewhere in the murk and blur of the real world, I sensed Rogaji showing off my room's ten thousand luxurious features—but I just didn't give a damn.

Even after she settled me in the bed and tucked me in, it took a full five minutes before I realized she'd left. These were some damn good drugs.

Time squirmed around me, the minutes bleeding into hours in the cool, stale darkness. No matter how long I pondered, though, I was out of insights. Running in circles.

My addled mind decided that the only solution to this was a second opinion. And the only second opinion within reach was my old friend Jekra Modri.

The instant I activated our consciousness link, he tore into me.

"You're a real piece of shit."

"Thanks," I replied in an inner voice that was still half my typical speed.

"Oh, not even gonna talk to me?"

"Talking takes too long. Too many muscles."

"Huh. Yeah, you are pretty fucked up." He snorted out a dark laugh. *"So, uh, you wanna talk about . . . everything . . . that went down?"*

"What's there to say?"

"That I was right?"

I sighed. "All right, fine. You were right. Narbu was a treacherous dick, Akasha has some scary secrets buried in her, and—"

"And this Rogaji chick is gonna slice you open once she gets what she needs."

That was enough to snap me back to semi-functional consciousness. "Huh?"

"You're tellin' me you don't see it? She's usin' you."

"I know that. She told me as much."

"No. She told you what she wants you to know."

"Listen," I said, inwardly grimacing, "you think everybody is out to get me."

"That's how it works for Purifiers."

"Right, but—"

"Wise up, Purifier. She's the contender."

"Huh?"

"Remember when you were in that worm thing's dream world?" Modri asked. *"It said there were three challengers for you. The first was the Duplicitous Contender. Contender . . . one who competes. She's a goddamn simmer. Haven't you put the pieces together?"*

For once, Modri was making a *lot* of sense. The notion chilled me. Was it possible that she *was* the contender from the monks' visions? If so, would I have to kill her? That seemed to be the dominant theme in my interactions with others. Especially others with aspirations of power.

I didn't have time to consider that much, though. Modri plowed ahead with his commentary as though he hadn't dropped a ten-megaton warhead on me.

"And don't even get me started on that Izymom . . . Izoom . . . Izazom . . ."

"Izamem."

"Yeah, him. Don't get me started on him. He's a little weasel, too. Put that in the bank and cash it."

The strange, seemingly contradictory nature of that last sentence threw my sedated brain for a loop, but I set that aside. "Modri, what I really need is your help. I've got nobody in here. Nobody that I really know, I mean. We're closer than ever to getting to the Unmade, to stopping this damn game, but I feel we're about to walk into a trap."

"Kid, you've been walkin' into traps since day one. You ask me, I think you oughta keep Akasha on ice for the foreseeable future."

I groaned. "She's innocent. Just caught up in it."

"Caught up in it? She's the Unmade's fuckin' mother."

"In a past life."

"Yeah, maybe, but . . . bad mojo. Hell, maybe you can convince your new crush to toss the old one out the airlock. Right into a star or something."

"First off," I mentally growled, "neither of them are my 'crushes.' And second, if you keep talking like that, I'm going to hush you again. And I'll keep you hushed for good."

Modri seemed to acknowledge the point—or at least respect it—seeing as he quieted down to the occasional mutter.

I understood his frustration over being silenced the majority of the time, but right now, I couldn't deal with the constant paranoia. Maybe it was just part of his conditioning as a soldier. Whatever the case, he wasn't lifting me up as I'd hoped he might. If I kept listening to his conspiracies about everyone and everything involved in this affair, it wouldn't be long before I triggered the base's nuclear-meltdown protocol.

"Listen, you and I'll sort this out," Modri said, backing off his war-hawk tone. *"What you've gotta do is keep your head on a damn swivel, trust nobody, and, most importantly . . . put a goddamn lock on your thoughts around that Purifier. She's no good."*

"Anything else?"

"Yeah. Quit turnin' me off every few seconds. This is the craziest, most batshit goddamn thing I've seen in a hot century. Mind magic and mush-rooms and whatnot. Least you could do is let me comment on it. Sick and tired of talkin' it all over with the Purifier party in here."

I furrowed my brow. "Wait, are you and all the other dead Purifiers talking shit about me?"

"Huh? Us? Nah, never . . . "

"You are, aren't you?"

"We've just got a lil' bet cookin', y'see . . . "

"On what?"

"Better if you don't know. Catch some dreams, you gullible bastard."

I let out an exasperated breath and flopped over in bed, trying to forget the hellish facility (and general situation) I now inhabited. Unlike most occasions, however, I didn't hush Modri—and in turn, he didn't bother me. There was something comforting in that. Not quite the feeling of being supervised by a deity, exactly, but close enough.

Midway through the hazy wobble of falling asleep, however, a coherent line of thought bubbled into awareness. It wasn't a conscious thought—it was far too refined, too brilliant for that. More a stroke of genius, really. And what was this insightful thought?

We're treating past lives as real.

That lone sentence, little more than the seed of an actual idea, was juicy enough to wrench my eyes wide-open. I stared into the darkness, teasing out the implications in twos and threes.

The surface meaning was clear enough: Modri and I were both dealing with Akasha's nature as though Narbu had told the truth. As though she'd *actually* lived in an ancient society guided by oracles. As though she'd *actually* been an empress. Nothing else was capable of explaining the undeniable karmic links between her and her spawn. Sometime long ago, in a distant land, her past incarnation had given birth to a son that would eventually become the Unmade.

If that was all real . . . If Narbu's account of reality held any weight whatsoever . . . it meant the Godmaker might be doing more than conjuring waking dreams out of brain activity. Perhaps it was drawing from reality. From my life.

Just not *this* life . . .

9

The next day—assuming a day had passed, which was damn near impossible to tell in a windowless room—I awoke with a blaze of inspiration. An afterglow from my last-minute revelation, it seemed.

After far too long stumbling around the still-dark interior of my quarters, waving my arms and slapping random wall panels to raise the lights, I managed to get my bearings and locate the stash of eerily well-tailored clothing Rogaji had left for me. I shaved, showered, and dressed with all the efficiency of an amphetamine junkie, far too exhilarated for the meager amount of sleep I'd gotten.

Even when I staggered out into the corridor, jogging in the vague direction I assumed led to the breakfast area, my mind worked overtime to slice through the sedatives' lingering haze. Thoughts and speculations emerged like wild, intermittent jets from a pressure washer.

If the Godmaker's showing my past life, does that mean I was also *part of Akasha's empire? Was I her bodyguard, her husband, her bed buddy? Was that . . . thing . . . really my original species? Is the Godmaker showing me only my past lives, or is it somehow tapping into Akasha's mind? How was I able to teleport? Did I have special powers in my old lives? Do I have powers now?*

My first impulse was to barrel straight into Rogaji and unload my half-baked theories. She was, after all, the owner of that bizarre contraption, and she'd surely have some insights as to what kind of hardware had gone into its construction. Or one of her crew members would, anyhow.

But somewhere in my frantic rush, I started to rethink my initial choice. My brain throttled down, and so did my pace. Soon I was just wandering forward, half dazed, half anxious, though I wasn't immediately sure why. Until I thought about Modri's words.

Maybe he was right. Maybe I couldn't trust Rogaji. The woman had spent years perfecting her role as a Purifier, no doubt selecting her upgrades and path with extreme deliberation. She was the sort to always have a plan, and a backup plan, and a backup plan for a backup plan.

What were the odds that an insanely powerful Purifier—one who'd had precognition and infinite funding, no less—would overlook something as substantial as the Godmaker's true function?

I stopped entirely and leaned against a bulkhead, pondering that.

Thus far, she hadn't actually said anything that indicated she believed in past lives. From the sound of it, she assumed the Godmaker was rendering physical "dreams" for its users. A valid and materialist interpretation of the phenomenon, I supposed. Hell, there was a good chance that it was the correct interpretation and that my drug-stewed lump of a brain had just popped out an answer that *seemed* plausible.

Even so, something kept me from racing onward. If I told her my theory, and it turned out to be *true*, I had zero leverage in this game. Right now, my only true role was to serve as a guinea pig. She had no idea what value I held or how I might aid her in accomplishing her aim of beating the Unmade. All she knew, with any degree of certainty, was that she needed me.

On the off chance I'd hit the mark and was indeed interfacing with a past-life simulation, there was a clear and present risk of my mind being cracked open like an egg for research purposes. After all, there was no need to keep a fellow Purifier around once the secret came out. If her true objective was the knowledge locked inside my skull—knowledge no other being could possibly provide—why waste time feeding, housing, and training me in her secret machine?

That raised another question, though one that took me a moment to fully spell out in my own head. Here was the line of logic.

Rogaji's future-seeing fungus had obviously had a plan in mind for her, and that plan included me and the Godmaker. All good and well, until you get to the past-life part. If the Godmaker was pulling from that source, it meant the fungus had also known about that feature. Which meant the fungus was also playing a role. Advancing a cause.

Whatever that cause was, it had me playing just as much a starring role as Narbu had foreseen. This, in turn, meant I needed to bridge some crucial gap in the whole plan. I had an objective that the fungus had spelled out long ago, with or without my permission. Somewhere in the Godmaker—in my past lives, more precisely—there was *something* I needed to kill, find, learn, see, or experience.

But what the hell was it?

"Don't do it," Modri growled in my ear.

Having had him shushed for so long, the intrusion made me flinch. "Goddammit. Can you avoid that? Making me think I'm having a psychotic break."

"What's the matter, chief? Not a fan of sultry voices in your ear?"

I scowled. "Not in this context, no. Now what are you saying?"

"I'm sayin', don't bring your little hunch to Rogaji."

"Am I that transparent?"

"Shit, you were mumblin' the whole night long about past lives and Godmakers and Jalisa. If you ask me, you're scrambled."

Crossing my arms, I slid farther back against the bulkhead and let a procession of labor fabriques march past. "But you believe it, don't you? That there are, uh, past lives?"

"Not a good judge of reincarnation theories, bud. I died, but I sure as shit ain't in a new place."

"Yeah, well, maybe you're the best judge of reincarnation for that reason. You're still here."

"Thanks for remindin' me," Modri deadpanned.

I decided to recenter the exchange. "You really think she'll use it against me?"

"I've met plenty of folks like her. She wants power, and lots of it. Anything she's got to worm under your skin is fair game."

"But if I'm right . . ."

"Then you'd especially *wanna shut the fuck up about it,"* he said darkly. *"You realize what kinda pandemonium you'd cause if she leaks this?"*

"What, that people are reborn after they die?"

"Uh, yeah? Pisses in quite a few religions' oatmeal bowls. Including the Hegemony's."

"Sure. Because parasitic alien superweapons, dimensional rifts, and mechanized monks are completely fine in the eyes of the masses."

"It's different," he warned. *"All the shit you just mentioned has been around for millions of years, and it all happens in the world of the living. The ones who know . . . well, they know. And the ones who don't know don't need to know. But rebirth's talkin' about death and what comes after it. That's a whole 'nother beast."*

"Why? Maybe if people knew there was another life around the bend, they'd tone down the shithead behavior."

Modri chuckled. *"Or they'd go goddamn nutty."*

"Either way . . . If it's the truth, it's the truth."

"Too much truth ain't a good thing," he whispered.

I ran a hand through my hair, sighing. "Since when did you become so concerned for the religious sensibilities of the entire universe?"

"I'm not." His grunt proved he truly, deeply did *not* give a damn about that. He seemed almost offended by the accusation. *"What I'm 'concerned' about is how much rain they'd dump on this facility if even one transmission got out. Rogaji ain't shyin' away from spotlights. She was a pro simmer, for fuck's sake. She says a word—just a word—and you've got some scary sons of bitches stormin' this place in a heartbeat."*

"You sound paranoid."

In truth, though, he didn't. He was being the most reasonable he'd been in some time. I had no idea how long it'd take to reach an acceptable level of power in the Godmaker, let alone how many experiences I might need to find the critical information stored therein. It wasn't as though an information leak would bring an invasion in a matter of minutes, but it also wasn't much better than that. Modri was justified in bringing up "scary sons of bitches" here. Between esoteric research funds, religious paramilitary cadres, and the simple yet crushing hand of the Hegemony, there were plenty of possible danger sources. Hell, for all I knew, rebirth had been proven time and time again throughout the cosmos, only for its proponents and religions to be crushed into oblivion by the powers that be.

"Fine," I thought at last, "I'll keep it under wraps. Nobody except you and me will know."

"Smart thinkin', chief. The last thing you need is another—"

Modri's sudden silence jarred me, though not for long. Less than a second later, I heard a curious *tik-tik-tik* approaching from farther down the corridor.

I glanced in that direction to find none other than old Izamem, who—despite his furious movements and huffing—was advancing with the pace of a paraplegic snail. He looked utterly ridiculous, almost like a hallucination, as he shambled beneath the corridor's garish lights.

"Good morning," I called to him, adding under my breath, "or whatever time it is . . . "

He withheld any response for an awkward forty-five seconds, during which he continued to shuffle toward me with a vengeance. His gait was so spirited I actually worried he might strike me upon getting in range.

Thankfully, he was more cordial than that. Once he'd come within battering distance, he sank down on some kind of haunches within his robes and glanced up at me. Thick lines of bluish sweat poured down his face.

"Boy," he said in that quiet, croaking voice, "we must speak at once."

I squinted at him. "I'm on my way to breakfast. We can go together?"

"No time to stuff your meat sack," he snapped. "You have found it. The truth. The cutting vision."

His fervent delivery left little room to wonder about the nature of that truth. Still, he spoke in a manner that was somewhat guarded. Verging on heretical.

"You must come with me at once," he continued. "We shall talk in shadows. In silence."

With a "request" like that, how could I refuse?

Izamem's upscale storage closet was just as dim and musty as yesterday. The only change was that he'd brought out a slightly larger cushion, allowing me to sit on the other side of his strange crystal. Whatever herbs he had burning in his various incense dishes did nothing to ease my migraine.

The moment he shut the door, my question came bursting free. "How did you know?"

Izamem giggled and limped over to his seat, then sank down heavily. "With a mind so raw, it's no wonder Madam Ro is able to pry it open at will."

"You're saying she knows?"

"Of course not," Izamem said, sneering. "My mind is sensitive. More sensitive than hers. Even in your dreams, you called out. It is a blessing that I intercepted your whispers. There are many, *many* beings who would not be so kind with such a secret in their jaws . . . "

I glanced about, suddenly wary of what might be lurking behind my back. In a voice so low I could hardly hear myself, I asked, "You were listening to me? To my mind?"

"Naturally. It is my task."

"From who? Rogaji?"

Izamem settled his walking stick in his lap. "From the cosmos itself."

"Thank you for that. Helpful. Not at all vague."

"You've confirmed what my visions told for a long while," he went on, blatantly ignoring my snark as he sprinkled more powders into his incense bowls. Each handful burst with a vinegary puff that made my eyes water. "The Godmaker *sees*. It revives. It unveils that which was hidden by the mesh of karma."

"So . . . it's real?" My jaw gradually dropped. "Like, *real* real?"

He offered a grave nod. "Not all details are present, but it is the best your mind can assemble at the moment. A window into that which came before."

"Just say it plain, would you? Am I *really* experiencing *my* past life?"

"One among the infinite, yes," Izamem grumbled. "It must be where the answer lies. The response to a riddle with no name."

Much as I was growing sick of the seer's roundabout language and imprecise descriptions, I'd come to accept it as part of the job when it came to eccentric folks like him or the monks. Besides, I was genuinely desperate to learn more about this. Unlike karma and all the other big-brain concepts I'd been presented with previously, this one had real, immediate consequences. I just didn't know what they were.

"So," I said at length, staring into his eyeless face, "why didn't you just tell me that?"

"One should not speak until they are certain."

"But you clearly knew it was a possibility. I'd even wager you were eager to confirm it."

Izamem shrugged. "What would it have mattered if I slipped such words into your ears? You needed to see for yourself. To see in my stead." When I gave him a questioning look, he went on. "This machine wasn't constructed for those of my composition. It is for humans. Meat dwellers."

"How do you know I'm not wrong?"

"I have one gift that Madam Ro does not," he said with a note of amusement. "She cannot witness what you experience within its depths . . . while I can."

I scooted closer in a rush of excitement. "So, you saw it? I mean, you saw what I saw?"

"All of it," he said, nodding. "A clarified mirror of my visions. Unsullied. Pristine."

"Your visions showed you *my* experience in the Godmaker . . . before I even had them?"

"The world you witnessed is familiar to me," he said in lieu of a direct answer. "When one's mind is bright and plain, the strands of karma are not so difficult to tease apart." He tossed another handful of powder into a nearby flame. "It's no accident that I'm here, boy. You, me, Akasha . . . we are coiled in the same serpent."

"I don't know what the hell to make of that."

Izamem growled low in his throat. "I'll fill up the empty vase of your mind. After a few preparations, that is."

By this point, the haze in the room had grown so thick I couldn't inhale without a burning streak going down my throat. My nose prickled at the sheer volume of noxious fumes.

"Is this really necessary?" I coughed, swatting helplessly at the air.

"A ward," the seer said quietly, dangerously. "A lock for the mind, boy. Madam Ro won't recover a word of this. As it should be . . . "

Midway through hacking my lungs out, I recovered enough to form a sentence. "You're locking her out of my mind?"

"Not entirely. Just the sensitive words. The words I'm about to share."

"Why?"

"Because this doesn't concern her," Izamem snapped. "I may take her wages, but I am not her dog. It falls to *me* to ensure this wisdom remains between us. Do you see, boy? Her mind is too untamed to be entrusted with this."

"Great. My first full day in the facility, and I'm already engaging in treason against the owner."

Izamem waved off my complaint. "There. The ritual cloud is finished. Now we may speak openly!"

"About?"

"As I was *saying*," he muttered, "we're linked in ways you can't yet understand. Bound by the anchoring ties of the past."

I let out another dry, hacking cough from the haze, then glared at the seer. "Are you trying to tell me that you've seen the world I experienced? I mean, before you saw it in my visions?"

"You don't believe me, eh?" Izamem gave me a wonky smile. "Try this on for size, boy. Your little world was one of reeds, wasn't it? An empire pinched between tradition and modernity. A land of monsters . . . such as the beja."

The reeds part gave me some pause, but when he mentioned the word *beja*, I stiffened on the cushion. There was no way that had been a lucky guess.

"How do you know about it?" I pressed. "History books? Scanning other minds?"

"My people have an excellent memory."

"Memory doesn't cut it. There's no way any of that happened in the last thousand years."

"Who said it did?" He smirked. "Just as you're able to walk through the lives before this one, my people are able to walk through the lives of those who came before us."

A few days ago, I'd have declared Izamem mad and gone skipping off to tell Rogaji that her little "consciousness specialist" was trying to cut her out of a deal. Not now, though. Assuming I really was seeing past lives via the Godmaker, there weren't many hard lines of logic remaining in my world. Including the concept of species-based "karmic" memories.

As I mulled this over, though, a fresh realization occurred to me. "Wait a second. If you saw the same world through your ancestors' memories..."

He nodded with grim satisfaction. "That's right, boy. My people inhabited the same world."

"Uh-huh. And you think *I*—"

"Was also there," Izamem finished, grunting. "Yes."

"As a beja."

Again, he nodded. "You carry their hammer, no?"

I glanced down at the weapon. "Huh?"

"The beja's hammer is said to be the blade that slices the worlds open. Made from very . . . *very* rare materials."

"Sparkseed."

"And more, perhaps." He cocked a grin. "From what I saw, you already met the empress. Jalisa, if I'm not mistaken . . . "

"Is that . . . her?" I asked, barely above a whisper. "Was Akasha really *that* empress?"

"Now you're starting to understand." With a grating laugh, he picked up his nearby mortar and pestle, along with a handful of dried herbs on a towel. "You might think you're going crazy, boy, but you're not. It's *them* who are crazy. The nonseers. The unanointed."

Despite Izamem's words—or perhaps because of them—I wasn't feeling very grounded. He wasn't exactly the most stable source of information, let alone a good judge of what constituted reality. At the same time, however, I couldn't discard him or his insights. If even 10 percent of what he was saying turned out to be true, he was my best (and only) guide for navigating a dangerous dimension.

It wasn't just Izamem's outward lunacy that gnawed at me, though. Back when I'd been on Chanzig's world—which seemed like a lifetime ago but was closer to a week—I'd finally started coming to terms with my lack of importance in the universe. I'd been comforted by the notion of being a nobody, of owing nothing to anybody. I'd been a clean slate with a universe to explore.

That self-image had flipped while in Narbu's custody. In there, I'd received a diametrically opposing message—I wasn't a nobody, but a specialized, predestined "chosen one" ordained by the Absolute itself. Another hard pill to swallow. In fact, the notion had only been palatable because of what Narbu said about my blank, empty nature. I'd truly believed I was separate from the Wellspring and karma and all the sordid plots that went on beyond our fragile, three-dimensional reality. A free agent, if you will.

Now, however, I had something in between. A model of my existence that seemed to take the worst from both perspectives.

If I *was* the true rebirth of someone who'd existed on Akasha's world, it meant I'd also played a role in this entire catastrophe. I didn't know what it was, not yet, but I would find out. This realization alone filled me with cold guilt.

Worse than that, though, was the implication of how little my choices actually mattered. Narbu and Akasha had taught that karma shaped one's incarnations. In other words, a murderer was likely to be born in a truly shitty universe compared to a charitable person. Fine and well on the surface, but not when it came to my case. What had I done to justify being dragged *back* into this affair? What possible action could I have taken to avoid the gravitational pull of Narbu and the Unmade and their power games? Hell, had I even done anything? Or had I just been another pawn to the Wayfarers that resided in our corner of the cosmos? Whatever the answer, one thing was obvious: I wasn't the snow-white dove Narbu had taken me for.

The only redeeming quality in Izamem's account of my existence—and I do mean *only*—was that it painted me as something integral in the universal order. Multiversal order, if you went by Narbu's model of reality. I *hadn't* just been poofed into existence by Chanzig. I *hadn't* been pulled out of some formless oblivion to serve in an impersonal war. In one form or another, I'd existed for a long, long while. I had real roots. History. A trajectory.

"Are you finished with your navel-gazing?" Izamem growled.

I shot him a vicious look. "You're dumping a *lot* on my plate right now. Us humans need a little extra time to think it all over."

"Pah. You humans and your *logic*. A slippery, slimy thing only good for men of numbers and men of corruption."

"And engineering. And city planning. And—"

"Even now, you want to squirm away from the matter at hand," he said curtly. "What's the matter, boy? Too scared to confront what you are?"

"I don't even know if you're telling me the truth. Like I said, you could be pulling *all* of this out of my head right now."

"Absurd."

"Is it?" I asked, scoffing. "The head monk told me *nobody* else knows what really happened on that world. Not even his brothers knew, courtesy of mind wiping. So forgive me if I have a little trouble buying your tell-all."

Izamem settled back and resumed his mortar-and-pestle session, crushing a few small, hard seeds into the herb paste. After a long and anxious pause, he lifted his head toward me. "You saw a procession, boy. A procession for Empress Jalisa Nodran. On the way to the capital, you were ambushed by hordes of thin, frenzied beings. Am I correct so far?"

"Yes. And *all* of that could've come from reading my mind."

He shrugged and kept working the paste. "I know more than you think. I know more than that accursed monk, even. But I can tell you don't believe me. You're too . . . skeptical. Human."

"Prove me wrong, then."

"I don't need to. Truth proves itself." He grabbed a small bottle of what appeared to be oil from the shelf behind him, then drizzled it into the herb-and-seed mix. "The world within Madam Ro's . . . machine . . . is not an exact replica of your experiences. It is a diorama, boy. A living theater. Your mind fills in details where they ought to be."

"What's your point?"

"The *point*, you myopic little fool, is that the experience responds to you. Suppose you kill the empress. Ah, ah, ah, you've fallen off the tracks. Fallen, never to return."

"You're saying I have to toe the line."

"Yes, but not only that. It is possible to drift farther from the truth of how it all occurred . . . yet also to gravitate toward that truth."

"Go on."

Izamem smirked. "Madam Ro will bring you to an armory today. You'll know what you must take, and what you must leave behind." When I just blinked in confusion, he (somewhat) clarified with, "If you wish to know how you lived, you must live the same way. Do you see?"

"You're saying that I should try to align everything with my past life. What I say, what I wear, where I go."

"Indeed I am."

"How the hell am I supposed to know any of that?"

"By *becoming* what you were," Izamem croaked. "Fill your mind with the knowledge of a beja, and you will know what you ought to do. You've already done it before, after all . . . "

"The 'knowledge of a beja' part is where you lose me."

"If my words are true . . . and they are . . . you'll find what you need precisely where I say it is."

I frowned at his words, which reminded me of a high-tech scavenger hunt. Not that I had many other options. In fairness, being able to locate something within the Godmaker based on Izamem's hints *would* confirm that he had knowledge beyond my understanding. That, or it would confirm he was able to manipulate my mind. At least the idea was better than "just trust me."

"What's your proposition, then?" I asked. "Give me a landmark in the city, let me explore it?"

"Sure."

"How do you know I'll emerge in the same spot? It might throw me into some random corner of the planet, or some other section of . . . *my* . . . life. Assuming it even puts me back into the same life."

Izamem mostly ignored me, busying himself with stirring and then bottling the dark mixture he'd been brewing. "That's what this is for, boy." He dangled the small bottle as though it were a piece of candy. "It will activate the mind. Invigorate it!"

"More drugs? How about no."

His smile turned to a sneer. "This is not a *drug*. It's a sacrament. One you should be kissing my claws to receive!"

"The monks called their fungus a sacrament, too."

"What a horrid comparison," he snapped. "If you wish to see clearly, you'll consume this. Do it an hour before you enter the Godmaker. No sugar. No salt."

Against my better judgment, I took the bottle from his hand when he extended it to me. "What'll it do, exactly?"

"Hold the image of the empire in your mind's eye," he whispered. "It will restore your sight. Then you'll be able to control the experience."

"Control?"

"I see *all*, boy," Izamem said, bristling. "Your mind was too unsteady to maintain continuity. You see, ah? That's why you were transported without willing it. Eh, but . . . you *did* will it . . . you just didn't know you did."

None of his verbal babble made much sense, but I got the gist of what he was saying in regard to the concoction's effects. If it worked as described, it would allow me to navigate the Godmaker without any "glitches" in the experience. I'd be able to go where I wanted, when I wanted—whatever that meant.

"All right," I said begrudgingly. "I'll take your little poison. Then what?"

"Then . . . you look for what I tell you."

"I'm all ears."

Izamem sucked down a rattling breath. "Within the empress's palace, there is a structure covered in the faces of the dead. Archives."

"I don't much like archives anymore."

He ignored me, though not without a familiar *harrumph.* "You were a beja, boy. They will not stop you. Go, let your eyes feast upon the echoes of that dead place. Then you will know if I speak truly."

"I still have no idea what a beja is."

"You will learn," he said, giggling. "You and I aren't so far apart. Your mind creates that divide. Beneath the flesh . . . beneath all your defilements . . . "

I tucked the tiny bottle into my pants pocket, unable to hold back the chill generated by gazing into the seer's face. He *knew* things, even if I didn't want to admit it.

"So, what's the end goal of it?" I asked. "Let's say I *am* a reincarnation of that beja, and Akasha *is* the reincarnation of that empress. You got a grand plan for that?"

Although I should've seen it coming, I didn't. Izamem's walking stick flashed up and *booped* me atop the noggin in less than a heartbeat.

"Goddammit," I hissed. "Would you stop doing that?"

"I will . . . when you stop being such a damned fool. Think, boy. Use the *meat* in your skull."

"About what?"

"You've been given direct access to the archives of karma," he explained. "Through this, you will *know*—not merely *believe*—what happened to the empress. You will *know* how the monks bound her mind in the darkness. You will *know*, most vitally of all, how the empire burrowed to the very heart of the void. To your . . . Unmade. And you will be able to repeat the ritual."

Considering Izamem's prickly, evasive nature, his words made a surprising amount of sense. That, or he'd managed to properly scramble my head with a concussion. If our joint theory was true, there was nothing stopping me from reliving the crucial moments Narbu had described: the Unmade's birth and death, the thinning of the veil between worlds, the opening of the first gateway. I would be able to see, with my own eyes and ears, what Narbu and the others had done. And maybe . . . just maybe . . . I'd be able to figure out the solution to it all.

"How do you know it'll work?" I asked. "It's probably been thousands of years since all that happened. Information tends to degrade over time."

Izamem chuckled. "Karmic records are not stored in the brain, boy. They are immaterial, incorruptible. The mind forgets *nothing*."

Confident I wouldn't be getting much more until I carried out Izamem's assignment, I nodded, stood, and headed for the door.

Once again, however, he stopped me—this time by rapping his walking stick on the floor.

"What is it now?" I said.

"You said it's been thousands of years," Izamem croaked, "but you're not thinking far enough. This saga has been in the making longer than your people have recorded time." He angled to face me. "Welcome back to the fold, Beja. It's good to finish things."

10

staggered into the breakfast hall feeling more like a corpse than ever. Part of that was surely due to the sedative hangover, but the real kicker—as evidenced by a mild rash up and down my forearms—was whatever "herbal remedy" Izamem had pumped into the air.

In the interest of keeping Modri in the loop, I'd made sure to confer with him while in transit. Unsurprisingly, his take had boiled down to "Izamem is bad." After politely thanking him for his advice, I'd stuffed him back into hushland. The last thing I wanted was his unsolicited commentary while spending time with Rogaji—especially now that I was, in some way, a double agent.

Judging by the look of the breakfast hall, I'd arrived at the tail end of mealtime. Most of Rogaji's crew sat sprawled out on their metal benches, dirty trays lining the table and various inhalant sticks dangling from their lips.

The only one still engaged in eating was the young scrapper—Bodhi Drezek, if memory served. The reason for his slow consumption was immediately evident. While most of Rogaji's crew members were the strong and silent type, Bodhi was the "Holy *shit*, would you shut up?" type. I half listened to his yammering as I crept over to the self-serve kiosk, received my allotted slop tray, and then crept back over to an empty table. The kid had been talking for two minutes straight, all the while holding the same spoonful halfway between his lips and his tray.

That's not to say he annoyed me. Quite the opposite, in fact. I was grateful for his distraction, as it allowed me to eat in relative silence and run through everything in my head. And there was a *lot* in my head.

Foremost among these considerations was the nature of Izamem's species. The way he'd explained it, it sounded as though his people—or at least, some evolutionary ancestor of his people—had shared the planet with Akasha's people. This was hard to verify, though. None of the beings I'd seen in the Godmaker had even a passing resemblance to Izamem, unless you wanted to lump all generally monstrous-looking species together. No, everyone in my experience had been a bipedal humanoid. Not a single sighting of tentacle legs.

This, in itself, wasn't a huge deal, but it did open up new realms of questions, such as . . . which species counted as his ancestors? If he'd evolved as an offshoot of the empress's people, then why didn't Akasha look anything like him? On the flip side, if he'd evolved from the brutish creature I dispatched—yes, the one that also looked like past-life me— where did his loyalties really lie? There'd been virtually zero context to the battle I fought, but even a simpleton like me was able to recognize the animosity between the empress and her foes. It was hard to imagine that the empress's eventual choice to open a gateway and doom their planet would've been received favorably. How much of that resentment had bled through into Izamem?

Then there was a slightly more meta question. According to Narbu, nobody had truly survived the opening of the gateway on the homeworld. He hadn't specified how much time passed between the empress open- ing the gateway and total collapse—at which point he and the monks had fled—but I had to imagine it couldn't have been more than a few years. With that kind of speedy devastation, what were the odds anything aside from the most privileged of citizens had been able to flee? My working hunch was that Akasha's ancestors, the ones intent on destroying the chok'tals, had probably belonged to that rich-and-powerful category. Iza- mem's slimy-looking ancestors? Maybe not.

"Hey, newbie!"

The distinctively smarmy voice of young Bodhi snapped me out of my thinking session. I glanced up to find the breakfast hall utterly deserted— with the exception of the kid and myself, naturally. It seemed that the oth- ers had evacuated not long after I sat down, their abandoned trays serving as the only indication they'd ever been there.

I dragged my spoon through the slop. "Newbie?"

"Oh, yeah!" Bodhi flashed me a disreputable salesman's smile. "You see, I *was* the newbie. For a long while, actually. But now that *you're* here, you count as the new newbie. Which makes me an old newbie. Or maybe just a normal crewman."

"I'm not sure it works that way," I explained flatly. "I'm not really a member of the crew. More like a temp worker."

"Nonsense! Anyone inside these fine walls is most assuredly a full member."

"Even the seer, Izamem?"

Bodhi's face soured. "Oh, I don't much care for talking with him. A codgy little fellow, isn't he?"

"Seems that way . . . "

"You know, just last week, he threw an iron ball at my head. Right at my head! Can you believe that?"

I reluctantly shoveled down a spoonful of slop to delay our conversation. It was dreadful, though about on par with having to listen to this kid. "I can't imagine why he did that."

"There was a reason," Bodhi said darkly. "Anyhow, enough about that. Why don't you tell me all about yourself? I'm something of an aspiring novelist, really. I'd like to write a memoir someday. My own memoir, mind you, but I wouldn't be too bothered about *also* penning someone else's. For a fee, that is. Although the royalty payments alone might be tremendous if I can capture the story of a verified Purifier. How does 50 percent sound? Well, I'd do forty. Thirty-five, if you twist my arm. I'm telling you, Purifier stories will be in hot, *hot* demand in a few years. Miss Rogaji, well, she wouldn't let me transcribe any details from her life, but you? That's a—"

A hard cough was enough to stem his verbal discharge. "No offense, kid, but I'm not much of a talker right now. I'd just like to eat and find Rogaji. Lots to do."

He just grinned. "A man of business. No nonsense. I like that. Hey, what do you think about adapting that as a title? *The Man of Business.* Pretty good, right? Just you wait. I'm a fountain of ideas. Last week, Toast was trying to figure out a converter malfunction, and I—"

"Bodhi," I snapped, causing his face to instantly shrivel. "I really, *really* don't want to be rude. Can I . . . please . . . eat in silence?"

Suddenly, the boy looked so crestfallen I worried I'd broken him. It was certainly moving enough to make me feel as though I'd kicked a small animal. Still, I *did* want relative peace. I could apologize to him later.

No sooner had I started eating in earnest, however, than a metal tray clapped down on the tabletop across from me. I looked up to find Bodhi, mischievous grin and all, settling in to join me.

"You really are a man with a strict sense of how to do things," he commented, seemingly unfazed by my boiling expression. "No wonder Miss Rogaji didn't kill you like the others. Hah!"

My spoon was already between my lips, but I eased it back out and set it into the gray slop, then fixed Bodhi with a serious look. "What did you just say?"

"Oh, she didn't tell you? Yeah, there were actually a few Purifiers in her future visions. That's what Holmes says, anyway. Guess she didn't like the others."

"You mean . . . she brought other Purifiers . . . here?"

Bodhi shrugged, obviously not as invested as I was in the truth of the matter. "All I know is that she killed 'em real good. Skinned, burned, dissolved, mashed, obliterated. You name it, Miss Rogaji's done it to a Purifier."

I hunched over the table. "Why?"

Right at that moment—just my luck, of course—Bodhi decided to tuck into his meal with gusto. Through mouthfuls of gelatinous *stuff*, he managed, "Miss Rogaji likes a *challenge*." That last word sent flecks of spit and slop all over my own tray. "She, uh, she doesn't care for killing things that are weak. Likes to make them nice and strong. Then . . . *krrt!*" He mimicked a blade running across a throat.

I stared at him for a while, waiting for him to walk back his words or add more context, but he didn't seem to grasp even one iota of what he'd just said. Then again, what did I expect from a kid who was two shakes away from becoming a con man?

"Bodhi," I said slowly, "are you trying to tell me that—"

"Good morning!" Rogaji came striding into the hall like a living ray of sunshine, her black dress replaced by a frilly, all-white jumpsuit that probably passed as fashionable . . . somewhere. "What, oh, what are you boys talking about?"

At the same instant, we delivered two very different answers.

"Purifiers," Bodhi garbled around his food.

"Memoirs," I sputtered.

"I . . . see," she said as she approached our table. "May I join you?"

Bodhi answered in my stead, offering a flourish-filled bow to the seat beside him. As before, Rogaji giggled like a blushing schoolgirl, then sat primly.

"You slept later than I estimated," she said to me. "Perhaps I *was* somewhat overzealous with the sedatives."

"Sedatives?" Bodhi put in. "Oh, Miss Rogaji, I've never forgotten the time you spiked my food. I passed out before I even knew what was happening!"

The two of them shared a strange little laugh, after which Rogaji tousled Bodhi's hair. "And do you remember why I did that?" she asked him sweetly.

"Yes, Miss Rogaji! I believe it was because . . . I played with your guns without permission?"

"Just so. And what did I say?"

"Behave like an animal and you'll be put to sleep like an animal!" Bodhi exclaimed, repeating the words as though they were a nursery rhyme.

"That's right," she said, more muted now. "I hope you haven't forgotten."

"No, Miss! As I recall, that dose almost killed me!"

"Yes . . . " she mused, smiling yet meeting my eyes with an irritated look. "*Almost.*" Sighing deeply, she turned to Bodhi and patted his shoulder. "Why don't you run along? Dak and I have a lot to discuss."

"Ah," he said, nodding. "Sophisticated things, I'm sure."

"Very sophisticated."

"Hrm. Very well. I'll leave you to it." After a moment of very adult-looking nodding and humming, Bodhi stood, took his tray, and headed off toward the exit. On his way out, however—and out of Rogaji's line of sight—he repeated the same knife-across-the-throat gesture.

Comforting.

"An incredible child, but a colossal pain," she said once he was gone. "Moving along . . . how are you faring today? Any steadier, mentally speaking?"

I grunted. "Hard to tell. Sedatives and sharpness don't tend to mix."

"Oh, come now. You were in distress, exhausted, and completely incapable of requesting treatment for yourself. You'd probably have had a nervous breakdown if I didn't intervene."

"You could've put me in a coma."

"You're a Purifier, Dak. If your body processed substances at the same rate as any run-of-the-mill humanoid, you'd have had problems . . . but it doesn't. Trust me."

Not wanting to get too emotional over the incident—emotions tended to let things leak, such as confidential information from seers—I nodded diplomatically. "So, what's on the agenda? You said something about Polyps, didn't you?"

"That I did," Rogaji said with a sparkle in her eyes. A sparkle that was outmatched only by the fresh coat of glimmering, slithering, *living* makeup pasted all over her eyelids. "I'd have shown you my collection yesterday, but, well . . . I don't think you were in much of a state to appreciate what I had to offer."

"Probably true," I conceded. "So, what've you got? Swords? Axes?"

She broke out in a hollering laugh. "What am I, some sort of primitive warlord?"

"Hey, it's what the monks had."

"Well, generally speaking, monks are rather ignorant about what constitutes real power. I prefer a more . . . modern . . . arsenal."

Although I was trying *very* hard to keep my mind on track, skillfully diverting it away from any thoughts of Izamem and what we'd discussed, I found myself excited at this latest development. By Halcius, I'd *finally* get my hands on some high-powered firearms. Maybe even the fun things I'd thus far been denied, like tungsten-core launchers or drone flocks.

There was just one issue.

"Don't you think it, uh, would come off a little strange to be using a high-tech weapon in the Godmaker?" I asked. "Just going by what I saw, there wasn't much in the way of destructive equipment."

She quirked a brow. "Do hunters opt to kill their prey with fists and feet?"

"Well, no, but—"

"You need to get over your notions of fairness," Rogaji explained. "Within the Godmaker, you aren't killing *people*. You're killing . . . things. Things that might scream, or cry, or flee, sure . . . but *things* nonetheless. Besides, you aren't in a game. It's not about fitting in, let alone forced immersion. Efficiency is the only metric worth consideration."

I nodded, once again unwilling to lock horns over an issue that might provoke unwanted mental seepage. Rogaji's points were all valid, but only when dealing with the Godmaker as she understood it. To her, there was zero reality conveyed through the sessions. Knowing what I knew, however, I had my doubts about her logic. Sure, the people in my past-life world might not be the real deal, as far as people went, but to me—unlike Rogaji—immersion *did* matter.

Izamem had more or less confirmed that. From the moment I set foot in that world, I'd accidentally acted as though I was a beja, and in turn, people in that world had treated me as though I really *was* the beja. Unlike Rogaji, I wasn't after mere Kill Points; I was after the information held by the people, places, and events present in the world. If I stepped too far out of line, perhaps by nuking a city or killing the wrong person, there was a *very* real chance that my experience in the Godmaker would decouple from my actual past-life memories, which would then leave me stranded in a world truly of my own design.

To put it simply, I believed Izamem's theory about needing to act the part of a beja. There was surely some wiggle room here and there, as evidenced by the empress taking mercy on my ignorance, but I couldn't go overboard. If I did, there was no guarantee I'd be able to recover the "real" experience . . . including the lost knowledge of how to reach the Unmade.

Not that I could say any of that aloud.

Instead, I pulled on a polite and hopefully sincere smile. "I'd *love* to see your armory."

Ten minutes later, we reached the facility's magnetic tram station—yes, she'd had a goddamn magnetic tram line installed—and entered the waiting car. A chime of pleasant music, a warning on how to avoid decompression fatalities, and then we were off. Soft, trendy music designed for upscale nightclubs came over the speakers as we zipped into a lightless tunnel.

I settled into a plushy seat while Rogaji went to the head of the car, where she'd evidently seen fit to place a semiconscious coffee dispenser. To my amusement . . . and slight discomfort . . . the machine refused to provide espresso until its labor grievances had been addressed. Well, that was sorted with a quick bonk from Rogaji's fist.

She came back with two small, steaming cups, smiling as though nothing untoward had happened.

I gave her a thin, nervous smile and took my espresso. It wasn't half-bad. "So, you mentioned you've got some Polyps . . . "

"Yes?" she asked, sitting beside me.

"If you don't mind me asking, where'd you get them?"

"Purifiers, obviously."

"Yeah, but which ones? I mean, did you hunt them down? Did they come after you?"

Rogaji studied me while blowing on the espresso. "Did Bodhi say something to you? He has a habit of telling fibs, you know."

"Bodhi? Say something? To me?"

The impressive verbal fumbling wasn't made any better when I reflexively squeezed my cup, causing scalding-hot liquid to dribble down my hand. Thankfully, the pain at least redirected my mind for a split second. Less meat for Rogaji to pick through.

"You don't have to hide anything from me," she said, her coy, fox-like expression revealing just how screwed I was. "I see *everything*, Dak. I know what you've been discussing."

My life flashed before my eyes. It wasn't a particularly great life, either. Judging by the glint in her eyes, Izamem's magic dust hadn't done a goddamn thing aside from giving me a rash. The espresso in my grip suddenly felt like a doomed prisoner's last meal. I tensed up, waiting for Rogaji's pistonlike punch to blow my brains through the tram window.

"What you've heard is true," she said quietly, though not without a hint of malice. "I *have* killed many, many Purifiers, some of whom were even brought here." She straightened, looming over my semislumped form. "Do you know *why* I killed them, Dak?"

I had to force my windpipe to unclench. "No?"

"Because it was predestined," she said with a zealot's smile. "You can think what you want about me, but such judgment is derived from the relative freedom of being able to choose your actions. For years and years, I had no such option."

"But . . . shouldn't knowing the future—"

"Have altered it?" she interrupted. "Changed it? Created some sort of divergent path through chaos theory?" That got a laugh out of her. "There's a world of difference between hearing a madman's prophecy and witnessing *every single occurrence* at the level of quantum particles. The fungus that guided me was beyond time, space, logic. Whatever it showed . . . I did."

I resettled myself, now feeling about 10 percent more confident she wouldn't kill me. "Even if the people you killed were good?"

"Even if they were good."

"So, you *didn't* lure Purifiers here to murder them for sport."

She sighed and took a long sip of her espresso. "Ever since I learned of the Unmade's existence, I've lost interest in that sort of thing. The Unmade *is* my sport. I intend to claim his head." Noting my guarded expression, she tried on an awkward smile. "Besides, Dak, I don't believe the blame rests on my shoulders. The Unmade produced the chok'tals."

Though I'd sprinkled hints about the concept, I didn't feel comfortable enough to disclose that she wasn't exactly right. The official canon behind the chok'tals was more nuanced. In that account of things, the Unmade opened gateways by tapping into preexisting desires. Power, glory, domination—any and all of these ambitions could serve as fuel to weaken the divide between dimensions. So, in a sense, people like Rogaji had contributed to the Unmade's quiet takeover.

"Just promise not to kill me," I said at last.

"All right," she said with a friendly nod. "I think we can make that work."

Shortly thereafter, the tram slowed to a halt and deposited us in an identical station. Rogaji took me down a set of stairs, up a lift, and then down *another* lift—though this last ride had a few key differences. The lifts we'd taken up until that point had been small, dark boxes, clearly suited to whatever corporate business had taken place on this world prior to Rogaji's acquisition. In contrast, the final lift we took was akin to a large cargo elevator, with high, transparent panes on all sides.

"Aren't glass elevators usually for skyscrapers and orbital stations? Y'know, places with an actual view?" I asked as we descended into darkness.

"Usually," Rogaji said with a knowing smile.

I glanced at her with puzzlement, only for the ride itself to immediately fill in the gaps. Our lift sank straight down an *enormous*, cavern-like space, its design so familiar I initially feared it was a second iteration of the God-maker. It wasn't. Hundreds of lights flickered on in sequence, revealing a five-story structure with too many shelves and display cases to count. Seeing as we were descending down a central channel, Rogaji's collection literally surrounded us. There were so many distinct objects and gallery sections that my eyes would've gotten lost if not for the polished railings and staircases that separated each level.

"*This* is your armory?" I sputtered.

Rogaji approached one of the transparent walls, hands meshed behind her back. "The main one, yes." She glanced back. "Don't worry, though—if you can't find something that tickles your fancy here, we've got three more to peruse."

"And they're all this size!?"

"Of *course* not," she said, borderline offended. "This is the smallest by far. Reserved for my most prized pieces."

"I see . . . "

When the elevator *finally* reached the bottom, Rogaji guided me out along a wide catwalk that spanned . . . a massive pit below us. Thus far, none of this woman's design choices had convinced me she wasn't an evil genius. Well, come to think of it . . . she really *was*.

Our first destination was a rather unassuming terminal located near the stairs to the first level. Rogaji strode up to it, tapped the screen to wake it up, and began pecking through various menus.

"In case you're wondering," she said while she worked, totally absorbed in her task, "this is something akin to an archive's search directory. Just . . . a bit different."

She stepped aside and gestured for me to have a browse. Sure enough, it was exactly as she'd described it. Instead of featuring categories such as time periods or research areas, it listed the following:

>GUNS
>MELEE WEAPONS
>ARMOR
>EXPLOSIVES
>POLYPS
>GADGETS

I cocked a brow, intrigued by the menu's apparent similarity to the genofacturing list. It was a fairly light selection, given everything around me. I decided to start with an innocent enough peek at the GUNS category. The ensuing submenu was where things got spicy.

GUNS
>HANDGUNS
>ASSAULT RIFLES
>BATTLE RIFLES
>SHOTGUNS
>MAGNETIC RIFLES
>SPECIALIST RIFLES
>SNIPER RIFLES
>LIGHT MACHINE GUNS
>HEAVY MACHINE GUNS
>SUBMACHINE GUNS
>PERSONAL DEFENSE WEAPONS
>ANTI-MATERIEL RIFLES
>ANTI-SHIP RIFLES
>PARTICLE RIFLES
>KINETIC LAUNCHERS
>CARBINES
>PLASMA
>ION
>GAMMA

The sheer quantity of categories suggested Rogaji had been *extremely* busy procuring and itemizing weapons over the years. There had to be hundreds of each type.

"Impressive," I said, whistling faintly. "How many of these were genofactured?"

She scoffed. "Do you *really* think I'd be so shortsighted as to offer you weapons you're genetically incapable of using?"

"I suppose not."

"Genofacturing is important, though it leaves something to be desired in the realm of weaponry," she explained. "Much more worthwhile to use your points on tonics and other enhancements."

"Easy to say when you've got trillions of bux."

Rogaji waved away my comment. "A few hundred thousand is enough to get your hands on the latest devices."

Seeing as I had exactly *zero* bux to my name, it made sense why I'd been relying on genofactured weapons. It seemed it was now time to upgrade.

"So, I figure we'll start you off with Polyps," Rogaji began, pacing in a tight circle. "Then we can move on to weapons, then armor, then your gadgets. Anything beyond that is, of course, more than open to you."

As I studied the terminal's yellow-on-black screen, however, a whiff of something like intuition came over me. At the same time, the hammer strapped to my belt took on a warbling vibration. It had already been "active" for the past day, probably in response to Rogaji's ongoing presence as a Purifier, but this was . . . new.

Rogaji watched me with pinched eyes as I let my finger hover over the display. "I presume you disagree with my order of procurement."

I didn't bother replying. Too much was churning in the undercurrents of my mind. Without knowing why or even how, I deftly navigated back to the main menu, selected ARMOR, and took in the following list.

ARMOR
>KINETIC GEL
>VACUUM-PROOF
>MODULAR
>LAMELLAR
>BIOFILM
>CLOAKING
>ARCHAIC

The majority of options dealt with armor kits I'd never even heard of, let alone seen deployed in the field. As a matter of fact, at least three of them were officially illegal, in the eyes of the Hegemony and other regulators.

None of these contraband picks mattered to me, though. Instead, I let my finger creep all the way down to ARCHAIC.

What appeared was a sprawling catalog of old-school armor, each marked with data about its intended species, culture of origin, metallurgical or biological composition, and so forth.

"You really *do* like a challenge, don't you?" Rogaji said with a sly grin, seemingly proud of herself and her collection as I scrolled through the thousands upon thousands of options.

Again, I said nothing. My mind was still somewhere else. In some other time. There wasn't a single thought floating through my skull, and yet I had an overpowering notion that I knew precisely what I was doing.

Before I consciously registered it, I found my finger poised just above one entry in particular.

>BEI-JHO BATTLE VESTMENTS
Origin: UNKNOWN
Age of Manufacturing: UNKNOWN
Style: Full-body
Composition: 73.1% Unidentified Titanium Alloy, 16.3% Graphene, 4.9% Uranium, 2.1% Turquoise, 1.9% Bone, 1.7% Mercury
Intended Species: UNKNOWN
Provenance: Private auction

"Quite the *random* pick," Rogaji commented.

"This one," I said softly. "Where did you find it?"

"It says it right there, Dak. A private auction."

"But why buy it?"

She shrugged. "Part of predestination, remember? I wasn't fortunate enough to understand why I did half the outlandish things I did."

"What would you say if I told you I wanted this?"

"Oh, Dak. It's not meant for humans. Far too large. Too . . . misshapen."

"Could you retool it? Fit it for me?"

After a moment of trying to gauge whether I was serious, Rogaji laughed. "You haven't even seen it."

"Let's just say it's important to me. You know. As, uh, an archaeologist."

"Well, it *was* rather expensive, and it won't be easy to convince Toast and Jar to return to their fabricator days . . . " She blew out a breath, feigning indecision, then smiled. "It's all yours, of course. Hasn't been much more than a footnote in my collection since I acquired it."

I wasted no time in tapping the LOCATE key beside the description.

Somewhere behind me and far, far up, a chime sounded. Turning back, I found a small patch of the fourth floor illuminated by green light.

Time to become a beja in the flesh.

11

D o you see the mottled plates on the black one?" Rogaji asked, pointing out yet another suit of armor suspended in a silicate case as we walked toward the real prize. "As far as I recall, that cuirass was a gift from a vizier on the world of Utreika. Quite a lovely man, though he—and the rest of his people, in fairness—had the nasty habit of making soups from humanoid skin. Something about the collagen, I believe. Well, anyhow, the armor itself is made . . . "

Rogaji kept going, delivering factoid after factoid, but I'd already tuned her out long ago. I was faintly aware that she was, in fact, speaking, but I couldn't tell you anything of substance about her collection.

Now, you have to keep in mind that I was a legitimate archaeologist. And yes, before you say it, that was all due to my implanted memories from Chanzig, which themselves were hollow recreations of Mr. Korasa's memories . . . but the end result is the same. Regardless of the dubious origins, I did, in fact, have a great deal of knowledge about ancient things—and the curiosity to match it. So, my lack of attention wasn't at all in response to the subject matter. There just wasn't enough room in my brain.

The mental power that would've been reserved for analyzing Utreikan viziers, bifocal targeting overlays, and all the other knickknacks Rogaji presented was, instead, diverted to making sense of what I'd just done.

Even at that moment, a good ten minutes after my "spell" had worn off, I still didn't know where my armor-selecting confidence had come from. How had I even known it would be listed in the database? It wasn't as though I'd had the harebrained urge to tab over to the search bar and enter *beja*. Somehow, some way, I'd wanted what I wanted before even knowing it existed.

And on that note, the name. The curious name. Bei-jho? Somewhere during our stairwell ascent, I'd realized that I had never seen the word spelled out—not that it mattered much, seeing as written languages didn't tend to hold up well over millions of years. Even so, I was almost certain the error existed on the side of modern transcribers. That clear, decisive part of my mind *knew* it was just "beja." This being the case, name recognition wasn't enough to explain my actions.

It did cross my mind, while half listening to Rogaji's lecture and nodding and walking, that I'd grown overconfident in my intuition. There was a solid chance that, upon reaching the actual armor set, I'd find something more suited to a twelve-armed arthropod than what I imagined.

This turned out to be a pointless worry.

The instant we rounded the next corner, I stopped dead in my tracks. The beja armor—bei-jho, if you want to be pedantic about it—stood upright in its case, gleaming under the soft lights that framed it from all sides. It was very much humanoid . . . and familiar to me.

More than familiar, even. It gave me the same blend of relief and chills you might experience after finding an old, beloved piece of clothing you'd forgotten ever owning.

"*This* is what you were looking for?" she asked, grinning. "Dak, this is practically a museum piece. Come to think of it . . . did I steal this from a museum? Hmm."

I just kept walking forward, transfixed by the suit.

It was a broad, towering assemblage of corroded titanium plates and inlaid gems, mostly in the form of turquoise studs. Flakes and pitting across the armor itself suggested it had once been dipped in a dark, almost tar-like coating. To my amazement . . . and slight concern . . . the proportions matched perfectly with my body as I'd seen it in the Godmaker. That is to say, they were *brutish*.

Almost as brutish as the enormous gloves and boots, both of which had plainly been forged for the purposes of smashing and stomping. They were covered in short, thin spikes that resembled teeth, and though most of their decorative accents had shriveled or faded over the years—including the exotic fur strips, which had only survived due to vacuum storage—they still bore hanging strips of beads and bone.

The helmet, however, was what held my focus. It resembled an alien mixture of a scarab and a serpent, with a wide, intimidating collar and far too many pointed studs. If you looked at the headpiece like a living animal—which I *knew* was the intent—you'd note that the wearer's head was nestled inside the "mouth." The space was obviously empty at the moment, but it didn't take much imagination to picture my face in that void, hemmed in by rows of protective fangs.

Perched above the head hole were strange, angular glyphs and a trio of finely forged "eyes." The most prominent of the three, naturally, was the massive (and very much open) eye directly above the helmet's mouth. Motifs of legs, pincers, claws, and wings ran down the sides of the collar.

"It's beautiful," I breathed, only to catch myself a split second later.

Rogaji came up beside me. "What was that?"

"Nothing. I . . . just didn't think there were any left in the 'verse."

"The beauty of an infinite reality, Dak. There's always more of something." She joined me in marveling at the armor, tilting her head as though she'd suddenly become an art critic in a gallery. "Then again, perhaps you're right. This is one of the stranger pieces in the collection. Perhaps you can tell me about it?"

"Oh. I don't think I'd be a good judge. Not yet, anyway."

"Hmm?"

I shook my head. "Forget it. It's just . . . from a very, very old culture. We don't know much about them."

"Not even a name?"

"Not even a name."

Rogaji made an acknowledging *hrm* sound, then moved closer to the display case. "Well, they were quite obviously humanoid. A few exceptions, granted, but the general shape is beyond question. I've always wondered about the slots around the shoulders and arms. They feel . . . random. Perhaps some kind of ventilation system?"

Trying not to let anything from my Godmaker experience filter into my mind, I recalled the exact reason those slots were there. They'd been shaped to accommodate the scythe-like growths that sprouted from the creatures' shoulders and arms.

"I've often speculated that the creators were part of a shepherd species," Rogaji went on.

I glanced at her sidelong. "Shepherd?"

"An archaeologist who's never heard the term?" She scoffed. "My, that's a new one. Then again, I suppose the Hegemony doesn't include anything that verges on esoteric wisdom in their academic programs."

Still, I wore a blank expression.

She sighed, then asked, "Please tell me you've at *least* heard of the Great Maker."

Now that, I *had* encountered—but not from many reputable sources. As the theory went, the Halcius Hegemony wasn't the first faction to claim the stars in the name of humanity. Crackpots, human exceptionalists, and cryptic alien wanderers all shared one thing in common: a devout belief in the existence of the Great Maker, a godlike human that had tamed the cosmos long before the start of recorded history. So long before it, in fact, that there was no trace of his empire *anywhere.*

That isn't to say there was no evidence of his empire, of course. When the Microbe Tide swept through the universe and took out alien populations left and right, some had survived. Done better than survived, even. They'd flourished. And what were these species? Why, the ones that had *already* possessed humanoid DNA, of course. Species like Akasha's. So it wasn't totally out of left field to claim that somebody or something had "humanized" alien species at a genetic level before humanity's eventual extinction and resurrection.

The contention, however, was the exact cause for that humanizing. The Halcius Hegemony's muddy position was that the Great Maker had been Halcius's first prophet, laying the seeds of progress by "gifting" alien species with immaculate humanoid DNA. Most serious and neutral academics, however, disputed that account, mainly on the grounds that the Hegemony was using the concept of a Great Maker to justify reconquering the universe. A deified, all-powerful human who'd once lorded over all of existence was a powerful propaganda tool for a human empire.

All this is a long-form way of explaining why, in answer to Rogaji's question, I gave a simple "I've heard of them."

"That's something, at least," she said with a wink. "According to the stories, the Great Maker claimed dominion by crushing every species he encountered. But his territory was too vast to control through fear, naturally. His solution was to force humanoid DNA onto every conquered species. To create a sort of unified universal order, bound in harmony by nucleic acids."

I narrowed my eyes, already feeling like this was a wild conspiracy theory. "Okay . . ."

"The ones that refused his offer were exterminated outright," she explained. "The ones that accepted, however, were merged with humanity through eugenics." She paused, studying the armor. "There were a few species the Great Maker didn't simply tolerate, however, but truly admired. Species he perceived as an asset to his empire. Some were gifted in the arts, others mathematics, various sciences . . ."

"What's it all leading to?"

She lifted a hand, signaling for me to shush. "The Great Maker needed a hierarchy to ensure the 'cooperative' species didn't begin rebelling the instant he left their world. That's where the admirable species came in. He tinkered with their genetics to make them even closer to humans, then designated them as shepherd species."

"Right . . . " I said at length, nodding skeptically. "So, they were sort of like overlords. Slave masters to keep the less human species on their planet in line."

"That's how I've heard it, yes. And in exchange for their fealty, they were given immense wealth. Power. Mastery of creation." As if proving her point, Rogaji swept her hand toward the armor in the display case. "Could this be the work of one?"

From the tone of her voice, I could tell she took it a little more seriously than as a thought experiment. And now, suddenly, against all logic, I did, too. *Shepherd species.* The idea rolled through my head, picking up steam as I weighed my experiences in the Godmaker. Sure enough, the world I'd seen had been a pastiche of different species—the brutes, the scrawny ambushers, the luxurious beings from the procession . . . including the empress herself.

The latter species, assuming it *was* a separate species, had looked undeniably humanoid. But it was more than just surface impressions. The genuine beauty in their appearance suggested a sort of engineered synergy between the features of their base species and humans, almost as though they'd been crafted by an artist to look that way.

Was it really so absurd to think that ruling species had been placed in power by another empire? Placed there to rule over "lesser" species, more accurately? If true, it certainly went a long way in explaining the animosity between the so-called cultists and the empress herself. Either way, it still didn't address the root question of who or what a beja was. What *I'd* been. Had they once been members of the more numerous species, mutated into a new form? Had they been their own species? Had they—

"It's all just a speculative theory, of course," Rogaji interrupted, snapping me back to the present. "Something fun to ponder."

"Yeah," I muttered. "Fun to ponder . . . "

She tapped on the display case as though she were a ship merchant showing off her merchandise to a prospective buyer. "So, this is the one? You're sure?"

"Assuming they can resize it without destroying it."

"Oh, that won't be an issue. *But* I can't guarantee you'll enjoy the fit very much. It'll be bulky at best and entirely inflexible at worst."

I let my head loll from side to side in mock deliberation. "Let's do it."

"Suit yourself, Dak. No pun intended." She winked at me, then led the way back to the main area's railings. "I was *hoping* to use my original order so your equipment choices would complement one another, but seeing as you've discarded that course of events, I'll leave the order to you."

I mulled her words over, trying to determine what I actually needed in my kit. I was highly, *highly* interested in getting my hands on an arsenal capable of dissolving a planet at two light-years away, but recent encounters had changed my mind on that point. Assuming my gear really did play a role in how accurate the Godmaker's rendering of my past life was, it was best to stick to the "canonical" gear. That meant no guns—you know, since I hadn't seen any there.

It also, unfortunately, meant I was probably better off without scooping up a Polyp. I needed my voice, and *only* my voice, to serve as the primary decision-maker in the experience. There was a slight chance Rogaji's collection contained a specimen capable of aiding me inside the machine, but I doubted it. I'd gotten lucky enough with the bei-jho armor; the odds of her having a Polyp from the empress's time were slim to none.

Besides, I hadn't even unlocked the second Polyp slot. Which brought me to another question . . .

"How many Polyps do you have?" I asked her.

Her original question had pertained to gear choices, so it came as no surprise that she looked, well, surprised. Only for a moment, though.

"Six," she said warily. "Why?"

My eyes went wide. "*Six* Polyps? Your back must look like a feeding ground for leeches."

"They're one of the only ways to gain permanent boosts to your Rank Timer and overall power," she explained. "I can't believe you've made it this far with only one."

"He's a bit of a handful."

Rogaji smiled. "Speaking of which, how's your Rank Timer doing?"

The question was phrased casually enough, but it made my chest clench up. *Shit.* I hadn't checked the damn thing since flying to the compound, and even then, it hadn't been fully topped up. Was I dipping into my Storehouse Time *again*?

Not wanting to drop out of reality while in Rogaji's presence, I pulled up the truncated view.

Rank Time: 3 Hours, 49 Minutes, 51 Seconds
Storehouse Time: 17 Hours, 37 Minutes, 4 Seconds
RANK-UP NOT AVAILABLE

Well, that was a relief. I was cutting it real close on Rank Time, but it didn't bring out as much fear in my current circumstances. After all, there was a time-distorting machine working overtime just a few modules away. From that point of view, I actually had something closer to four hundred hours before I started chewing into my Storehouse Time.

Not bad.

The only wrinkle there, of course, was that I wasn't sure my mind could handle that long of an experience. The first session had damn near broken my brain, and that had been less than a minute of real-world time. With any luck, Izamem's little potion—and my sweet new armor—would be enough to keep me grounded.

Then another pestering thought overtook me.

The armor.

"Can you have Toast and Jar get to work on that armor?" I asked.

The urgency in my voice didn't go unnoticed. Rogaji fixed me with a blank, questioning look, then said, "*Now?*"

I nodded. "I've got a little over three hours on my Rank Timer. I'd like to wear it in the next session."

"Is there some kind of fetish thing that I'm missing?"

"Just . . . call it immersion."

Though she didn't exactly seem to buy my explanation, she gave a relenting shrug. "I'll transmit the work order now, have one of the fabriques deliver it. In the meantime . . . gear?"

"Let's take a look."

About an hour later, I was kitted out to the gills. As mentioned many, many times, I intentionally went out of my way to avoid picking any weapons or gadgets that would draw attention in the Godmaker's world. This ruled out most of the fun items, including a warhead-launching sofa that guided its payload using eye contact.

Still, I was satisfied with my haul. I'd managed to snag a bunch of ration kits, a large pack made from unidentified, scaly leather, a magnifying lens that affixed to my eyeball . . . Basically, anything that would simplify my work without becoming a cause for alarm.

Rogaji didn't seem too happy with my paltry loadout, probably because she took it as some kind of petty comment on the state of her collection. In some ways, I understood her upset. She'd amassed millions of pieces, ranging from the exotic to the industrial, only to have her honored guest pass it all up in favor of an antique armor set and a handful of assorted thingamajigs. Most upsetting was my choice to skip even *looking* at the Polyps; it would've wasted too much time.

Nevertheless, she eventually gave up on pressuring me to take more and instead complied with my request to help me reenter the machine.

As we backtracked through the facility, switching from tram to lift and all the rest, I took the opportunity to uncork Izamem's little vial and drain its contents. Amazingly, it didn't taste too bad. It was mostly that damn smell. A smell that *would've* spelled disaster, had Rogaji not been occupied by her arguments with Toast and Jar over the transmitter lines.

"I don't *care* how much power you have to divert," Rogaji growled as we headed down a linking corridor. "No, Toast. No bonus pay. Yes, I'm serious."

The tiff was mostly settled by the time we reached the Godmaker's control room, though I got the feeling I'd have to check the armor suit for hidden surprises before putting it on.

Rogaji and I sat in the same chairs as before, twiddling our thumbs and waiting for the delivery. It'd been about twenty minutes since I slurped down the concoction, and there weren't any effects yet. Not consciously, anyway. No shifting walls, no metaphysical revelations.

"I've got a question," I said at some point, breaking the silence. She nodded for me to continue. "If the Godmaker is capable of constructing and deconstructing matter at will, why can't you use it as a fabrication module?"

She let the question hang for a moment. "You mean, why I can't I use it to produce infinite copies of something?"

"Well, yeah. Ships, weapons, sim servers, whatever."

"The machine recognizes its own, and it takes its own back."

"Huh?"

"The matter it generates is proprietary," she said with a trace of annoyance. "The moment the machine powers down, everything it's created is reabsorbed. Probably for the best."

"Why's that?"

"Because the Godmaker doesn't just generate inanimate objects," she said. "Can you imagine the existential hell of producing living beings, then bringing them into a world they can't possibly understand? I'm not even certain their bodies would function outside its influence."

"Oh," I said, instantly abandoning any hope of bringing the empress or another being back through the exit lift. "That's a good point."

Out of nowhere, Rogaji straightened in her chair and frowned at something on her wrist. Something on her wrist's transmitter node, anyway.

"What is it?"

She glanced up at me, still frowning, then back down. "Nothing. I think."

"You *think*?"

"Just some strange readings from orbit. Like I said, nothing."

"But . . . couldn't those readings be ships?"

She waved off my concern. "If they are, it's just the Hegemony doing another surface sweep to complete their investigation. Don't worry about it. In their mind, you're already dead. Nothing but a clump of molten plasma."

"So, nobody knows I'm alive except you and your crew," I said drolly. "Good to know."

"Anonymity is a virtue, Dak. Trust me on that one."

Just then, the door leading to the control room hissed open. Heralded by a chorus of angry grunts, Toast and Jar soon came through the entry-way—backward. The reason became clear when I saw what they were hauling.

Against all odds, the two mad bastards had managed to downsize the bei-jho armor to a far more workable—and human-friendly—state. Aside from a few ugly welding lines and dappled spots where they'd been a tad too aggressive with a particle smoother, it was perfect. A miniature clone of the original.

The armor was upright, affixed to the hover-cart being pulled by the two men . . . though it was fairly obvious the cart had seen better days. Its left-side repulsors had failed, leaving the cart's underside dragging across the floor in a spray of sparks. No wonder the two mechanics were tossing me sweaty, red-faced stares of hatred. What should've been a job any ten-year-old could handle had turned into a battle of brawn.

"That took you long enough," Rogaji said, eyeing them distastefully.

"Fucking . . . cart . . . is bonked," Toast growled.

"Well, whose job is it to repair that?"

Toast and Jar gave each other a look I can only interpret as, *Do you think we'd succeed in killing her?*

The answer was a hard *no*, given how quickly the two of them sank from anger to defeat. After a sloppy salute—and one last *I'll get you* look in my direction—the mechanics lumbered out of the room, leaving their prize behind.

"I apologize for their surly demeanors," Rogaji said, shaking her head and watching the door close. "How *uncouth*."

I, on the other hand, only had eyes for the armor. It was . . . stunning.

"Would you prefer to change here and now, or shall I leave you alone?" Rogaji continued.

My face immediately skyrocketed in temperature. "Uh . . . "

"Oh, I see now. You've never even kissed someone. I'd imagine nudity around the opposite sex might make you a bit skittish. Unless you're some sort of voyeur pervert?"

Well, that right there was my proof that I hadn't yet learned to counter Rogaji's mind-reading ability in *all* situations.

"Right," she said, grinning. "I'll wait outside."

12

Ten minutes (and a lot of cursing) later, I stood alone in the Godmaker's black entry chamber, stuffed inside the bei-jho armor like some kind of gargantuan lobster. It didn't take long to realize where Toast and Jar had compromised in their redesign.

As I said before, the exterior was immaculate. Somehow, they'd managed to variously curve, flatten, and merge the individual components to leave the basic design intact. The *interior* was a different story—and one that, logically, I should've seen coming. Anytime you downsize a set of armor, there's bound to be additional material left over. In most cases, that material is trimmed away. That wasn't the case here.

Toast and Jar, either innocently or out of malice, had opted to fold the extra material inward. This created dozens of small, sharp spots that pinched my skin like a torture machine, especially around critical joints. If I'd had extra time, I might've asked Rogaji to fetch me a second set of clothing to further protect my skin—but I didn't. Izamem's potion was coursing through my veins, and there was no telling how long it might last.

The second issue was the weight. The suit had obviously been designed for a creature three or four times as strong as a human, as even with Overclock running at full power, it required a good deal of strength to lift a single leg. I wouldn't be doing any crazy acrobatics in the near future. Then again, if all went to plan, I wouldn't need to fight for quite a while. My primary goal for this session was to get in, find the critical information, and get out.

By Halcius, I was starting to feel like a bona fide spy in Izamem's service.

"Good to go?" Rogaji asked through the intercom.

I gave her an awkward thumbs-up—I was still getting ahold of the gloves' less-than-ideal maneuverability—and approached the chamber's center. As before, a green glow emerged at the base, then began snaking up as I drew closer.

Just before I reached the green cylinder itself, a loud, earsplitting noise ripped through the intercom. Rogaji's voice came through the garbled signal. I spun around, trying to figure out what the hell was going on, only for the Godmaker to engage.

Another flash of light, another instance of obliterated sensory data, another trip through the rinse cycle of dimensional warping. Just like that, any concern for the "real world" vanished. There was only the Godmaker.

This time, however, there was an added stability to the transition. Even when stripped down to pure awareness, I didn't have a sense that I was lost in the deluge. I was able to orient myself, feeling into and through the bubbling phenomena, trying to discern the nature of this strange limbo. By the time the Godmaker's reality began loading in, I was almost reticent to leave the quantum sprawl behind.

For some reason—probably because it had been my first and only experience in the Godmaker—I expected to be deposited on the same road as before. That wasn't the case. Instead, the world that came together around me was far closer to the interior of the royal palace. *Closer*, but not an exact match.

I was in some sort of small, candlelit vestibule, a gentle breeze pushing through the cloth door-hanging at my back and whispering through tiny gaps in my armor. Within seconds, I knew things felt *different*. Not dangerous, but *different*. There was a renewed sense of solidity to the experience, and though it may have been my imagination, I swore the environment was twice as detailed as before.

Take the vestibule's decor, for example. The overall design choices, from the ceiling height to the color scheme, were a perfect match for the empress's royal chamber, right down to the black-and-gold trim running along the floor. Only it wasn't simple trim anymore. Now it was adorned by a row of tiny, intricately etched soldiers—thousands of them, in fact, almost like a miniature army marching all around the room. Upon noticing this, some déjà vu corner of my mind assured me that the empress's royal chamber had *also* featured the motif and I just hadn't noticed it.

Well, who's to say what the real truth of the matter was? I can't. All I know is, if you aren't aware of something, it doesn't really exist for you.

The longer I spent just standing there, watching and listening and sniffing, the more the world seemed to introduce itself to me. Before long, I was grinning like an idiot at the scents of fresh bread and cardamom on the wind.

Now, in the interest of fairness, could this have been caused by some kind of psychedelic additive in Izamem's vial? Of course. But seeing as I lived through these events firsthand, you'll just have to take my word when I say that wasn't the case.

If I had to compare it to anything, it would be the opening of a flower. The flower, in this case, was the Godmaker itself. Deep in my mind, I sensed a gradual leaning in, almost as though my consciousness was urging the experience to unfurl itself and present its vivid reality. In the first session, I realized in retrospect, the mental reaction had been the complete opposite. I'd *feared* the Godmaker's power. Its capricious nature. Its strangeness.

I was so entranced by my surroundings, which in any other case would've been considered mundane, that I almost ignored the question of where the hell I was. *Almost.* Turning in place, I got a good look at the vestibule as something more than an art project.

Two wide, striated columns—basalt, I presumed—sat opposite the cloth hanging that led outside. Each of their bases held a variety of candles, bundled herbs, trinkets, and loose gems, almost like an offering site. Nestled between the columns was a tall, dark set of wooden double doors decorated with iron studs and beautiful carvings.

Most of the door designs matched the trim, featuring row upon row of marching soldiers. Sprinkled between those rows were similar motifs, such as priest-looking figures carrying urns and laborers carrying sacks. But my eyes lingered for a different reason—and no, it wasn't because of beauty or anything like that.

Running down the central seam of the doors was some type of writing. Not just any writing, either, but the sort I'd seen in the empress's chamber and on the bei-jho helmet. That is to say, glyphs instead of individual letters. They were large and incredibly detailed, and their gold inlay suggested they said something important.

The longer I gazed at the glyphs, the less . . . alien . . . they seemed. Their angles, their curves, their spacing—all of it was *just* barely beyond the scope of recognition. It was like a language I'd learned as a child but neglected to practice. After a good twenty seconds of just staring, which resulted in little more than a mild headache, I decided to give it up. What was I even thinking? That I'd just pop in here and read my mind's abstract clone of a dead language? It was ridiculous. Whatever relationship I had with these glyphs had probably come from seeing them in other locations.

I shook my head, glanced away, and—and understood. In one snap, the confusion vanished. Wisdom broke through my muddled thoughts like a lighthouse's beam through fog.

With no conscious understanding of how or why, I *read* the glyphs from the bottom to the top.

"The Sacred Council of Pristine Wisdom," I whispered.

I rubbed my eyes and looked at the glyphs again. Sure enough, they were as legible as anything written in my native tongue. Instead of registering as foreign shapes, they were actual sounds in my head. Sounds that related to ideas. Objects. People.

Before any of you linguistics nerds start getting too excited, no, I had no idea what to make of their grammar or syntax. It was just another flash of insight, not a textbook-style breakdown of the language as a whole. I mean, come on. I didn't even have a name for the language itself. All I had was the meaning.

Both puzzled and intrigued, I looked at the doors as a whole once again. The doors to a council building, it seemed. Only . . . there was something extra beyond simply knowing what it was. I had a *feel* for it. A sense of the place as it related to my own life, my own memories. That sense, by the way, wasn't one of overwhelming excitement. It was closer to skull-numbing tedium.

Even so, something pulled me toward the door and its carved-horn handles. *I'm supposed to be here.* The thought arose unbidden, almost startling me with its clarity. *I'm running late.*

Still, I hesitated. More precisely, I debated turning around, walking outside, and immediately locating the archives Izamem had specified. That *was* the mission I'd been given, after all, and I didn't want to waste the effects of the seer's little potion. That got me thinking. Was my new glyph-reading ability a product of the drug? Would it wear off before I reached the archives if I dallied? I didn't want to find out.

With my mind semi–made up, I moved toward the exit door's hanging cloth. If I hurried, I could probably—

"Ah, blessed stars," a raspy voice said from beyond the fabric. A moment later, the owner of that voice—a thin, skittish-looking man from the empress's species—began ducking his way into the vestibule. Between his loose cerulean robes and the stack of scrolls gathered under his arm, I gathered that he was some kind of official. "I thought I was the only one who'd be late, but—"

Upon seeing me in full, he nearly dropped his scrolls. His eyes went wide enough to serve as tea saucers, and he half slumped back against the doorway.

"M-my apologies, Beja," the man said, gulping hard. "I—I didn't—"

"Apologies for what?" I asked.

He gave a nervous little chuckle. "For . . . interrupting you, Beja. May . . . may your blood run strong. May all foes be reduced to dust."

Without further explanation, he sank into a low bow, averted his gaze, and sidled past me, almost frantic in his efforts to get through the door. Frantic . . . and pathetic. No matter how hard he tugged on the doors' horn handles, all he received were groans from the wood. Midway through his scrabbling, grunting, and heaving, he flashed me an awkward—and *terrified*—smile, though it didn't last long before being swallowed by a look of horror.

"Here," I said softly, moving in beside him. He let out an instinctive squeak and shrank back, almost knocking himself out on a wall panel. I just rolled my eyes. "Let me, uh, help you with that."

Maybe it was my still-active Overclock, or maybe the man was just a pitiful public servant, but I tugged the doors open with ease.

The mouse of a man mumbled some words of thanks and made another bow, then scurried down the long, carpeted corridor before us. At the far end of that corridor, illuminated by candlelight, stood four guards in ceremonial armor that wasn't *quite* as ornate as mine. Their interlocked staves formed an X-shaped wall that barred entry to an adjoining room.

I followed the man down the hall, my loud, clanking steps doing nothing to ease his anxiety—he must've glanced back four or five times in terror. When I came within earshot of the guards, I picked up on the man's dilemma.

" . . . don't understand," he hissed, waving his scrolls about in an unintentionally comedic display of all bark, no bite. "I *must* get inside! Empress Jalisa is waiting on my report!"

One of the guards—their leader, based on the red serpent coiled atop his helmet—looked at his comrades, then laughed at the much, *much* smaller man. "What's this? Planner Hijeksos, late for his precious meeting? Don't you find it ironic?"

"Let me through, or I'll—"

"Kill me?" the guard growled. "Try your luck, Planner."

"I'll report you!"

"So you may . . . *after* this meeting is adjourned." The guard pushed Hijeksos back a step with the tip of his staff. "I don't know how seriously your report will be taken, however."

"Oh, you wait!"

The guard took a step forward, easily towering a full head over the planner. "There aren't many of us willing to shed blood for the empire, Planner. It takes *conviction* to spit in the face of karma." He leaned down, causing the planner to shrink in turn. "Now, sycophants and armchair emperors . . . plenty of those. Enough for you to be replaceable."

I frowned and began stalking toward the interaction. It was time to see just how far my sway went in this world.

"What's the matter?" I asked—just as the guard went to grab the planner by his robe's lapel.

Everyone froze up, looking at one another with plain confusion.

I crossed my arms. "Well?"

"The usual rabble, Beja," the guard said. "Planner Hijeksos claims he deserves entry."

"He certainly does," I said.

This appeared to shock everybody present, including the planner himself.

Now, I had no idea whether the planner actually deserved entry or not. For all I knew, the guy could've been some random quill pusher eager to impress the empress with budget cuts. Still, he seemed earnest enough. And the guards seemed like real dicks. Most of all, though, I wanted entry to the meeting myself. There had to be a reason my intuition had pushed me toward it.

"Beja," the guard said in a quieter tone, releasing the planner as though he'd never laid hands on him, "this . . . *man* . . . is nothing more than an academic. You surely don't believe the empress would've allowed—"

"I heard the order myself," I lied. "Stand aside and make way for us. Or else."

Once again, I had *zero* clue what kind of status I actually held in this world. My only clues, thus far, had been my consorting with the empress, the fact that my name had been chanted, and the reaction of these folks— all of which had indicated I was a moderately big deal. And as you surely know, regardless of your species or culture, the words *or else* are always suitable as an intimidation tool.

The same held true here, judging by the fearful crinkle in the guard's eyes.

"Of course, Beja," he said quietly, lowering his head. "May your blood run strong. May—"

"Yes, yes, enemies and dust," I finished with a groan.

The guard looked as though he wanted to say something, but one of my cocked brows was all it took to issue a hushed order to the men under his command. As one, the guards peeled back their staff barricade. The two men closest to the inner doors peeled them back for us.

Planner Hijeksos, who'd remained silent and more or less motionless during the entire exchange, passed me a guarded little smile.

I motioned for him to enter the dim, curving stairwell beyond, then followed—after a parting glare at the leader of the pricks.

Only in the murk of the stairwell, long after the guards had sealed the doors shut behind us, did the planner summon the nerve to turn and look at me.

"Th-thank you," he managed. "I—"

"Don't mention it, Planner. Brutes just like to use their power on those who are smaller."

It took me a moment—and a weird look from the planner himself—to realize the irony in my statement. My "true form," which was closer to the monstrosity I'd killed on the road than any of the locals, was the walking epitome of a brute. Good thing I hadn't clapped a hand on the man's shoulder to sell the sentiment. He might've had a heart attack . . . assuming this species *had* hearts.

At some point in our ascent, a mixture of voices flowed down the stairwell. Voices of contention. This, in my mind, was far more worrying than any battle sound could ever be. Throughout my brief life, I'd gone out of my way to avoid meetings and debates and brainstorming sessions wherever possible. More often than not, these well-intentioned gatherings often ended with a whole lot of migraines and stuffy air.

It was too late to turn back, though. Soft light painted the stairwell's curving wall, and soon Planner Hijeksos and I were marching up toward the doorway, equally timid despite the contrast in our appearances.

Thankfully, Hijeksos was brave enough to make the first entrance. I followed behind him, peering around his shoulder to get a look at this hellish event.

What I saw looked straight out of a swords-and-sorcery sim. The meeting room itself had something like a bell shape, its floor circular and walls curving upward to meet at a central point in the dome ceiling. Everything from the tiles to the table to the high-backed chairs had been carved out of that spotless basalt, giving the space a distinctly murky feel despite the plethora of candles and chandeliers throwing light everywhere. The only things that shone in that relative darkness were more gold-inlay glyphs lining the wall panels.

At a glance, there appeared to be roughly twenty people seated around the table. Most of them were the same species as Hijeksos and the empress—who, by the way, was also present and perched in an elevated black throne—but there was also a pair of outliers. These two sat on either side of the empress's throne, clearly alert yet unruffled by the spirited discussion taking place around them.

As Hijeksos and I moved farther into the room, staying in the shadows and behind the guards by skirting the wall, I got a better look at those two attendees.

They were dressed the same way, bundled up in thick, snow-white robes with wide hoods, but I didn't pay that much mind. No, what caught my eye was the twinkle in their faces. Maybe *twinkle* isn't the right word, but something akin to it. Light glinted off their features as though they were made of diamond, or glass, or—

Metal.

My steps faltered as yet another pulse of vague familiarity swam up. I knew what they were in an instant, even if I didn't have the words for it. The closer I looked at them, the more certain I became.

Their faces were completely metallic, the features far too jagged and sunken to be a mask. Their three eyes glimmered with the pinpricks of optical sensors. What should've been a mouth was instead a short, cone-like protrusion lined with vocalizer studs. Even their hands, which just barely protruded from oversize, gold-threaded sleeves, were crude imitations of a humanoid's. The fingers were little more than multi-jointed hydraulic worms.

Monks. They're fucking monks.

Just as I noted this, however, the room went silent. Hijeksos and I stopped our slow, creeping incursion toward the empress's throne.

"Planner Hijeksos," the empress said with a warm smile. "I was beginning to think you'd ignored my summons."

He threw himself into a back-breaking bow. "Never, Empress! Never! Never!"

She pointed to one of the remaining empty chairs. "Sit and speak, please. I believe we could all use a shift in focus." As Hijeksos did as ordered, the empress looked my way. "Beja?"

Though I'd wagered things couldn't get more awkward, they somehow did. Given the fact that the empress had been about to ravish me in bed the last time we departed, I wasn't sure what to make of this rather pedestrian greeting. And that was just one point of confusion. Overall, I had *no* idea what I was doing in this world, much less what role I might serve at a stodgy meeting. Still, it wasn't like I could tell them that my dimension-hopping intuition had told me to join the party.

So, I tried the safest response. Meshing my hands behind my back, I nodded and said, "Empress."

"Does something require our attention?" she asked.

After a moment of contemplating how out of place I was, I opened my mouth—and was saved by Hijeksos's pointed coughing into his fist.

"Actually, Empress," he began while laying out his scrolls, "I . . . I believe the beja should be here for this. Much of my work concerns him. His role, that is."

One of the monks—the one seated to the empress's left—let out a synthesized scoff. "Empress, this is highly . . . irregular. Animals have no place in this congregation."

The other monk's "eyes" flared at that. "Oracle Narbu, this is *not* the time or place."

I just about shit myself.

Narbu! Here! Even dead, the son of a bitch just wouldn't get off my back. I was so stunned by the revelation that I missed the rest of the spat between the two monks—or perhaps I should say oracles.

What I *didn't* miss, however, was the empress's booming interruption. "*Enough.* Oracles, I ask that you reserve judgment. Planner Hijeksos has consulted with me extensively. If he believes the beja's presence is warranted, it is warranted."

The empress indicated a chair near Hijeksos, and I numbly wandered over to it, staring at "Oracle" Narbu the whole time. No wonder he'd felt so familiar. Then again, he was a far cry from how he'd looked in the real world. I suspected the reason had little to do with my mind's distortion of karmic memories and more to do with the fact that he'd swapped out bodies at some point. His current model was slightly larger than the organic bodies of those in attendance—good for engaging with society, but probably not so good for waging war on the Unmade.

That gave me an idea. Provided my theory was correct, the oracles swapping bodies to larger variants would serve as an excellent heads-up warning that some shit was about to go down.

Even when I settled down in my chair, I found that Oracle Narbu was still watching me with plain disgust. As to how I knew it was disgust, given the oracle's robotic form? I don't know. I just knew. It was almost like a hot breeze, roiling off him and smacking me across the table.

"Please, Planner," the empress said, fixing Narbu with a warning look, "explain your vision."

The planner to my left nodded fervently and worked to unfurl the last of his scrolls. "Yes, Empress, thank you. I, uh—" He looked up, met the expectant gazes of the room, and seemed to wilt into himself. It took a good while before he summoned the nerve to continue smoothly. "As I've detailed in my reports, the interlopers have grown increasingly bold in recent seasons. They've carried out massacres at Ranswala and Kathad, and there are even reports of enslavement among the nomads. This indicates that our strategy of containment is not working."

Several members of the gathering—those of the empress's species, mainly—burst into an uproar at that. The empress was quick to silence it.

"I will not have my advisers *heckled* while presenting such findings," she growled, her imperious gaze sweeping over the faces all around me. "Perhaps you should wait until the planner has finished his remarks before intruding."

That didn't stop one of the attendees—a woman with red-hued makeup—from shaking her head and offering her thoughts. "How much more must we hear, Empress? What he is suggesting is heresy."

"He's proposed nothing," the empress said curtly.

"But he will! He wishes to mobilize the force of death."

"Nothing of the sort has been said."

Planner Hijeksos raised a weak hand. "Actually . . . Perceiver Nukran has the right of things."

Again, there was a furious outburst of emotion.

One voice, however, was clear and sharp enough to pierce the commotion. That voice belonged to Oracle Narbu, who only spoke after receiving some sort of confirmatory nod from his partner.

"Planner Hijeksos may speak crudely," Narbu began, quelling the worst of the noise, "but he speaks in truth. The empress is aware of our concerns. She knows what must be done."

A man on the far side of the table rose from his chair. "Empress, what is the meaning of all this?"

After a moment of contemplation, the empress glanced at Narbu and gave a subtle wave.

He seemed to grasp precisely what this meant, because he was quick to stand and begin addressing the gathering as though he was the proper ruler. "Dark forces are at work beyond the realm of our dominion. Forces that wish to rend reality, to defile its beings, to undo all that we have sought to construct. Wisdom itself has counseled us to move against this darkness. If we do not act now—and act with overwhelming force—all may be lost."

At this, everyone went quiet. Well, except Hijeksos, who was still madly fussing with his scrolls as though they might speak in his stead.

"Now you understand why I've sought out the planner," the empress said in the thick silence. "If there were any other way, I would not advise preparing such plans. But all beings have their limits. Their lines in the sand. This empire has carried on the flame of gods and Wayfarers, and it *cannot* be snuffed out. Our survival depends on the following months."

The same woman as before, Perceiver Nukran, shook her head viciously. "A few malcontents are *not* grounds to wage war. The deepest wish of the defiled is to drag the pure into their hell." She grimaced at Oracle Narbu. "And *you*. How dare you? Your order is tasked with promoting the refinement of the mind. Why do you speak of killing?"

The empress turned to Narbu, evidently deferring to him. That alone was a clue as to the influence of the oracles in this society.

"Perceiver Nukran," Narbu said at length, drawing out her name, "do you understand the nature of compassion?"

"Of course I do," she snapped. "The fundamental value from which all others are derived."

"You understand the palatable sort of compassion . . . but do you understand what it truly is?"

Nukran folded her arms, watching him warily.

"Compassion is love," Narbu said. "Love is not always pleasant. It is not always tender. Love does what it must."

"What are you trying to say?"

Long, cold seconds passed as Narbu stared her down. "Suppose a spider takes up residence where your children sleep. What do you do?"

"I would remove it," she said quietly. "I would not kill it."

"And what if it decided to return?"

"Then it is welcome to share this world beside me."

Narbu nodded. "Suppose two spiders take up residence, then. Three, perhaps, or even four. Suppose that they create a nest there."

"I would *remove* it," she repeated.

"So you would. You would remove them . . . remove them . . . remove them. And each night, hours after their removal, they would return. They would continue to build nests and spawn their young . . . until one day, seemingly without cause, your home is awash in spiders. They sting your children while they sleep. They devour the countless other beings that reside in the walls and floor of your home. They leave corpses in every corner. Within weeks, your home becomes a shrine of death. A temple of decay."

"What is your point, Oracle?"

Narbu lifted his chin. "My *point*, Perceiver, is that negligence is not love. If one ignores a small woe, it will not dissipate. It will blossom and flourish, expanding until it has become an unthinkable woe. Then . . . you will not have any choice of compassion. All that will remain is death."

"The interlopers are part of our empire," Nukran hissed. "They are not pests. We took an oath to preserve them, and we have always maintained it."

"And yet," Narbu said, lifting a skeletal finger, "we have always served as their keepers. We have relied on death"—he threw me a pointed look— "to prevent death. If we do not quash one spider and its young, we will be forced to kill millions. *That*, Perceiver, is compassion. It is love."

After that mic drop of a finale, the room lapsed back into tense silence. The fight didn't exactly leave Perceiver Nukran's face, and certainly not her eyes, but she had the wherewithal to avoid wandering back into any of Narbu's traps. Hate him or love him, the man was unparalleled when it came to picking apart matters of philosophy.

Strangely, it was none other than Planner Hijeksos who broke the stalemate. He lifted one of his crinkled scrolls in the air—a map, judging by the grid lines—and cleared his throat.

"Empress?" he squeaked. "If I may?"

After a brief glance at Nukran to ensure she'd given up the fight, the empress nodded at Hijeksos.

"I've conferred with the reconnaissance units over the past cycle," he began, "and we've managed to pinpoint the location of an interloper compound. We believe that they've been using it to breed, train, and arm warriors for combat. In fact, we've managed to track several of their ambushing units back to the compound's general vicinity."

He gestured to the map in his shaking left hand, using a small red stylus to indicate something in the upper-right corner. "As you can . . . see here . . . there's plenty of natural cover for the compound. Plenty to, ah, hide it, I should say. They've gone to great lengths to obscure their intentions in the area."

Another woman near Perceiver Nukran lifted a finger. "Planner, this is highly speculative. Do you have any idea what this might cause? The clans would see *any* mobilization as a declaration of war, defensive or otherwise."

"And yet there are few other courses," Narbu cut in. "Their minds have drifted away from the radiant. If we refuse to act, it will be perceived as weakness."

"Let us appear weak, then," Nukran said. "Better than as butchers."

Sensing another imminent conflict, Planner Hijeksos tapped the map again and resumed his presentation. "The compound is just over two days' journey. If the . . . strike . . . is performed properly, there should be minimal casualties. The true aim is to assess the scope of their operations, you see. If the beja encounters anything that indicates extensive arming . . . " He paused and looked at me nervously, as though he'd just remembered I was there. "That would be a future conversation."

In the gathering quiet, the empress stood and surveyed the group. "I believe that Planner Hijeksos has shared enough. It's best to keep our discussions restrained, given the sensitivity of the matter." She pulled in a long breath—one that seemed to catch in her throat. "Cast your votes with pure minds. The empire depends on it."

At first, there was little more than a smattering of coughs. Everyone seemed to be too nervous, or just plain uncertain, to make a move one way or the other. Then, to my surprise, Perceiver Nukran raised her hand, a defeated and utterly disturbed look on her face. One by one, hands went up around the room, ending with those of the oracles.

Hell, just to feel less alone in the group, I even put mine up.

That seemed to be a mistake.

All eyes immediately whirled toward me—and stayed there. Even as I let my hand slink back down, their attention lingered. It was as though I'd just suggested beating an infant to death.

"What is the meaning of this?" Narbu asked the empress in that icy, detached tone.

She met my gaze, though I didn't get a single thing from it. "Even the beja recognizes the holy nature of this task. Let us praise his sacrifice."

By this point, I was *thoroughly* confused, though I didn't let any of it show. By the sound of it, I was going to be the only one carrying out this compound-buster mission. Not a big deal, given my need for Kill Points, but the circumstances surrounding my participation were more than a little odd. The guy expected to put bodies in the ground didn't even get a vote?

And yet . . . one thing confused me above all else. Confused, and then frightened. You see, when the empress stood this final time, I spotted something I should've seen long before that point.

She was pregnant.

13

Everything about that damn city screamed luxury. Not the sort of luxury connected with high prices, mind you, but the sort that implied exclusivity. Prestige. Arrogance. It felt as though it had been designed as the afterlife for a dying emperor—or *empress*, I mused.

"There's nothing like the air in late spring," Empress Jalisa said as we descended an alabaster staircase, lifting her beak mouth and sniffing deeply. "When I was a little girl, my father took me for walks along this promenade. He said . . . "

She kept talking, but I wasn't paying much attention. There was far too much on my mind. Foremost among my concerns was the *highly* visible curve to her belly, atop which her dangling necklaces jingled.

We'd been on this evening stroll for well over an hour—at her request, naturally. The ease with which she'd requested my presence told me this was a fairly common occurrence. Despite the length of our walk, however, I hadn't learned anything of value about my identity or expectations in the world. The only other clue I'd received had been while departing the meeting; there, Narbu had tossed me a nasty scowl and referred to me as a "pitiful beast."

The whole experience had me feeling quite dizzy, and it had nothing to do with the gravity-defying bridges or drifting, jellyfish-like beasts criss-crossing the skies above us. It was a case of psychological whiplash, really. See, in most normal situations, you're treated in accordance with your rank—and that rank is typically clear. That wasn't the case for me. At various points, I'd been viewed as a hero, an unwelcome pest, and a dangerous monster, with those perceptions sometimes overlapping in ways that were far too nuanced for me to grasp.

What *was* obvious, though, was my extremely niche position in society. I was valued enough to serve as the empress's only bodyguard while walking through the capital city but reviled enough to warrant fear or outright disgust from those beneath the empress. However I sliced it, that contradiction just didn't make sense. Were they jealous that I shared a bed with her? That I'd seemingly impregnated her? The latter idea made even *my* skin crawl.

But it wasn't until we reached that point in our walk, heading down toward a vast and festive public square, that the real implications of the pregnancy hit me. What were the odds that *wasn't* the Unmade in her stomach? More to the point, what were the odds that was my doing? It was almost enough to make my legs drop out beneath me.

The concept of being a father was daunting enough, but being the father of the Unmade? I wasn't sure my mind could handle that.

"Are you listening?" she prodded.

I shook myself back to awareness, only to realize we were threading through a massive crowd of civilians. The majority of them were singing and dancing and tossing colorful dust around, feeding off the energy of spirited yet ethereal music. Not all of them, however. Many regarded me with thinly veiled terror, backing away or prostrating themselves. Even those who seemed poised to throw flower garlands on the empress didn't dare approach.

"Isn't this . . . a little dangerous?" I asked her.

She stooped down and smiled at a young girl, then hurried back to me. "Dangerous?"

"All these people, and no security."

"You *are* my security," she said, giggling.

"I'm one person," I said. "A crowd this size . . . "

"Are you certain you're all right?" She ran her gaze over me, perturbed. "There's no threat here, Beja. The people are pure of heart. They would never compromise their minds."

"Good people sometimes do bad things."

Her smile faltered, just for a second. "What concerns you? Is it the task ahead?"

"No, I—"

"You don't leave until tomorrow," she said. "We have all night to enjoy the splendor of reality."

The way she said *all night*—with a mischievous grin, that is—gave me the same visceral reaction as before. My eyes went to her belly, lingering, wondering.

"Do you remember when you guided Dojat and me down these streets?" she went on, evidently missing where my attention had gone. A wistful smile came over her. "Those were some of the happiest nights of my life, Beja."

I hummed as though I had some idea of what the hell she meant. "Ah, yes. Dojat."

She spared a smile and a prayer gesture for a group that had stopped to kneel before her, then let her expression dissolve into something more somber. "He was the greatest emperor of this era. The greatest man, perhaps."

Ah, an emperor. The plot thickened. I still had no idea what she was going on about, so it was time for a bit of well-intentioned prodding.

"You . . . loved him, didn't you?" I tried.

After a moment of contemplation and a brief sparkle in her eyes, the empress turned to study me. "*Love* is not grand enough a word to express what we had."

"You, uh, made a wonderful couple."

She gave me a curious look, probably to suggest I was speaking far too rationally for a dedicated killing machine, then nodded. "He was my guiding presence. Maybe more." There was a brief, halting pause, with words bubbling up and then disappearing after spurts of soft noise in her throat. "The oracles say that when two beings truly love one another, they will reunite in future lives. Their karma binds them."

To my chagrin, that was enough to make me blush. "That . . . sounds plausible, I think."

"You believe it?"

"Sure."

She seemed satisfied by the answer, but she was strangely silent as we ascended a marble ramp and came to overlook the greater sprawl of the city. Beneath us, rivers threaded through the districts, their courses marked by the soft, bluish glow of the water. They reminded me of liquid turquoise. That, or radioactive sludge.

I couldn't deny the beauty of this place, however. After the "royal" city I'd witnessed on Chanzig's world—shit, after the cities I'd witnessed across several worlds—this place was almost impossible to accept as real. There were no screams, no gunshots, no spurts of fire rising up to denote fresh explosions. The only sounds were those of music and laughter.

The empress wandered up to a railing that overlooked regal gardens, and I followed. "Do you think he's already been reborn?" she whispered after a time.

It took me a moment to parse her meaning. "Emperor Dojat? I don't know."

"I wonder where he is," she said, more to herself than me. "I wonder what sorts of marks he's left on the other worlds."

"Probably a question for the oracles."

After several seconds, she seemed to snap out of her near trance. Then she smiled at me, sighed, and looked down at her stomach. "At least his progeny will make a mark here. They will know what sort of man he was."

It felt like a dam burst inside me. A dam of relief, just so we're clear. The kid *wasn't* mine. If not for my better judgment, I'd have been leaping for joy against that railing. Only . . . the feeling didn't last. It just felt wrong, being so violently happy about the revelation in light of the empress's pain. It was obvious she'd loved the emperor. Loved him enough to defend him even after his death, with nobody around to punish her for flippant words.

Of course, this *still* didn't explain why the empress had tried to drag me into her bed the night we returned from the cross-city trek. That was a question, and a concern, for later.

Right now, it was information-gathering time.

"Do you think the council made the right decision?" I asked.

Again, she gave me a weird look. It was obvious she wasn't used to a beja—whatever the hell it was—being so talkative. So . . . approachable. Even so, her shoulders lost some of their stiffness when she began considering my question.

"Right and wrong are dualities," she said, almost as though reciting a script. "The true path is not marked anywhere, even among the stars."

"But you still support it."

"If there were any other way, I would not."

"Because of our . . . oath," I said, drawing on the term Perceiver Nukran had used to support her disagreement.

The empress nodded slowly, her gaze tracking over the glimmering spires. "I used to believe they were simply ignorant. Beings with minds that could not comprehend the path of purity. I believed that they wished to be good and to live in accordance with our codes." Her face slackened, taking on a numb, icy veneer. "But when they took Dojat's life, I knew there was no redemption for them. They're not people, Beja. Not anymore."

I just stood there, unsure what to say.

The empress noticed after a short while. Her eyes crinkled in distress, and she looked almost . . . ashamed. "I'm sorry," she said faintly. "They are still your people, and they are not all under the grips of the same defilement. With the blessings of the oracle, you may still be able to save them. Some of them."

"Save them from what?"

"From their impurities," she said with unexpected force. "The oracles, particularly Narbu, are correct in their assessment. It's better to destroy the cancer now. If we allow them to thrive, to bear children and teach them their defiled ways, your blade will never again be clean."

The sudden shift in tone took me somewhat off guard, but given the revelation that "my people" had slain her husband, it wasn't all that unwarranted. That being said, it did loop back to a massive question I was nowhere closer to figuring out.

Why the hell is one of their enemies serving as the empress's bodyguard!?

Asking that outright would draw too much suspicion, however. Going by Izamem's warnings, it might even be enough to throw me off the established track of history. Better to avoid rocking the boat, I supposed, by sticking to questions that felt logical—or, at least, driven by my intuition rather than impatience.

"How many troops are marching tomorrow?" I asked.

She frowned. "Troops? Marching?"

"Well, yes? We're attacking—"

Before I knew it, her hand was clamped over my mouth. She gave me a hushing gesture—the universal *shh* finger, that is—and glanced about anxiously. Then, in a low voice, she said, "This will be the first offensive action in four hundred years. It cannot be spoken of lightly. Especially among the people."

I let her hand rest on my mouth, too mind-boggled to offer a fitting reply. Four . . . hundred . . . years, and all without a strike on enemy territory? No wonder they'd made such a fuss about taking down a compound. Some planets couldn't go four hundred days without a war breaking out.

"But tell me," she continued quietly, "why are you speaking of troops?"

Her hand came away, and I considered the question at length, trying to determine what those words implied. I didn't have a good answer.

"If we're . . . marching out," I said, picking my best euphemism for *attacking*, "we'll need to have enough . . . company . . . to ensure it's successful."

She studied my face for a moment, then broke out in a rash of giggling.

"What?" I pressed.

"I almost thought you were serious, Beja."

"About what?"

Her expression soured. "You're not speaking in jest?"

"I don't think so."

"We really should have you examined by the oracles before you depart," she said, shaking her head. "You've not been the same since we returned from the pilgrimage. Something happened to you. Perhaps it's what Narbu's always warned about. The bloodlust. It addles the mind."

Had she not been staring right at me, I'd have rolled my eyes so far back they fell into my brain. Narbu, lecturing people about the dangers of bloodlust and corrupted sanity? It was just too rich to let go. Regardless, this wasn't the time, and certainly not the place. To the empress, Narbu was an infallible genius. A visionary.

And that was why he'd fucked everything up.

"I . . . was not being serious," I said, trying to recover from my overeager push for details. "Of course I know what will happen tomorrow."

"Do you?"

"Of course. I'll move out with—" I stopped upon seeing her brows crease again. "Alone," I amended. "I'll be moving out on my own. Because I'm a one-man army."

Despite a few seconds of skepticism, her light smile suggested she'd accepted my answer. "We can head back to the palace, Beja. My heart is heavy, and your mind is . . . strange . . . but I believe we can enjoy one another's company to resolve that, no?"

She reached out for my gloved hand, but I was quicker in tucking it against my side.

"If it's all the same to you," I said, wincing at the awkward surprise on her face, "I have some business in the archives to deal with."

"The archives? What for?" She let out a pip of laughter. "Besides, it's your final night before—"

"Call it curiosity," I cut in.

"Very well," she said, narrowing her eyes with what might've been amusement. "I suppose you haven't earned anything yet, have you?"

Though I had no idea what she meant by that, I nodded politely and offered a matching smile. "I also, uh, had a request. A small one."

"Yes?"

"I'd like Planner Hijeksos to accompany me tomorrow."

She pursed her lips, mulling it over. "Why?"

The real reason, which I'm free to share with *you*, was that I had a strange and impersonal bond with the man. I'd saved him from the wrath of cruel guards, and for that, he surely owed me something. Besides, as much as I hated to admit it, the man seemed to genuinely fear me. He'd answer anything I asked him—and all without raising any alarms, given our lack of any true connection. Oh, and that was another thing. Our connection. Because we didn't have many ties, and I was quite certain "real me" had just been a standard, brutish dick to the man during his encounter with the guards, there wasn't much risk of me derailing the timeline. He was almost like a freebie. A walking information desk.

Naturally, I couldn't explain *any* of that to the empress. So I went with the most logical, albeit boring, reason.

"He knows the terrain well, and he's clearly done his research on the enemy's layout. He'd be a true asset to me."

"Planner Hijeksos is an academic."

"I don't expect him to fight, Empress. Just . . . to fill me in on some things."

This time, her silence didn't feel nearly as damning. She considered my words with obvious gravity, her gaze sweeping back and forth across the impressive skyline. After what felt like an hour, she turned back to me and nodded. "So long as you ensure he's removed from any fighting."

"Of course," I said.

"The death of a citizen would be devastating," she continued. "There will be blood in their streets tomorrow, Beja, but I will *not* allow his pure blood to flow among it."

"You have my word, Empress. I'll keep a close eye on him." I stared off and over the buildings, studying the flat, windswept expanse beyond the city. "A *very* close eye."

Even after we returned to the royal palace and its maze of exotic multi-tiered gardens, it took another three hours for the empress to finish her nightly rituals. And by *rituals*, I don't just mean her beauty regimen—though that was part of it. Throngs of oracles and servants and madmen masquerading as holy men came and went, each fulfilling some vital role I couldn't understand.

Then again, I didn't need to understand it. My only job was to sit in the corner, half-asleep, ensuring that none of the visitors intended to slit the empress's throat. Much like the commoners in the city below, however, these people didn't present much of a threat. In fact, they all seemed ecstatic to have the privilege of bathing her in fragrant oils or chanting mantras at her feet. This was the population every ruler dreamed of having.

When the parade *finally* ended, allowing the empress to slip under her blankets and drift off to sleep, I hauled my aching body out of the chair and headed back out through the main doors—all six sets of them, mind you, each with a different lock. At some point during the day, I'd switched off Indomitable to conserve energy and avoid wasting away from the sheer caloric drain. That meant I moved with all the grace of a geriatric elephant.

Despite the fact that "I" had never explored the palatial compound, it wasn't hard to find my way. As before, there was a slight, almost nagging sense of déjà vu behind my navigational choices. Besides, once I located and started tailing a procession of scribes moving through the eastern cloisters, it was easy sailing.

The archives were located in perhaps the largest building within the palatial walls: a tall, sturdy block adorned with gigantic statues of what I assumed were former rulers. Only two guards stood watch at the grand entrance—no great surprise, given the lack of security elsewhere—and even then, *stood watch* might be too charitable a description. Both men leaned on their spears as though flitting in and out of consciousness, sparing little more than a passing glance at the scribes filing in.

That changed when I approached, however. The guards snapped to attention, examining me with the strangest of scrutiny. Well, maybe not so strange. The empress's reaction to my idea of visiting the archives had given me some advance warning. Around these parts, it seemed, a beja was not a usual sight.

Even so, neither man dared to meet my eyes, much less make any snide comments. That was good. What wasn't so good was the hubbub I accidentally caused. Antihubbub, I suppose. Let me give some context.

You see, much like Rogaji's armory, the archives consisted of multiple floors, with the ground level's obsidian flooring left relatively open to allow for congregation. And congregate those scribes did. Unlike your typical library, in which silence is regarded as a sacred law, this place was abuzz with lively discussions and arguments. It was closer to a bazaar than anything else.

That all changed, however, the moment I descended the small steps and wandered onto the floor. Silence swept through the five-story structure like a tidal wave. Most of the scribes had the presence of mind to turn away and look busy, while a handful of stragglers gaped at me with open mouths and wide eyes. A select few even tossed their scroll cases and bolted for a rear exit.

Note to self: people are not *happy to see me anywhere.*

Ah, well. There wasn't much to be done about that. Besides, it wasn't like I was battering down the doors and raiding their shelves. I was (probably) a royal figure, and that gave me all the permission I needed to look at whatever damn scrolls I desired.

Speaking of which . . . I had no clue where to start. The place was gargantuan, and Izamem hadn't exactly been specific with his instructions. At least Narbu, for all his *many* faults, had possessed the decency to offer me a reading list.

I also realized, with great concern, that I didn't actually know if I could read anything here. Sure, I'd been able to comprehend the glyphs on the council door, but what if that was just some artifact of my past life? A fluke, in other words? Whatever the case, it was clear I'd need a helping hand of some kind.

My best guess was on the uppermost floor, which contained an office-style partition bathed in candlelight. First stop.

While strolling about, looking for some type of staircase, I caught sight of glowing, borderline celestial discs floating up and down in the building's corners. It took me a solid minute of squinting to realize what they were: elevators. Some variant of elevators, anyway. Thus far, I hadn't been able to determine this empire's true technology level. Almost everything had the look and functionality of a wealthy yet preindustrial society, yet there were . . . outliers. Outliers such as enormous skyscrapers, flying bio-ships, and these floaty, ghostlike discs. It was hard to imagine a people that had invented all that but hadn't yet cracked the code for firearms or propulsion systems.

Anyway, that was just one of several topics to investigate—and I'd come to the perfect place for investigation.

I spent several minutes watching scribes enter and exit the discs at varying levels, trying in vain to figure out how the hell they worked, not to mention how to operate them. After some time, though, I gave up the attempt and settled for sneaking aboard a disc already loaded with scribes.

After a brief stop at the second and third levels, the disc took me and my *very* uncomfortable passengers all the way to the top. A small line had formed near the door to the office thing, but upon seeing me—and, more accurately, my armored bulk—heading closer, that line dissolved to nothingness. There were some perks to being the beja.

Inside the little room, a single woman worked behind a desk that was positively littered with scrolls, tablets, ink jars, and wax. Her gaze came up toward me with a veil of annoyance, but that vanished the moment she recognized me.

"Beja," she said breathlessly, "I didn't know we were due for an inspection. Forgive me, I'll—"

I gave her a lopsided smile. "No, no need. I'm not here for an inspection."

"Oh. Does the empress . . . require . . . ?"

"Personal matter," I said. "I'm hoping to browse some materials."

She gave an urgent, snappy nod and leaned over to access the desk's side cabinets. "What do you seek, Beja? I have the registry here. Somewhere . . . "

"It'll be a few things, probably." I rubbed the back of my head, trying to puzzle out how to tell the woman what I needed. "If I gave you a general topic . . . or five . . . could you point me to the best resources on them?"

A moment later, the woman popped back up with the registry—which turned out to be a *fat* book—and flipped it open atop the desk. "Certainly. What is it?"

There was an empty, albeit uncomfortable-looking, chair across from her desk. I pointed at it with a limp finger until she gestured for me to go ahead.

Once I'd taken my seat, I meshed my hands atop her desk. "All right. Off the top of my head, I'll need resources on the history of the empire, the royal line, the factions outside our territory, and the beja."

She just stared at me, her hand halfway between flipping pages. "That's . . . extensive reading, Beja."

"Can you do it in three scrolls or less?"

"It depends how thoroughly you wish to investigate these topics."

"Surface knowledge is fine, for now."

"I see," she said, though she didn't look all that convinced. "Would you like me to deliver the materials somewhere?"

"They're for me. To read. Here."

"Oh." She kept staring at me, occasionally nodding, though my words didn't seem to reach her in earnest for a few moments. "*Oh.* You . . . want to read them."

"Yes?"

"Oh."

The way I'd been treated thus far, it felt like I really was nothing more than a beast walking upright. This was no different. The woman looked at me as though I were a small infant pawing at a high-powered piece of machinery. How damn *dumb* had I been in my former life?

"So," I said, trying to move things along, "three scrolls or less?"

"As a matter of fact, I believe one will suffice," she murmured, scanning the registry with hawklike eyes. "Ah, there we are. *Suhar: A History*, by Venerator Tamblas. A few decades old, but already a classic. Perhaps you've read Tamblas's other—" She caught herself, perhaps remembering she was speaking to an uncultured beast, and offered a weak smile. "Allow me to fetch it for you, Beja. We have a private reading gallery."

I gave my most dignified nod of thanks. When she rose from her desk, however, I raised a finger and said, "If it's no trouble, I'd ask that you don't mention this to anyone. It's . . . classified. Very classified."

Her eyes widened with understanding. "Of course, Beja. Not a word shall pass my lips."

Excellent.

It was time to get myself an education.

14

ight about now, you might be worried I'm about to deliver an hour-long lecture on the history of the empire. Well, today's your lucky day, because I'm skipping most of it. What you'll get instead is a bare-bones, need-to-know-basis summary of that hellish scroll.

Speaking of scrolls, this was perhaps the longest scroll ever created by man or machine. Its platinum, gem-encrusted case, which hadn't been much larger than the thousands of other cases around it, turned out to be a bit of a ruse. The scroll had been packed so tightly it resembled a rolling pin, and on top of *that*, the author—one Venerator Tamblas—had written text so small it required the use of a room-size magnifying apparatus to read.

My one saving grace was the fact that I *could* read it. Much like the glyphs outside the council chambers, the text had begun as a meaningless yet beautiful jumble but quickly resolved to the point where I could read it at a glance. This was fortunate, given the aforementioned size of the damn scroll.

At several points I considered activating Modri and even letting him summarize giant blocks of text, but that wouldn't do. This was *my* past life. *My* history. I needed to read it alone, if only due to the possibility that I might awaken some latent memory through my slog.

Now, then, with all that aside . . .

The planet I was currently standing on—or rather, *had* been standing on in my past life—was named Suhar, as you might've guessed from the scroll's title. This city, the capital, was Suharyama. And, keeping with the theme, it appeared I was part of the Suharkayan Empire. Great.

There was a *lot* of prehistory to cover, but as I said, I'll spare you the mind-numbing stuff. Better to just set the stage.

Millions and millions of years ago, Suhar was nothing but a tribal bat-tleground. The various sentient species (we'll get to those later) warred with one another, exterminating this group, exiling that one. As you might expect from a history text written by a Suharkayan scribe, of course, the scroll was exceedingly generous toward the Suharkayans. They were practically painted as saints or, at the very least, as unwilling participants in the slaughter.

The scroll mentioned a few species that had competed with the Suharkayans for control, but most of them weren't around anymore. Their most dangerous foe was said to have established their own empire, and even to have created . . . undead creatures? A little random, but it added some spice to the reading.

Anyhow, this all changed when—drum roll, please—the Great Maker and his interstellar fleets stumbled across the world. The Great Maker wasn't a very kind individual, having slaughtered several quadrillion beings during his reign (the scroll's words, not mine), but he *did* have a soft spot for sentient species that might benefit his human empire. To that end, the Great Maker singled the Suharkayans out as excellent candidates for integration. Humanoid DNA integration, that is.

Through genetic engineering, some truly hideous eugenics, and what the author described as "magic," the Suharkayans were elevated to their present state of existence. That is to say, extremely humanoid.

So, in short, everything up to that point perfectly accorded with Roga-ji's "just for fun" theory regarding the species' origins. She also turned out to be spot-on in regard to the shepherd species idea. Although it wasn't explicitly called that in the text, it was quite clear the Great Maker had gifted the Suharkayans with advanced technology and weapons to let them subjugate the "lesser" species. You know, the ones the Great Maker had deemed too alien to integrate.

Things got a little wonky here, however. The Suharkayans rapidly became the leaders of the planet, but not without a price. Their dominance led to a war that persisted for several thousand years, ending only after untold bloodshed and several apocalypse-level catastrophes. *This* was about where Akasha's rosy recollection of her ancestors kicked in. The Suharkayans, having witnessed the widespread devastation and blood-shed, resolved to give up their imperialist ways and embrace a new phi-losophy: that of "pristine wisdom." Immediately thereafter, they disarmed, dismantled their most advanced devices, and pledged unity with all beings in all realms of all . . . Well, you get the point.

To make their switch to pacifism official, the Suharkayans devised a treaty. In exchange for the Suharkayans *not* killing them, the planet's other species would deliver varying forms of tribute. One such component of that tribute—and this is where things get *quite* interesting—was a beja.

This was obviously a big deal, because the author went out of his way to include an entire chapter on the subject. A beja, to put it simply, was an elite warrior bred by one of the enemy species. According to the prehistory section, they were pretty frightening. Blood rituals, sacrifices of entire cities, insanity . . . not good. It didn't include much information on *how* a beja was made, but they were, in fact, *made*, not born.

That's right—I was a vestigial symbol of the Suharkayan conquest. Only it was more than that. The idea of paying a beja as tribute to the empire wasn't just cultural, but practical. As you'll recall from above, the Suharkayans totally abandoned any notions of war, or killing, or even enslavement. To make up for this, though, they needed a creative loophole.

A loophole such as using a "barbaric" tribute beja to do their dirty work.

This made a whole lot of sense to me. Back at the roadway ambush, the empress and her soldiers hadn't carried any weapons; they'd deferred to me, allowing them to keep their hands clean and minds pure. It *also* now made sense why I was assaulting the compound alone. They didn't have soldiers. Just me.

Now, you might be thinking, *So why did the empress try to screw you?* That's a great question, and one that wasn't addressed for quite some time. But it *was* eventually addressed, and I wasn't sure I liked the answer.

According to tradition, the empress and emperor were bound by monogamy, expected to keep their royal blood (and consciousness) confined to the dynasty. This made sense, seeing as the entire empire had been built on the notion of inborn supremacy. In their minds, they were living in utopia because they were pure, and the "lesser species" were living in hell because they were impure. It was simply the way of things. The natural arrangement of life.

This "cosmic order" idea carried all the way down to individuals, including royalty. In the eyes of the common Suharkayan, the ruling family and their heirs were tantamount to gods. They ruled the empire because they deserved to rule. Three cheers for circular logic.

In any case, let's loop back to the beja. The author noted that when the spouse of a leader died, they were expected to procreate with noble concubines—but never, *never* with their royal protector, the beja. As a matter of fact, the emperor and empress were forbidden from any and all "untoward contact" with the beja, whom they regarded as the ultimate sign of their "animal past." A necessary yet much-hated member of the empire.

In short, this meant Empress Jalisa's seduction was *not* part of standard operating procedure. Hell, it was closer to a treasonous act than anything else. By extension, this also meant the empress was risking her neck to nibble on mine. This left me with even more questions, but deeper still, it left me wondering how much of the empress was Akasha.

Finally, I came across one minor yet rather interesting tidbit about the hammer on my belt—one that seemingly explained Akasha's cube. Sure enough, just as Tekshim had told me on the monk planet, there was a form of Sparkseed (here known as Dalaya) in the empire. The scroll didn't give many details regarding how it was created, but it *did* mention that it was extremely rare, difficult to harvest from "the requisite," and used for one purpose: the creation and maintenance of the beja's ceremonial hammer. I had no idea what differences existed between the monks' Sparkseed and this empire's Dalaya, assuming there were any differences at all, but that was something to handle later.

The one detail about the hammer I absolutely couldn't parse—and one that would soon become important—related to its core. The text referenced something "unspeakable" at the very center of the hammer. Something not even the author dared disclose.

All right. You've now made it through the history portion. Give yourself a pat on the back and give yourself a second pat if you understood it. That same understanding took me millions of words and hours of skimming. Not bad for an impure animal, though, if I may say so myself.

As I sat at the reading table, drumming my fingertips on the finished scroll, I tried to make sense of it all. It was certainly easier to follow than Narbu's monologues had been, but it also made me doubt some of what Akasha had first told me. Back on Chanzig's planet, for example, she'd mentioned that her people were guided by "shamans." As it turned out, though, the shamans had belonged to one of the species *her* people exterminated. Similarly, her people hadn't been nearly as peace-loving as she led on.

There were a few possible explanations for the contrast, but all of them circled back to Narbu and his oracles. They were the ones who'd assigned her birth to a specific spot in space and time, which also meant they'd glimpsed the future and seen the circumstances of that birth—including her chok'tal-hunting ancestors. If Narbu had successfully altered the memories of his own brothers, fellow oracles, was it really so hard to believe he'd also tampered with the memories of those ancestors? The answer was *no*.

This, however, led to the question of why he'd done it. Had it been to spare Akasha from the truth of things? To distort her perception and make her hate the chok'tal more? I just couldn't figure it out. All I knew was that he *had* altered things, and he'd done it for a reason.

I sighed and pushed the scroll away. As bloody as this world's history had been, I couldn't ignore the obvious: matters were about to get much worse, and there wasn't a damn thing I could do to stop it. Not without possibly fucking up our one chance to stop the Unmade, anyway.

While heading out of the archives, however, another thought occurred to me. Throughout the text, the oracles hadn't been mentioned much. In fact, they'd almost exclusively been described as the lapdogs of the empire, divining prophecies and performing rituals at the direct instruction of the royal family. That didn't seem to be the case anymore. The vibe I'd gotten from the council meeting was closer to the opposite, with Narbu and his oracles serving as the guiding voice to the empress.

What had changed in the few decades since the scroll was written? How had they managed to accrue so much power?

Whatever the case, I would surely find out in time. And I had *time*. Thinking back on Narbu's words on the mountaintop, I recalled that they'd botched their ritual and killed the empress's son around his sixteenth birthday. Sure, there was a chance their years moved slower or faster as dictated by orbital patterns, but thus far, the hours had more or less matched up with the universal constant for sentient species. I shuddered at the thought of having to spend sixteen real-world years in the Godmaker. Then again, if that was what we needed to win once and for all . . .

I pushed it out of my head and lumbered back toward the royal palace, where I would surely have to poke around to find my assigned bedroom. Grayish, predawn light told me I wouldn't have long to do that, much less to sleep.

Then I'd be off to war.

After a few hours of fitful sleep, most of which was plagued by indistinct nightmares I couldn't recall, the preparations began. Thankfully, I didn't need to do much of my own volition. After a stomach-busting buffet breakfast, the empress directed most of the show, instructing her servants to bring me to the royal baths, lather me up, and douse me in the same fragrant oils she'd received last night.

I wasn't exactly thrilled about being disrobed and scrubbed by strangers, but some of that anxiety disappeared when I realized there was no harm to my emergency exit gadget. The servants were quite diligent about stashing my armor within visual range, and they didn't appear at all bothered by—or even conscious of—Rogaji's button. Similarly, there was no indication that they found my species and size strange . . . even though the "beja tub" was comically oversized for my body.

I also wasn't about to make a scene over what I presumed was a standard occurrence for a beja. The texts had spoken at length about the "inborn impurity" of my kind and how their entire consciousness was dominated by the binary spectrum of pleasure and pain. This meant that the Suharkayans treated their beja—yes, it was both plural and singular—as an oversize dog in need of conditioning, lavishing them with food, drink, and sex. Not constantly, though. To make it brief, a beja was only "rewarded" at two key times: prior to killing and after killing. This ensured that, in a beja's mind, bloodshed was always linked with pleasure.

From that angle, the empress seducing me during my first trip into the Godmaker had been a customary thing. Obviously it had been a perversion of that ritual, since the text had *very* clearly stated a beja was to be rewarded with "the velvet touch of concubines." Whatever the hell that meant.

Once the soap-and-suds business concluded, I forced myself back into the armor and followed the gaggle of flower petal–tossing servants out of the palace. They led me through the royal gardens, clearly intent on the huge tower that dominated the royal compound's northeastern corner. It wasn't your ordinary tower, however. Whereas most had a cylindrical shape, sometimes tapering inward near the top, this one was closer to a mushroom. Its smooth, black stone ascended several hundred meters skyward, then billowed outward to form a wide yet flat top.

Only about halfway up the tower's seemingly endless floaty-disc ride did I grasp what this place was: a launchpad. This was further confirmed when, upon reaching the tower's gusty top, I spotted one of the city's flying jellyfish undulating at the far end of the platform. Gathered around the creature were frond-bearing servants, oracles, and the empress herself.

When the petal throwers and I drew nearer, the platform erupted in more rituals. Servants lined up on either side of me, misting the air with various perfumes, chanting, kneeling, weeping. Even the oracles appeared to be possessed in their own way, curling their mechanized fingers into various positions—mudras, as I'd learned from the monks—and shouting unfamiliar words over the wind.

Despite the hubbub, Empress Jalisa stood beside the creature with ramrod posture, her face muted but still carrying a soft smile.

There was someone else beside her, though: a thin, cowed-over man in cerulean robes. Planner Hijeksos. He was busy pleading with the empress about something, and I had a decent guess regarding the nature of his grievance.

" . . . highly irregular!" he was saying as I approached. "Empress, please. I'm willing to forgo my wages. My year's wages."

Almost as though the planner hadn't spoken, the empress turned to me with her usual smile, but her words weren't directed my way. "Planner, this was the beja's request. I don't believe he would've submitted it without proper reason."

Only then did Planner Hijeksos seem to truly notice my arrival. He sized me up with a gaze that flitted between outrage and deference. "Beja?"

"In the flesh," I said. "Are you ready to travel?"

He struggled to gulp through a trembling throat. "Beja, with *all* due respect, I believe my presence would be nothing more than a nuisance. We've supplied all the maps and reports you'll require."

"Give yourself more credit, Planner. You'll be invaluable."

"But—I—"

"Don't get overexcited. We're nowhere near the battlefield."

The empress gave me a knowing grin. "I wouldn't fear that, Beja. It took no less than four attendants to drag him here this morning."

"Beja, please," he said in a breathless voice. "Perhaps you'd reconsider, if only for my wife and children?"

I did take a moment to think over the planner's request. Last night, I'd only asked the empress for permission to take him along because I needed information. There hadn't been a single trace of malice in my body. *However* . . . things had changed drastically since then, mainly due to my deep dive into the nature and role of a beja. It just didn't feel fair for Planner Hijeksos to send me into combat while he lounged about in his villa, munching on grapes. So, with that in mind, I was able to *easily* strike down whatever pity arose from his appeal to emotion.

"Sorry, Planner," I said with a shrug. "It'll be brief and simple, just the way you said it would be at the meeting. Right?"

He could barely meet my eyes. "Of course . . . "

"All is settled, then," the empress said, clapping her hands together. "I believe it's time for you both to depart with glory. When you return, there will be a festival."

Hijeksos looked as though he desperately wanted to argue some more, but he didn't follow through with it. Instead, he nodded dutifully to the empress, turned, and palmed a metal panel that had been lodged in the jellyfish's flesh.

To my amazement, an entire strip of the creature's striated flesh slurped out of place, then peeled back to reveal . . . an interior. Not goop, or organs, or even tissue, but a proper living space. It seemed the "engineers" responsible for creating this thing had hollowed the jellyfish out like a ripe vegetable, then stuffed it with a habitation module and standard amenities. Perhaps I should've been nervous about the idea of flying inside it, but I was far too busy wondering how the creature was even alive, much less conscious enough to comply with instructions.

Such questions didn't seem to matter to the planner. He dragged his skinny bones up the living ramp and into the cabin, his head hanging lower than ever before.

The empress joined me in watching him board, then turned back to me with unbidden concern in her eyes. "Promise me that nothing will go wrong," she whispered.

"He'll be safe," I said. "I'll probably keep him inside the . . . " I trailed off upon realizing I didn't actually know the thing's name.

"I'm not talking about him," she said, saving me. "*You.* Promise me you'll return."

I glanced about, suddenly nervous to speak with her so candidly on account of what I'd learned, but it seemed safe. The oracles were currently occupied with the task of berating servants who didn't toss the flower petals high enough.

"I will," I said, though I doubted my words were backed by the same kind of emotion she felt toward me.

That didn't mean I felt nothing, though. In fact, perhaps I felt too much. I couldn't look into her eyes for more than a few seconds before I began seeing her as Akasha. As the woman I *did*, in fact, feel something about.

Maybe that transferred affection was all it took, because the empress nodded and smiled, seemingly content with my answer, then turned to deliver a hand gesture to the oracles. In response, the oracles angled themselves toward me and dropped into spontaneous lotus postures. A low, chest-rattling thrum filled the air—it seemed some monk traditions hadn't died over the millennia.

"Wield your weapon with love," the empress called as I started up the spongy ramp, "but show them no mercy."

Talk about a strange society.

15

The moment the jellyfish's ramp coiled up and re-formed into a solid, albeit organic bulkhead, I turned around to examine the cabin module. Living space. Whatever it was called in this thing. Any way you sliced it, it was little more than a solid cube of unknown, glossy material—metal, wood, some sort of fusion?—equipped with the minimum complement of furniture to support life: a row of beds, a washing basin, a rations container, a small table. End to end, it probably only measured ten or twelve meters. The whole module was bathed in eerie blue light, which I soon realized was a byproduct of the jellyfish's organs pulsing through a silicate panel in the ceiling.

In short, it was equal parts strange and boring. It had just enough comforts to make me forget I'd be flying inside a gigantic jellyfish. That being said, there was just one tiny, almost irrelevant matter I couldn't figure out.

How to fly the damn thing.

Thankfully, I had a way to figure that out. "Planner Hijeksos, how do I fly this?"

The man was hunched over in a corner booth, breathing heavily into his hands. If I didn't stop him soon, he'd probably pass out from the stress of it all.

"Planner?" I nudged, somewhat louder this time.

That got his attention. His head snapped up, and he looked at me as though I'd wandered into his bathroom while he was showering.

"Wh—" He swallowed a lump, then tried again. "What?"

I strolled over to join him, moving slowly so as to avoid triggering a full panic attack. "I need to know how to fly this creature."

"But . . . this is *your* vessel, Beja . . . " That was all he got out before he lapsed into another round of short, gasping breaths.

Something told me he wouldn't derive much comfort from suddenly having my hand slapped on his back, so I opted to remain a few meters away. That didn't stop him from burying his face in his hands and muttering frantically to himself. Clearly, I would need to take a different tack if I wanted results here.

"Planner, listen," I said in a low voice. "I'm going to level with you, but you have to promise that you're not going to try and bolt out of here."

He peered at me through gaps in his fingers. "Huh?"

"I'm not what you think I am. I'm a—" I caught myself, realizing it probably wasn't wise to spill the *full* container of beans to a man on the verge of going into a catatonic state. Besides, there was a real risk to the timeline in this world. I could probably fudge it a bit, but there was a breaking point I didn't wish to reach. "The point is, I'm not a killer. Not like the other beja that have served the royal family. I don't want to hurt you, and I don't want you to get hurt on this mission. What I need from you is help."

Whether out of genuine interest or just surprise, Planner Hijeksos lifted his face with a placid expression. "What are you, then? One of the cult's creations?"

"What? No. Forget the cult shit for a minute." Sighing, I moved closer and slumped down across from him in the booth. "Let's put it this way . . . I'm the nicest, most intelligent beja you'll ever meet."

"How?"

"What do you mean, how?"

"How did they change you?"

I rolled my eyes. "Magic, okay? Just . . . magic."

His eyes went wide. "*Ooh . . .* "

"Yeah, *ooh*," I said, scoffing. "Part of that, uh, magic ritual involved the loss of some memories. Important memories for a beja. That means I need someone to fill in the gaps for me."

"I don't understand, Beja."

"I know you don't. It's very convoluted." I nodded vaguely in the direction of the jellyfish's head. "First order of business is flying this thing. Do you know how to do it?"

"Of course," he said with a touch of stammering. "I'm less of a pilot than you, surely, but . . . "

"You'll do just fine."

"You . . . mean it? You wish for me . . . a lowly planner . . . to fly your vessel?"

I shrugged. "Consider it your lucky day."

The lingering anxiety on his face assured me that this would not, under any circumstances, be considered a lucky day for him. I understood. From his point of view, he was still trapped, forced to attend a dangerous mission with a vicious brute who'd somehow been screwed up via magic. A scary situation for anybody, let alone a spineless pacifist who'd probably never touched a blade in his entire life. And now he was being asked to fly a royal vessel . . . into an uncertain combat zone.

"Look," I said, trying to assuage his fears, "if you pull this off, and you do it well, I'll put in a glowing recommendation for you. The empress will probably make you a full-time member of the council."

Now *that* . . . that got his brain working. In a matter of seconds, he went from petrified to perky. A dim smile formed on his lips.

"But of course, Beja," he said as he leaped up and headed across the module. "You won't sense a smidgen of turbulence!"

Not long after, we were skimming the flats outside the city at an incredible rate of speed. You wouldn't have known it as an ordinary passenger, however, given our module's impressive velocity-dampening capabilities. While sitting in the booth, I felt little more than mild, intermittent shudders from wind streaking over the jellyfish's exterior.

Given the lack of windows, you might suspect I was merely guesstimating our speed. Not the case. You see, the jellyfish was controlled using some kind of neural-bridge device at the forefront of the module. Planner Hijeksos sat in the pilot's chair, completely limp, his entire head and both hands encased in the vessel's pucker-like filaments. The biomechanical appendages seemed to function as relays for the jellyfish itself, translating Hijeksos's nerve activity into aerial maneuvers.

These maneuvers were displayed through the use of a giant, in-bloom flower dangling above the pilot's chair. And no, I'm not kidding. The center of that flower held something like a giant bead of water—though it was really closer to a gelatinous pearl—that projected a dizzying fish-eye view of the vessel's exterior. The image was murky but clearly being generated by some kind of front-facing camera. The jellyfish's eyes, maybe?

In any event, the effect was the same: I was able to get a rough sense of our speed, though staring at the image for too long was a nausea risk. That was all right. With Planner Hijeksos confidently handling the flying, I was able to catch up on some critical work. By work, of course, I mean napping.

Lots of napping.

Sometime later—the jellyfish didn't have a clock, unfortunately—I woke with newfound freshness . . . and a puddle of drool on the tabletop. A quick glance at the flower camera revealed a dusky landscape, which was now painted in some form of infrared. My first instinct was to panic about my Rank Timer and whether I'd begun dipping into Storehouse Time, but thankfully, that fear didn't last long. I was in the Godmaker, after all. Time was a slippery thing.

Determined to stay on top of things, though, I pulled up the abridged display.

Rank Time: 2 Hours, 13 Minutes, 21 Seconds
Storehouse Time: 17 Hours, 37 Minutes, 4 Seconds
RANK-UP NOT AVAILABLE

The number initially spooked me, if only due to its relative closeness to the Storehouse Time reservoir, but again . . . time dilation. After a bit of mental math, I determined that I'd spent just over an hour and a half in the real world between visiting Rogaji's armory and loading into the Godmaker. Since my arrival, I'd probably only used a few minutes, if that. That gave me more than enough time to show up to the battle, wipe the floor with my enemies, and hit the next rank. I did worry slightly about the number of Kill Points I'd earn, as my first and only encounter in here hadn't given much, but what else could I do? I had to trust in Rogaji's promise that the Godmaker was capable of scaling encounters to suit my needs.

The downtime also gave me the opportunity to try something I'd wondered about for quite a while.

"Can you hear me, Modri?" I asked quietly. There was probably no need for caution, seeing as Hijeksos's entire consciousness was fused with the jellyfish, but I didn't want to risk it.

"You're flyin' . . . in a jellyfish."

I grinned. "I'll take it that's a yes."

"A jellyfish, Purifier."

"Yeah, I'm well aware."

Modri did a little mental bristling, then gathered his wits. *"Looks like that seer Izzy wasn't totally bullshittin' you after all."*

"What, you mean about the past lives?"

"What else would I be talkin' about?"

I shrugged. "If you've been here and conscious the whole time, you're probably proud of me right about now, huh?"

"Why's that?"

"Because I'm a goddamn warrior champion? Just like you were?"

"Nah. You're a glorified security guard, Purifier. No offense."

"Are you kidding? I'm the one who fought *all* the wars for this empire."

"Probably because the empire's only wars are fought against farmers and whatever the fuck they're herdin' on this shithole of a planet."

"Hey," I said testily, feeling a pang of outrage over the attack on my past life's people, "I'll have you know that this was a highly advanced civilization."

"And yet . . . you're flyin' in a jellyfish."

"See? Advanced biotechnology." I shook my head and grimaced. "The point is, I'm a big shot here. Well, I *was*. And now I know I've got a straight shot to figuring out the Unmade's portal shenanigans."

"Unless you deviate too far from the real timeline. Izzy didn't say you'd be gettin' any second chances if you fuck it up."

"That's why I intend to *not* fuck it up."

"But you already are, genius."

"How?"

Modri gave a growling laugh. *"You brought along that bozo of a planner . . . and you're lettin' him fly the jellyfish."*

"What's the problem?"

"How do you know he's gonna fly the same way you did? For all you know, he might crash you into a mesa or some shit."

I rolled my eyes but still took a nervous peek at the flower screen. "He's a good pilot, okay? A great one. Unless *some* people I know . . . "

"Make your jokes, Purifier," Modri grumbled. *"You ask me, he's gonna get you in trouble. New variables always do. Ain't that the whole premise of chaos theory?"*

"Imagine that. A meathead soldier discussing chaos theory."

"A'right, y'know what? I'm hushin' myself. I don't have to take this shit."

"You can't hush yourself."

"Oh, yeah? Watch me."

"I'm watching." Despite my watching, however, he didn't say anything for the next ten seconds. Or thirty. A full minute went by without a peep. "Modri?"

Still nothing.

"Listen," I said, sighing, "I'm sorry for what I said. You're a smart soldier. One of the smartest that ever lived. Now, quit trash-talking our pilot and—"

An eardrum-rupturing *kloom* rocked the module, bucking me sideways and then slamming my head into the table. I rolled onto the floor in a haze of pain and utter bafflement, only to realize I wasn't lying there. I was sliding. A second later, I struck the far wall of the module. When I touched my face, trying to find out if everything was intact, my hand came away bloody. The sharp, throbbing aches around my nose told me it was probably broken.

"Hold on, Beja." The monstrous, distorted voice exploded through the module's concealed speakers, jarring me almost as much as whatever had just hit our vessel. It took me a solid few seconds to recognize the voice as a fusion of Hijeksos and the jellyfish. "We're descending rapidly, so, uh . . . Well, ah . . . you should brace for impact!"

The planner's warning was appreciated, though not well timed. Glancing about, I found absolutely zero things to grab. I was lying in the newly formed canyon between the wall and floor, which now formed a perfectly smooth deathtrap. Each time I tried to haul myself toward a piece of furniture, my boots squealed back down the panels and left me in the same spot.

"Any moment now!" Planner Hijeksos announced.

All I could do was sit there, bloody and bruised. "Well, fuck me, ri—"

Then we made impact.

At least, I think we did. When I returned to consciousness, I found myself in a dark, silent cube lit by the occasional red strobe. Thick, odorous liquid of unknown origin was pooled beneath me—and spread in all directions, I soon discovered. But that was far from my biggest problem. My skull felt as though it'd been speared with a shard of rusty iron.

Mentally, I made a note to begin recording how many times I'd been knocked out.

"Hijeksos?" I called, though my words came out in a strangled yelp.

At first, nothing came back. Right then and there, I wrote Hijeksos off as a casualty. He'd probably been liquefied by the crash or had his mind evaporated due to his link with the (presumably) dead jellyfish.

Then, through the ringing in my ears, I heard it.

"No, no, no . . . I said no . . . I said I didn't want to . . . "

The halting, nervous voice immediately identified the man. Based on sound alone, Hijeksos was somewhere ahead of me, shrouded in the darkness.

"Hijeksos, are you all right?" I asked.

This time, I got a more spirited response. "Beja! You're . . . alive."

"Yeah, though I'm not sure I want to be." Struggling through the pain, I worked my way onto my hands and knees, then rubbed my eyes to clear the remnants of the blood. "Are you hurt?"

"I'll survive. I hope."

I nodded to myself, relieved I hadn't lost my only companion on the mission, then took a more thorough look around. Somehow, a myriad of objects had gotten stuck to the ceiling. *Wait.* After squinting and checking again, I realized the truth of things: I was on the floor, which had formerly been the ceiling. The module was inverted.

"Can you get the exterior doors open?" I called across the room. "We need to get out of this thing, take stock of our situation . . . "

"I'm . . . not so sure that's a good idea, Beja."

"Why not?"

Only *then* did I lock on to the incessant squelching somewhere beyond the module, which I'd initially mistaken for the jellyfish's decomposition. Someone—or something—was trying to hack through the jellyfish's flesh. Trying to get to the meat inside. After all I'd been through, I wasn't naive enough to assume those were the sounds of rescuers.

"Planner, you should probably plug your ears," I said, slipping the hammer off my belt in defiance of the throbbing. "Your people are a little sensitive to things like this."

He babbled on in protest, but I couldn't spare any attention for his dramatics. Instead, I struggled to my feet—not easy, when the floor is mainly goop—and headed toward the sound of the commotion. Upon reaching the wall panel, I could plainly discern the *thwick-thwack* of blades ripping through the exterior flesh.

"Planner," I called back in a whispered hiss, "where's the release panel?"

He didn't get a chance to answer. The thwacking cut off, only to be replaced by the slurp of something moving through the jellyfish tissue. A hand, by the sound of it. No sooner had I hefted the hammer into both hands than the wall panel flipped open—upward, to be precise, due to our inversion.

It was gloomy as hell outside, but I instantly spotted the five silhouettes gathered before me. Two were carrying curved, pickax-style tools, while the others hung a bit farther back, carrying . . . guns?

My HUD lit them up with blue boxes.

Armed Ambushers (HUMANOID) (5)
CALCULATING . . .
Estimated Kill Points: 36,100

That was all the confirmation I needed. Dashing toward the nearest enemy, I twisted at the last moment and caught his chin with a vicious upward swing. His head damn near came off his body. Before the corpse had even hit the dust, I was on the next pickax wielder. He brought his weapon up in a feeble block, but I ducked low and caught him in the ribs, then the side of the head. There was no scream, only the pattering of blood.

The three gunslingers behind the entry team seized up, clearly unprepared for what was about to happen. One of them lifted their barrel and took aim, but he never had a chance.

In a flash, I triggered Telekinesis, thrust my awareness outward, and took control of the quantum particles comprising the gun. One impulse was all it took to rip the weapon from his hands and deposit it in mine. The unarmed ambusher's comrades frantically worked to line up their shots, only to drop in solid heaps when I put a trio of bullets into each of their chests. Well, maybe not bullets. The rounds emerged as hyperfast neon streaks—some kind of particle accelerator, probably. The details didn't matter much, though, given what the rounds did to the gunmen's bodies.

That just left the man with no gun. He let out a howl, then turned and began fleeing across the murky flats. I wish I could say that I let him go, but I didn't. One shot to the back of the head was enough. He didn't make it more than ten paces before he went down, lost to the growing darkness.

ENCOUNTER SUCCESSFUL
Kills: 5
Kill Points Awarded: 36,100

I lowered the weapon and let out a long, tense breath, only to be interrupted by fresh clamor.

"Stop! Stop!" Planner Hijeksos shrieked, rushing through the slippery module behind me. "I wasn't supposed to be here! Only to bring him, as we agreed! Now it's done! I—"

Both his voice and his footsteps faltered when I turned back to him.

"Oh, Beja," he squeaked. "I'm so glad you're—"

Rather than even responding, I directed Telekinesis to the man's robes and hauled him into the air like a puppet.

"What did you just say?" I hissed, stalking toward the man as his legs pedaled uselessly.

"I—"

"If you lie to me, I'll gut you."

"This is a mistake," he said, trying to laugh but not quite succeeding. "Beja, I would *never . . .*"

"Never what? Send me on a mission you *knew* was a trap?"

"That's preposterous!"

"Is it?" I moved right up to him and pressed the gun's barrel into his stomach. "If you tell me the truth—*all* of it—you've got a small shot at returning to the city alive. That shot is shrinking by the second."

To my surprise, he responded by breaking into full-on wailing. "I'm *sorry*, Beja! I didn't want to, but . . . but . . . "

"But?"

"They made me," he said through his sniffles. "They said the time was near. That the empire was falling to a great darkness. And . . . I *saw* it. I saw the darkness, Beja. I saw my family being butchered! This was my only chance. *Their* only chance."

I rammed the gun's barrel farther into his stomach, eliciting a wince. "I'm getting *very* sick of betrayals."

"Beja, I'm—"

"Sorry. Yes, I know. You should be." I sighed, trying to make sense of this entire situation. "Right now, I only need to know one thing. That compound you sent me to attack—is it a true threat?"

"Yes!"

"And are we near it?"

"Uh . . . it—it's not many leagues from here."

"So, we can hike there."

The planner swallowed harder than ever before. "*We?*"

"Yes, we. You got me into this, so you're coming along. And if you fuck me with any more, no matter how small the fuckery, you'll be returning to your family as a box of ground meat. Is that clear enough?"

"Amazingly clear!"

In any other situation, I wouldn't have believed a single word. But between the man's terror, seemingly genuine remorse, and frail-ass frame, I was willing to take the risk. In the original timeline, after all, he'd probably gotten away with his crime until the beja—I—returned to the city and delivered unholy justice to his skull. So, for the time being, it was best to keep him alive.

Groaning, I released the Telekinesis and let him flop to the floor. "Get up. We've got a lot of hiking to do."

At my request, Hijeksos told me the entire saga of how he'd gotten wrapped up with the enemy while we marched across the alien flats. The abridged version went as follows: The planner had been captured while surveying this region, then subjected to some kind of bizarre cult ceremony that involved . . . you guessed it . . . drinking some type of hallucinogen to divine the future. As he'd mentioned in the jellyfish, that future had been nightmarish. The details, however, piqued my curiosity. He'd seen burning cities, portals to other dimensions, and silvery slugs.

In short, Hijeksos had legitimately seen the future. The arrival of the chok'tal, to be precise. I had no doubts as to the intensity of the experience; given his loyalty to the empire, it seemed unlikely that he'd have flipped sides for anything less than the unthinkable.

When it came to the topic of why they'd wanted to ambush me, however, Hijeksos was rather mum. That or oblivious. The surface reason was clear enough—kill the beja and the empire is left defenseless—but I suspected there was more to it than that. What proof did I have? None. Well, nothing beyond the circumstantial. While inspecting the corpses of the jellyfish attackers, I'd found a variety of netting, tranquilizers, stun rounds, and other oddities that suggested their intentions had been to capture rather than kill. Now, could they have been trying to snatch me for some kind of elaborate cult sacrifice? Sure. I still didn't buy it, though. There was something bigger at stake than my death.

On and on the hours went, the hills and gulches around us completely silent aside from the occasional call of unseen creatures. It wasn't a boring hike, though. It was a new world—and a beautiful one, at that. Patches of enormous, glowing tubers gave some light to our voyage, and we measured the distance using spires of coral-like growths that dotted the landscape like trees.

Eventually, though, Hijeksos grabbed my arm and . . . *tried* . . . to tug me behind a cluster of rocks.

"What?" I hissed.

He leaned out and pointed at something with wide eyes. My gaze followed, landing on a clump of dim, guttering lights in the distance. Smoke coiled into an aurora-laden sky.

"Is that it?" I whispered to him.

He nodded excitedly. "Yes, Beja! That's it! The horrid compound!"

After a moment's consideration, I crept out and advanced to a higher position. Hijeksos's soft, plucky steps assured me he was on my tail. From the new vantage point, I got a fairly comprehensive look at the target . . . which didn't say much. The compound was little more than a collection of squat, mud-walled buildings and ramshackle watchtowers, all ringed by a wall that appeared to be bristling with sharpened stakes, much like a porcupine.

"*That's* what we came here for?" I asked.

"It is," Hijeksos confirmed. "It's a foul place, Beja. Their magics are . . . powerful."

"Yeah, well, mine are, too," I said, drawing the hammer from its belt loop. "Let's find out who holds the crown."

16

In spite of Planner Hijeksos's attempt to have me killed, I trusted him enough to hang back at the overlook while I dealt with the compound. The wilderness went on for hundreds and hundreds of kilometers, ensuring he wouldn't be able to get very far if he ran.

Besides, the man was a walking bundle of nerves. If anything, he presented a greater risk in battle than outside it. The last thing I needed was for him to shriek while I was halfway to assassinating a target.

This is an especially good example, because at that moment I *was* halfway to assassinating a target. To get more precise about it, I was crouched in the shallow, reed-filled drainage canal that ran along the compound's southern side. Pacing the wall overhead was a sentry. Even with Nocturnal activated, it was difficult to get a read on their species—not that I needed one. I kept forgetting this, but there was no legitimate danger and hence no need to study enemies for their weaknesses. This was nothing but a steamroll simulator.

In light of this remembrance, I sprang out of the ditch, grabbed hold of the wall's mottled exterior, and began worming up through the gauntlet of spikes all around me. Near the top, the sentry's footsteps stopped. Then came the grinding of dust under boots, signaling his turn in my direction.

So much for the stealthy approach.

Boosted by Indomitable and Overclock, I launched myself off a spike and atop the wall—bringing me face-to-face with the unfortunate sentry. They were the same species as the ambushers from both the roadway and the jellyfish. No great detail, but it might explain why I hesitated for a moment. There was very real, very humanoid fear in their eyes.

That second of hesitation, however, was all the sentry needed to snatch something off their wicker vest and puff into it. Their puff turned into a rolling *kwoom* that nearly deafened me.

I hefted my hammer, ready to split the sentry in two, only to realize it wasn't an audio-based attack. It was a warning.

In a matter of seconds, the dirt pathways below became flooded with dozens of ambushers, not to mention a few specimens from my own species—aka brutes. All at once, my visual field was reduced to a patchwork of mud buildings and blue boxes.

[SLAUGHTER EVENT]
Compound Ambusher (HUMANOID) (16)
Defiled Champion of the Western Horde (HUMANOID) (3)
CALCULATING . . .
Combined Estimated Kill Points: 801,500

I didn't give my foes any time to properly arm themselves, much less organize. With one merciless swing, I caved in the sentry's face. Caved it in a little too well, perhaps. Even as the bastards below began gibbering and rushing my position, I worked to rip the hammer out of the man's face. It was *firmly* lodged in place.

Just before one of the champions managed to scrabble up the inside of the wall, however, my weapon tore free in a spray of gore. I spun around and slammed the hammer's glinting head straight down, punching through the champion's helmet and into rubbery brain tissue.

The corpse dropped, and the guns started firing.

I threw myself over the wall's edge and into the compound, rolling hard and coming up with my hammer in both hands. An ambusher came barreling around the corner, finger already on the trigger, but I wasn't having that. One spirited push from Telekinesis was all it took to latch on to the particle inside the gun's chamber—and hold on to it.

When the ambusher fired, the gun exploded in a spray of sparks and black smog. It didn't kill the poor son of a bitch, but it sure took him out of the fight. I finished the job by racing over and crushing his skull. At the instant of his death, another pair of ambushers cleared the corner and bumped straight into me.

Without thinking, I snatched the barrel of one enemy's weapon and shoved it toward the other guy. The ambusher fired in terror, ripping massive chunks out of his comrade's face and neck. He screamed in horror, eyes wide as he watched the man's body slump, but I put him out of his mercy, too, with an Overclock-infused backswing.

Glancing over, I caught sight of a spear-wielding ambusher running up on me. It was almost too easy. Still tapped into Telekinesis, I grabbed hold of the man's boot and yanked it upward, flipping him straight onto his back. Then I seized the midair spear and drilled it down through his eye.

That gave me some pause. As awesome as this was, and as fluid as I'd been since the start of the encounter, it was obvious that the scenario was heavily manipulated by the Godmaker. There was no way ordinary me could've pulled off these moves with even a tenth of the grace.

That was a thought for later, of course. The pair of champions racing toward me with shoulder-scythes on full display were a more pressing concern. As they lumbered within hammer range, however, I realized they *weren't* a pressing concern. The mental shift was ludicrous enough to make me laugh. Yes, laugh. Out loud. The unreality of the Godmaker was staring me in the face. The minute either of these enemies took a swipe at me, the entire system would slow to a crawl and give me the wiggle room to deliver a killing blow.

The two champions glanced at one another, probably wondering why the hell a beja was cackling at them, then continued advancing. Slowly advancing. It took me a few seconds to realize that it wasn't them slowing down, but time itself. Even the granules of sand along the roadway tumbled past as though suspended in syrup.

I glanced about, trying to determine the origin of the threat, only to *finally* glance up and spot an ambusher on the awning just above me. He had his gun's muzzle firmly fixed on my head, and his finger was most certainly squeezing the trigger. There was even a tiny blossom of energy forming inside the gun's barrel.

You poor, dumb bastard.

I casually walked backward, which then caused time to snap back to its normal speed and send a superheated pellet sizzling into the dirt. The ambusher took a few moments to piece together what had happened, visibly struggling to make sense of how his target had zipped out of the crosshairs in less than a microsecond.

He didn't get long to ponder that question, naturally. A few spurts of Telekinesis later, his own gun took his head off.

I turned my attention back to the champions. "Ready to tango?"

The one on the left responded with a bloodcurdling howl, bounding toward me on all fours like a rabid lizard. Time to test a theory. Kicking

Telekinesis up a notch, I worked my awareness into the densely woven quantum mesh of the creature's helmet. By the time I had a firm grip, the champion was less than a meter from me. Predictably, however, time was creeping toward a total standstill. This meant I had infinite chances to do what I'd planned.

Try, fail. Try, fail. Try, fail. Over and over I worked on the metal helmet, clenching my jaw and swiping away the trickles of blood that came leaking from my nose. It took far longer than it should've, but eventually, the helmet gave a hollow *kwop*. A sizable dent had formed on one side. Grinning at my partial success, I pushed even more energy into the act.

Just as I was preparing to let go, convinced my body would rattle itself into dust, the helmet buckled inward, then completely imploded. The momentum of the mental crush was too strong, though. The helmet kept crumpling until reddish paste—formerly the champion's brain and face—came bursting out through the eyeholes in slow motion.

With the enemy dead, time resumed.

I stepped back as the pulpy mess splattered across the road. The champion's companion, who'd been creeping up on me seconds prior, became enraged. I could only sigh as they charged me in total defiance of self-preservation. Just before the creature reached me, I blindly reached back with Telekinesis, got a grip on the dead ambusher's spear—which was still embedded in their face, mind you—and hurled the weapon just over my head.

The spearhead skimmed my helmet with a supersonic clap, indicating it was traveling closer to a bullet's speed than anything else, then ran through the champion. I mean that literally, by the way. The champion staggered to the side and clawed at the coin-size hole in its chest, spurting blood as it trampled through clay jars and barrels and crates.

The commotion caused the ambushers at the end of the dirt path to freeze up—and also gave me a moment to run some quick mental math.

Six ambushers down, and all three champions.

Ten to go.

At a glance, there were probably seven or eight of the ambushers clustered before me. Most of them held simple weapons such as swords and spears—clearly this compound wasn't an armory—though one or two held long, flickering guns that looked a bit deadlier than the standard variant. This would've caused me concern had there been any real risk of death.

Seeing as there wasn't, I stepped over the helmet-crushed champion's corpse with the confidence of a man in a lucid dream. "You all should probably hit the road, but I doubt you'll do that."

In response, the remaining ambushers bared their teeth and came charging in.

"Well, can't say I didn't warn you . . ."

Three minutes later, the last of the ill-fated bastards hit the sand, the left half of their body completely pulverized. The system's encounter update appeared as I stepped over a dismembered arm and shook the blood from my hammer.

SLAUGHTER ENCOUNTER SUCCESSFUL
Kills: 19
Kill Points Awarded: 801,500
Storehouse Time Awarded: 2 Hours

A quick glance at my Status Display revealed that, in spite of the oceans of blood I'd created, I'd only racked up 1,044,100 Kill Points—nearly six hundred thousand short of the next rank. Not the worst progress in the world, though. This fight, at least, suggested the Godmaker was scaling up my rewards over time. Learning and straining my capabilities, perhaps.

Strained, however, I was not. Most fights in the real world, minor or otherwise, tended to have me gasping for breath the moment they ended. That wasn't the case here. In fact, my heart rate was barely elevated. Respiration was normal. This turned out to be a boon, because my lack of panting allowed me to hear a sound so faint I initially thought I'd imagined it.

Wandering around the inside of the compound, I picked up further on the sound. It was coming from the largest building, which also happened to be located smack-dab in the center of the compound.

Lifting my hammer, I crept toward its low door. With every step I took, the sound grew louder and . . . weirder? It came in fluttering, nearly sub-audible pulses that put me on edge, mainly due to their similarity to what I'd heard from the Throne of Radiance and other "not quite right" entities.

As soon as I ducked and entered the building, that sense of wrongness only grew. The room around me was cramped and dark, its only light coming from a candle tucked in one corner. That candle also illuminated the room's sole notable feature: a rough, irregular hole that had been drilled down into the dirt. Even as I approached it, the ominous sound reverberated up through my boots.

Aside from the small sliver of the hole cast in flickering candlelight, the hole was completely black. Not a great sign. My only pseudocomfort was the presence of a rickety ladder that appeared to lead all the way down.

I stared down into the void for a few moments, trying to hype myself enough to descend. With or without the Godmaker's immortality, self-preservation instincts didn't shut off easily.

After far too long spent on deliberation, I groaned, squatted, and began climbing down the ladder. My weight made a few of the thin rungs creak, but nothing snapped. As I descended with Nocturnal on full blast, I used Telekinesis as I had in the junnara-gol pit, combing the walls and immediate area below me to detect any traps or other oddities. There was nothing dangerous, as far as I could see, but at about twenty meters down, I started passing smaller subchambers filled with crates of *stuff*. I say stuff, of course, because I wasn't stupid enough to dismount the ladder and poke around in them, and Telekinesis revealed little more than some kind of paste within.

Down and down I went, my depth crossing thirty meters, then forty . . .

Suddenly, my awareness snagged on something. Solid dirt, mixed with a few patches of bedrock. This was it—the true bottom. As I toggled off Telekinesis, my ordinary sensory awareness trickled back to full force. Only then did I detect how pronounced the warbling sound had become. The powerful, skin-buzzing pulses felt like growls moving up a massive predator's throat. I also became aware of something that no sensible person with night vision should've missed: long, dark streaks of blood striping the dirt on all sides.

Certain I was about to get a fatal case of the heebie-jeebies, I slid down the remainder of the ladder and hopped off with my hammer in hand. I even gave a spirited shout in hopes of intimidating whatever was making all that noise.

The chamber around me was dim and low-ceilinged, but Nocturnal made up for that. And my, what a sight it was.

Piled high in the central space were corpses. Hundreds of corpses. They'd been tossed into a pit that was surely much, *much* deeper than looks suggested. As my vision adjusted, I realized they were a mixture of various species—Suharkayans, ambushers, champions, and even a few oddballs that seemed more beast than humanoid. The entire mass was stained with varying shades of blood, forming a splotchy, brownish coating that had attracted all manners of maggots and flies and other nasties.

Amazingly, there was no smell coming off the bodies, probably as a result of the innumerable herbs and oil dishes that ringed it all. Out of this central heap flowed six wide yet shallow channels, all sloping downward toward the chamber's still-dark edges. The liquid flowing downward was, at this point, closer to a sludge than anything else.

"Beja," rumbled a low, croaking voice.

I spun in place, trying yet failing to source the noise through all the echoing.

"You finally return . . . to deliver a killing blow to your own people."

Far across the chamber, a small, rusty flame sparked to life, revealing . . . Izamem? No, not Izamem, but something frighteningly close to him. The same lipless mouth, the same lack of eyes, the same gnarled, jagged "hands." The only discernible difference was that this specimen was taller, though not by much, and cloaked in all-black robes.

"You mind explaining what the fuck all this is?" I called, gesturing to the pile of corpses.

In response, the diminutive alien just giggled and kept creeping closer. "*This*, Beja, is the rebirth of this fallen world. It is the promise you couldn't keep."

"Do you know how many of your little goons I just slaughtered?"

"All of them, I would suspect," the alien said. "That is what a beja does, isn't it? Kills for sport?"

I studied the candlelit creep. "Are you the one who wanted me dead? The one who tried to turn Hijeksos on me?"

"It is not *me* who wants anything, Beja. It is the gods. The ones beyond—"

"The Flesh Plane," I filled in.

"Very good. You haven't forgotten your roots . . . not entirely, anyway."

"All right, listen up. You've got about a minute before I bash your brains in."

The shaman cackled. "You don't even understand the weapon you wield, do you?"

"It's a hammer."

"That and more . . . so much more . . . "

"Are you going to tell me what this place is or do I have to beat it out of you?"

"Settle down, pup. Settle down." The alien waddled over to me—a personal-space invasion I allowed, given the fact that he presented zero threat. "You really shouldn't work yourself up. All that must be done is already done. The landslide has begun."

"You're really starting to piss—"

My voice trailed off when I noticed that the alien had turned and begun moving to the edge of the chamber. His slow, limping walk surely wasn't an attempt at fleeing. Shrugging, I followed him into the darkness. As we neared the wall, Nocturnal picked out some fresh details: a crop of tall, thin flowers growing in the gathered filth of the corpse pile. Each of the flowers was topped with a bright-red pulp and serrated crimson leaves.

"So, what is it?" I asked, now more curious than angry. "Some kind of gardening project?"

The alien laughed. "It is the song of vengeance, woven through soil and death."

"All right, hammer time it is."

That got a better response. The alien hefted his candle up as though it might shield him from my fury.

"This is your last chance, Beja," he hissed. "Your final opportunity to return to your kind and fulfill what you were meant to do."

"Whatever all *this* is, I want nothing to do with it."

"You choose the oppressors, then."

"I choose the side that isn't making blood flowers."

"No matter. The sacred seeds will do what you could not. You betrayed your own kind, Beja. You betrayed all of us. Now it falls to the gods to finish your mission."

"My mission? The fuck are you on about?"

"What's this? A beja with a bruised memory?"

"Yeah, I had it all wiped by the empress," I lied, rolling my eyes. "Why don't you just treat me like I'm a fool, fresh out of the womb?"

"You will *never* be one of them," the alien hissed. "Had you accomplished your holy task, you would have lived as an emissary of the heavens. You would have danced in the eternal halls. Now . . . now, you will die a coward. A failure to all those who gave for you."

Again, I lifted the hammer between us. "Are those your last words?"

"No, Beja. Listen well, for my words will echo at the moment of death." He shuffled closer to me, his fishlike mouth stretching into a hideous smile. "It is too late to stop what's coming. Your Suharkayans, your precious oracles, your empress . . . all of them will burn in the flame of their own sins. Not a single word you speak will prevent it."

"What, did you poison the water supply or something?"

"Why poison water when you poison minds?"

That was the last straw. Enough of the cryptic threats, enough of the riddles, enough of this fucking guy overall. Before he even saw it coming, I thwacked him upside the head with the hammer.

He went down in a tangle of robes and tendrils, but he didn't cry out. Instead, he began laughing. Even when the sounds became gurgled from the blood in his mouth, he kept on going.

"Claim my life, Beja," he rasped. "You are *nothing* but a traitor to this world. A thousand years in the hells for you . . . and ten thousand of domination for our people. An eternity of glory! We will reign forever! Until the stars burn out! Until—"

One swift, pitiless downward swing silenced the fucker.

Then it was just me, the silence, and the muted *pwaps* of blood draining into the earth. Oh, and a shitload of blood flowers.

Around half an hour later, I stalked back up the slope where I'd left Hijeksos. Part of me worried he'd fled in spite of my commands, but the other, more sensible part knew he'd be waiting for me.

Just to ensure he remembered what I could do to an escapee, however, I'd set fire to the entire compound. The landscape all around me blazed in angry orange tones, and embers drifted past me like fireflies on the wind.

Sure enough, I found Hijeksos hunkered down behind the same rock as before, his eyes wide and glowing with the inferno's blaze.

"You . . . you did it, Beja!" he exclaimed.

He ran in for a hug—one that I promptly shut down by nudging his chest with the hammer to keep him at arm's length.

"Hijeksos, I have some questions," I said quietly.

"Uh, questions? Yes. Ask, Beja! Ask!"

"What do you know about me?"

"About . . . you?"

I dragged him behind the rock, if only to escape the heat. "I met a tiny shaman in the bottom of that compound. He said he knew you."

"Oh, yes . . . Shaman Lukrati, I imagine."

"Well, he's Shaman Bashed Head now. And unless you want the same fate, you're going to answer me *very* specifically. If you tell one goddamn riddle or try to make me guess something, you're going to have a terrible time. Understood?"

Hijeksos nodded passionately. "Yes, Beja!"

"First off, me. The shaman made it sound like I was some kind of traitor. Explain."

"I . . . Beja, I thought it was common knowledge."

I lifted the hammer in warning.

"Okay, okay!" he squealed. "You were groomed to be the empire's beja. They, uh . . . they spent years teaching you dark rituals, giving you medicines, making you a warrior . . . in the hopes you would assassinate Empress Jalisa."

"What?"

"You . . . don't remember?"

"Magic mind erasing, Planner," I said, reminding him of my ridiculous story. "What do you mean, groomed? Wasn't I born in the empire?"

Hijeksos frowned at me and opened his mouth but then seemed to quickly reconsider whatever snarky comment he was about to make. "Among your . . . *people* . . . one infant is selected at the request of the royal family as the old beja nears death. The child is given all the clan's food . . . all its education and resources . . . to ensure that they'll grow into the next beja."

"What do you mean, all their food?"

"Ninety-six percent of your people's young starve," Hijeksos said, though he spoke without a shred of concern over that fact. "They assumed you'd be the one to carry out their plans. For centuries, the royal family *theorized* that there might be a traitorous beja coming from the flats, but . . . "

"How do you know all this?"

"It was . . . told to me," he whispered. "Through visions, mostly."

"You mean blood flowers."

He scrunched up his face, momentarily confused, then caught on to what I meant. "Yes, Beja . . . the seeds of the flowers, to be precise."

I nodded slowly. "So, why didn't I carry out my 'mission'?"

"I . . . I don't know, Beja. You could have."

"You realize what that means, right?"

"No?"

"It means you're even worse of a weasel," I said, jabbing the hammer into his ribs. "I was born and bred to be a traitor, while you did it out of free will."

"Beja, please!"

"Relax. I'm not going to kill you. Yet."

"Yet?" he squeaked.

I shook my head. "The shaman mentioned something about wreaking vengeance on the empire. Poisoning minds. Has to do with those blood flowers, I'd imagine. What do you know about that?"

"Uh . . ."

"Speak quickly, Planner."

He tried and failed several times, finally coming out with, "They . . . were paying laborers to smuggle the seed paste into the city. I don't know what happened to it after that. I promise, I don't."

"You've got to be shitting me."

"Beja . . . ?"

"Not only did you try to kill *me*," I whispered, "but you let them poison your own fucking city. You're a waste of air."

"I had no choice!"

"There is *always* a choice!" I drew the hammer back, ready to kill him, only to rein my temper in at the last instant. He looked like a cockroach, shriveling under the hammer's head. "How long has this been going on?"

"Less than a year . . . "

"How . . . long?"

"Ten months?" he said, wincing through his attempt at a smile.

"You're going to find us a swift ride back to the city," I said, stepping forward so he shrank down farther. "You won't disappoint me, will you?"

"N-no, Beja!"

"And you most certainly won't mention a *word* of this . . . any of this . . . to anyone. Am I correct?"

"Beyond correct! Impeccable!"

I nodded, satisfied with his fear. "Good. Now get walking. If you slow us down, you'll be taking your rest under the sand."

17

Fortunately for me (and Planner Hijeksos), we didn't end up searching for long. Just before dawn broke over the glowing flats, another jellyfish swooped down from seemingly out of nowhere to rescue us. As it turned out, the imperial crew had been combing the area for several hours. Evidently "operational expediency" was an unspoken quality of all bejas, and us missing the deadline for a safe return had prompted Empress Jalisa to dispatch a search party.

The ride back was blissfully silent, especially on Planner Hijeksos's end. The squirrelly little Suharkayan sat in the module's booth with ramrod posture, a fake, too-wide smile squirming on his lips every time I glanced in his direction.

Much as I wanted to use the ride to get Modri's take on things, I didn't. For two reasons. First of all, he'd shushed *me*, which was a move so disrespectful I didn't want to converse, no matter how hypocritical that sounds. Second, I tended to make absurd faces while talking to him, even if our exchange was purely mental. Given the craziness of the compound and what I'd learned—namely, the fact that I'd been groomed from birth to kill the empress—I was almost guaranteed to start making faces if we got into it.

The moment we touched down on the landing platform, we were met by a team of advisers who had clearly been camped out there for some time. My initial fear was that they'd pegged me as the traitorous beja the shaman painted me as, but that wasn't the case. In fact, they'd come to discuss something more alarming. Something they refused to say aloud.

Something so severe that it required my immediate presence in the oracular chambers.

Naturally, I agreed to go with them, though not without a parting glare at Hijeksos to remind him of our little agreement.

Then we were off. The advisers hurried me down the stairs, through the palatial compound, and down a network of narrow streets that were apparently restricted to royal personnel. Before long, we came within sight of the aforementioned oracular chambers: a cluster of vast, gleaming spires covered in gold and obsidian streaks. Their presence was made even more foreboding by the various mandalas that had been etched into the masonry.

Gathered in the gardens outside were several hundred oracles, all of whom stood perfectly still and gazing reverently at the massive front gates—which, by the way, were guarded by a group of royal Suharkayans. Although I knew absolutely nothing about this culture and how it dealt with scandalous events, it didn't take much context to realize that this was highly unusual. I mean, why else would you have to kick all the oracles . . . out of the oracular chambers . . . then have them guarded by the empress's forces? Whatever was being discussed inside had to be well beyond the pay grade of these lower-ranking oracles.

That being said, the guards were quick to step aside and haul open the gates as the attendants and I approached. This exposed a long, empty, obsidian-floored corridor better described as an atrium than anything else.

The moment I entered, though, I heard only my footsteps. I looked back to find that not even the attendants had accompanied me. They stood beside the guards, sheepish and plainly nervous about . . . something. Another great omen.

Moving down the giant hallway, I found that the ceilings were so high I couldn't spot their rafters. The expanse was lined with pillars that had been carved into serpents and other fantastical designs, all of them looming over me like the judges of life and death. Was I about to be executed, perhaps due to charges Hijeksos had falsely conjured? Only one way to find out.

At the far end of the walkway, and after more grueling and unnecessary marble stairs, another pair of royal guards opened yet another set of gates. Inwardly, I pondered how much of the empire's budget had been spent on wasted interior space.

The chamber that lay beyond these gates, however, instantly vaporized my snark. Although it had the same general bell shape as the room used by the council, it was three or four times as large, with every single surface—from the floor to the walls to the octagonal ceiling panel—all inscribed with glyphs and elaborate murals. These glyphs shimmered in the light of the central spectacle: a churning, airborne vortex composed of blue particles.

As I wandered forward in a daze, I realized it was the *only* source of light. And by Halcius, did it give off light. The levitating configuration swam and coiled in on itself like a hurricane, its movements so graceful yet chaotic that the thing seemed to be alive. Some kind of fission reactor, maybe? No, that couldn't be. There was nothing visibly shielding or containing it, and besides, that kind of energy would've stripped the skin from my bones in seconds. The sounds emanating from it weren't those of a reactor, either. Long, rolling chains of *whump-whump-whumps* echoed all around me.

That isn't to say it was powerless, of course. Even at a distance of fifty meters or more, I sensed its effervescent waves fluttering over my face, tingling all the little hairs across my brow and upper lip. More than that, though, I sensed its intelligence. Its consciousness.

Despite my hesitation, I kept wandering forth, basking in its radiance. The same part of my mind responsible for translating the glyphs flicked on by degrees. I had no idea *why*, but I knew this entity deserved my reverence. My fear, even.

Only about halfway through my semiconscious walk, once my vision had compensated for the brilliance, did I spot something curious on the walls. Scattered among the columns and panels of glyphs were monks—er, oracles. They were all suspended upside down, their legs joined but arms spread far to either side. They would've resembled bats sleeping in a cave, if not for the clear tubing that ran from their mechanized chests into the floor. Most of the tubes were empty, but a few sparkled with leftover drops of golden fluid.

Sparkseed.

In a flash, all the nonsense I'd encountered in the archives' books made sense. The vague explanations and hints came together to paint a perfect picture of the situation. To the oracles—indeed, to the empire—their most venerated practitioners were more than just living representatives of their religion. Toward the end of their lives, they became a sort of living battery. Fuel for a reservoir of Sparkseed that was surely located just under my feet.

Didn't change much in the formula, did you, Narbu? I thought, shaking my head.

Whereas the monastic order had used the junnara-gol to convert sentient minds into Sparkseed, this empire used some other, less hideous method. Probably, anyway. As mentioned, I had no idea what was beneath me. For all I knew, there was a grandpappy junnara-gol soaking up all those mind fluids.

Again, though, my thoughts turned to the discrepancy between Narbu's account and the truth of things. Why hadn't he mentioned his people having access to Sparkseed long before they arrived on the planet? It was possible his memories had been purged or otherwise corrupted during the monks' interstellar journey, but if that was the case, why had it been so selective? Why had he recalled some things with perfect clarity, while others just didn't jell?

"Beja," someone called, directing my attention to a group of humanoids gathered near the base of the floating particle entity. Between their relatively tiny size and the eye-scorching brightness of the entity, it was no wonder I hadn't seen them first.

As I hurried over to them, I realized it wasn't *all* humanoids. Narbu stood among the small cluster of Suharkayans, embroiled in a debate that was far more serious than I'd first expected. The oracle was even thrusting his fingers about in accusation.

The empress ran to me the moment our eyes met. "Beja! Are you all right? Is everything well?"

"Yeah, it's all good," I said distractedly, trying to make sense of the kerfuffle. "What's going on?"

"Come," she said in strained tones, seizing my wrist and guiding me over to the group. "You *must* make him come to his senses."

"On what issue?"

Thankfully, Narbu answered that question for me. Just as I broke into the gathering of tense—and, dare I say, angry—faces, he began ranting in his typical sanctimonious manner. "I have already offered two choices for the boy. If neither is accepted, there is nothing more to be done. My visions were *not* incorrect, nor were they premature. I have seen the collapse. I have seen the end of a thousand worlds."

Oh, so it was *this* moment. The one where Narbu divined the corruption of the empress's son. The one where he began the accidental creation of the Unmade.

"You must listen to the beja," the empress urged, nudging me forward. "He went to the root of this evil, just as we discussed, and he vanquished it. Tell them, Beja."

I glanced about at the waiting faces. "I'm not so sure I should be involved in this."

Narbu crossed his arms. "It seems that even animals can occasionally drink from the well of wisdom."

Empress Jalisa grabbed my arm again. "Beja, Oracle Narbu believes my son to be corrupted by those of foul blood. He claims they will move against—"

"I *claim* nothing," Narbu cut in. "I convey the truth of reality. That is all I have done, Empress."

A grim-faced Suharkayan scoffed at that. "Your own brothers stand against your so-called visions."

"Because they are *blind*," Narbu boomed. "You are free to ignore my counsel, but there will be consequences. A mighty plague will fall upon this world."

"The beja has been to the defiled lands," the empress said weakly. "He has seen their plans, and he has dismantled them."

Narbu's gaze shifted to me. "Tell them what you know, Beja. I am certain it will affirm my words."

Now *this* was a spot I did not want to be in. For perhaps the first time, I *truly* understood the real danger of my time in the Godmaker. It had nothing to do with physical danger and everything to do with losing our only shot at fixing this mess. Just as Izamem had explained, this timeline could easily go off the rails if I didn't watch my actions closely. Whatever I said here, even if it outwardly aligned with the real timeline, carried the risk of permanently altering the course of things. That was the paradox, really. There was no way to determine what I had or hadn't done in my past life.

Considering all this, I decided to play it coy. "How do you know all this?"

If robotic looks could kill, Narbu would've had me turned to ash in that moment. "The methods of my divination are beyond the minds of my brethren, Beja. Why do you think you could possibly grasp them?"

Cold, dreadful realization washed over me. "Did it have something to do with the seed paste?"

Artificial or not, his eyes responded to that. They dimmed just a shade—just enough to let me know I was right. "Such sacraments are part of my *private* cache. What would you know of it?"

It seemed the shaman hadn't just been talking a big game after all. It took every ounce of my willpower to avoid ripping Narbu's Godmaker avatar apart. *He* was the cause of all this. His need for power, his ambition, his circumvention of the empire's laws—all of it had driven him to sourcing those goddamn blood-flower seeds for his own rituals. And those seeds, in turn, had planted wicked visions in his head. Visions that would drive him to murder a royal child.

The conclusions rolled through my mind in a torrent, but I couldn't voice a word of it. Couldn't let my anger overflow. If this was how it had happened, I couldn't do anything but play along.

"Nothing," I whispered. "Just a hunch."

Narbu nodded sharply. "As I thought." Turning back to the empress, he softened his voice to a more agreeable level. "The purification ritual would be painless, Empress, and it would ensure a ruler of tremendous power for our people. One that might even bring an end to this conflict before it begins."

"You were supposed to prevent this from ever happening," she hissed back.

"My brothers and I have done what we could for his mind, Empress, but this is the way of things."

"I gave you fifteen years . . . "

I spun toward her. *Fifteen years?* What the hell did she mean by that? There was no way Narbu could have known she'd get pregnant that far in advance, unless his predictive powers were *truly* that on the nose, and—

Narbu suddenly turned to a shy, drawn-in Suharkayan standing beside him. One marked by sets of parallel crimson lines running across his cheeks . . . and fear in his eyes. "Perhaps we should ask the boy what he feels is best."

"Tarkal will *never* be one of yours," the empress snapped. "You told me his tutelage was temporary, Oracle Narbu. You promised me."

I couldn't believe what I was hearing. Not at all. For a good ten seconds, all I heard was a ringing in my ears. My eyes tracked from the Suharkayan boy—Tarkal, it seemed—to Akasha's stomach, then back again . . . and again . . . and again. If the child in her stomach wasn't the boy in question, that meant . . .

The Unmade looked up from his navel-gazing and gave me a clumsy smile.

In a single rush, thousands of fears slipped free of their leashes and ran roughshod through my awareness. How had I been so stupid? So blind? Here I'd been, thinking I had well over a decade to get my ducks in a row and sort out the flow of events . . . when in reality, I probably had a few months at most. Certainly less than a year.

"You have another child coming, Empress, and it will be healthy," Narbu said calmly. "Should young Lord Yurma take up the blessed robes, your daughter will ascend the throne." Silence fell over the gathering, which Narbu used as an opportunity to push his point. "Whatever decision is made, the integrity of the empire—of benevolence, of wisdom, of purity itself—will remain intact. Disaster shall only come if you disregard this prophecy."

After several moments of letting the tears fall unbidden, the empress looked at me. "Beja?"

I was in no place to respond. I was still trying to figure out what the fuck was happening. What I did know, however, was that I needed more time. More power. I'd planned on spending the equivalent of years and years in here, and now my timeline had been slashed to a tenth or less. In short, I needed a way to keep things going. A slight delay. To that end, I began calling upon factoids I'd learned in the archives. Avenues to keep the show going without anybody noticing my ploy.

Awkwardly nodding at the boy—the same boy who would later cause untold slaughter and chaos—I delivered my proposal. "We should refrain from the ritual for now. It would be much safer for me to investigate if there are any . . . mitigating factors at work."

Narbu began seething. "What is the beast even saying?"

"Empress," I said slowly, "I discovered clear signs of the enemy rearming at the compound. Their entire coalition will surely mobilize in a matter of months, if not sooner. I'm prepared to go to war with them, if it means extracting information or recovering texts that can solve this issue."

"There is no solution to be found among the defiled," Narbu said.

I cocked a brow. "Aren't they the ones who grow your sacraments?"

The empress, on the other hand, was ecstatic. She smiled at her son, then at me, wiping away her tears with newfound resolve. "Yes, that's it, Beja. This could all be the work of their foul magics, couldn't it?"

"If what their shaman confessed to me is true, yes," I told her.

"It makes sense," she said, though it was obvious her desire to save her son had overpowered any form of logic. "Perhaps their ancient tombs contain a way . . . a remedy for the sickness they've brought upon us . . . "

"This is unthinkable," Narbu growled. "I have seen the course of reality, Empress. Would you really shatter centuries of peace on the words of a monster?"

"I would."

In turn, the oracle fixed me with a gaze so cold I wanted to crawl out of my skin. "Very well. Do as you will, Empress. I will continue to maintain the ritual world . . . for the moment when you realize this is untenable."

The empress studied me sidelong, the hope glimmering in her eyes. "If the heavens align, we will not need that world."

Later that evening, I stood on a fern-laden rooftop within the palatial compound, staring out at the lights across the city and trying to make sense of the day's happenings. That, and what I'd eaten for my postbattle feast. Half the foods had lacked any obvious analogue from my own life, and the other half had tasted so utterly alien I'd eaten them without any reference points in terms of flavor. There *had* been piles upon piles of strange, peppery meat that I'd quite enjoyed—up until they hit my digestive tract, that is. Some foods just weren't made for humanoids, I supposed.

My experience at the oracular chambers, however, disturbed me far more than whatever gastrointestinal distress I was enduring. There was so much to unpack. So much to worry about.

When you got right down to it, though, all those worries were really one massive worry, just cropping up in different forms. It was all about the timeline. The flow of decisions that had led to the creation of the Unmade. Try as I might, I couldn't think of any way to measure my own course against the one I'd experienced in a past life. Back then, I hadn't even been working with human consciousness. What if real me had let Narbu attempt to turn the boy into a machine, or simply allowed him to perform the ritual posthaste?

And speaking of the boy . . . Tarkal, or the Unmade, I supposed . . . I was still at a total loss. My mind was nowhere near powerful enough to read a person's state of consciousness, as Narbu could, but I still considered myself a decent judge of character. There hadn't been a single shred of malice in that boy. If anything, he'd been exemplary in terms of a peaceful mind. He'd exuded a sense of nervous innocence, much like a small, startled animal.

I put my hands on the alabaster banister and gazed out at the skyline, wondering how Narbu had gotten it so thoroughly wrong. Again, I don't think he was evil, nor that he ever had a truly cruel intention . . . which only made things more perplexing. Obviously, there was a lot of power in those damned seeds. If they could cause a decent oracle—a being with an exceedingly sharp, clear mind—to indirectly assassinate the empress's son, they could easily drive other, more susceptible beings to states of total depravity.

That seemed to make something click.

The flowers. The hordes. The cult.

Those seeds hadn't just popped into existence of their own accord. They'd clearly been cultivated, over a period of long and grueling centuries, to pack maximum defilement power. That required intention. Conscious direction. By extension, that also meant somebody—or a group of many somebodies—had been planning this far longer than anybody in the empire understood. These seeds were nothing but the tip of an iceberg, hinting at the vast hatred lurking outside the Suharkayan territory.

Back in the oracular chambers, I'd largely been lying to the empress when I explained my plan. In truth, I'd had almost no clue whether there really was an answer to her son's predicament among the sands. It had been a last-ditch, blurted-out idea intended to buy me more time to keep ranking up and honing my skills.

Now, though, I wasn't so sure. I turned my attention to the dark, rolling hills that contained the enemy. *Somebody* out there had engineered the creation of those seeds and, in turn, the entire plot to corrupt and kill the empress's child. If I could find them and make them talk, I might be able to learn *all* their defiled secrets. Including the method to opening a direct gateway.

Again, I was struck by another ping of seemingly obvious insight. Back on the monks' world, Narbu had mentioned Akasha looking through ancient, long-dead tomes to uncover and perform the ritual. That she'd found those tomes out in the deserts wasn't a foregone conclusion, but it *was* likely, given Narbu's hatred of the cult and its dark ways. There wasn't a chance in hell the oracles would allow that kind of knowledge to exist within the empire's domain.

Find the knowledge myself . . . and skip the rest.

The thought arose seemingly of its own volition, throwing me into total confusion. It was a stupid idea, wasn't it? After all, I was here to follow the timeline to a T, not carve out my own path. If I said *fuck it* to the course of things and went straight for the goal, I might royally screw myself (and Akasha) over. But somehow, it just felt right. Whether or not the inhabitants of the Godmaker counted as real people, they sure seemed real enough. Their eyes held the same fear, pain, joy, and surprise as mine. That was doubly true for the empress's son.

If I could skip the entire collapse-of-the-empire scenario, it would save untold oceans of suffering. Whether that suffering was for flesh-and-blood people or mental echoes didn't feel particularly important anymore.

There was, of course, the issue of Akasha's catatonic slumber. As Izamem said, I was really here to kill two birds with one stone: find the method to open the gateway *and* figure out how to unlock Narbu's mind prison. I had a plan for that, though. One I won't disclose just yet.

After what felt like hours of wandering through my own thoughts, however, I was interrupted by the whispers of satin shoes on stone.

I turned back to find the empress and her attendants crossing the rooftop.

When she drew nearer to me, she turned back and signaled for her followers to hang back. They respected her gesture without hesitation, descending the staircase back down into the palace proper.

"Oracle Narbu wishes to apologize to you," she said as she came to stand at my side. "He was . . . careless in restraining his tongue."

I offered a thin smile. "Did he really apologize, or did you ask him to?"

"An apology is an apology, Beja."

"Fair enough. I'll take it."

She rested a hand on my wrist. "I was told you didn't find your concubines pleasing."

Oh, right. The concubines. How could I forget? Upon returning to the palace, I'd been greeted by no fewer than four Suharkayan women in varying states of undress, all of whom were giggling like mad and serving as sentient bed warmers. Well, I'd shut that down right away. Simulated or not, I didn't feel it was proper to engage in an alien orgy as my first sexual experience. Certainly not one involving concubines.

"No offense to them," I said, shrugging. "I just wanted a clear head this evening."

"Shall I arrange for others?"

I shook my head so quickly I nearly pulled a muscle. "No, no, it's fine."

"Ah . . . are you saving yourself?" Her hand crept up to my elbow, then my shoulder.

I rested mine atop hers to stop it from advancing any farther. "Can I ask you something?"

"Anything, Beja. You've earned whatever answers you seek, given what you've done for my child."

"Why me?"

"Come again?"

I leaned on the banister. "It's quite . . . unusual . . . for an empress to take a liking to a beja. Much less for them to enjoy their company physically."

My explicit reference to our *contact* had a profound effect on the empress. She withdrew her hand and worked to pull on a crooked smile, though it didn't look right beneath furrowed brows.

"I care for you," she said at last. "I don't believe you're a beast."

"But I could've been. I still could be, I suppose. That's the nature of a beja."

"You've grown so . . . philosophical lately." She shifted closer, resting her weight against mine. "Sometimes, Beja, a beast is necessary. A beast is able to devour sins without being infected by them. It shakes the earth in ways that its prey cannot."

"Are you asking me to do something?"

She looked at me for a long while, a question quite obviously poised on her lips, then shook her head and glanced away. "I just feel, at times, that this is all a world of illusion. The oracles speak of its insubstantial nature, its impermanence, its fragility . . . but it extends deeper than that."

Was I *really* about to have this talk . . . with a simulated person?

I cleared my throat, preparing for a highly unpleasant and awkward discussion, only to be saved by the empress herself.

"It's an illusion of power," she continued in a whisper. "For thousands of years, the dynastic bloodlines have held sway over this empire. Now, though . . . now, the wind speaks of grim affairs."

"What do you mean?"

"Have you ever lifted a heavy object with a companion stronger than yourself, Beja?"

I blinked at her, unsure of the relevance. "Yes?"

"In the beginning, you feel the strain equally. Then, gradually, the strain grows lighter. Before long, you feel as though your strength is tremendous . . . as though you could move mountains with a single finger." She stared out at the city, hollow-eyed. "Only when your companion drops their side of the object do you grasp the truth of things. You were never *really* bearing the weight. They always held the control, and they always dictated how far you would carry it."

"The oracles," I guessed.

Her eyes went wide, though only for a moment. Almost as though I'd spoken a curse her brain wasn't prepared to register.

"Never in our entire history has there been a schism between the royal blood and the oracles," she said softly. "But now . . . they speak of my son, my blood, as though he is defiled."

Before I could stop myself, I firmly said, "They're wrong."

"You're certain, Beja?"

"I am."

She had to trust me on that, though. Although I'd committed myself to a chaotic path of wisdom via conquest, thus abandoning the original timeline, I couldn't risk deviations that completely overturned the established course of events. Telling her about Narbu's corruption—hell, even about the seeds—would bring about changes I couldn't possibly foresee.

But by Halcius, did I want to spill the oracle's secrets. She didn't deserve to live in the shadows of those lies, and she absolutely didn't deserve to see her own son butchered due to faulty conclusions. Maybe that was why I was so intent on doing things my way. Maybe it wasn't about the masses but about one woman and her children. About redeeming what I'd failed to stop the first time around.

"We'll need a full report, a course of action, and clear directives," she said quietly, letting out a long-held sigh. "Then we'll need to—"

I stopped her by raising a hand. "None of that. All I need is another ship, a good pilot, and Planner Hijeksos. I can leave tonight."

She tossed me a puzzled look. "Planner Hijeksos?"

"He knows more about those hills than I thought," I said. "Plus, he assured me he'd be honored to help with any future activities."

"Oh," she said, her face brightening despite the plain absurdity of the idea. "Very well, but . . . I don't think it's wise to press into their territory so soon. Such a decision has not been undertaken in countless years." She regarded me seriously. "We're speaking about war, Beja. A war against an entire army."

"No, Empress. We're speaking about your son's life."

Her eyes crinkled. "You mean it? You truly wish to leave . . . tonight?"

"If all goes well, I'll have what we need within a few days. A week, at most."

"I see." She looked out across the city once more, then shifted her hand from the banister to the pronounced lump in her belly. "Nobody except us can know about this, Beja. The advisers are already on edge. If they find out you've entered open combat without approval . . . "

"They're free to try their luck at skinning me."

A solid minute passed between us, entirely silent apart from the wind whistling through crenellations. Then the empress turned to me with a face caught between hope and abject terror.

"You promised you'd come back to me, and you did," she said. "Would you make the same promise now?"

Something came over me in that instant—something I hadn't even considered, much less debated as a possible action. Before I caught myself, I leaned over, took her head in my hands, and kissed her forehead. My first instinct was to seize up and apologize, but when I saw the smile on her face, I let my mind relax.

"I *will* come back," I whispered. "But not until this is finished."

18

This is the part where I summarize a war (and how I became a god). I know, I know—you were probably clamoring for a proper slog of blood, guts, and bullets, but hear me out. Even if you don't know it yet, there are plenty of reasons why you don't want to get my detailed account of the fighting. Most of these reasons are due to my own miscalculations, and, on a broader level, the problem of scale. We'll get to that.

On a more immediate and literary level, however, it's simply not *fun* to read about an entire war battle by battle, kill by kill. This isn't some grand saga where a hero and his plucky pals take on an evil force for the fate of the world, undergoing phenomenal character growth and learning about themselves along the way. Instead, it was *one* guy—me, very much not a hero—carving his way through thousands upon thousands of poor, starved, seed-corrupted nomads under the command of shadowy forces. How many times can you *really* read about the different ways in which I shot, stabbed, crushed, strangled, or exploded living beings? More to the point, how many different ways are there to make death sound interesting?

Not enough for this war.

Anyhow, let me move onto the calculation issues. You see, I'd ballparked that it would take me roughly a week to ferret out the ancient, spooky temples of the cult, kill the leaders, and recover the magic formula needed to open a rift straight to the Unmade. I'd also estimated, based on Hijeksos's reports, that there were between two and three thousand total soldiers in the enemy ranks.

Well, I was miserably off on both counts. My "one-week war" lasted about eight months (just shy of two days in the Godmaker, if you're wondering), and those two to three thousand soldiers ended up being nearer to one hundred and twenty thousand. The fighting ended up being so widespread, so thoroughly destructive, that the empire was forced to create a hundred-kilometer-wide no-man's land that ringed their territory. Scattered throughout this no-man's land were pulsating relay towers to send requests to and from the front line, as well as various stations stocked with rations, clean water, and weapons.

Day in and day out, I slaughtered the enemy. I woke up and went to sleep covered in blood. I faced battle lines so long I couldn't see their edges . . . and I sent every member of those battle lines to the afterlife. Or rebirth. Whatever. The point is, there was no glee or glory or even satisfaction in my war. It was eight months of crusading, flying from one region to the next, dismantling entire cities and their populations without a shred of mercy.

The reaction wasn't phenomenal in the empire, as far as I'd heard, but there wasn't much Narbu or any other adviser could do about it. This was the first war in seemingly forever, and as such, the empress's will reigned supreme. Every so often, Hijeksos described the "riots" that had been quelled within the capital or another Suharkayan metropolis. Riots, of course, is an overreach for what these events really were. In general, they never got past the point of a few dozen Suharkayans congregating in public and complaining with soft voices.

On the other side of the aisle, however, the reaction was more . . . unexpected. Among the foreign species that comprised the enemy, my name came to describe something akin to a demon. A monstrosity from beyond this world. By the second month of combat, every new town I entered was covered with effigies resembling me, complete with baskets of bread and fruit—some kind of superstitious belief that they could sate my bloodlust with offerings, I supposed. On other occasions, they littered the walls of their settlements with dead bodies to scare me off. No such luck. With every battle fought, every enemy slain, my reputation and mythological status expanded further.

The campaign consisted of three stages, which seemed to repeat infinitely. The first stage was entry, in which our unnamed royal pilot (and a groveling Hijeksos) guided me to the outskirts of an unconquered region. The second stage was assault, which here means "killing every enemy within visual range, then interrogating them for information." The third and final stage was scouring, aka exploring bombed-out ruins, half-buried temples, and vaults that had lain dormant among the swamps and deserts. Once I'd picked through everything I could—and invariably found nothing of substance—the empire's security team would move in to control the local populace, and I'd loop back to the first stage in some new corner of hell.

Sound boring? Yeah, it was. Even if you don't *yet* buy my explanation, just take it on faith—I'm doing you a favor by sparing you the torment of reading my exploits. Even if I wrote in such a way that one sentence equaled one battle, you'd still be asleep before dissecting the first month of combat.

There were a few highlights thrown in, of course. It wouldn't have been a proper war without them. Most of these highlights were a result of the cult army's menagerie, which consisted of beasts that had been trained and abused to the point of vengeful madness. On varying occasions, I took down colossal mothlike creatures, massive spiders that dwelled beneath the flats, leathery beasts that boasted entire fortresses on their backs, and birds with reptilian tails and pincers. Much like the defiled champion I'd first faced on the roadway, these beasts were regarded as demigods—which meant their deaths were especially traumatic to enemy morale.

That being said, it clearly didn't psychologically damage them enough to make them give up the fight and turn over their dark materials. Each engagement seemed to grow longer, more vicious, especially when I took the front line to the east. It felt as though I was nearing something they didn't want me to access. As though they'd needed to marshal the bulk of their forces to protect something.

That might explain why, on the eighth month, third week, and first day of the war, I found myself standing atop a small, mossy rise overlooking a dead forest. Arranged within that forest were thousands of enemy soldiers, all of whom had smeared their bodies with ash and blood. Even at almost half a kilometer away, they stood out like ghosts among the barren trees.

By this point, my vision had gotten so good I could see the hazy courage in their eyes. The dark, sappy discharge of the seeds running from the edges of their lips. The starvation in their shriveled limbs.

Days prior, this forest had been teeming with exotic, colorful life. Not anymore. The moment the enemy heard I was carving a trail through the region, they'd gone full scorched-earth policy—literally—by burning the trees and fields. Now it was a land of ash and blood. I'd already conquered two cities in the region, both of which had been relatively undefended compared to prior targets. This only made the enemy's gathering here more conspicuous. There was no good reason for them to have abandoned a fortified position and taken up arms in a swampy, humid forest—unless there was something juicy in the wilderness behind them.

I whirled the hammer in my hands, preparing for yet another messy engagement. "How many, do you think?"

Planner Hijeksos, seated on a nearby stump beside our stoic pilot, lifted his eyes from the latest battle map. "Oh, I don't know, Beja. I'm not so skilled with numbers . . . "

One might expect that the wily planner hadn't changed much in eight measly months, given his species' long life span, but he had. He'd changed a lot, in fact. He was quieter these days, more guarded in what he said or how he moved. There were long, wrinkled lines beneath his eyes and mouth. Sometimes, the night after observing a large battle, he'd wake with screams.

So, in short, I'd probably traumatized Hijeksos. Not to say he didn't have it coming, of course. I still felt a touch bad about it, however, considering the circumstances. Neither he nor his people, nor his parents, nor his grandparents had ever experienced the horrors of killing. He'd been thrown into the deep end of the pool. Despite all that, he seemed to have adapted reasonably well to serving by my side. In eight long, bloody months, he hadn't made a single attempt to escape or sabotage me. Even when left unattended by the empire's security teams, he'd kept his mouth shut.

Somehow, some way, he'd become the closest thing to my friend in this blighted land.

"Keep an eye on the left side of the battlefield," I told him as I began moving down the slope, my gaze fixed on the enemy ranks. "I need some data on the shock wave."

If you're confused by the words *shock wave*, don't be. That will require some explanation. But to explain *that*, I need to explain my Status Display, which I pulled up in full before reaching the bottom of the slope.

STATUS DISPLAY
PURIFIER RANK: 23
RANK-UP NOT AVAILABLE (1,677,721,600 KP required)

Kill Points: 1,304,804,400
Genofacturing Points: 120,402,300

Rank Points: 0

Rank Time: 21 Hours, 52 Minutes, 12 Seconds
Storehouse Time: 239 Hours, 38 Minutes, 41 Seconds

Anima: 560%
Dominion: 0/8

That's right—Rank 23. And yes, that's also right—1.68 billion Kill Points needed to advance. Thanks, multiplication.

In the interest of fairness, I hadn't gotten all those points by blindly wandering around and dismembering villagers. By this point, I'd unlocked both Genofacturing III and IV, granting me access to top-of-the-line consumables. As you've probably guessed from my girthy stockpile of Genofacturing Points, I didn't have any trouble producing those, even in excessively large batches. At any given time, the rucksack slung over Hijeksos's shoulder contained no fewer than twenty tonics—most of them engineered to boost Kill Point acquisition, but not all.

Here was my precise stack as I marched toward the mass of gibbering enemies in the dead forest.

Kill Point Boost IV: Quintuples the number of all Kill Points gained for six hours. All encounters affected by this boost must end within the six-hour window to gain increased points.

Chain Kill Boost IV: Grants additional compensation for kills completed within ninety seconds of one another during encounters. After successfully killing an enemy, gain 250 extra Kill Points for the subsequent kill, and 250 more for each kill thereafter, with a maximum gain of twenty thousand Kill Points per enemy. All kills affected by this boost must have their Kill Points assigned within the six-hour window to qualify.

Rank Timer Delay IV: Freezes the Rank Timer's countdown for four hours.

Given this cocktail of pharmaceutical goodness, it shouldn't come as any surprise that I was able to keep my rank-up momentum going. Even without tonics, I was a verifiable murder engine. *With* them, I was a god of war. Some small, petty side of me desperately wanted to return to Kagu-9 and mash the faces of any leftover Chanzig sympathizers, but I knew that just wasn't feasible.

Although . . . I *was* rather intrigued by Genofacturing IV's assortment of high-end, exotic weaponry, and those bastards seemed like excellent test subjects. Up until this point, I'd barely browsed them, much less considered producing them. Even if it was pure superstition, it felt too dangerous to switch from my hammer to an advanced weapon. I'd already thrown enough new variables into the experience.

As for which shiny new upgrades I'd gotten? You're about to find out.

At just over a quarter kilometer from the enemy forces, I squatted down, gritted my teeth, and flipped on Soaring Death. Pain sizzled through my upper back as a pair of monstrous, bloody wings tore free and extended to both sides, perfectly threading the slots I'd had chiseled into the back of my armor. Believe me—damaging the beautiful breastplate had hurt almost as much as using this goddamn upgrade.

The wings snapped against the breeze, their thin, translucent panels of flesh vibrating like eardrums within cartilage frames. I breathed through the discomfort. It'd been one hell of a surprise when I first hit Rank 14 and nabbed the ability—made even worse by how miraculous and majestic it had seemed in the description—but by now it was closer to a diffuse, lingering ache that eventually faded into the background.

Even so . . . wings. Come on. Each growth was around two meters long, forming a silhouette that was unsettling enough to have sparked mass panic in at least half the cities I'd assaulted.

That effect hadn't stayed forever, of course. A consequence of adaptation. With each new force I faced, they seemed less and less intimidated by my appearance. Terror had been replaced by rage. The kind of rage you don't find in purely simulated beings.

This might explain why, as I was midway through flapping the blood off my wings, the enemy lines came alive. The deep, rolling bass of war horns filled the valley, and soon there was a mass of flesh rushing straight toward me, blades and spears and shields held high. The ground itself quaked as the army's heavy hitters—mutated specimens or plain abominations—lumbered forth, dragging the rusted chains that had kept them bound to stakes in the earth.

Time to handle business.

Squatting down, I simultaneously directed power into my heels and the base of the wings. With one mighty flap, I shot airborne. Each pump of the wings took me higher, higher, higher . . . Before long, I was over a hundred meters above the horde below, circling along the edge of their front line to get a better view of the action. Bullets zipped past here and there, but they were empty threats. Much like blades or any other melee weapon wielded by my enemies, the projectiles triggered god mode and allowed me to rather leisurely thread the chaos.

At a glance, there were about five thousand troops below. A mass of ants broken into manageable, grid-like battle squares, occasionally divided by the presence of the aforementioned beasts. In some ways, their lack of evolution in tactics still blew my mind. Their forces had been decimated in every single interaction—once again, by *only me*—and yet they still insisted on using the same lazy maneuvers.

Beyond them and their dead forest was a dark, placid body of water that resembled an abscess on a corpse. Jagged, mossy shapes rose up through the surface in places, suggesting the presence of buried ruins. Past even the water was the highest point in the valley: a tall, calcified wall of stone that had either been carved out or formed through natural erosion. None of these seemed like particularly juicy targets, but then again, the enemy army hadn't made much tactical sense to me in prior engagements, either.

After zipping through a spirited burst of flak—some kind of caustic debris loaded into homemade cannons—I banked to the right and cut downward. Wind bit at my face and howled in my ears as I picked up speed, but I paid it no mind. I was focused entirely on the largest square of their force, which, as I'd told Hijeksos, was located on the left-hand side of the battlefield.

This wasn't because I wanted to shatter their morale or pull off an impressive strategy, mind you. The real reason was more practical. In almost every other engagement, the enemy had broken ranks and begun fleeing the moment I dealt any serious damage to their formations, even if said formation was the smallest on the field. This made reaping Kill Points a pain in the ass. It's no fun having to chase down and butcher individual soldiers for hours.

Hence, I started with the biggest, densest knot of troops. That way, when the enemy inevitably turned tail and routed, I'd be sure to wind up with a decent payout.

I descended at incredible speed, keeping myself locked on the enemy's banner to avoid losing focus amid the flurry of movements and color. Adrenaline sharpened my vision and sent warm, throbbing tingles down my wrists. Well, maybe it was adrenaline. See, this wasn't just another fight. It was my favorite kind of fight: a test fight.

After hitting Rank 23, I'd held off on purchasing a new upgrade for a while. There was a lot to choose from, after all. But earlier that day, I'd pulled the bullet and selected a Mutation ability known as Shock and Awe. The description had promised a novel experience, to say the least.

Shock and Awe (REQ Rank 23): Converts the desired tissue into a directed-force blast by dissolving nuclear bonds. *Does not require a Dominion slot.* (1/3)

The tissue-conversion aspect had given me pause—and still did—but I figured it was worth a shot. Besides, it was Rank 23. Newer is always better, right?

. . . Right?

In any case, I'd decided against testing it in boring, noncombat conditions. Better to see it used in all its glory on the field of slaughter.

When I came down to an altitude of ten meters, skimming the jagged, ashy tips of former trees, I directed my will into my left hand and thrust it palm out toward the center of the enemy mass. My HUD sprang up and labeled the encounter, but I waved it aside. I was committed. Excited. When I felt a split-second tingle and jolt of pain in my wrist, however, I realized I might've fucked up. Too late.

In a microinstant, my left hand unraveled at a quantum level. Due to either the upgrade itself or my mental conditioning, I sensed every . . . single . . . happening. The cells burst open; the DNA unraveled; the atoms sizzled; the quarks strained against the very fabric of existence. Before I could even cry out, my hand was gone.

It was replaced by a blinding cone of light that ripped into the earth—and bodies—beneath me. My vision went black, my hearing vanished, and a counterforce slammed into me so hard that I went careening backward, tumbling, screaming, cursing. Not that I heard any of those screams or curses. I just knew I was sailing blindly in a tangle of ruptured wings and limbs, the sides of my head and ears growing warm with fresh blood.

Bit by bit, second by second, my vision swam from darkness back to clarity. By the time I was able to see again, I found myself drifting several hundred meters away from the battle, my wings tattered yet still holding. The black waters of the valley's lake rippled beneath me, evidently still carrying the colossal aftermath of Shock and Awe.

Only while looking down, deaf and baffled, did I note the remains of my left hand. It had obviously been blasted to smithereens, but it was already beginning to re-form, one nub and tendon at a time, courtesy of my 560 percent Anima.

Goddamn, that hurt.

The revelation was strange to me. Since entering the Godmaker, I hadn't really felt pain. Nothing could injure me, after all. The closest thing

I'd felt had been chafing or itching, but those weren't really comparable. Here and now, however, I understood that I needed to take caution. The enemies couldn't do shit to me, but I sure could.

Oh, right. Enemies.

I spun around in midair, catching the breeze and circling back toward the . . . battlefield? Even from this distance, it was clear the battle part was over. The enemy ranks were in total disarray, breaking apart and fleeing in all directions. Not fleeing from me, though. Fleeing from the gigantic, smoking crater that had been a stretch of forest just moments earlier.

Every tree in sight had been flattened, and even the soil itself bore concentric rings that indicated the sheer power I'd directed into the ground. Needless to say, there were no corpses at ground zero. As I soared overhead, the most substantial evidence of life I found were cast-off arms or legs that had been thrown hundreds of meters from the blast site. Everything else was just burned carbon.

I sighed, very much not looking forward to the postbattle cleanup. Thankfully, I'd picked up an upgrade that somewhat sidestepped that chore. In the old days, I'd had to manually eliminate every foe with a hammer swing to the head—unless I confiscated a gun and practiced my target shooting, that is. Any way you sliced it . . . tedious.

Enter Pestilence.

Pestilence (REQ Rank 21): Generates a swarm of microscopic insects capable of devouring living tissue within a fifty-meter range. *Does not require a Dominion slot.* (1/3)

Halfway through a barrel roll, I waved my right hand over the fleeing masses and triggered the upgrade. The skin of my palm boiled and bubbled, hinting at the writhing creatures beneath, then split completely open like a sheet of thin paper. Out poured a stream of swift, black insects that resembled floating grains of sand. One shred of my willpower was all it took to direct them down and into the thick of the enemies.

Like clockwork, screams filled the forest no fewer than ten seconds later. I cringed at the sounds. Even so, I couldn't resist the morbid curiosity of glancing down and watching the feast. My enemies slapped at themselves and convulsed on the soil in agony, their bodies covered in shifting patches of the black death. There wasn't a drop of blood in sight, but that didn't mean there was no damage. Even as I watched, their limbs and faces and fingers disappeared as though they'd been targeted by an invisible eraser.

Dropping a bit lower, I flitted through the trees and took stock of the situation. By my count, nearly a third of the force was already dead. By the time I unleashed a few more clouds of Pestilence, that kill count would rise to half. Still, there were a few nasties that continued to stand defiant.

Foremost among them was some hybrid I can only describe as a mad scientist's attempt to blend a scarab and a rhinoceros. The six-legged, twenty-meter-tall monstrosity lifted its head toward me, revealing a pincered maw with thousands of smaller, blood-soaked scarabs scurrying across its three tongues. Then the insectoid panels all along its armored flesh lifted in unison and rattled a solemn song.

I was up for a challenge.

When the creature reared up, attempting to snap at me with a mixture of fangs and flapping tissue, I easily dashed over its nose and delivered a backhanded hammer swing to one of the beady eyes. Blood misted the air, and the thing sank back down with a chorus of howls. Didn't take it down, though.

Circling back, I swept low and spotted a string of discarded guns that had been trampled into the soil. An idea took shape and further solidified when I realized my Shock-and-Awe-exploded hand had fully regrown. It was time for my next trick—a little second-tier upgrade known as Tumorous Grasp.

Tumorous Grasp (REQ Rank 18): Sprouts two additional arms from the midsection. (2/3)

Yeah, you read that right. *Two additional arms.* The moment I triggered the upgrade, ligaments and strands of muscle burst through the good-size holes on the side of my armor, emerging just beneath my actual arms. Even as the stubby limbs formed, I sensed my nervous system connecting with them, integrating them.

Within five seconds, I was able to lift the bloody, misshapen paws at the end of the new arms. Within ten, I could open and close the fingers as a whole. And finally, within twenty, I could operate one finger at a time as though using my normal body. That meant I was ready.

Dodging a low swing from one of the scarab-rhino's bladed legs, I followed the curvature of the ground, frantically weaving and dipping to avoid the remains of trees in my path. As I sped over the soil, I plucked at the firearms littering the earth as though they were collectibles in a gaming sim. One gun, two guns, three guns, four . . .

By the time I angled skyward and got a good look at the beast, I had all four guns ready to go. Hell, I'd even nabbed three more using Telekinesis. Just for fun.

With a smooth smile, I turned the weapons on the rhino-scarab's face and let loose.

To my amazement—but also slight disappointment—the beast died in no less than three seconds. Weak. Its remains crashed to the ground, now resembling a large pile of ground meat. The last of the dying Pestilence bugs swarmed the corpse and ate their fill, then dissolved into the gore.

SLAUGHTER ENCOUNTER SUCCESSFUL
Kills: 1,603
Kill Points Awarded: 25,618,200 (TONIC BONUSES: 106,491,320)
Storehouse Time Awarded: 82 Hours, 20 Minutes, 0 Seconds

Sighing, I dropped all the guns and let them plop to the earth some fifty meters below.

That had barely been a fight at all.

Off to the right, the last of the army's survivors fled into denser forest and narrow canyons. They weren't too far to catch, but they *were* too low in Kill Points to justify a chase. Besides, I was damn tired. Shock and Awe had taken a lot out of me—including a hand.

In general, tiredness seemed to have become the dominant force in recent months. There was no joy left in fighting. No excitement. Every single encounter had become, disturbingly, a competition to see how creatively and efficiently I could extinguish life. The fact that my body now resembled a literal monster's didn't help with that feeling. Furthermore, the Kill Points per individual had continued to diminish, as expected and even explained by Guide, which meant I needed to obliterate even more people to keep going. The issue was, I just didn't want to.

I knew what was at stake, and more importantly, what was waiting for me in the Unmade's dimension, but I just couldn't find the killer determination I'd had in the early days of the chok'tal. I was, quite frankly, overpowered. Especially with no risk of death involved.

Still, there was no sense complaining. Rogaji's invention—this damned machine—was the only reason I was still in the game. Without it, I surely would've died shortly after the fight on the monks' planet.

When I finally headed back to the hilltop where Hijeksos and my pilot were posted, I was met with a curtain of strangled silence. Both men were in a state of vague shock, or perhaps fear for their own lives. Whatever the case, neither of them was capable of meeting my eyes, much less greeting me.

Turning back toward the battlefield, however, it wasn't hard to understand why. There was practically nothing left. My Pestilence doses had consumed half the trees in the immediate area, and the other half had been splintered beyond recognition due to the blast and subsequent trampling by beasts. Even the black water of the lake, which had previously been obscured by the forest, was now clouded with all manner of blood.

"So, how'd I do?" I asked as I faced the men, only to discover another casualty: The tents, bedrolls, and pot of soup had all been blasted down the back side of the hill. I rubbed the back of my head and let out a weary sigh. "Sorry. I didn't know it would be so forceful. I'll stick to using a finger next time. Maybe just a fingernail."

Hijeksos struggled to lift his gaze. "Beja . . . we received a relay from Suharyama. Your presence has been requested."

Toggling off my wings and extra arms, I fixed the man with a severe expression. It was clear he wasn't offering the full story. "What is it, Planner?"

"Per—" The word got lodged in his throat, and he coughed before trying again. "Perhaps it's best we don't speak of it. The empress will surely want to discuss it."

I took a warning step forward. "What . . . is . . . it?"

"Beja, it's not my pl—"

"Is it about the child?"

Hijeksos's lip quivered as he nodded.

"Which one?" I pressed.

"Well, that's . . . the rub of it," Hijeksos mumbled. "It's both of them."

19

The moment our jellyfish touched down on the landing platform, I pushed past the waiting, somber-faced attendants and ran straight for the palace. Where I'd once seen throngs of gardeners and servants and dancers, I saw only stragglers with downcast gazes and shriveled postures. *Something* was wrong. Horribly wrong.

My fears only mounted when I entered the palace proper and found it full of weeping, trembling crowds. The entire atrium looked like a funerary site. Pots that had always been stocked with fresh, radiant flowers were now little more than altars of decomposition. Enormous shutters had been drawn down to mute the midday sun. Rancid incense burned on tiny platters.

At that moment, my heart dropped. What had I done? Had I driven Narbu to madness—to the point of killing the empress, even? Had my absence allowed an assassin to enter the royal grounds?

All thoughts fled my mind, and I shouldered my way through the masses with twice the vigor, nudging aside the mourners and dead-eyed officials. When I reached the door leading to the royal chambers themselves, I found myself facing an even larger gathering of broken souls. The various offerings and knickknacks ringing the doors did nothing to put my mind at ease.

Fortunately, the two guards assigned to the entryway spotted me the moment I came barreling up. They were quick to clear the way and usher me through the doors. When the heavy wooden slabs creaked shut at my back and the next set of carved doors stared me down, I paused, drawing a deep, shuddering breath in the darkness of that makeshift airlock.

I needed to be ready to confront whatever lay beyond this point, even if that meant the empress's cold, perfumed body lying on a slab. I just wasn't sure I could. Even if she wasn't *real*—even if *none* of this was real—her death would break me. Part of that was due to her importance in the grand scheme of things, but the greater part came from my attachment to her. To Akasha. The empress's simulated death spelled the end of my very tangible quest to undo Narbu's mental locks and awaken the woman I cared for.

Just keep going, I told myself.

Somehow, though, I couldn't. My feet were unwilling to move. All this work, all this death . . . I didn't know whether I wanted to scream or just pound the exit button on the Godmaker.

Then a curious thing happened. Almost as though a small, invisible fissure had formed in the back of my mind, a stream of calmness bubbled up and flowed over the deluge of thoughts. A clear, radiant calmness I'd only felt on the verge of death. It saturated the contents of my mind, holding the fear, the anger, the bitterness, soothing them until they were nothing but looping words amid the vast sky of consciousness. The confidence I'd felt in the junnara-gol's mind returned with fresh intensity.

I will face whatever has happened. I will set it right.

To my own surprise, I opened the next set of doors with steady hands. Then the next, and the next . . . Soon, I stood before the final barrier. The last thing shielding me from the truth. Before I had time to evaluate my decision or turn tail, I took hold of the handles and tugged them open.

The royal chambers were a den of shadow and swaying silk. A soft, whining breeze moved through the space, fluttering the thick tapestries that had been suspended from the rafters. Every so often, I caught a hint of motion, a whispered word.

Despite the ache in my gut, I took a step forward, then another. I moved toward the empress's bed as though caught in a witch's spell. All the while, my body resisted me. The muscles in my legs quivered and threatened to buckle beneath me. Air stopped halfway down my throat. This continued until I'd reached the wide, mica-encrusted tapestry shielding the bed itself.

With a silent prayer and no shortage of dread, I nudged it aside . . .

And found a living empress lying there.

Try as I might, I couldn't stop myself from rushing to her side and sinking to my knees. I grabbed her hand—her soft, warm hand—and pressed it to my lips. Her startled attendants shrank back and murmured among themselves, but I paid them no mind. She was alive. All was well.

At least, it seemed that way for a moment.

Only as I held her hand, shaking from pure excitement, did I realize she wasn't moving to reciprocate. Even though I felt a pulse moving beneath her skin, there was no spark in her, no desire to move or touch me in turn.

I lifted my gaze and found her looking at me. Well, not quite *at* me. It was as though she were looking through me, studying something far, far in the distance. Her eyes weren't quite cold, just . . . dead. Hollow.

Frowning, I let my attention wander down the length of her body. She was covered in thin, pale sheets that generally followed the curve of her form, and yet . . . there was no bump on her stomach. No sign of a child. My initial reaction was one of strange joy. She'd given birth, after all. She was probably just dazed from the effort.

That impression died the instant I saw bloody splotches lower on the sheets. Some was fresh, while most was darker, oxidized, indicating it was at least several hours old. Why hadn't they changed out the sheets after labor?

My lips tumbled open. "Wh—What—?"

The empress just studied me, her face so neutral it yielded nothing as to her inner state. Even when she spoke, her voice was thin and detached. "They let me hold her for a few minutes."

A vacuum formed in my rib cage. I sank back, gaze tracing the tiles blindly, trying to make sense of it all.

"The oracles said her mindstream was subtle and untainted," she whispered, still looking at me without truly seeing anything. "She might have become an oracle herself."

"How did—I . . . " The words just wouldn't come.

"Her karma was not suited to this plane," the empress went on. "She's been reborn somewhere else. To a new mother, a new father."

My tongue felt as large and coarse as a brick, but I struggled around it. "Did the oracles do this?"

She shook her head after a long, long pause. "It was her karma, Beja. *Our* karma."

"What do you mean, your karma?"

"That of my blood." Her focus gradually slid down to her stomach. "Oracle Narbu said it was a sign of defilement. The sins of one child . . . haunting another."

Narbu.

I took hold of her hand again, firmer this time. "Empress, where is Narbu now?"

"Departing. Journeying. Purifying the boy . . . "

"Where?"

"The Ladders of Ascendence," she said flatly, still gazing at me but letting her finger trail vaguely to the west. "Let him go, Beja. He is doing what he must . . . "

I was on my feet and sprinting toward the exit before she'd even finished speaking.

Simulation or not, I was going to rip Narbu's fucking head off if I found out he'd had anything to do with the stillbirth. There was a good chance he had. What better way to prove your theory about an evil child than killing its sibling before it even had a chance to live? In a superstitious culture like this one, there probably wasn't much that couldn't be sold through such a theory.

Even more maddening was the realization that my entire war had probably been one long distraction. The enemy had lured me from place to place, trying to buy time for the ultimate implosion of the empire. Maybe they'd succeeded in the end.

All that was old news, though. I had a score to settle.

I'd never heard of these Ladders of Ascendence before, much less visited them, but it wasn't hard to figure out. After screaming in the face of a few patrolling guards for directions, I activated Soaring Death and went airborne.

A hundred meters up, I immediately spotted my target: a vast, gleaming square of polished alabaster just outside the city's walls. Sitting on that square was an enormous ship that resembled a cylinder of solid black metal. Rings of warbling blue energy orbited the vessel, climbing up and down its length as though powering up some alien machinery. Gathered on one end of the platform were the small, thin shapes of humanoids. Oracles, most likely.

These people and their fucking names, I inwardly raged as I swung into flight. *Ladders of Ascendence, my ass. They're called launchpads.*

Judging by the number of people clustered directly around the base of the ship, it seemed they weren't preparing to launch in the next few seconds. That was good, because I had a few words to exchange with Narbu. And maybe a few things to blow up.

The people below noticed my arrival long before I'd come within landing range. They began hurrying about, pointing and shouting as though I were a mythological beast about to rip them apart. Good. They had every reason to be afraid.

Fifty meters out, I spotted Narbu—and Tarkal at his side. Gritting my teeth, I tucked one wing and fell into a rolling descent, calling on every shred of impulse control in my body to stop myself from plowing straight through Narbu and turning him into an oily streak on the landing platform. Through some miracle, I succeeded at that. Instead of killing him with a hawk's dive, I buffeted my wings to slow myself, then dropped to the alabaster a few meters shy of my target—hard.

Several of the surrounding oracles had tensed up, hands raised as though in preparation of violence, but Narbu dismissed them with a shake of his head.

"You're not taking him," I hissed.

Narbu just stared back at me, his mechanical frame catching the sunlight and glinting just as much as the alabaster beneath us. "I have nothing to say to you. This is between the royal blood and the oracles."

The boy, for his part, just looked between us with wide eyes. He didn't seem particularly happy to be standing there, awaiting his exile to a barren world, but he also gave no indication he planned to break his composure or come to my side, even when I beckoned.

"Leave him be," Narbu said. "His mind is defiled, and we will cure it . . . before anyone *else* is harmed."

At those final words, Tarkal glanced away from me with a crestfallen look. It was clear he blamed himself for what had happened to the child. That he truly saw himself as evil.

"If you want him, you'll need to kill me," I said.

Narbu lifted his chin, considering my point, then said something hushed to the boy. After a moment's hesitation, the boy nodded and began shuffling toward the vessel's boarding ramp. A pair of oracles moved to escort him.

"There," Narbu said coldly. "Now we can speak with privacy."

I kept my eyes trained on the boy's receding form, which now shimmered like a mirage due to the alabaster's heat. "You're *not* taking him. I know what you are. What those seeds have done to your mind."

"You're nothing but an animal, Beja. A blind, stupid animal who sticks its nose where it is not warranted." He shook his head. "Already, you've cost the empress one child. Would you ask her to sacrifice both? What, then, will remain of the emperor's progeny?"

"What did you do to the child?"

His carbon-studded eyes narrowed. "*I* did nothing. This was the consequence of the fabrications you shared with the empress. Just as I said, there is no cure for the boy's defilement among the outlying lands. We will provide it, and the empire will thrive."

"You're wrong."

"History will decide such matters."

I stepped forward and drew my hammer. "No. *I'll* decide them."

Despite the lack of articulation on Narbu's face, I swore he smiled at me. "Do you really think this can be undone through violence, Beja? There is a course to all things. A time and place. Radiant wisdom would not deceive us."

"Yeah, well, just wait a few thousand years. Then we'll talk."

I'd tossed that out as a thoughtless zinger, but something about it lingered in Narbu. He stood just as straight and dignified as before, but now there was a shadow in him. A gnawing, vicious shadow.

He moved closer, stopping a mere two or three paces away. His voice took on an edge that chilled me to my core. "If you slay me and return the boy to the empress, you have no chance of finishing this."

"Finishing what?"

"You know exactly what I mean." Now the shadow left him, and I felt it creeping through my own flesh. His eyes became daggers that pierced straight through the air between us—between the comfortable veil provided by the Godmaker, even. "I see you, Dak Korasa. I see the machinations churning in your head. Restrain yourself and calm your mind, or you will *never* see the end of things. Some blood is fated to be spilled. If you can grasp this—if you can stay your hand and wait for the sap of wisdom to flow of its own accord—you will learn what you seek."

For the first time, I felt true, genuine danger inside this simulated experience. I shrank back a step, trying to figure out what the hell had just happened.

"Did you just . . . ?" I couldn't even finish the sentence. "Is that you, Narbu? Are you—"

In an instant, the sharp prescience that had inhabited the oracle's eyes vanished. Replacing it was the same haughty, arrogant disposition I'd seen in the simulation's version of him.

"Return to the empress, Beja," he said, crossing his arms as though nothing strange had happened. Almost as though he'd been reset with the flip of a switch. "When the boy's defilement is cured, there will be no need for such hostilities. Attend to your duties, as I shall attend to mine."

He then turned and began heading toward the ship, not a care in the world. All I could do was watch him and fumble with slipping the hammer back into my belt. With a head empty of everything aside from vague, creeping unease, I finally headed back to the city on foot. I was too shaken to even consider flying. At some point in my walk, while crossing the ocher soil beyond the alabaster landing pad, I heard the engines throttle on with a static thrum. The vessel's long shadow swept over me, and soon it was just a fading buzz in the atmosphere . . . then nothing at all.

My feet moved mechanically, driven by something other than my conscious will. He'd seen me. Really *seen* me. Not as a beja, but as Dak Korasa. Somehow, some way, he had peered beyond the veil of the Godmaker. The thought was as absurd as it was chilling. These people weren't just globs of organic matter and energy—not all of them, anyway. There was living, pulsing consciousness in this domain . . . even if I didn't know who it belonged to.

This last point stayed with me during my long, silent trek. The more I reflected on it, the less certain I was that the "presence" had been Narbu. After all, back on the mountaintop, both he and the Unmade had been certain that his fate was a grisly one. Narbu's mindstream was probably in that twisted dimension, not inside the Godmaker.

If that was the case, however, it birthed even more questions. Who or what had spoken to me? What did they know about this entire affair? More importantly, what did they know about what I was seeking?

I didn't know, and I had no idea where to dig for answers. My only course was to do as I'd been instructed: settle back and do nothing. It hurt like hell, especially given the empress's woes, but I didn't have another choice. Just like the presence had said, I needed to wait . . . supposedly for the "sap of wisdom" to flow. Whatever the hell that meant.

What I did know, unfortunately, was that the next few days wouldn't be easy. I was many things—a clone, a killer, and a Purifier—but not a source of comfort. Dealing with the empress's shattered spirit would likely be the hardest battle I'd ever fought.

Days passed without weight or meaning, each one bleeding into the next like overlapping shadows. I spent most of my time by the empress's side, occasionally venturing to speak with her but receiving nothing in return. Through it all, she remained in the same bed with the same bloody sheets, only rising at the suggestion of her servants to receive a bath or eat a small meal. Sometimes, in the deep hours of night, I'd wake to the sound of her whimpering in her sleep, only to find her holding the bloodied sheets to her chest as though they were a child.

Just as I'd predicted, it was a grueling time. One I almost wished I could've skipped through the use of whatever time dilation had overtaken me in my first Godmaker experience. That wasn't an option here, though. I just had to sit . . . and listen . . . and wait, all the while enduring the guilt of knowing what I had—or rather, hadn't—done to bring this about.

The worst part had nothing to do with the tedium or the empress's heartache, however. In fact, it was the worst precisely because it hadn't come yet. Sooner or later, Narbu's vessel would return and bring the news that was fated to shatter the remnants of the empress's mind, and there was nothing I could do about it. In fact, perhaps more tragically, I didn't *want* to stop it. My own intuition, as well as the presence within the God-maker, were certain that this needed to happen. This was the very moment I'd been waiting for since I entered the chamber.

That didn't make any of it easier, of course. If anything, the inevitability of it all only strained my heart further. I couldn't help but feel I was one of the many butchers involved in the empress's life.

About a week after Narbu's departure, I was awoken by the whiplike crack of a vessel reentering the atmosphere. The narrow windows lining the upper crest of the royal chambers flashed from black to blue as concentrated energy rippled through the clouds.

To my surprise, the empress rose before I did. She wandered over to her balcony and stood against the railing, blending in with the murky night.

I followed her with great concern, praying she wouldn't preemptively jump. Thankfully, she did no such thing. She was just there to watch. See, if you leaned over the railing and strained your eyes, you could just make out the pale square of the Ladders of Ascendence. By the time I'd joined her, the vessel was already touching down with impossible grace. Its orbiting rings cycled faster and faster as the base neared the landing platform, rising to a crescendo at the very moment of impact. After a few brief, tinny whines, the engines powered down, and the ship's lights winked out.

I looked over at the empress, but there was nothing to see. Her stare was as vacuous as ever, trained on the ship as though it were a dead sea creature that had washed ashore.

After far too long for my nerves to handle, the boarding ramp slid down to the landing pad and the doors rose. Framed in the ship's interior lights was a group of oracles with their hoods raised.

The empress stared at the procession as they came down the ramp. Judging by the microtwitches in her pupils, her vision was probably better than mine. Good enough to know who was and wasn't among the oracles' ranks, that is.

When the group made it out onto the landing pad itself, the empress's brows relaxed as though she'd spotted what she came for. Her eyes lost whatever small, budding spark of interest had taken refuge there. She glanced my way, and despite seeming to have just noticed me, there wasn't a hint of surprise, or affection, or even disdain. Without so much as a blink, she turned away and walked back to her bed, then lay down again.

It was time for the long, horrible task of waiting for melancholy to turn to madness.

20

Empress Jalisa Multheri Nodran drew the obsidian dagger across her left forearm, leaving a thin, twinkling line of blood in the candlelight. She set the blade down on the wicker mat, extended both arms to her sides, and smiled in ecstasy as her ritualists slathered the wound in a mixture of honey and ash. She didn't cry out, just as she hadn't cried out during the preceding sixty-four cuts.

All across the small, hazy chamber, ritualists draped in furs and scaled hides pressed their lips to flutes of carved bone. Their collective breaths filled the gloom with a deep, echoing call reminiscent of an entire herd crying out at their own slaughter.

On either side of the mat on which I knelt, heavy drums pounded and herbs blackened in small, rusty dishes. The air was practically boiling, and sweat ran in itchy streaks down my naked back. Somewhere in the rear of the chamber, attendants dunked bushy fronds into holy water and shook them over braziers, intermittently dousing me with blasts of steam.

"With this pain, reach across the divide," the empress shouted, furiously rubbing every patch of flesh on her exposed body to smear the ash-honey-blood pulp. "With this agony, know the furor of my heart! Gaze into the yearning of this mind!"

I just kept my gaze low, having learned by now that I could not stop her.

At least we were well beyond the melancholy phase.

This ritual was the latest in a long, outlandish series that had been going on for nearly a month. This was the part of my past life that most closely aligned with Narbu's series of events. The empress had indeed buried herself in the lexicon of dead, heretical practices, even going so far as to deny the oracles entrance to the palace. From the atrium to her royal chambers, every open space had been converted into a ground of dark magic. Silk ribbons had been replaced by streamers of dried flesh and berries; cushions had been tossed out in favor of nail-studded prayer mats; fruit bowls had been displaced by mounds of raw meat dedicated to entities beyond my understanding.

Despite acknowledging the importance and even necessity of this phase in the empress's life, it wasn't easy to witness. All I could do was bite my tongue and obey her commands each time a ritualist fetched a new grimoire or scroll from the palace's forbidden vaults. Many of these texts had been looted by the royal "occupational peacekeepers" during my war campaign, though I hadn't understood their importance at the time, given the overwhelming assortment of local languages and dialects in which they'd been written.

There *was* something new with this ritual, however. Seated around the empress and swaying in private trances were members of Izamem's shamanic species. They'd been captured and brought here on the empress's orders, and although nobody else sensed it—willful ignorance, maybe—it was all too clear that they got a sick sense of delight from being here. This was their quiet victory lap . . . and I couldn't say a damn thing about it.

Some blood is fated to be spilled.

Those words, along with the uncanny gaze of Narbu's possessing presence, had haunted me every night in my dreams. Although I couldn't prove it, I was certain that presence still lingered in every nook and cranny of the Godmaker. It certainly lingered in nightmares. For the past few days, I'd dreamed of squirming, shadowy figures lurking just outside the edges of my perception. They constantly grew closer, louder.

My waking nightmares, however, all took place in this chamber—a dead, decrepit place buried beneath the royal palace.

Even as I watched the empress, she swayed unsteadily, the honeyed blood and sweat dribbling off her hands in dark ribbons. She couldn't take much more. Then again, that was the whole point of these rituals. According to the alien shamans, gnosis—a direct, blinding breakthrough of wisdom—only occurred when the mind began to detach from the body. One way to achieve this was through "sacraments," in the form of psychedelic plants, which had been the monks' favored method. The trouble was that she'd already tried (and overdosed on) every type of sacrament known to the empire. That left the second method of insight, which was seldom used by the oracles but praised among the cultures I'd conquered.

Agony.

If one sufficiently tortured the body, there was a point at which consciousness retracted into itself and left the pain behind. That was the *idea*, anyway. Thus far, the empress hadn't gained anything except deeper, more stubborn madness. Outside her daily rituals, which now occupied more than half her time, she did little more than resting in bed and murmuring to herself. It seemed more likely for these exploits to end in death than a profound awakening.

Right on cue, the empress's face slackened, and she toppled forward in a limp heap. The muscles across her emaciated back twitched violently.

Rather than helping her, the ritualists and shamans intensified their routines. The drums beat louder, the flutes began shrieking, and steam billowed across the chamber as though forming a bridge to some new and hellish world. According to the forbidden texts, this was the crucial moment. The fleeting opportunity for one's mind to access that which they sought. The heat, clamor, and chanting all mingled and rose to an absurd boiling point.

My eyes never strayed from the empress, however. By now, I'd grown perceptive to the subtle shifts in her body. I could tell the difference between mild unconsciousness and the precipice of death. On this particular occasion, it leaned toward the latter. The instant her back ceased its spasms and relaxed, further folding her over, I leaped to my feet and used Telekinesis to rip the flutes straight out of the shamans' mouths.

The abrupt shift in volume brought an end to the rest of the madness. One by one, the ritual's participants slowed and finally abandoned their tasks. It wasn't the first time I'd done this—far from it, actually. This being the case, everyone around me knew precisely what I expected. The two attendants posted at the rear popped the seals on the doors and threw them open, flooding the chamber with comparatively cool air and torchlight. Next, the ritualists with the drums moved to the empress's side, eased her up, and began carrying her out into the corridor.

Within five minutes, the candles were extinguished, the blood was mopped up, and the grimoire was wrapped in its ceremonial leather. The attendants and ritualists had all gone to help the empress recover, while I remained with my two "friends."

The shamans were coy, slimy fellows, which further convinced me that being a cryptic ass was just the nature of their species. From what I knew, both of them had been wrangled up from a temple complex in the northeastern highlands. They *claimed* they'd never had any direct contact with the blood-flower shaman I killed at the compound, but I hadn't accepted that at face value. Like I said, they were slimy. They knew how to get under your skin but also remain as cordial and outwardly innocent as possible to avoid having their faces smashed in.

Well, enough of that. I'd given them two full weeks to prove they were different from their kin, offering them free rein when it came to the arrangement and performance of cultic rituals. Hell, I'd even treated them as though they were possible allies. This *was* their traditional magic, after all, and I'd hoped to have them on our side as facilitators—until the empress learned what we needed, at least.

As I mentioned, though, they weren't here to help. They were here to drag their feet, to inflict pain, to misdirect, to placate. In short, to do anything *except* get us closer to the goal. Most of the others, including the empress, were blind to this interference.

Unfortunately for them, I was not.

"We're going to play a game," I said quietly, shutting the door with a gentle backward kick and plunging us all into darkness. After flicking on Nocturnal and studying their eyes, which glowed like melted wax in my altered vision, I got the sense they didn't like where this was going. "You're going to tell me the *real* ritual she needs, and in exchange, you live. If you decide to fuck with me, I'll take you each apart . . . one centimeter at a time."

In truth, I was half bluffing here. I had no desire to torture people, much less in a still-superheated room that was equally unpleasant for *me* to be in. What can I say, though? I was out of options. All I had was my intuition, and in this case, my intuition told me that the beja—past-life me, that is—had stepped in and handled business with these clowns. It wasn't just a matter of urgency, either. I had a nagging feeling that, if left unchecked, these shamans would guide the empress down a long, brutal road that ended in death. It was time for some course correction.

The shamans exchanged obvious, cheeky glances, and then the one on the left stared me down with a slender grin. "Why do you threaten to open our flesh, Beja? You believe *we* are the keepers of the profound wisdom?"

"The thieves have forgotten the treasures they stole," the right-hand one growled.

"They are blind. Swimming in oceans of their own filth."

"Defiled."

"Foolish."

Back and forth the two of them went, rattling off enigmatic phrases as though they meant a damn thing to me.

"All right, *enough*," I hissed. "What do you mean by *thieves*?"

"You have forgotten the sacred verses of your people," the shaman to the right said.

The left one nodded. "Poisoned by the lies of the occupiers."

"The demons."

"The foul ones."

Rather than interrupting them again, I flipped on Telekinesis and took mental hold of the drawstrings within their robes. The slightest nudge of intention was all I needed to turn those drawstrings into miniature nooses. The shamans sputtered and twisted as I pulled upward, keeping them just low enough to ensure they couldn't fully stand on their tentacles.

After half a minute of this, I released the hold and let them flop back down. "Are you ready to talk like normal people yet?"

The one on the right clawed at his throat, wild eyes boring into me. "The Addled Regent seeks what is already possessed."

"Just out of reach," the left-hand shaman continued, coughing all the while.

"Held in the clutches of the bloodless deceivers."

"The engineers of chaos."

"Butchers of the mind."

My mind did something like a double take, circling back to a few words that ordinarily would've meant nothing to me. Words that had, at first, registered as little more than the shamans' ongoing charade. Then it hit me.

The Addled Regent.

In an instant, I yanked them both up to stop the verbal flood. As they hung there, twice as pissed off and noisy as before, I recalled the words of the ghostly monk that had inhabited the junnara-gol's purgatory.

First, they end the life of the Duplicitous Contender. Then they slay the Addled Regent. Finally, they destroy the Sun Eater. With each victory, the power of the Purified One increases. Their mind gains insights into the Unmade's nature.

All thoughts vanished, leaving a void that was quickly filled by dread. If I *was* following a fated path, it meant I was also fated to kill those targets . . . in that order. Was the empress truly the Addled Regent? As of this moment, she certainly aligned with that description. But that couldn't be. What about the Duplicitous Contender? My blood ran cold as I considered the possibility that I'd done things out of order. That I'd ignored Modri's warnings about Rogaji. Had I been expected to kill her before entering the Godmaker?

That was a big enough issue, but it still didn't address the regent part. Whether or not I'd skipped a step, it was beginning to look like the empress was on the chopping block. How, why, or when, I couldn't say, but the conclusion was all the same: If I wanted to end this, I needed to spill her blood. There was no other interpretation.

I unceremoniously cut the Telekinesis and let the shamans plop down again, at which point they unleashed a barrage of curses and hateful gestures.

"Settle down," I said, lifting my hand to signal that I could do the same trick again . . . and again . . . and again. That did the trick. "I want clear answers. No more language games. Who holds what?"

"Oracles," the shaman on the left said, sputtering. "The defiled oracles hold that which was our birthright."

"The shining gem of our people," the right-hand one added.

Before they could fall into another nonsensical exchange, I lifted the same shaman who'd just spoken, using Telekinesis.

Then I turned my glare on the one still sitting. "*Talk.*"

"The oracles pilfered our wisdom," the shaman barked. "They imprisoned it. Darkened it. Held it in their thieving little palms!"

"What wisdom are you talking about?"

"The Wellspring!"

I cocked a brow. "What did you just say?"

"Well . . . spring."

Mention of that strange, presumably dead hive mind immediately set off my internal alarms. The monks had all practically salivated upon hearing the word, yet thus far, despite all the times Scryer Narbu had mentioned it in his monologue on the mountaintop, there'd been no sign of any Wellspring in the empire. Weirder still, the way it had been described made me think it was closer to an immaterial concept or dimensional portal than a physical object. That wasn't the case here. If the shamans were telling the truth, it *was* real, and it *was* here.

"They *stole* the Wellspring from you?" I asked.

"From *us*," the shaman whispered. "It was taken . . . hidden . . . denied to its shepherds. The betrayers will not loosen its chains. They obscure its brilliance."

After glancing at the dangling shaman to ensure he was still alive, I turned my attention back to his comrade. "You're saying the empress needs the Wellspring to learn the ritual."

"Yes, Beja."

"And the oracles know that, but they're hiding it from her."

"Yes!"

"So I need to go have a talk with them."

"Yes!"

Now there was real glee on the shaman's face. Rising bloodlust at the mere idea of me wreaking unholy vengeance on the machines.

Sighing, I dropped the other shaman and let him roll back to a sitting position.

"You've both been very helpful," I said, my gaze swiveling between them. "That being said, you'd better hope the oracles have what I need. Because if not, I don't need *you* anymore. And that would not be good for your life expectancies."

Wisely enough, the pair of jokesters held their comments and settled for shaky nods. That was probably the best I'd get out of them.

Ten minutes later, I was pushing my way past the royal chamber's guard duo, my mind a haze of violent thoughts. Just how deep did this corruption run? The empress had mentioned her suspicions about the oracles and their silent transfer of power, but she'd never mentioned a word about their "ownership" of the goddamn Wellspring. From the sound of it, they'd been relying on their ill-gotten treasure for a long, long time, extracting its wisdom yet keeping it all to themselves.

Ordinarily, I'd have thought this version of events was just fiction conjured up by shamans eager to send me into a rage, but this was different. With my own eyes, I'd seen the whirling blue vortex that dominated the oracular chambers. I'd felt the immense energy pouring out of it. That same vortex now appeared to be nothing but the tip of a larger, more impressive iceberg that had been hidden in the chambers' depths.

I moved through doorway after doorway, unsure of how to broach this with the empress. Unsure of what to think, even. She clearly knew about the oracles' divine methods of perception—it had been discussed several times, not to mention its starring role in the title of the council's meeting area—but perhaps she didn't know *everything* about how they accessed their visions. Was it possible that the oracles were lying to everybody, passing off the blue vortex as the genuine article itself? If so, what was the reason behind it? What influence could it exert that was powerful enough to challenge their rank?

I didn't know, but I would find out.

When I entered the royal chambers themselves, the empress was in her customary position: lying in the bed with her eyes fluttering, a damp cloth on her forehead and attendants gathered all around. Bloody, ash-smeared rags had been piled high on a nearby platter.

"Everybody, out," I commanded as I went to her side.

Several attendants looked up at me with concern, but none were bold enough to say a word against my order. After setting aside their sponges and bandages and salves, they bowed their heads and filed out through the servants' door.

I knelt down beside the empress and took her hand in mine. "Empress, there's something I need to tell you."

At first, she remained as still as a corpse. Then I felt the subtle shift of muscles in her hand, and her bloodshot eyes rolled toward me. "Oh, Beja . . . you're here."

"I need you to stay awake for this. It's important."

She just stared at me, her soft smile indicating her mind was nowhere to be found in this dimension.

"What do you know about the Wellspring?" I asked.

"Wellspring," she said, tasting the word. "Wellspring . . . Wellspring . . ."

"Empress, please."

I squeezed her hand; a tremor of life passed through her gaze.

To my amazement, she began squirming up in her bed, obviously try-ing to shake some consciousness back into herself. Her cracked lips trem-bled as she said, "What is . . . a Wellspring?"

"I'll show you." Rising, I leaned over her and tenderly pulled her across my shoulder. To my relief, the attendants had given her the dignity of cloth wrappings. "You might not like what I have to do, but it's for the good of us both. Do you understand?"

Her frail, bruised fingers swept through my hair like a child stroking a pet's fur. "I have always trusted you, Beja," she whispered hoarsely. "I always shall."

I'd expected my empress-over-the-shoulder appearance to cause a bit of commotion, but what I got was well beyond anything my imagination could produce. Just minutes after I shoved the guards aside and headed into the streets, hell-bent on the oracular chambers, crowds formed and began shrieking like banshees. People fell to their knees by the dozen, clawing at their own faces or calling out for divine aid.

Given my status as the empire's hired killer, nobody dared to get close, but it was obvious that a good number of civilians wanted to skin me alive. I understood. These people hadn't seen the empress's true state for several weeks—an attempt to keep things kosher, I wagered—and as such, they were unprepared for her bleeding, babbling, scar-covered form. It didn't help that we were still technically in an unprecedented war with the very same species that had raised me. In their eyes, I was probably the same vile, double-agent beja the shamans proclaimed me to be. More to the point, I looked as though I were responsible for the empress's wounds, both physical and mental. Most of the crowd perceived my actions as those of a conqueror showing off their victim.

Of course, I was too intent on tearing Narbu's limbs off to stop and explain myself to these people. What could I even say? *Don't worry—she did this to herself?* Or how about, *We're just on our way to slaughter your precious oracles and learn a death-defying ritual?* Yeah, no. Nothing would go over well at this point.

By the time I came within sight of the doors to the oracular chambers, the crowd had turned into something of a funerary procession. They strode behind me, weeping and screeching and pounding the tiled roads, occasionally growing bold enough to ineffectually throw a wicker basket over my head. If anything, they just made me more annoyed. More pissed off.

Luckily, I had a building full of simulated oracles ready to soak up my wrath.

Several of those oracles prowled around the gates, seemingly drawn out by the din in the streets. As I approached them, the foremost oracle—marked by a robe with a purple sash—raised a hand, urging me to stop.

I didn't.

"Remain rooted where you stand, Beja," the oracle called, their high yet clear voice indicating this had likely been a woman prior to their conversion into a machine. "This sanctum is guarded by wards your mind cannot grasp. No defilement may enter."

I readjusted the empress, then looked at the handful of oracles one by one. "You're kidding, right?"

"We shall not move. Oracle Narbu has forbidden your wicked presence from proceeding."

"Funny you should say that. Narbu's the one I'm looking for."

The oracles shared looks that, due to their mechanical nature, were completely unreadable to me. Then, as though coming to some silent conclusion, the one with the purple sash advanced a step.

"Turn back, Beja, or be torn apart by the brilliance of primordial radiance," she called.

"Primordial radiance does sound frightening," I said, nodding, "but not quite as frightening as Telekinesis."

With little more than a raised hand and a dash of focus, I seized hold of the alloy chassis that contained the oracle's still-organic brain. She stared at me in confusion, but only until I started squeezing. Like a python of the mind, I tightened my grasp around the torso itself, ratcheting up the tension until the oracle began screaming through her vocalizers. Panels quivered and buckled, and soon rivets were popping free, clinking against the stone below.

The crowd initially broke out in screams, but all that ended when I lifted the oracle several meters off the ground. A deathly stillness settled across the square. Even the woman's fellow oracles shrank back with their heads bowed low.

Satisfied I'd made my point, I tossed the oracle to the side. She landed hard and slid to a stop, trembling, leaking small pools of coolant that soaked into her robes. She would live, I guessed, but she wouldn't be fighting me off anytime soon.

"If all *that* is done, I'd like to enter now," I said to the ones left standing. "Oracle Narbu has a lot to answer for."

21

Moving down the central aisle of the oracular chambers, I picked up on long, resonant echoes that were a perfect match for what I'd heard on the monks' world. The nearer I drew to the inner sanctum, the louder it became. Soon it was a thrum deep in my rib cage. A dirge for a dying world. The origin was just ahead, behind the thick barrier that concealed the Wellspring's vortex.

When I threw those doors open, the sound hit me like a living wall. Hundreds of oracles had gathered in the vortex's light, arranged in the same concentric circles they'd employ farther down the line of history. As one, they raised their hands, let out a harmonized *auuuuum*, and then prostrated themselves. The cycle continued in ten-second intervals.

"Isn't it beautiful?" the empress whispered in my ear, giggling. "Their sounds take refuge in my weary bones, Beja. They congregate."

Rolling my eyes, I headed deeper into the madness.

A lone figure stood directly ahead of me, arms splayed out as they soaked up the vortex's energy. Their shadow stretched back toward me like a black road. It didn't take much thinking to suss out the identity of that figure.

"Narbu," I shouted, bringing an immediate end to the oracles' chanting. "Turn around and face me with dignity."

After a long, awkward period of basking in the blue light, Narbu did indeed turn around and face me.

"Dignity?" he called over the vortex's *whump-whump-whumps*. "You dare to violate this hallowed ground with harm, then speak of dignity? Only an animal could do such a thing."

I advanced in the oracle's shadow, all the while keeping the empress balanced and angled away from the blinding light. "At least I'm brave enough to do my harm in the open."

"You know nothing about what you proclaim. You have brought a reckoning upon this empire. Upon wisdom in all corners of existence."

"You *really* don't want to go down that road."

He gave me a strange look. "We acted on the counsel of a force beyond your comprehension. You, in turn, have fed the flames of the empress's defilement. You have broken her mind. Whatever follows this moment is your karmic fruit."

"Funny you should say that . . . when you're hiding the answers to her problem."

"Do not mince your words, Beja."

"You've lied to these people," I said, sweeping my hand across the assembly of oracles. "You've lied to your own citizens. To your own empress."

"What are you—?" Narbu stopped, then moved closer to meet me in the middle. When he was just a few paces away, his eyes took on a calculating sheen. "Ah, I see now. You've learned of what we have endeavored to protect for so long."

"That's right. The Wellspring."

"Such a name is too pure to be *defiled* by your mouth," he said dispassionately. "You're just as I have always said, Beja . . . an animal incapable of understanding that which is proper. You allow your emotions to dictate every twitch of your nerves."

Much as I wanted to drop the ultimate bomb by informing him of the Wellspring's fate—that is, being devoured by the Unmade—I restrained myself. Maybe he was correct in saying that I'd let my emotions run wild. I was here to get information and get out; anything more was purely a display of pride.

This being the case, I settled my voice and met his gaze squarely. "I know that the Wellspring contains what the empress needs. If you refuse to show it to me, I'll rip the floor apart by myself. We both know I could do that easily."

"Yes, you could." Narbu studied me for several seconds, and although it may have been my imagination, I swore I detected something new in him. Something . . . curious. "I do not wish to see harm come to any who abide here. If it will stay your hand, I am willing to show you what you seek."

I narrowed my eyes. "What's the catch?"

"The empress must remain here."

"Not a chance."

"I have no intentions of deceiving you," Narbu said, and his voice was genuine enough to make me believe that. "As you yourself have pointed out, we are incapable of harming you."

"The empress isn't so indestructible."

"No, but she is also a being of tremendous potential. To strike her down—even to harm a pore of her flesh—would be a sin worthy of rebirth in the lowest hells. Then again, I should not be so surprised that a beast would fear innocent minds. You exist in a world of blood and meat. In your deluded perception, all faces are those of monsters."

Despite practically seething with rage at Narbu's continued hypocrisy, I gave a stiff nod and eased the empress down from my shoulder. When she touched the floor, she looked up at me in obvious confusion, but I was quick to still her with a smile and a soft kiss to her forehead. It didn't take long for her to begin gazing into the burning core of the vortex, lost to its radiance.

"All right," I said to Narbu. "Now show me what I came for."

The process of opening the descending staircase was absurdly complicated, ritualized, and downright stupid from an engineering perspective, so I'll spare you the novel-length description. Suffice it to say, it consisted of many levers, puzzle-like sliding grids, illuminated glyphs, and pulleys. If we're being honest, the sheer complexity of the process made me doubt I could've accessed it on my own, no matter how strong I was. My only path would've likely been to use Shock and Awe to blow open the floor panels, but that wasn't very palatable, either—primarily because it would've meant the loss of a limb, but secondly because it might've destroyed the Wellspring itself.

However, that didn't mean Shock and Awe wasn't useful in this situation. Just after Narbu finished gaining access to the stairwell, which looped down in a corkscrew shape beneath the vortex, I used the very tip of my index finger to create a deafening blast . . . which accidentally caved in part of the ceiling. Overkill? Probably. A good way to ensure the oracles didn't fuck around and seal me inside after I descended? Absolutely. No matter how much you shed your fear of death, you'll still be somewhat concerned about a madman with nuclear weapons camped out beneath you.

Just before we descended, Narbu had one of his students bring us a pair of boxy lanterns with small, bright cores of golden energy pulsing within.

We moved down the steps in awkward silence. Just five meters down, the air changed drastically, shedding the warmth of the surface in favor of the cold, windless void found in places abandoned to time. Before long, there were no traces of the vortex's presence; its turbine-like *whooshes* were gradually replaced by a deeper, more threatening sound that reminded me of a caged predator.

"So, what was the endgame?" I asked as we headed lower.

Narbu turned back, seemingly surprised I'd spoken. "What are you referring to?"

"I had a word with some of the enemy shamans," I explained. "They said you stole the Wellspring from them and kept it locked up. Why the secrecy?"

"So many falsehoods . . . " Narbu muttered. "The Wellspring never belonged to them, Beja. It formed of its own accord. Their defiled minds could not accept that it was fated for a higher purpose."

"Who are you to judge how they ought to have used it?"

"They sought to manipulate reality. They wished to mold it into their sick, cruel vision. It is always the duty of the just to deprive evil of its instruments."

"All right, fine," I said, sighing. "Let's say 'my people' were in it for the wrong reasons, and you were in it for the right ones. Why keep it hidden from the royal family?"

Narbu let out a sputtering sound—presumably a laugh. "You believe we hid it from them?"

"You did."

"How could that be, when it was this empire's route to flourishing?"

I lowered my lantern to get a better look at his eyes. "What are you saying? You used it without them knowing about it?"

"Such foolish words." Narbu kept moving farther down, and I followed. "Perhaps I should not judge an animal by its cries. To understand the history of the Wellspring—indeed, to understand why the empress should not know of its presence—you must first understand the history of this empire."

"I've read it. All of it."

"You cannot read that which has been erased from time."

At that moment, our lanterns' collective glow began etching strange shapes in the smooth rock wall to our left. Moving closer, then stepping back, it was revealed to be a massive depiction of a humanoid. A Suharkayan, to be precise. Unlike all the Suharkayans I'd seen, however, this one featured a long, pointed beard . . . and a sword in each hand. The image was roughly two-dimensional, reminiscent of the ancient artwork found in pretechnological warrior cultures—that is, full of small, time-intensive details, but lacking in any real emotion or realism.

Thousands of small oracles, scaled down to the level of ants, knelt down in wavelike rows around the central figure. They appeared to be worshipping him as he presided over the corpse of a shaman. Well, a being from the shamanic species, anyway. A member of Izamem's people. Only then did I realize he was standing atop a mound of similar bodies, their blood forming a ritual pool rendered in glimmering black stone.

Overhead, a comet streaked through the sky, leaving dark, spiraling trails . . .

"A Suharkayan killing someone," I said, whistling. "That's new."

Narbu glared at me, then looked back at the image with plain reverence. "This is Sagarika Tabir, First of His Name, Devourer of the Living. The first emperor of the Suharkayan Empire."

"A conqueror."

"Yes, a conqueror." Narbu ran his metal fingers across the etching, producing a horrible scraping noise. "Armed with the Great Maker's gifts, he brought order to a world of chaos and despair. He tamed the animals that had preyed upon minds since beginningless time."

"He exterminated my people and took their artifacts."

"You judge what you cannot understand," Narbu whispered. "He may have brought death to our world, but it was death in service of life. Of rebirth. He was a blazing fire that consumed the dead wood to make room for saplings."

"Why the hell is he here, then? I thought this place was all about nonviolence. Seems more fitting to keep his image in the palace."

"Because he recovered the Wellspring," Narbu said, indicating the comet in the etching.

"Stole it."

"Your perception does not change the way of things," Narbu explained calmly. "The Wellspring crashed down from the heavens—a gift from higher planes—only to be seized by those who reached it before us. It was never meant for them, and yet they hoarded its wisdom. Only the emperor understood the great power contained within the Wellspring. He created our order to protect it . . . to preserve it . . . to use it for matters of guidance. Through the Wellspring's wisdom, he fostered a world without defilement. We were tasked with ensuring it continued to advance this goal."

"Okay . . . "

"He also stated, however, that a time would come in which our leaders would grow spoiled by their birth. They would forget the great law of balance. For all times of purity, there are times of defilement. Times when cruelty must be used to prevent greater cruelty."

"Ironic, don't you think?" I said, gesturing to myself.

Narbu ignored that little jab. "It only took three generations of blood-less rulers to forget their place. They knew nothing of order. Nothing of purity. Thus, it fell to our order to carry the burden they had left by the roadside."

"Meaning?"

"We could not entrust the Wellspring with the whims of capricious rulers," Narbu said. "We purged its existence from the minds of all who knew its existence. We destroyed the records of those who had recovered and safeguarded it. All we left was the energetic formation on the surface. A token gesture of our power."

"I have to admit, Narbu . . . you've got a few predictable strategies."

Again, he gave me a look that just *begged* to know what I was on about. I didn't give him that satisfaction.

"So, you've been running the empire as quasi rulers since . . . forever," I finally said.

Narbu lifted his lantern higher, staring into the bloody scene. "We have done what is needed for the stability of the teachings. Our mission is too vital to be left in the hands of those who cannot understand the face of true wisdom."

"How many times have you wiped the empress's memory?"

"None," he said. "There is no need anymore. Things have proceeded with smoothness . . . until now."

"I just don't get it. What's so dangerous about the Wellspring? If it just gives you insights into reality, shouldn't you *want* your people to access it?"

"Not everything it whispers is palatable to the mind," Narbu said darkly. "You came here because you believe the empress's solution is found within its depths. Perhaps it is. But the secrets of life and death are not meant for the masses, Beja. They can hardly understand their own consciousness. The Wellspring, in the hands of ignorant children, is a weapon. It is a risk to all of reality. Especially in its current state . . . "

His words reminded me of the strangeness of this entire journey. There was nowhere I could truly pinpoint as the beginning of the long, convo-luted steps that had birthed the Unmade. At every stage, something had gone wrong. Long-dead things had come to life. Even their miraculous Wellspring, in the end, had become a curse. Maybe he really *did* have a point.

"The first emperors and empresses understood this risk all too well," Narbu said as he guided me lower, using his lantern to expose dozens of similar etchings, all of which depicted different figures slaughtering their foes or interacting with mysterious energy.

I clicked my tongue. "Damn. How much art is down here?"

"It is not just art," Narbu said. "This place is a mausoleum for the forgotten. A final resting place for the bodies and minds of those who were stricken from the consciousness of this empire."

"You mean . . . you buried the early leaders down here?"

Narbu glanced over his shoulder at me. "They are not buried, Beja. They are slumbering. Forever carrying out their oath."

"Which is?"

"To protect the Wellspring."

"Is this some kind of curse situation?" I asked.

"Not a curse, but an anomaly. A place in which life and death are forever held in balance."

I kept glancing at the etchings as we descended, shuddering each time their dead, stony eyes made contact with mine. "If you've all gone to such lengths to keep this hidden . . . why show me? Why tell me any of this?"

"Because I have hope that your mind, defiled though it may be, is still capable of clear seeing," Narbu said. "I will reveal the Wellspring to you, but only so that you might abandon this quest and rid the empress of her delusion. Her children are no longer in this realm. They will *never* return. Not as she wishes them to be."

"I know that," I said quietly, bringing Narbu to a halt, "but this needs to happen. And I know there's *something* inside you that agrees with me."

"You always were defiant," Narbu said. "I still recall every detail of the day they brought you to the city. You were nothing but an engorged, mewling pup." He shook his head. "Even then, I saw that you could not be tamed."

"Huh?"

"You carry the defilement of those who spawned you, Beja. Your magic . . . your strength . . . your intellect . . . all that you are stands in opposition to what you were created to do."

"What are you trying to tell me?"

Narbu continued down the steps, talking as he went. "Do you really think our enemy provided the beja of their own accord? It was a demand made by Emperor Sagarika."

"To have a bodyguard?"

"No. To destroy."

I paused midstep. "Destroy what?"

"This," Narbu said, turning and gesturing at the complex around us. "The beja was not made to be loyal to those in power, but to those who labor in the shadows. To the oracles."

"Bullshit."

"You resisted your conditioning, Beja. You were a failure. A wretched, impure experiment."

"Shouldn't you be celebrating that?"

"I am not referring to the conditioning of your blighted people," he spat. "Can you not recall the long hours spent in these chambers, Beja? The days and weeks spent trying to tame your mind? You opposed me at every turn."

"That's starting to sound like a good thing," I said, rather amused at "my" past exploits. "I'm nobody's pet, Narbu."

"Ah, but that isn't true," he said coldly. "You were the beloved of young Jalisa. She admired your sharpness, your power. Your loyalty to *her*. Her father would not allow me to dispose of you like the filth you are."

I rolled my eyes. "All right, pretend I'd done what I was supposed to. What was my task?"

Again, Narbu gestured to the walls. The scenes no longer depicted emperors, but bejas. Hordes of bejas, all hunting down their foes and tearing them apart. Etchings of bloody rivers spiraled down the stone we passed. Upon reaching one etching in particular, Narbu stopped short and raised his lantern to illuminate it.

The scene depicted a beja towering over a Suharkayan, ready to crush their skull with the same golden hammer on my belt. The etching's glow suggested they'd put real Sparkseed in the grooves.

"What is this?" I asked.

"The beja's role was never to wage war on the rabble outside," Narbu said, gazing at the image longingly. "You and your ilk were created as a fail-safe. A vengeful tide that would sweep away any royals brazen enough to advance their claim on the Wellspring."

"Hold on," I said, baffled. "You're telling me that the beja were made to *kill* the royal family?"

Narbu nodded. "This system functioned without a single flaw . . . until you. How ironic, Beja, that you refuse to draw blood despite it being the foundation of your nature."

"You mean to say that I'm the first beja with a mind better than yours."

Narbu whirled on me, the anger clear in his synthetic eyes, but he was quick to settle down and angle away. "What do you know of the hammer in your hands?"

"It's a beja's hammer."

"I am referring not to the form, but to its essence."

"Sparkseed?" That earned me a strange look. "I mean, Dalaya."

Again, Narbu nodded. "And what do you know of Dalaya?"

"It's golden," I said, shrugging. "You harvest it from the minds of dying monks or something."

Rather than replying, Narbu kept heading down the steps. I followed, mildly confused, until we reached the very bottom of the chamber.

The space was enormous, and its only light came from the forest of curling tubes that snaked across the bowl-shaped ceiling. To be precise, it came from the brilliant gold fluid that filled those tubes. The network provided just enough illumination to reveal a packed-earth floor, a narrow central column covered in Sparkseed etchings, and . . . bumps on the walls.

Hundreds upon hundreds of bumps, each of them capped with some kind of valve and a plaque. It took me just a few seconds to realize what they were: tombs.

"You are mostly right about Dalaya," Narbu said, wandering toward the ominous column before us. His voice echoed around me like an ethereal guide. "However, you misunderstand one crucial aspect. Dalaya is not harvested from the dying; it is a work of alchemy."

I stared up at the pulsing tubes, transfixed. "Meaning?"

"When one full of wisdom is on the verge of death, they come here, to this place," Narbu explained. "They abide within the Wellspring until it has permeated every fiber of their form. Until their mind is replaced with its intentions. At that point, their vital essence is nothing but Dalaya."

"I . . . don't get it."

Narbu spun around and lifted his lantern. "Dalaya is the product of two things: the mind and the Wellspring's insights." He gazed skyward, eyes running over the shimmering tubes. "The Wellspring is not only a source of knowledge, Beja; it is the very tool that allowed us to reclaim our world from defilement." Before I could once again ask him to clarify, he approached me and tapped the hammer on my belt. "Dalaya is the one substance capable of destroying that which has crossed the boundaries between worlds. It is not physical, nor is it immaterial. It is the bane of that which should not exist."

Instead of pestering him with stupid follow-up questions, I put my beja brain to work and tried to make sense of what he'd explained. If I was correct, he was saying that the Suharkayans had desired the Wellspring for its ability to create Dalaya, which in turn allowed them to destroy interdimensional . . . things . . . and subjugate the entire planet.

In many ways, this process was just a more refined version of how Narbu and his monks had created Sparkseed on the fallen planet. Only instead of marinating monks in a Wellspring, they'd used their own discount-version Wellspring—the Throne of Radiance, that is—as a percolator that produced the golden stuff.

"Can it harm the Wellspring itself?" I asked, figuring that the Wellspring would also be a suitable target on account of its interdimensional origins.

Narbu looked genuinely surprised by such an astute question. "Of course. That is why it remains sealed in Dalaya . . . and why we *must* retain control of the substance. It is the only way to control the uncontrollable. Your defiled people never understood this responsibility . . . which is why they unleashed so many horrors."

Suddenly, I understood why Akasha had carried that cube—the same cube that Narbu had transformed back into my hammer. It was the one substance capable of keeping the Unmade *out*. The one thing it couldn't crack open and devour. At the same time, I also understood how Akasha had been speaking in a metaphorical yet largely incorrect sense. Her cube hadn't contained the actual minds of her people; it *was* her people. Dalaya itself—Sparkseed, in common vernacular—was nothing but minds made manifest.

I now also grasped the reason Akasha and Narbu had worked so hard to protect the cube. It wasn't *really* a living memory of her people; it was a weapon. Perhaps my *only* weapon suited for the task of killing the Unmade.

"Don't you think you've made it angry?" I asked.

Narbu stared at me. "Speak plainly."

"You've kept it caged up for thousands of years, constantly taking from it. Is it any wonder it started to spit out faulty prophecies?"

He set his lantern down. "Somehow, Beja, you see the same flaws in the Wellspring that I perceived. I saw its slow corruption, its impurity, its death. My brethren would not listen to me. They were—"

"I know," I said, groaning. "Trust me. I've heard the whole story."

"Even so, the Wellspring is our greatest treasure," he said quietly, though not without a weird, questioning look. "I do not wish to see it destroyed . . . but if you reveal it to the empress . . . if you fill her mind with its secrets . . . I ask that you destroy it."

I took one look at the column, then shrugged. "Yeah, okay. Now show me the goddamn thing."

After a few moments of hesitation, Narbu nodded and led me to what

I sought. Up close, the column turned out to be far, far wider than I'd ever expected. It was covered in glyphs and scenes so small that they had to have been done with the help of magnification. Its most striking feature, however, was the charge it gave off. Even without its blue light or rushing noise, I could feel the energy rushing through its frigid stone prison.

"I thought this was a congregation of Wayfarers," I said as I rounded the structure.

"Wayfarers?" Narbu asked.

"Never mind. You'll find out someday." I sighed. "What I mean is, I thought a Wellspring was just a term to describe a group of beings beyond physical reality."

"All beings require a medium with which to interact with a world system," Narbu explained. "The congregation of these beings is a Wellspring . . . but this, too, is one of their many faces. A manifestation of the unmanifest."

"So, the Wellspring is both the battery *and* the electricity inside it."

"It is path, conduit, and gnosis."

I had no idea what the hell he was talking about, but I was just about done with the metaphysical games anyway.

By the time I'd finished inspecting the circumference of the column, Narbu was halfway through another long, intricate sequence to unseal an obvious-looking door panel. I went to ask him how long it would take . . . at which point a series of locks clunked out of place. A spray of pressurized air coiled down as fog.

Narbu and I stepped back as the door swung out on hinges and lifted, revealing an outer core of solid Sparkseed. My skin tingled at the mere sight of it, and the taste of blood formed on my tongue.

"Are you certain you wish to see?" Narbu asked.

I nodded.

In turn, he raised his hand and began emitting some kind of telekinetic force on the Sparkseed, more or less repeating the effort needed to form a mandala.

The golden ocean flowed in strange whirls, bending back on itself, glimmering, breaking apart and reforming in jigsaw segments. Slowly, in dim patches and flashes, I saw *something* through the veil. Something moving.

In a move that defied conventional physics, that massive *thing* came leaping out of the Sparkseed in a blur of stretched limbs and condensed matter. It walked on two legs, but it was far from a humanoid. Backlit by the Wellspring's glow, I saw nothing but six bladelike arms, a pair of blazing eyes, an elaborate headdress, and a conical beard.

"What the fuck is that?" I whispered.

Narbu simply took a step back. "The price of your ambition, Beja. The same price paid by all who dared to enter this sanctum."

The creature lumbered toward me, extending its blades into a peacock-like display around itself. As it moved farther into the shadows, I saw it in all its terrible beauty. Its garb was a dead ringer for the etching of Emperor Sagarika, right down its purple-colored regalia, and yet . . . it wasn't him. It was something horrible, something mutant. Each movement had a halting, frantic quality, as though it were a machine powered by hydraulic pumps.

Mostly because it *was*. The four-meter-tall behemoth clearly had a set of gears and pistons working under its clothing, animating everything from the eyes to the blades. The slithering gold of Sparkseed pumped through small "veins" across its porcelain mask. It was a goddamn mummy.

Upon drawing my hammer, the HUD and its blue box appeared.

[NEMESIS EVENT]
Sagarika, First Protector of the Wellspring (UNKNOWN)
CALCULATING . . .
Estimated Kill Points: 1,904,600

Sighing, I turned back to Narbu. "This isn't the fight you think it is. It's annihilation."

Narbu's eyes flashed, betraying his bafflement, but I didn't give him the chance to respond. I didn't have the time for it—nor for this monstrosity.

The instant the mummy leaped at me, I raised my hand, seized hold of its body with Telekinesis, and began squeezing. Just like the oracle that had tried to stop me outside, it resisted at first, then began buckling with deep, shuddering *klonks*. Within five seconds, I'd bent the blades back, snapped them, and driven them through the machine's leaking center. After ten seconds, I was doing nothing but compacting my ball of scrap metal. As a coup de grace, I grabbed the Sparkseed within its body and tore it free, snuffing the light from its eyes.

NEMESIS ENCOUNTER SUCCESSFUL
Kills: 1
Kill Points Awarded: 1,904,600
Storehouse Time Awarded: 8 Hours

I'd expected the fight to take twice as long, given Shock and Awe posing an existential risk to the Sparkseed within the column . . . but it hadn't been my worst work. Clearing the blood from under my nose, I let the mummy's spherical corpse drop to the earth in a solid heap, then turned back to Narbu.

"No," Narbu whispered, backing up with his arms raised. "It's not—"

With one flick of my mind, I crushed both his legs. He fell to the ground in a heap, squirming and whining through his vocalizer, trying desperately to crawl away from me.

I approached him with a leisurely walk. "I just need to know something."

He just kept clawing his way back toward the steps.

Well, I put an end to that by pressing a boot down on his back panel. He went still beneath me, head buried in the dirt.

"This will sound strange, but answer me honestly," I said, squatting down. "How would one unlock a curse you put on their mind?"

Narbu craned his head to the side, then rotated it fully around, staring up at me flatly. "You will get nothing from me, betrayer."

"Listen to me. This isn't about you, or your empire, or anything else." When the defiance remained in his eyes, I changed my tack. The days of half-truths were over. "I'm from an alternate timeline, Narbu. A timeline in which *you* birthed something so horrible you couldn't stop it. You put a lock on someone's mind to separate it from their body. If you don't help me right now, right here, there's going to be a lot of death. So tell me . . . how do I unseal a mind?"

A thread of comprehension passed through his stare. "How do you know of such a ritual?"

"Did I not just say it?"

"Now it is your time for regret," Narbu said softly. "There is no solution, Beja. Such a lock is not made to be undone."

"Bullshit."

"I have no reason to deceive you. I am already dead."

"Well, you're right on that account. But if you don't tell me the truth, it won't be good for you."

Narbu's eyes locked onto mine, staring straight through me. "There . . . is . . . no . . . way."

My entire body shook with rage. All this work, and there was no route for Akasha to come home. No way to circumvent the damage this fucker had done.

"You have no idea what's coming, do you?" he managed.

I glared at him. "What?"

"At the moment of death . . . you'll have no defense. Your weapons . . . your strength . . . nothing will protect you from the winds of fate. Every drop of your tainted karma will rise and blossom . . . and you will be left in a hell beyond your imagination. The gods will *laugh* at your torment."

Before I could stop myself, I crushed his head with a blast of Telekinesis. Blood poured from my nose, mingling with the spatters of oil and other fluids.

Then I stepped back, breathless and quaking. The chamber lay still around me, thick with the presence of death.

My only comfort was the blazing barrier of Sparkseed. A barrier Narbu probably didn't think I could access without him.

I gritted my teeth and stared down at the hammer in my hands. Swirling within its structure were the minds of infinite people, some of whom had probably lived here at this moment in history. Some were Akasha's direct ancestors—the ones who'd hunted down and murdered chok'tal for a living. The latter group was the one I addressed as I bowed my head.

"Let's finish this . . . together."

22

My back was nearly broken by the time I'd finished carrying the empress down those murderous steps and into the beating heart of the chamber. Without Anima running at well over 500 percent, I'm certain it *would* have broken.

The nearer I drew to the inner core, the more the empress began to stir. Step by step, meter by meter, life returned to her tortured body. The light of consciousness filled her eyes. At five meters away, she was walking on her own, gazing wordlessly into the golden tapestry.

"Are you ready?" I asked.

She looked at me, but I could tell she didn't truly *see* me. All she saw was the light . . . and the energy it contained.

Figuring that was the most confirmation I'd get, I lifted my hand and mimicked what Narbu had done to shift the veil. Fortunately, the Sparkseed was relatively easy to mold. It seemed to engage in play with me, coiling around my touch and guiding itself as it saw fit. But damn, was it deep. The Sparkseed parted like a living sea, unveiling more and more of itself to form a glimmering, narrow canyon. To my relief, nothing else came popping out, even as we reached the four-meter mark. It was just slow, nosebleed-inducing work.

Then, finally, something shifted. The last membrane of Sparkseed hissed inward, lost to a writhing yet indescribable center. Literally indescribable. As of the time of writing this, my mind can recall nothing of its true form. When I glanced sidelong, however, I was able to discern rainbow-shaded motes of light drifting toward us, then dispersing. Its ambient light registered as something of a soap bubble.

The empress's stare met mine, and I nodded.

She didn't hesitate to begin wandering forth on thin, bleeding legs, running a hand along the Sparkseed as she went. Before long, and seemingly in an instant, I lost sight of her. Phantom traces of a humanoid shape strobed up and down the tunnel, as though she'd slipped through a hole in time itself.

Seconds went by, then minutes. Through it all, I just sat in front of the doorway, staring into that void I cannot recall. If I thought anything during this period, it was erased from my mind.

The next memory I have is of her emergence. After how long, I can't say. All I know is that she came striding toward me, her eyes resolute and posture so straight it gave me flashbacks to the mummy.

I scrambled up onto my feet. "Did it—"

She pressed a finger to my lips, then gave a soft, sad smile. "The cost is too great, Beja."

"*What?*"

"It demands a sacrifice I cannot ask you to make."

"Empress, no. Whatever it is, we'll do it. You have to."

She let her smile deepen. "But I don't want to."

"Just tell me what you need, and we'll figure it out."

"Death," she said softly. "It demands death."

"I've dealt with plenty of that."

She stepped back and studied me from head to toe. The sadness, which had formerly been balanced by something sweet, now soured on her face into outright despair. "It's more than that, Beja. The death of a mind. Its imprisonment."

"I don't unders—"

"I know," she said, nodding fervently. "I know you don't. Nobody does. Nobody but us. I hold the keys to life and death, Beja. I have seen everything."

"So, what is it?"

"One mind for another," she said breathlessly. "To recover my son's being, you must descend into the darkness. Into the deepest hells."

"I'll have him back in a snap."

"Listen to me," she said, suddenly furious. Her voice exploded through the chamber. "If this exchange is made . . . if the veils of reality are breached . . . you will be killed here and now. Your mind will sink to depths you cannot fathom, and you will not return. I cannot ask that of you."

"But if we just need *someone's* mind . . ."

She shook her head. "The mind of one who is willing."

"We can—"

"Beja, there are none in this empire who would condemn their own mind to the hells. They are selfish. Addicted to pleasure and wisdom. I see now . . . I truly *see*."

A curious cocktail of intrigue and dread passed through me. Was this how it had really happened? Had her beja—me—given their entire existence to save her child? Obviously I'd royally screwed the timeline, and yet . . . there was something about this moment that rang through me like the last echo of a tolling bell.

Her words also brought terror, however. *One who is willing.* I didn't know anybody who would pay that price in the real world, unless I counted Akasha . . . who was unconscious.

Even so, there was only one way to know if *this* was the magic bullet.

"All right," I said quietly. "I'd like to do it."

"No, Beja."

"Yes. Just think of your son. Think of his eyes."

Small, silvery tears flowed down the empress's cheeks, marring her smile. "You do not know what you're asking."

"Oh, but I do. I'd like nothing more than to give you this, Empress. Please."

"You would give your mind for this child?"

"Yes," I said, moving closer and embracing her. "I would give anything."

She stood in place, nodding for far longer than any normal person, then stepped back and flicked away the last of her tears. "You asked me why I cared for you, Beja . . . I feel I owe those words to you."

Even as I squinted, trying to predict what she might say, she lifted her hand and shut her eyes. Sparkseed began peeling off my hammer in large, scintillating clumps. She maneuvered them past herself and then between us, flattening them until they formed a wide, hovering disc.

I instantly recognized it as the seeds of a mandala.

"You always made me feel safe," she said as she extended the spokes of the formation, bringing them to sharp, fractal-like points. "You cared for me when others refused to. You did what was just, not what was simple. You spoke with the kindness of one beyond your station."

Now the mandala was a shivering beast, expanding to shroud my entire body. The inner point loomed ahead like the eye of a black hole.

I stood there, rapt, as the empress telekinetically lifted my hammer between us. Only it wasn't my usual hammer anymore—it had been stripped of its Sparkseed "flesh," exposing a squirming, oily core. My breath caught in my throat.

The hammer's true substance was *literally* the Wellspring. No longer bound in place by the Sparkseed, the clump of Wellspring began revolving into a sphere that occupied the very center of the mandala. All along, I'd been carrying a bona fide shard of the Wellspring. It had been obscured, hidden behind a veil of powerful minds . . . all to conceal a key between this world and others.

That was why the Unmade feared it. Why Narbu had gone to such lengths to protect and preserve it . . . and, eventually, deliver it into my hands.

"Most importantly, Beja," the empress whispered, bringing my mind back to the present, "you are a part of me. The best part of me. You are the light that held back the shadows of this world. And for that, I love you. I will always love you."

In a moment of pure, unbridled energy, the Wellspring-fueled center of the mandala came screeching toward me.

Then I died.

Physically, at least.

Even as the empress's final words ran through my head, distorting and crumbling into the void, I sensed the end of all that I had been. Memories flaked away and descended into blackness. Spotlights formed in the dark, illuminating strange, murky vignettes of places I'd been . . . but the moment I tried to focus on any scene in particular, their spotlight faded, and another took its place. There was no pain, no fear, no sense of being anybody. I was simply . . . whatever I was.

And then the world came screaming back in blood and agony, and I saw nothing but looping, slick intestines, and the innards of stomachs, and flashes of skin being peeled from muscle. My body formed and dissolved a thousand times a second. More blood. Howling. Vast, monolithic shapes drifting overhead, raining bodies and impaling haggard forms. Spiders larger than stars trundled over heaps of flaming beings. Needles ran through eyeballs, and creatures of a thousand eyes eviscerated me, and there was nothing but pain. Pain, pain, pain. Before long, I was lost in the deluge, stripped of any sense of existence whatsoever. All I knew was that fucking pain. Hatred. Misery.

Only in retrospect can I say that this endured longer than any star system that will ever exist. There was no order in that place. No hope. Nothing at all. I must have spent a trillion years floundering in the hells, reduced to screaming into the emptiness, suffering death after death in forms so vicious I cannot recall them—and even if I could, I would purge them. Even now, I am left with nothing but glimpses, mere whispers of a torment beyond all imagination. There was no recognition of my name, let alone where I'd come from. Rogaji, the Godmaker, the empress—they were all forgotten in the face of that eternal brutality.

And then . . . after a period so muddled I cannot even say it existed . . . a glimmer of light pressed forth from behind my eyes.

As my skin was shredded and eyeballs scorched and tongue pried apart, a single thought formed.

This, too, is the Absolute.

The suffering carried on in the background, but I was no longer afflicted by it. My mind drifted free, expansive in all directions. The influx of freedom was strange. Alien. In bits and pieces, I recalled my experience in the junnara-gol's nightmare. I recalled the presence of light. The savior within myself.

Through my own deeds, I have built this fallen world. Through my own deeds, I will liberate it.

Despite the fingernail peeling and flesh melting, I felt that I was not constrained by anything. I was unbound, unsullied by whatever destruction came to my body or mind. I was infinite. Unstoppable. Vigorous.

Then there was a rush of déjà vu, a certainty that I had been here before. This opened just the slightest crack in the facade of it all. This wasn't the real thing; it was merely my own mind's recollection of the experience I'd undergone in a time I could scarcely recall. An experience, in fact, that I had undergone just before taking birth as Dak Korasa. In my prior life, just as I'd done in the Godmaker, I had sacrificed myself. Brought myself to this hell.

The crack in my psyche expanded. Streamers of memory coiled out and enveloped me.

This isn't real, I thought, half in self-assurance and half with total confidence. *None of this is real.*

More memories piled in: Akasha. Chanzig. Barren planets.

I was still in the Godmaker.

That simplest, most obvious fact immediately nullified the pain. It was as though I'd woken up from a dream, or perhaps disconnected myself from some hallucinogenic drug being pumped into my veins. The unreality of this hell realm—indeed, of all my trials and tribulations—ceased like a storm tapering into soft rain.

Phantom impressions of this world's sights and sounds and feelings rolled out into the endless horizons all around me. The barbaric visions and searing aches faded back into that familiar blackness, and I was left adrift.

Well, momentarily. Seconds later, hazy blue light threaded across the blackness. It coagulated and spooled into thick, rolling shapes, much like the accelerated formation of a nebula. I had no body, but somehow I was able to "rotate" myself, at which point I discovered there was no true center or direction to any of it. All around me, three hundred and sixty degrees, the creeping blue light continued its blind expansion.

Before long, there were shapes nestled in the omnipresent haze. Humanoid shapes. First one, then two . . . and soon enough, there were too many to count. They fizzled in and out of existence, as though birthing themselves from the clouds and dying back into them.

I tried something that, in hindsight, should've been my first course of action. "Hello?"

My voice didn't emerge as sound but rather as a mental flicker across the emptiness. The very intentions that formed the word rippled out, gently displacing clouds and drawing what seemed to be curiosity out of my formless watchers. Inwardly, I sighed, concerned that I'd somehow trapped myself in a new realm that consisted entirely of shy energy knots. I was also somewhat worried about my lack of body, which meant a lack of an exit button for the Godmaker, but that was a secondary problem. Sort of. You see, I just didn't feel fear. It was as though something here was keeping me calm, sedating me. Preparing me.

"WE COME TO YOU IN WISDOM."

The voice seemed to burst from every point in space simultaneously, jarring me so intensely that I shut down for a few moments. It was fortunate I didn't have a physical heart, as that likely would've burst in my chest at the sheer fright.

"Uh . . . greetings," I tried.

A great stir of whispers went through the assembly, and when the voice spoke again, it seemed to belong to neither one being nor many. "WE ARE THE WELLSPRING. WE HAVE ARRIVED TO TELL YOU WHAT YOU MUST KNOW."

"Yeah, well, I've had *plenty* of people telling me what I 'must' know, so—" I stopped, my sluggish mind latching onto one word in particular. "Wait. Did you just say you're the Wellspring?"

"WE SPEAK IN TRUTH. WE ARE HERE. WE HAVE MADE THIS SPACE TO SPEAK WITH YOU."

"Holy *shit*," I whispered, mainly to myself. "Are *you* the presence that spoke through Narbu on the landing pad?"

"WE ARE."

"No way . . ."

"YES, WAY."

Dropping back into my clearly artificial calmness, I asked, "Why am I not freaking out right now?"

"WE HAVE STABILIZED YOUR MIND. HELD BACK THE AFFLICTIONS."

I considered their words for a while, still not entirely believing my perception. It's hard to trust reality when you've just been tortured for a trillion simulated years. "I . . . thought you were dead."

"DEATH IS MERELY THE OUTCOME OF A CONCEPT YOU CALL LIFE."

"Deep. But that doesn't answer my question."

"WE FORESAW THE DEFILED ONE'S REIGN. WE MIGRATED."

"Migrated?"

I chewed on that, wondering if it was a mistranslation or simply a consequence of two vastly different intelligence levels interacting . . . then stopped. *Migrated.* I thought back to the pulsing presence inside the hammer, to the Sparkseed "coating" that Narbu's monks had died to create.

"You hid yourselves as the core," I said faintly. "As the hammer."

"YES. WE CONCEALED. EVADED. WE CLAIMED THAT WHICH THE DEFILED ONE COULD NOT DESTROY."

"So . . . he really *did* devour your dimension."

"YES."

"And all of you made it out?"

There was a long, unsettling silence. "ONCE THERE WERE MANY. NOW THERE ARE FEW. WE CANNOT SHAPE THE INFINITE WORLDS ANY LONGER. THUS, WE TURN TO YOU."

"You're Wayfarers, then."

"THAT IS THE NAME PROVIDED BY YOUR REALM."

I sighed. "You mean to tell me that I've had a bunch of Wayfarers hidden in my hammer this whole time, and not one of you decided to help me out?"

"OUR CONCEALMENT WAS NECESSARY."

"Necessary for what, exactly?"

"TO DELIVER US INTO YOUR HANDS."

Well, that tracked. It made sense that the Wellspring, with its near omniscience and power, had begun conspiring to defeat the Unmade long before Narbu ever knew about his existence. That didn't solve my main issue, though.

"You knew about this," I said. "You knew about all this, and you did nothing. You let Narbu create him."

"WE PROVIDED OUR COUNSEL."

"And what was his alternative? The deaths of trillions of beings?"

"YOU ARE NOT ADVANCED ENOUGH TO UNDERSTAND THE CALCULUS OF OUR DECISIONS. YOU ARE ONE COG IN A MACHINE THAT TRANSCENDS YOUR INTELLECT. ONE ASPECT CANNOT KNOW THE DESIGNS OF THE WHOLE."

A fair enough point, I supposed. Still, the whole thing didn't sit right with me. Nothing about this did. Analyzing the situation further, my thoughts worked down a brief yet profound line of logic. "Does that mean . . . Did *you* create the Godmaker?"

"WE PLANTED ITS SEED IN A WILLING MIND."

Rogaji's mind, I surmised. If I'd had a jaw, this is the moment where it would've dropped. "You built this whole thing for *me*."

"YES."

"How much of the experience did you control?"

"WE MERELY ILLUMINATED THAT WHICH YOU HAD FOR-GOTTEN. THAT WHICH HAD BEEN BURNED AWAY BY TIME AND OBSCURATIONS."

"But . . . how did you get my mind to remember it?"

"WE DID NOT NEED TO. WE REMEMBERED. WE SAW."

My mind exploded for the second time that minute. "It wasn't my mind creating that world," I said, breathless. "It was *you*. You were in the ham-mer, influencing the Godmaker the whole time."

"THERE IS NO SEPARATION IN TRUE, PRISTINE REAL-ITY. THE ARMOR UPON YOUR BODY . . . THE WEAPON YOU WIELDED . . . OUR INFLUENCE . . . YOUR OWN MIND . . . ALL WERE INSTRUMENTAL IN CALLING FORTH VISIONS OF A DEAD WORLD."

"Oh," I said, not quite understanding their point but guessing it had something to do with merging various streams of information to flesh out a single experience. "Can you get me the hell out of here?"

"YOU ARE ALREADY FREEING YOURSELF," the Wellspring said, "BUT WE CANNOT ALLOW YOU TO DEPART BEFORE OUR WORDS HAVE BEEN GIVEN."

"What exactly do you need to tell me?"

"SOON, THE MOVEMENTS OF THE MANY WORLDS WILL CONVERGE. YOU WILL FACE THE DEFILED ONE."

"Am I going to win?"

"WE DO NOT KNOW."

"How can you not—"

"YOU ARE BEYOND THE BOUNDS OF KARMA, AS IS YOUR FOE. WE HAVE DONE WHAT WE CAN, AND YOU WILL DO WHAT YOU MUST."

"Is that it? That's your goddamn pep talk?"

"LISTEN WELL, PURIFIER. DO YOU UNDERSTAND HOW YOU CAME TO THIS PLACE?"

"Sort of."

"WE DO NOT REFER TO THIS EXPERIENCE, BUT TO LIVES LONG GONE," the Wellspring boomed. "YOU DID NOT LEAVE THE HELL REALMS BY PROCESSING YOUR KARMA. JUST AS YOU HAVE DONE IN THIS LIFE, YOU MOVED BEYOND ITS INFLUENCE."

"I don't understand what that means!"

"WE WITNESSED YOUR BIRTH. WE WITNESSED THE OATH YOU SWORE."

I picked my brains, trying to recall what in Halcius's bleeding name they were talking about. I hadn't sworn an oath; I was certain of that.

"YOU DEMANDED THIS BIRTH TO REDEEM WHAT YOU HAD CREATED."

"What *I* created? Oh, fuck off. This isn't my fault."

"YOU HAVE SEEN THE TIES OF KARMA. YOU HAVE SEEN YOUR ROLE IN THE CREATION OF THE DEFILED ONE. WE REVEALED IT TO YOU."

Now that . . . that gave me some pause. On some level, they were right. My past incarnation had, indeed, sacrificed himself to give the empress what she desired. What they were suggesting, though, went far beyond the bounds of physical existence. They were claiming that I'd *chosen* to be born as Dak Korasa. That I had willingly taken on the suffering of this world.

"What *oath* are you talking about?" I pressed. "An oath to myself?"

"TO US."

A cold tremor passed through me. "*You* were the force that took me out of the hell realms and into my new birth?"

"YES."

"Damn, you're involved in a lot of my life. But . . . why?"

"YOU ARE A TOOL IN THE FINAL ANALYSIS," the Wellspring said without a hint of sympathy. "WE SAW YOUR PLACE IN THE TAPESTRY OF KARMA. WE PERCEIVED HOW IT COULD BE ALTERED WITH OUR INFLUENCE. HOW IT COULD BE ADVANCED TO COMPLETION."

I puzzled over their words. *A tool?* From the sound of it, they'd used me just as much as the Unmade had used Narbu. They'd quite literally torn open this "web of karma" to pluck me out of eons of damnation and incarnate me as Dak Korasa. The more I learned about this whole affair, the more it seemed like a giant, ever-expanding war taking place on all fronts, from the quantum level to the multiversal. The Wellspring, ultimately, was just a soldier on the side of purity, poised against the forces of defilement. In the overall scheme of things, I was nothing but the tip of a single spear on the battlefield.

The trouble was, I didn't know whose spearhead I was. The Unmade and Chanzig had boldly plotted to bring about my birth and corrupt Narbu's monastery, but now it seemed the Wellspring played an even deeper role in my creation. No matter how I sliced it, though, I was still just a pawn. A convergence of infinite factors beyond my grasp.

"That still doesn't explain why you accepted my oath," I said, shaking away the navel-gazing. "What did you get from this whole deal?"

"WE HAVE NOT YET RECEIVED ANYTHING. WE SOON SHALL. IF YOU SUCCEED."

"Go on . . . "

"YOUR MIND IS NOT CAPABLE OF UNDERSTANDING THIS SUBJECT, PURIFIER. ALL YOU MUST KNOW IS THAT YOUR OATH REMAINS."

"Right . . . so my *oath* is to kill the Unmade."

"NO." The Wellspring's blue energy coiled around me. "YOUR OATH IS TO NULLIFY THIS GREAT MISERY. KILLING IS NOT ENOUGH. HE MUST BE ERADICATED."

"And what happens if I fail?"

"WE WILL WITHDRAW OUR PROTECTION, AND YOU WILL RETURN TO THE SAME HELLS FROM WHENCE YOU CAME." The Wellspring paused, apparently for dramatic effect. It worked; their words rippled out across the emptiness, lapping over my invisible skin. "YOU ARE A TREMENDOUS PRESENCE OF VOLATILITY IN THE FOLDS OF REALITY. WE HAVE GIVEN WHAT WE CAN, IN ACCORDANCE WITH YOUR OATH. YOU MUST ABIDE BY YOUR WORDS. ALL DEBTS MUST BE SETTLED."

"Are you *shitting* me?" I hissed. "You're saying that if I fail here—if I die, or can't pull it off, or whatever else—you're sending me straight back to *that* place, with no way out?"

"WE ARE NOT RESPONSIBLE, PURIFIER. YOU FORMED THE OATH. YOUR CONTRACT IS NOT WITH US, BUT WITH EXISTENCE ITSELF. YOUR DEATH WILL BE A VACUUM. A VACUUM THAT MUST BE FILLED. BALANCED."

It was enough to make me want to claw my own immaterial eyes out. How the hell was it fair to expect *me*, the unwitting incarnation of a long-dead and forgotten warrior, to live up to a bargain I couldn't even remember? This rebirth stuff was maddening.

"Okay, fine," I growled, accepting that I was still in the same sticky situation as before. After all, if the Wellspring was correct, I'd *always* been at risk of being sent back to the hell realms. I just hadn't known it. "You said you needed to tell me something important. Get to it, please."

"WE HAVE ALREADY EXPLAINED THIS. IT IS NOT ENOUGH TO MERELY DESTROY YOUR FOE. THEY MUST BE SLAIN WITH PURITY. YOU MUST OBLITERATE THEIR MINDSTREAM FOR THE GOOD OF ALL SENTIENT BEINGS."

"Are you talking about Narbu's pure-killing idea?"

"HE COULD NOT GRASP THE MEANING OF THIS, BUT PERHAPS YOU WILL. THERE IS LITTLE TIME TO DO SO."

I thought back to that mountaintop encounter, to the sheer madness brought about by Narbu's arrogance. The notion of pure killing was still alien to me, outside the brief compassion I'd felt for the slain turtle. It was paradoxical, the notion of murdering something with joy in your heart. Maybe even sociopathic. Still, if I followed the muddy logic, it was the *only* way to destroy the Unmade for good. Anything less and he'd be reborn somewhere else. Perhaps in an even stronger form.

"Listen, while you're here . . . I need to ask you three things," I said delicately.

"INQUIRE. OUR TIME IS DWINDLING."

"All right, all right. First off, the empress did a ritual to try to bring her son back. But—"

"YOU FEAR THAT YOU CANNOT RECALL THE INTRICACIES OF THE PROCESS," the Wellspring cut in. "DO NOT BE CONCERNED. YOU WILL KNOW WHAT YOU MUST WHEN THE MOMENT IS UPON YOU. IT RESIDES IN THE STOREHOUSE OF YOUR MIND, WAITING. KNOWLEDGE WILL ARISE."

Once again, the phrasing was so muddled it might as well have been a different language. And yet . . . I caught some inkling of what they were saying. When I needed to perform the ritual, I would. I just had to trust in my own mind to drag the information up from my subconscious.

One down, two to go.

"How did this . . . happen?" I whispered.

"WE DO NOT UNDERSTAND YOUR INQUIRY."

"The Unmade. How did he become what he did?"

"WORDS WILL NOT SUFFICE. WE WILL REVEAL IT THROUGH VISION."

Before I could ask for clarification, I more or less disappeared. Rather than having a body or mind, I had "vision." As in, I felt like a floating camera. My only role was to view the images presented by the Wellspring. Their film, if you will.

That "film" began with pure blackness, which was soon filled by thousands upon thousands of lights. Somehow, I intuitively knew that this depicted the rise of Wayfarers in the multiverse. It was as though the requisite context was beamed straight into my consciousness.

Next, those lights swam apart and drifted together, spiraling out, forming small clusters that soon attracted other lights like a gravitational field. The birth of Wellsprings. The image magnified, focusing on one particular Wellspring. *This* Wellspring, to be precise. I felt the vast love and truth radiating from it, saturating the surrounding darkness.

Then the image shifted, and I saw *inside* the Wellspring. Inside its past version, anyway. It was . . . immaculate. A million lights, ten trillion hands and arms, eyes that stared into the hollows of dead universes, light bursting and blooming . . . At its center was a long, seemingly infinite column of pure energy, burning up and down into the infinite reaches of space. All the Wayfarers within the collective drew from that column of energy as though it were an umbilical cord.

Again, the image shifted. Now I saw what looked to be Narbu and his oracles on a windswept bluff, the empress's son cowering beneath them . . . Narbu's prayers to the Wellspring echoed like thunderclaps in my ears. My vision shifted back and forth, showing the bluff, then the center of the Wellspring . . . then the bluff, then the Wellspring . . . Over time, I noticed a subtle change.

The boy's mind was literally cycling between physical reality and the Wellspring. The failed purification ritual, I guessed. An attempt to send his mind to that pure, bright abode and have it cleansed of defilement.

Just as I'd expected, though, something went wrong. With the last and final repetition of Narbu's prayer—along with the last stab of a ceremonial knife—the boy's mind detached from the body and manifested directly inside the Wellspring's column of energy. Instantly, the energy soured. Curdled. Spotless white light became dirtied to shades of red and brown, bleeding out to the countless Wayfarers like poison in an IV drip.

Their world of light and gold began dissolving. Screams rolled through the collapsing dimension. The mind inside the column—that of the Unmade—expanded to colossal dimensions, drinking up the energy of the dying Wayfarers. A cold, biting laugh exploded through the darkness.

Suddenly, I was back before the Wellspring's audience. I drew a deep breath into lungs that didn't exist.

"Damn," I breathed. "So, they tried to send the boy here . . . to you . . . but you weren't strong enough to purify him. It backfired."

"YES. THE ORACLE ACTED AGAINST OUR WISDOM."

"What the hell was that column? The one with all the energy?"

"THE SOURCE. A SHARED MANIFESTATION OF OUR POWER."

"And . . . he stole it from you."

"YES. HIS MIND DIRECTS ITS ENERGY. IT IS LIMITLESS. ONCE, IT WAS FED BY OUR MERITS. OUR COMPASSION. NOW IT IS FED BY DEFILEMENT. HE IS TOO STRONG TO BE OPPOSED IN THE SPACE BETWEEN WORLDS. YOU MUST BRING US TO THE SOURCE DIRECTLY."

I ran through what I already knew of the prophecy. According to the monks, most prophecies ended in me killing the Unmade but being corrupted by his latent energy. That now made sense. Anyone who killed the owner of the dimension would have to soak up all the energy of that central "Source" and become its new handler. If I didn't do this *perfectly*, I'd easily become just as defiled as the Unmade, courtesy of all that raw power.

"All right, got it," I mumbled, though I really didn't. "Get you into his dimension. Kill him with love. Take over the Source."

"YES. NOW, BE QUICK. OUR TIME WILL SOON EXPIRE."

"Akasha's mind," I blurted out, cognizant of the fast-approaching end of this strange, immaculate moment. "How do I unseal it?"

"ONE'S OWN MIND IS THE PANACEA."

"Huh?"

"OUR WINDOW OF CONVERSATION DRAWS TO A CLOSE," the Wellspring proclaimed in a flash of light. "HEED OUR WORDS, PURIFIER, AND DESTROY WITH YOUR HEART AS OPEN AS THE

SKY. FATE IS NO LONGER WITH YOU. ONLY YOUR NATURE REMAINS."

"Wait!" I cried, trying to claw at them despite the futility. "You haven't explained enough! I need to know how to—"

"BIRTH DRAWS NEAR. GO FORTH WITH WISDOM, PURIFIER, AND DELIVER BALANCE."

I called out again, but the blue light was already gone, as were the humanoid figures that had formerly populated it. Now there was only blackness. Blackness, and my own mind. Somewhere far, far ahead, like the light of a train approaching from a vast distance, I saw a pinprick of existence. It shimmered like a kaleidoscope, turning, morphing . . .

Birth.

Without knowing how or why, realization came over me. That lone pinprick was my life. My physical, material life. If I plunged into it, I would return to the same body I'd hauled into the Godmaker. If I turned away, I would be . . . somewhere else. Somewhere far away from the Unmade and its torments. All this was as clear and open to me as my own name.

At that moment, however, the growing momentum of my journey rolled into a valley and ceased. I felt the true loneliness of it all. The impermanence. What did it *really* matter if I went back and ended this? Beings died. They died all the goddamn time. What was wrong with simply drifting through the crawl space of reality for the rest of time, seeing, hearing, feeling, yet always apart from true death? In fact, the longer I dwelled on the concept, the more nonsensical it became to consider returning. I was out of the madness I'd despised for so long. No chok'tal, no Unmade, no prophecies.

No Akasha.

The thought stilled my mind, bringing my mental gaze back to that pinprick of all that was, of all that could be. Right then, I knew I hadn't taken that oath for myself. I hadn't even done it for all sentient beings. I'd done it for one mind, one person. For one measly chance to see her exist in a universe without this horror.

Suddenly, there was no choice. There was only the pinprick. I stared into it, calling it forth, urging it to swallow me up.

"Here we go," I whispered to myself as the image stretched and folded around me, forming into shapes and moments and particles. "Here we fuckin' go."

My eyes shot open, unveiling polished steel and glass, and an involuntary, shuddering breath ripped down my windpipe. My heartbeat drummed in my ears. *My heartbeat.* I was alive, existing as a corporeal being once again. Everything from the buzzing in my fingertips to the prickle of cool air on my unarmored skin assured me that I was well outside the Godmaker's confines.

That only left one question.

Where the hell was I?

Blinking to clear the fog from my vision, I discerned that I was lying on a metal floor, staring ahead at a glass pane with a dark shape beyond it. No, not just a dark shape.

Rogaji.

Modri had been fucking right after all—Izamem, too, I supposed. She really *was* the Duplicitous Contender. She'd probably been monitoring me inside the Godmaker, waiting until the moment I was able to access the ritual that could take her straight to the Unmade. Now that she'd gotten what she desired, I was just a slab of meat. One she was comfortable trapping in a glass cube in preparation for execution, I presumed.

"I knew it," I growled, trying to summon the energy to get to my feet—and failing miserably. The result of a tranquilizer, I guessed. "You . . . were playing me."

Rogaji crossed her arms. "Those drugs really did a number on you, huh?"

"Fuck . . . you."

"Oh, kill me now," Rogaji huffed. My vision cleared just enough to reveal the annoyed scowl lining her face. "Dak, let your brain juices settle. Then take another look."

Despite my grimace, I did what she asked. The chemical haze affecting my brain didn't make it easy, but I managed to sit up, clear my vision to a workable level, and then perform a slow, calculated analysis of my surrou—

Aw, hell.

Like an optical illusion solved with one tilt of the head, I immediately understood the truth of the situation. Rogaji wasn't lording over me; she was trapped in her own transparent cube, which was identical to mine. Both our containers were sitting on a scuffed metal floor, surrounded in all directions by shadows and murky shapes. Conversely, we were lit up by powerful overhead beams. Almost as though being shown off like zoo occupants.

A sharp *click* echoed through the room, and then harsh, eye-gouging floodlights activated to drive out the darkness. What it revealed was green— Hegemony green.

It was a shade somewhere between emerald and forest, recognizable enough to catch my breath in my throat and drive home just how fucked we were. That devilish color was everywhere, from the ceiling struts to the wall panels to the armor that surrounded us. *Armor.* My gonked brain took several seconds to count how many soldiers there were, eventually coming away with the specific figure of "a lot."

The stocky, rifle-bearing troops were lined up in rows of ten, their weapons tucked against their chests in some sort of parade-style stance. As my vision adjusted more, I realized there were hundreds of them here . . . and, simultaneously, that we were in a room far too green and spacious to be part of Rogaji's compound.

Shit, shit, shit.

We were on a Hegemony ship.

Believe it or not, though, that *still* wasn't the worst of our problems. Situated between the rows of Hegemony troops was an elevated metal slab that might've been a repurposed surgical table, and situated atop that slab was a sleeping woman with blue skin and white robes.

I immediately sprang forward on my knees, colliding with the cube's glass wall. No matter how hard I struck the pane with my tranquilizer-weakened blows, however, I earned nothing but a blossom of condensation.

"That's quite enough," a throaty voice said, the words broadcast straight into my cube through hidden means. "Now that you're awake, we can converse with decorum."

That voice. Where had I heard that voice?

My question was answered a moment later, when the knobby, hunched form of Izamem the seer came slithering around the side of Akasha's table.

The Duplicitous Contender.

23

The average person in my position, upon learning of this betrayal, might've opted to scream *How could you!?* or some variant of that. Not me. I immediately toggled on Indomitable and Overclock, raising my fists in an apelike gesture of conquest that heralded the world's largest slam attack on the glass.

Rogaji stopped all that with a wag of her finger. When I glanced over, perplexed, she said, "I wouldn't do that. It's immune to everything short of quantum-disentanglement weapons."

Given the woman's absurd levels of power, I had no reason to doubt her. Diverting all my rage and confusion into an all-out beatdown on the cube was tempting but also a horrible waste of whatever calories I had left in my body. A quick look downward confirmed I was running on the leaner side of things *and* that I'd somehow been peeled out of my armor and stuffed into loose-fitting civilian clothes—namely, the standard Hegemony prison garb of a T-shirt and chafing pants.

That didn't deter me. I just had to work smarter, not harder. Lifting my gaze, I focused on Izamem's walking stick and poured Telekinesis into it. Tried to, anyway. It was as though my awareness stopped just shy of my face, absorbed straight into the cube's curious material.

"They're energy-insulated," Rogaji went on, seemingly bored. "Nothing that exerts physical force is getting in or out. Might as well let the smarmy bastard finish his monologue."

A small, vengeful part of me wanted to use Shock and Awe. Even if it cost me a literal arm or leg, I might have a chance of breaking the cube. I was quick to discard that, though. My extremely scant knowledge of physics assured me I'd be blown to bits by a confined explosion.

Thoroughly pissed off, I sank down against the glass and glared at Izamem. "So, what the fuck?"

Izamem's smile broadened. "You might—"

"Let me guess," Rogaji cut in. "You cut a deal with the Hegemony for retirement money."

"No," the seer said, his voice ringing with disbelief. "You see, I—"

"Oh, no, I get it. You're on their hook, and they compelled you to do this."

"No . . . it's—"

"What, did I forget to pay you?"

"Silence!" Izamem roared. Shockingly, Rogaji followed the request. After a few seconds of composing himself, he cleared his throat and began pacing like your average villain. "Dearest Madam Rogaji, I regret to inform you that this has *nothing* to do with you. In truth, it hardly has anything to do with Mr. Korasa, though he will understand my grievances."

I stared him down. "Is this about your people?"

His eyes flashed with fervor. "Very much so."

"Oh, for fuck's sake," I said, sighing. "Get over it, would you?"

Rogaji glanced at me. "Care to fill me in?"

I lifted a hand to stop her, my eyes never leaving Izamem's. "It's ancient history. Besides, I saw what happened there. You were both miserable to each other."

Once more, Rogaji tried to inject a question, but Izamem toggled a small device in his palm—and then her cube was silent. Soundproofed.

"Much better," Izamem said. "Now, then . . . I believe you are slightly mistaken, boy. I hold no grudge toward that wicked empire. As you say, those days are dead and fossilized. No. *Her* crime, that of this incarnation, is still raw. It festers."

"Does Chanzig have something to do with this?" I asked.

"Chanzig?"

The confusion in Izamem's voice gave me some relief. I explained, "A terrible guy who's now dead. He had a real penchant for recruiting the Hegemony, too."

"The Hegemony and I share a relationship of mutualism." The old seer resumed his pacing, each step punctuated by the clack of the walking stick. "They seek access to powers beyond this world, while I seek retribution."

I paled at the mention of *powers beyond this world*. "The Unmade isn't a *power*. It's a goddamn killing force. A monstrosity."

"Halcius resides in all places," Izamem said, quoting one of the Hegemony's more famous litanies. "He resides even in the hollow places, where flesh cannot enter . . ."

I began to put together what Izamem was saying without actually saying. These myopic, delusional fools really thought their one true god—that is, Halcius—was masquerading as the Unmade. Not only that, but they wanted to "free" him. To bring him into this world with renewed power. It was the same terrible prophecy the monks had mentioned over and over. Given the thinning of the boundaries between our dimension and others in this region of space, it was no surprise the Hegemony had thought this area to be their sacred ground for ascendence. They were *actually* going to unleash annihilation on an entire universe in their quest for glory.

"You can't be serious," I whispered. "Izamem, you know what he is. You know what he'd do if they managed to open a permanent gateway."

"That is a concern for those who cling to the Flesh Plane," he spat.

"Then I'll tell them myself."

Izamem coughed out a laugh, then turned and waved his walking stick toward the ranks of Hegemony troops. "You think they'll listen to you? You're a criminal . . . a sick, broken little child. They are guided by faith."

Seeing his point—they really *were* die-hard zealots—I switched my approach. "Fine. What guides *you*, then? What could possibly be worth inking a deal with the Hegemony?"

"Have my words slipped through your skull, boy? I am here for retribution."

"Over *what*!?"

Izamem pulled in a long, steady breath I recognized as the start of another monologue. "I may not be sore over the wounds of my ancestors, *Beja*, but their scars have shaped my existence. You saw what was done to them. The deception, the subjugation, the hypocrisy. You saw, even, how they snatched my people's font of wisdom."

"You . . . saw all that?" I asked quietly.

"Madam Rogaji may not be able to peer into the Godmaker—into your feeble mind—but I am." He stared at me for a long while, dark eyes burrowing through the cube and chilling me. "Bah. No matter what you have seen, you failed to witness the glory my people held. Once, they were masters of their world. Lords who presided over the weak. *We* knew the secrets of the Wellspring, boy."

"So, you *are* bitter about all that."

That seemed to have gone too far, judging by Izamem's lightning-fast decision to switch off my cube's microphone, too.

"Now you'll listen like a good pup," he snarled, fighting to calm himself. "Do you know what the empire did to our species, Beja? Do you *know*?"

It was purely rhetorical, seeing as I couldn't actually reply. "We were not only starved of wisdom. We were made to be beasts. Starved. Slaughtered. Our only relief came when the empire's ambitions devoured it. The day the gateway was opened, my ancestors sang songs of beauty and danced through the night! They watched, gleeful, as their blood-soaked cities crumbled and dispersed. The Wellspring had finally turned on its abusers, just as we had turned on them.

"When the chok'tal emerged—our sacred gift from the reaches beyond this plane—we gorged ourselves on its power. We slaughtered those who had slaughtered. We ate those who had eaten us. We reclaimed our world and turned it into a paradise your mind will *never* understand.

"But those who had destroyed and lied and raped could not release their pride. Cravens. Those who survived the purge fled into the stars, biding their time for the day when they could crush us beneath their heels once more." Izamem turned to Akasha and ran the walking stick just over her skin, from head to toe. "The Cobalt Ones pursued my people for ten *thousand* years. And for what? Because we were worthy of the chok'tal's blessing. Because *they* were not.

"We did not kill with the chok'tal. We did not oppress. We used its power to keep our lands safe from monstrosities, and to ensure we would never . . . ever . . . be conquered again. If only you could ask the Cobalt Seer yourself, Beja. She would tell you the same truth. We were *not* monsters. We were those who remained. In ten thousand years, not *one* of our Purifiers departed the surface of our worlds. We kept to ourselves . . . and yet they sought our destruction."

As I listened, it was hard to *not* feel a shred of sympathy for Izamem and his people. Sure, they'd been almost cartoonishly evil in the God-maker, but what had brought them to that point? The Suharkayans themselves had admitted their own genocide, their own repression. They *had* stolen the devices and knowledge formerly owned by Izamem's ancestors. They *had* treated them like animals.

Likewise, it was strange and even disconcerting to hear Izamem's take on what Akasha had told me long, long ago on Kagu-9. Akasha's memories, altered though they surely were, had painted her ancestors—the survivors of her homeworld—as being impoverished rebels fleeing an overwhelming force of evil. That didn't seem to be the entire truth. In Izamem's view, *his* ancestors had been the persecuted ones. Despite their judicious and reasonable use of the chok'tal to defend themselves, they'd been hunted down and destroyed as some kind of eternal blood feud.

"You may wonder, Beja, why I hold such contempt for *this* one," Izamem went on, poking Akasha's shoulder with the stick. "For that, I will refer to my own life. To what has been seen with these very eyes.

"My clan lived on a small, fertile world, subsisting on crops and berries. There was no war, no corruption. We had forgiven the barbarism of the Cobalt Ones. Among our people, the chok'tal was a sacred gift . . . a responsibility to protect one's clan with the power in their veins. *I* was to be the next Purifier, Beja. It was my time. My opportunity. As such, we held a feast to mark the end of one Purifier's life and the start of another's.

"Ah, if only you could have smelled the lilac in the air. Felt the breeze. Never had I witnessed such joy. Such compassion. It was a rare window on this tainted Flesh Plane . . . a view of primordial reality and all its splendor." Once more, he paced back to Akasha and tilted his head, studying her like a small child trying to make sense of a corpse. "Her vessel arrived just past sundown. *Her* ship. *Her.* We tried to flee, but it was too late.

"She destroyed our protector, our Purifier, and with it . . . our chok'tal. But did she stop there? Ah, no. No, no, no. She slaughtered us all. The children, the women, the old men . . . I had never seen such cruelty. Not even the darkest of tales prepared me for what she did. She laughed at our tears, Beja. She pushed us into the dirt and tore heads from shoulders. She *reveled* in the blood she spilled. I hid, and I prayed, but she did not stop. Only after the others were cold did she find me. She dragged me out of those merciful shadows and forced my eyes open and made me look at them. All of them.

"And then, just as I prayed for release . . . for the severance of mind and body . . . she mutilated my body. She tore out the holiest of all nodes in the body . . . the nerve endings that could bind with the chok'tal. The sum of all my hopes, my aspirations, my prayers . . . stolen." He stared at Akasha for a long, long while. "Then she left, Beja. With blood thick in the air and death all about, she *left*. Do you know why, Beja? Because she wanted me to remain with that death. To suffer. To know that I had failed my people, even in their darkest moment.

"She took *everything* from me," Izamem whispered. "And for that, she will feel true pain for the first time in her pitiful existence."

When Izamem clicked the little button to reengage my microphone, I had nothing to say. For the first time in seemingly ever, I was speechless. Floored. If even half of what he was saying had actually occurred, I understood his grievance. I understood every mote of pain in his shriveled little body.

"I'm sorry," I said honestly, "for all that happened to you."

"There is no room for apologies," Izamem said icily. "She will pay for her sins through the flesh. All that remains is her awakening."

I blinked at him, caught off guard by that last bit. "Come again?"

"You entered the Godmaker, Beja. You know what to do."

"I'm not—"

"You *know*!" he croaked. "Awaken the Cobalt Seer so that I may have justice."

"I don't know how," I said, "and even if I did, I wouldn't do it for you. This isn't how you do it."

"You cannot dictate anything."

"No, but I can tell the difference between justice and revenge. They slaughtered your people, you slaughtered theirs . . . it's a cycle, Izamem. A bloody cycle. Whatever you want to do won't bring any of them back."

"Unlock . . . her mind."

"I already told you that I don't—"

"*Lies,*" he snapped. "You hold the knowledge of her mind. Do not deny me this."

"If you really could see into the Godmaker, you'd know that's bullshit. There's no way to undo the lock."

Given what Izamem planned to do with Akasha, I was suddenly grateful I hadn't learned anything he couldn't just rip out of my skull with his mind powers. It was better for her to be unconscious.

"Play your games," Izamem said, leveling his stare on Rogaji. "I'll start with her."

I glanced sidelong at the woman, who was more or less spellbound by the entire exchange. "What do you mean, start with her?"

As if on cue, a series of red veins worked their way around the cube, enveloping it like artificial skin. Those same veins then began strobing with angrier and angrier pulses.

"If you refuse to help me," Izamem said, "she'll be torn apart. Piece . . . by piece."

I pounded on the glass. "This is goddamn insane! Let her go!"

"Three seconds, Beja."

"I don't know anything!"

"Two . . ."

"Listen to me!"

"One."

The network of red veins suddenly imploded, seeming to phase *through* the cube's exterior, then tore into Rogaji's body. Her eyes bulged in agony, and her screams—silent though they were—ate at my heart like battery acid. Chunks of her flesh peeled away and dissolved in the red lattice, only to regenerate nearly instantly from her frighteningly high Anima.

"Stop it!" I screamed, hitting the cube's pane once again to no effect. "I don't know anything!"

After nearly thirty seconds of the unwatchable torture, Izamem met my eyes, but his gaze was virtually dead. "I believe you, Beja."

I looked over at Rogaji's cube just in time to see the red veins perform their final dissection trick. Like a knot coming together with one pull, the energy converged on the cube's center and completely disintegrated Rogaji. I watched it in silence, baffled as to how a body had just disappeared. When the energy powered down, all that remained of the Purifier were a few motes of atomized carbon.

I fumbled for words. "You . . . you . . . "

"Killed her," Izamem said, nodding. "And since you haven't one clue as to how to awaken the dreamer, I will settle for having you watch. Consider this justice for your service as a beja, boy. A touch of payment for the betrayal you allowed to seep into your mind."

"You need her to open the gateway!"

"Ah, ah . . . a lie," Izamem said. "The Hegemony doesn't need her . . . just knowledge of the ritual. Which *you* possess."

Despite, well, everything . . . a grin came over me. "You don't know how to open it, do you?"

"I have seen enough."

"Beg to differ."

Izamem scowled. "Don't worry about *that,* boy. The Hegemony will have plenty of time to crack open your little head and make you dance when we arrive at their station. For now, just watch. Let the images consume you."

Once again, I went apeshit on the cube, slamming against it and kicking and punching. All I succeeded in doing was splitting my skin all over, though Anima quickly patched that up.

I was out of options. Done. I didn't know whether to keep fighting or lean back and await my death by laser, especially when Izamem drew a long, narrow blade from his robes and held it over Akasha's face. Perhaps it was best to look away, denying him whatever pleasure he might get from my reaction. On the other hand, defiance had always been my strong suit.

As the blade drew closer to her flesh, panic overtook whatever semblance of strength I'd tried to establish. My thoughts ran wild, assembling plans that went nowhere, formulating options I didn't have, picking at yet never penetrating the barrier of my utter defeat.

Then I caught a passing strand of memory. A cluster of words that felt half imagined.

One's own mind is the panacea.

I still had no idea what the Wellspring's words meant, but they lingered, turning and twisting into something more tangible. The decryption needed to be faster, though. The blade was nearly against her forehead. Ready to carve out her third eye.

One's own mind . . .

Revelation broke through the clouds of consciousness. *Mind. Mind Cascade.* It was a long shot—I had no idea if such an ability could escape the cube's dampening—but it was also my *only* shot. If this failed, everything failed. I'd be on an express line straight back to the hell dimensions.

The only thing on my side was the Rank Points I'd invested in Mind Cascade. Two more of them, to be precise. That meant, in layman's terms, I was working with it at 3/3. The only problem was . . . I'd never used it. I hadn't been bold enough to attempt using such a power on simulated beings. So, in essence, it was *theoretically* a powerful ability at max level, but theories didn't always hold up. This would be a true trial by fire.

Gritting my teeth, I stared intently at the target. You might think it was Izamem, given his control over the cube-altering remote and position of power . . . but it wasn't. His mind would surely be a fortress of terrifying proportions. A trap, even.

Which was why I targeted Akasha.

Just as Izamem's blade began a long, shaky cut, I poured every drop of my own mind into a connection I couldn't feel. I willed it to cross the divide between space and time. To transcend whatever physical boundaries separated us. To merge with her own consciousness, which I knew better than any other being's.

The cube resisted my invading awareness, presenting a black, impenetrable wall with quantum links so dense that I couldn't find a way through. That was all right. If I couldn't slip past, I'd shatter it. Even if it meant permanently losing the anchor of my own mind. Marshaling my focus, my inner reservoir of consciousness, I drew on something deeper than I'd ever accessed. Volatile jets of energy rushed forth from the apparent void behind my eyes, chipping away at the cube's structure, seeping through the dark mesh.

The more that strange, untapped energy emerged, the more I understood it. It was the Absolute. That primordial, timeless flux that formed *everything* . . . including the cube, and me, and my mind, and the minds of Akasha and everyone else aboard the ship. Abruptly, the direction of that energetic flow completely flipped. I was no longer drawing from power within myself, but the power latent in all things, at all times, in all places. The universe itself condensed and funneled through me as though I were merely a conduit in the folds of spacetime.

Breach.

My awareness—though, subjectively, it felt like *all of me*—surged through the cube and drilled straight toward Akasha. For seemingly the hundredth time that day, material reality collapsed into the churning sprawl of her mind. Only . . . it didn't feel like a mind at all.

Past uses of the ability had rocketed me into a shadowy, swirling realm of mental residue and chaotic emotions. This being the case, I expected Akasha's mind to look similar. It didn't. Whether due to her unique disposition or those two additional points in Mind Cascade, I found myself standing in front of a crystal dome so large it may as well have been a research installation on a dead moon. The world around me wasn't made of darkness, but rather a storm of drifting . . .

What the hell is that?

They weren't quite *objects*—not in the typical sense, anyhow—but they still filled the grayish expanse like frenzied sparrows, orbiting, tumbling, colliding with one another. I watched a tangle of them with cautious interest as they flitted past. They were devoid of any real qualities, almost as though they were bubbles in an ocean. Condensed knots of the same gray in which they floated.

That didn't mean they were empty, though. When one of the weird "bubbles" streaked over me, I heard it *speaking*. The language was unfamiliar, but . . . No. No, it wasn't. It was Suharkayan. A sound bite of a dead, fallen world encased in nothingness.

My breath caught in my energy-based body. *Memories*, I thought. *They're memories.*

I glanced back toward the crystal dome, a seed of understanding taking root. These motes were *all* Akasha's memories. Her past-life memories, that is. The only thing preventing them from reaching Akasha was that enormous dome—a physical embodiment of the mind-lock Narbu had placed on Akasha, I surmised. If I shattered that dome . . .

That train of thought ceased when I detected movement within the dome. Rushing up to its edge, I pressed my face to the crystal and cleared away the mild frost that had formed over it. What I saw wasn't Akasha.

The appendages of some horribly large, lurking beast swept past my field of view. I didn't see it for long, but it was enough time to make out its scaly, slimy flesh . . . its rotten talons . . . its dragging, pustule-covered tumors. The thing had to be at least fifty meters tall. It had worn a rut around the inner track of the dome, almost as though it were patrolling, keeping something back.

Her Accretion, no doubt.

I cursed and prepared to draw back, confident I was fucked, but then . . . then I noticed what lay beyond the Accretion.

A verdant, sparkling grove had claimed everything within the Accretion's circular patrol route. Small birds zipped between ancient, moss-bearded trees and stacks of lichen-covered stone. Soft amber light spilled down from some impossible source. Thin waterfalls the color of lapis lazuli descended from golden clouds, ending in gorgeous ponds with pebbled beaches.

It was a utopia, smack-dab in the middle of an existential hell.

More movement stirred deeper inside the grove, and though I initially assumed it was some kind of foraging animal, the presence of blue skin and white robes changed my mind. I cleared away even more of the frost and desperately tried to project my voice through the divide.

"Akasha!"

She looked up, though not toward me, almost like she'd mistaken my voice for a bird's song. I called again . . . and again . . . and eventually, her gaze met mine. I nearly screamed with joy.

"Dak . . . " she said quietly, wading through waist-high grass toward me. She stopped just before the Accretion's rut. "Where are we?"

The lack of concern in her voice concerned me. She said my name as though I'd dropped in for a surprise lunch.

"We need to get you out, okay?" I said.

"Out . . . ?"

"Yeah. Izamem—this, uh, seer guy—is about to kill you. I need to know how to open this thing up."

She smiled. "What thing?"

"The . . . dome?"

"I don't know what you mean."

I slapped my palm against the dome. "This thing!"

"Are you all right, Dak? I don't—"

"Just hold on, okay?" I stepped back and blew out a breath of frustration, knowing damn well I couldn't blame her for whatever magic was corrupting her mind. Part of Narbu's mental lock had to include a kind of ignorance regarding the situation itself. "Can you step back for me?"

Akasha tilted her head, seemingly amused. "What for?"

"Just humor me."

"All right, Dak. For you, I will. It's nice to see you . . . It's been so long . . . "

I smiled and nodded through her comments, biding my time until she'd backed up far enough to avoid any damage from what I was about to do. Then I pressed my hand to the crystal and injected as much of my inner light as possible. It wasn't a surefire solution, but it *had* destroyed multiple creatures in other instances of Mind Cascade, so—

Nope. Nothing. The light sizzled *around* the crystal, never truly penetrating or weakening it.

"What are you doing?" Akasha asked, more amused now.

I racked my brain, trying to figure out what the problem was . . . only to realize I'd already seen it. So long as the Accretion existed, there was no hope of breaking out. It had been sealed in there with Akasha as a protector, a guardian of the knowledge she'd been forbidden from accessing. And only one of us could kill it.

"Akasha," I said slowly, meaningfully, "do you see the creature with you?"

She turned back, apparently in the direction of the circling Accretion. "Yes. It's a dear friend."

"What does it look like to you?"

"To me?" she asked, laughing. "You can see it for yourself, Dak."

"What . . . does it look like?"

"Angelic," she said wistfully. "It's so . . . radiant. So pure."

Well, that proved my theory. I clenched my jaw and, not for the first time, hoped Narbu was suffering for what he'd done. "Okay, Akasha. I need you to do something I can't."

"What is it?"

"I need you to kill it."

She gave me a puzzled look. "Why?"

"Because you're the only one who can," I whispered. "I know it might seem like I'm mad, but I *need* you to follow through. I'm begging you."

"But if I harm it—"

"Please. Trust me."

Again, she angled herself toward the Accretion and studied it. I felt the urge to scream at her, to pound against the crystal . . . but I never got the chance. Even as I stood there, I sensed something both familiar and unexpected.

Something was pulling me *out* of Mind Cascade.

I glanced down at my hands, which were fast unraveling into strands of pure light that coiled back into the distant horizon. Something like dizziness spread through my body. I was being deconstructed. Ejected. I had just a few seconds to get my point across.

"*Empress*, please," I said, fighting to speak through the dissolution. "You have to remember."

Then the blackness claimed me, and I was swirling back through a vacuum, a great rush clawing at me and returning me to the physical plane. A mirror of the very same process through which I'd entered her realm.

I slumped to the side, gasping and choking. The garish light of the beam above the cube stabbed at my eyes.

When my headache subsided, I shook my head and looked out into the room. Izamem was still above Akasha, still holding his little knife. He wasn't cutting, though. Instead, he was staring at me with unbridled rage, the cube-controlling remote clutched in his shaking hand.

"You meddling rodent," the seer hissed. "Thought you could escape the confinement zone, did you? Well, my congratulations. You nearly did. Do you know how *dangerous* it can be to overload the cube's containment protocols?" He muttered something under his breath. "No matter. Nothing a touch of redistributed power won't fix. Oh, how I despise technology . . ."

I didn't say anything, mostly because I didn't know *what* to say. He'd beaten me. My last ploy, my last chance to see and comfort Akasha . . . and I'd failed. The best I could do now was close my eyes.

Just as I went to do that, though, I spotted a rare blot of motion among the stock-still soldiers around Izamem. A *blue* blot of motion, to be exact. Frozen, inwardly silent, I watched as Akasha's fingers curled at her sides. Then a leg twitched. Her belly rose with a deep intake of air. Finally, in a grand finale, her eyes shot open with inhuman clarity.

Through it all, Izamem just stood there, fiddling with the little remote and grumbling. He only noticed something was amiss when the soldiers behind him sprang into action, raising their weapons and barking commands.

By the time he turned around, Akasha was lording over him like the reaper. Not *my* Akasha, though. She was changed, somehow. Her eyes held no traces of warmth, and she carried herself with the unstoppable poise of a machine.

I watched on, breathless, as dozens of Hegemony officers emerged from the ranks in an attempt to control the situation. I used that opportunity to shout, "Don't fire or you'll *never* open the gateway!"

It seemed to be enough. The troops fanned out and kept their weapons raised, but not a single one dared move their finger over the trigger.

Izamem, meanwhile, staggered backward and bumped into my cube. "It's— I can't— What *are* you?"

Akasha lifted him with one hand, causing his leg tendrils to frantically batter the cube pane right in front of me. When she spoke, her voice carried the authority of a timeless deity beyond the laws of this dimension. "I am the Empress Jalisa Multheri Nodran, Third of the Blessed Name, Priestess of the Nine Realms, Radiant Guardian of Oracles and Sages . . . and I will deliver the vengeance of my people."

24

Istared on, slack-jawed and mind-blown, as Akasha lifted the blindfold on her forehead. Although I was shielded by Izamem's body and the protection of the cube itself, the light that screamed forth seared my eyes.

I twisted away, grimacing, but I couldn't help myself for long. Peering up through slits in my fingers, I saw pure carnage. Izamem's body was flaking away, painting itself on the cube in dark, atomized streaks, much like the victim of a nuclear blast at ground zero. Droplets of blood floated eerily, then boiled into fine red dust. Within just ten seconds, nothing of Izamem's upper half remained. His lower body plopped to the floor in a wet glob.

Finished with her grim task, Akasha approached the cube and stared down at me. "Arise, Beja. It is time to fight."

I could hardly believe what was happening, let alone respond to it. The only possible explanation was that she had, in fact, managed to slay her Accretion—which meant she was under the same spell Narbu had always feared. The weight of unbearable memories had fallen upon her, compressing her mind like coal being squeezed into diamond. Whatever she was, it wasn't the Cobalt Seer anymore. It was a force of pure destruction.

"Akasha," I breathed, "we can't—"

"That is not my name."

"All right, fine. Empress, we can't fight them. Not like this."

"Why does fear claim your heart, Beja?" she asked, casually kneeling to retrieve Izamem's cube-controlling remote. Just as casually, she hit a button that caused the cube's many sides to flip upward. "Come. Stand with me against the interlopers."

I glanced about in utter shock. She'd just freed me . . . at a time when I wasn't so sure I *wanted* to be free.

When she stepped aside, revealing the hundreds of weapons aimed at our heads, I was doubly confident in my assessment. As badass as that execution had been, we weren't going anywhere except another cell, a body bag, or straight out the airlock. My HUD sprang up, counting an ever-growing number of foes, but I didn't pay it much mind.

"For what it's worth," I said quietly, edging forward to climb out at Akasha's side, "I've had a good time with you. In all your forms."

She smiled at me in spite of the orders being barked. "We cannot fail, Beja. The weight of the infinite heavens will tip the scales."

Well, that was one way to face imminent death. I sucked down a deep breath, ready to charge to my inevitable demise (and, subsequently, hell) . . . then froze. Distant, shuddering jolts moved through the floor panels. The *whump* of muffled blasts bit straight through the many bulkheads around us.

The soldiers initially ignored the sounds, but when the room's lights began flickering and sputtering out in entire rows, they could no longer afford that luxury. Their helmets swept back and forth, and rifle barrels traced the rafters overhead.

I turned to Akasha. "What the fu—"

In a spray of black smoke, sparks, and white-hot shrapnel, the pressurized door to our left *exploded*. Before the debris had even settled, hundreds of neon tracer rounds came ripping into the room, tearing through Hegemony armor and rifles and columns with merciless indifference.

Thinking fast, I grabbed Akasha and hauled her behind Rogaji's cube, all the while ducking under the zip and hiss of bullets streaking just centimeters past our faces. Once behind that disturbingly transparent barrier, the impacts turned to solid, muted *kwoks*, leaving hardly a divot on the cube's front pane.

The protection proved ultra-useful, because no less than three seconds later, explosions started going off throughout the room. Body parts and superheated metal scrap thudded into the walls.

I glanced at Akasha, but she wasn't home at that moment. Her eyes were filled with righteous glee, basking in the all-out slaughter.

On the other side of the spectrum, I was just confused. Who the hell would be attacking a Hegemony vessel at this exact moment? I distantly ran through the possibilities, the majority of my attention reserved for the ongoing massacre.

Insurgents? No. It was *possible* they'd heard the Hegemony was carrying a high-value target and had thus planned a raid to nab us, but I doubted it. They just didn't have those kinds of resources. Not when an entire fleet was waiting in the wings, anyway.

Chanzig's surviving zealots? No, that was just paranoid conspiracy talk.

Rogaji's crew? Not a chance. They were either dead or twiddling their thumbs in a cell, probably on the cusp of killing that little shit Bodhi.

Just as I seemed to be out of options, I received a hint. Phantom images streaked through the Hegemony troops in twos and threes, seemingly materializing and vanishing in under a second. Each time those phantom images struck a target, they practically exploded in a geyser of blood and cartilage. Then I saw the afterglow of energy moving through skulls and chests . . . the distorted space of pressure waves ripping armor open . . . the glint of blades slicing through necks.

My gaze dribbled down to the pile of innocent-looking dust in the cube. Rogaji's dust. Sure enough, there was no immortal chok'tal squirming around in the powder. Which meant . . .

They killed another goddamn clone.

As if in response to my solving of the mystery, objects moving with the speed of meteorites crashed through the ceilings and walls and floor. Only . . . they weren't random projectiles. I followed their movements and quickly discerned that they were, in fact, Rogaji. *Dozens* of Rogajis. They zipped and teleported about, giggling, dancing, slashing their way through the dwindling numbers of Hegemony troops.

Then, suddenly, there was silence—apart from the screech of the ship's alarms, that is. The smoke thinned enough to present a single Hegemony soldier squirming toward the exits, leaving a bright, glossy trail of blood behind him. He'd lost both legs at the kneecap.

I looked about, trying to spot Rogaji—one of her, at least—but she was nowhere to be seen. All that remained were corpses and bullet-riddled panels and blood. Lots of blood.

Just as I moved to step out from behind the cube, however, Rogaji sprang into existence just behind the legless soldier. With a savage grin and a pip of laughter, she drove her fist straight through the back of his helmet.

I stood in place, shell-shocked, while Akasha just moved around me and toward the very much alive Purifier.

"What a grand display of power!" Akasha called. "You are truly a warrior of the heavens. My kindest regards."

Rogaji flicked the blood off her fist—not much use, as it was *all over* her—then smirked at me. "So, you managed to wake your girlfriend up?"

I staggered toward her with wide eyes. "What . . . the actual . . . *fuck* . . . is going on?"

Shrugging at Akasha, then looking my way, Rogaji explained, "Sorry I was a little late. I've been into meditation a lot lately, and I tend to lose contact with my doubles when I get deep in a session. Giving myself me time was Izamem's idea . . . though I guess I ought to be assessing his suggestions a little more prudently." She glanced at the remains of his body, then made an *ick* face. "Oh, well . . . that's that, then."

"That . . . " I looked at her, then at Akasha, then back again, trying to rephrase my *what the fuck is going on* question in a way that would get me a real answer.

She seemed to understand my brain's system crash. "Oh, come on, Dak. I'm practically a god. Do you *really* think I'd just be walking around my own base with my real body, waiting to be captured? That's just foolish."

"You . . . you're telling me . . . that this is the first time I'm meeting your real body. Again."

Rogaji nodded sweetly. "Nice to meet you, Dak. I'm Rogaji." Before I could even *think* of a suitable reply, over a hundred copies of her materialized like digital pop-up ads all around the room. In hypnotic unison, they said, "It's a real pleasure."

"How marvelous!" Akasha exclaimed.

All the Rogajis offered a bow in response, but I wasn't done just yet. "How far away were you?"

"Oh, a few systems away," her original version—hopefully—said. "So, what happened?"

"You tell me."

"Well, as far as I can surmise, Izamem betrayed us to the Hegemony once you accessed whatever you were seeking in the Godmaker," she said, tapping her chin. "Come to think of it, it was rather rude of you to hide your intentions from me."

"Sorry about that," I said through gritted teeth. I still wasn't done being pissed at her for hiding her *truly* insane abilities. "How do we get out of here?"

Rogaji narrowed her eyes in thought—a gesture repeated by her clones. "Once my crew gets here, we can think about an escape route."

"Where are they?"

"Oh, almost here," she said, glancing at the blown-out door she'd entered through. "I rescued them from the brig with one of my extra bodies."

"Are you serious? How many bodies do you have?"

"Two thousand and fifty . . . four? No, two. Just lost a pair to an infrared beam."

I sighed, no longer even questioning the absurd heights of her power. "What the hell are they doing around infrared beams? Those are—"

"Yes, ship-to-ship weapons," she said, bored. "I'm currently fighting the bulk of the fleet in zero grav."

"I call bullshit."

"Call it what you like." Smirking, she snapped her fingers and summoned what appeared to be . . . a vidscreen. It wasn't solid but rather a flickering, granular blob that reminded me of Chanzig's mind-made vidscreens. "Have a look."

The floating screen projected an image that was seemingly untethered to any one location, forming a pastiche of deep space from multiple angles. Everywhere I looked, I saw Hegemony ships bursting with silent explosions or letting off thousands of multicolored rounds. Just for shits and giggles, Rogaji magnified the detail on one of the nearest battles. True to her word, the ship's hull was being ripped apart by a team of Rogaji clones clinging to the surface. Panel by panel, they deconstructed the armor, allowing several of them to punch their way down and into the ship's innards.

"You've got to be kidding," I breathed. "You're literally fighting a Hegemony fleet . . . and winning."

She looked rather impressed with herself. "True, but not for very long. They have reinforcements coming . . . and I've got a feeling they'll be bringing a few special weapons for Purifiers in the wild. Best not to stick around."

Akasha cried out, jarring me—and all the Rogajis. She collapsed to her knees, clawing at her head and screaming like I'd never heard before.

"What's . . . wrong with her?" Rogaji asked.

I sank down at her side and put my hands atop hers. "Akasha? Empress?"

After a few more seconds of howls, she met my gaze with bloodshot eyes. "Dak . . . it's coming through. I can't hold it."

"Coming through?" Rogaji said.

"It's a long story," I said, though in truth, I didn't understand it myself. It was probably something to do with the Accretion. Maybe she hadn't killed it, or maybe she'd absorbed it . . . Whatever the case, there was clearly a problem. "Just focus. Stay with me."

Akasha nodded, but just then, I spotted blood on her robes. It was coming from her sternum and stomach. From the same rift that had birthed the Unmade on the mountaintop. Horror washed over me. *This* was the reason Narbu had sealed her mind. She was fractured, an unstable rift that joined this world and *his*.

"We won't have time to get away from here," I told Rogaji. "I know how to open the direct gateway, but we'll need to do it now."

She scoffed. "You can't be serious."

"Unfortunately, I am."

We locked gazes, stubborn as could be, until our contest was broken by the sound of drumming feet and panting. Looking up and past Rogaji, I saw her crew dashing through the doorway with a team of Rogaji-clone escorts in tow.

"The whole crew, together at last!" young Bodhi shouted, looking far too confident in his oversize prisoner's garb. His eyes moved to Akasha. "Oh, well, *hello* there . . . "

Krezz Holmes saved me from a homicide charge by slapping the bastard upside the head. "Not the time, boy."

"Hey," Bodhi said, shying away, "I'm a social networker."

Rogaji gave me a nervous glance, seemingly taking my words at face value, then faced her crew. "All right, listen up, everyone. The current fleet is managed, but there's going to be more coming. A lot more."

"Hell, yeah!" Bodhi said. "Time to earn my combat pilot's badge."

Again, Krezz gave him a tender smack.

"*Anyway,*" Rogaji went on, ignoring the rumbling blasts taking place throughout the ship, "what's the status of your ship?"

Krezz Holmes shifted his jaw as though chewing an unsavory wad of amp-snuff. "Docked in the impound hangar. Could probably pry it out, but it'll be hell gettin' through the crossfire. Not to mention any pinch jammers they've got . . . "

"Don't worry about the jammers," Rogaji said. "I'll take care of any ships with those. You just need to take Dak and, uh, Charming Blue Woman . . . and get far from here. Any system will do. We'll meet up on—" She stopped short, eyes bulging. "Shit. The Godmaker."

Toast and Jar crossed their arms, then asked as one, "What about it?"

"We can't let them get their hands on it," Rogaji said, pacing and blowing out hard breaths. "The things they'd do with it . . . the technology they'd develop . . . No. Not a chance. Mr. Holmes, I need you to escort the engineers back to the compound. Toast and Jar, I need you to wire the Godmaker for total collapse. Set it on maximum." She stopped again, frowning. "Where is Frownmaker?"

The crewmembers looked at one another, shrugging. Finally, Krezz Holmes said, "We lost sight of him a while back. Last we saw, he grabbed a gun and started goin' to town on the Hegemony."

Rogaji cocked a brow. "Ah . . . right, then. The rest of the plan stands. I'll send you a few of my doppelgängers as security, Mr. Holmes, but the rest will be left up to you. If all goes well, the implosion from the Godmaker should cover our tracks when we move systems. Why, it might even swallow up the entire planet."

"Entire system," Toast put in, frowning. "It's an unstable quantum contraption."

"Even better," Rogaji said. "So, are we all in agreement?"

I'd listened to the entire exchange, but only half-heartedly. My attention was on Akasha, whose wound was only growing. She wouldn't make it long enough to board that ship, much less ride it back to the compound and then onward to another destination. In just a few minutes' time, I wagered, she would become a host for the Unmade once again. And this time around, there was no telling how I might banish it—if I even could.

"We're staying," I said. "She and I need to finish this somehow."

My sudden intrusion into the conversation drew all eyes to Akasha's still-expanding wound.

"Oh," Rogaji said, seemingly realizing what I was so concerned about. "*Oh.*"

I sighed. "Yeah, *oh*. Remember what I told you about the mountaintop? It's happening."

"But . . . why?"

"A long story. Too long to explain right now."

Rogaji's gaze softened with the gravity of it all. "All right, us three will stay here and deal with it. My copies can handle the rest remotely."

"Hold on now," Holmes rumbled. "What about our payment?"

"I've got an escrow account for all of you," Rogaji said. "You'll get your funds once we're clear."

"Y'expect me to believe that?"

"Mr. Holmes, if you have a grievance that relates to your terms of employment, I'm more than happy to allow you to escape on your own and take this up in a courtroom."

He sneered at her, then let out a defeated puff. "Fine. We're rollin' out."

The grizzled captain whirled around and headed for the door, prompting his crew to follow. Most of it, anyway. Bodhi lingered awhile longer, looking between Rogaji and me with a distinctly guilty smile.

Rogaji frowned at him and plastered her hands on her hips. "I'm disappointed, Bodhi."

He shrugged and, with some difficulty, fished a golden hammer—*my* golden, Wellspring-containing hammer—from his rear waistband. He handed it off to me with a look that carried both pride and a sincere, unspoken request to *not* have his fingers broken.

I snatched it from his grubby grip. "Thanks. I guess."

"You're very welcome," Bodhi said, winking. "Bodhi Drezek, budding entrepreneur and venture capitalist. Spread the word. Look me up."

With that, Bodhi gave a theatrical bow and jogged off to follow his comrades.

"So, what now?" Rogaji asked me after a period of stunned silence, gesturing to Akasha's wound. "Does he just . . . climb out of her?"

I shook my head, eyes glued to the alien and her fluttering eyelids. "I don't know."

"Didn't you figure out the magic bullet inside the Godmaker?"

"Yes and no."

Rogaji folded her arms. "All that money . . . down the tubes."

"Not exactly," I said. "There *is* a way to reach his world . . . but we can't do it."

"Why not?"

"Because it needs—"

"A sacrifice," Akasha interrupted weakly. With each breath, the blood spread farther. All Rogaji and I could do was exchange a series of concerned glances. "I have witnessed the fate of this body, Beja. I have felt the threads of this world. There is no longer a question of what *can* be done . . . only what *must.* Just as you gave your mind for me, so shall I give my mind for you . . . and for all beings."

Rogaji started to speak, but I shook my head to indicate it wasn't the time. She had the tact to take my word on that matter.

"You don't know what you're asking," I said as I shifted her into my lap. Her breaths came in long, shaky rushes. "You don't even know what it's like to—"

"I know only that the hells will deliver that which I have earned through cherishing my own blood," she said, wincing. "This is not yet the end, Beja."

I ran a hand across her forehead, trying to soothe her, but it was no use. We were the only two beings in local space that had any idea what was happening. For once, at least, we were on the same level. We viewed this horror from a vantage point none would ever share.

"If you cannot recall the words," she said with a dribble of blood from her lips, "I will recite them with you."

"There might be another way."

"No," she said softly, sweetly, peering into my eyes with lucidity that would soon vanish. "This body . . . this mind . . . are gifts to the infinite worlds. Can you deliver them, Beja? Can you make them shine with radiance?"

I glanced away, but all I found was Rogaji's creased stare.

Akasha rested a trembling hand on my arm. "Do you remember what I told you, all those days and nights ago? Do you remember words of love?"

"Yes," I whispered.

"Then hold on to those words. Hold on to the love that survives in the face of great evil." Her hand strayed to my chest. "Let it reside there, Beja, and know that it is me. What I am . . . what you were, and what you are . . . cannot be destroyed."

All sound dropped away, and strangely, illogically, nothing seemed to exist except the two of us. When our eyes met, I didn't see another being. Not in the way I usually thought of them. Instead, I saw the very force that animated those eyes—indeed, the force that *was* the eyes, stripped of their rigid shape and color and DNA. I saw the Absolute itself staring back at me.

You can't die.

The thought didn't refer to Akasha's body or even her consciousness, but rather to the totality of what she was, to the endless web of causes and effects that had brought her and me and trees and water and stars into existence. *That* could never die, nor be snuffed out. It was nothing but existence . . . and existence had to exist. It was the simplest, most beautiful axiom, grasped in an instant without so much as a thought to confirm its logic. I just *knew*.

It felt like a download straight from reality itself—a summarized, wordless package of everything I'd seen and heard and read on the monks' planet, all distilled into one heartbeat.

The fear and the anger and the outright disbelief remained, but they were held in an ocean so much greater than themselves. They passed beneath me, through me. Even that selfish knot of clinging that wanted Akasha more than life itself was seen in its true form: another modulation of the Absolute. Everything was exactly what it was, and yet . . . different. In the Absolute, nobody and nothing was truly dying, nor were they being reborn, nor suffering.

It was all . . . exactly what it was.

Change. Endless, breathtaking change.

A lightness came over me. A certain confidence. The smile that came over my face—and, simultaneously, Akasha's—had to have looked utterly mad to Rogaji, given how quickly she threw up her hands and walked away to give us "our moment."

Without needing to think about my decision, and without even really knowing *how*, I began the ritual. I stood and stepped back, then began peeling motes and globs of Sparkseed off the hammer, molding it into my own mandala with a light touch. Whereas my first time creating the arrangement had been strenuous, even bordering on the impossible, this time was as simple as breathing. The golden threads wove together and flattened and curved, all the while assembling a formation that blocked my view of Akasha's tender stare.

The last fragments converged in a rush, and then the mandala hung before me, glimmering and pulsing with primal energy.

My mouth opened. My heart slowed. The words began pouring forth, ancient and extinct, filling me with a sense of mystery whose solution was just out of reach. Rogaji moved and said something in the background, but I didn't really notice. All I heard was my own voice, supported by Akasha's, as we called forth the unspeakable.

Just as I'd seen in the Godmaker, the exposed core of the hammer—an impossible, drifting glob of the Wellspring itself—drifted into the center of the mandala like a focusing crystal.

Word by word, breath by breath, the configuration receded into space that was not physical. It defied all laws of physics, stretching back and back and back until it settled in place as the end of a long and twisting tunnel. A final syllable escaped my lips, and then there was a flash, a ripple of force . . . and death.

I stepped back, my hands trembling, as the mandala dissolved and reformed as the hammer. Akasha lay on the tiles before me, eyes open but stripped of life. She looked so peaceful. So . . . hopeful.

"Is this . . . *magic*?" Rogaji's hyped-up voice drew my attention to her. She was walking toward me, somewhat unsettled by the corpse but largely transfixed by what hung above it. "Are you a magician, Dak?"

The esoteric knowledge that had possessed and guided me through the ritual began to taper off, ceding to a quieter, more refined sense of steadiness. I sensed the doors to the secrets of the universe closing, locking me out once again. And yet . . . I held a glimmer of what they'd taught me. A souvenir, if you will. It gave me the composure to avoid screaming at Rogaji for her pitiless comments.

After all, she, too, was just a form of the Absolute. She played her role as much as I played mine and Akasha had played hers. Given all the death she'd seen, and all the death she'd hand delivered, I couldn't fault her for speaking so casually around the body of a woman she'd never actually met.

There was, of course, another good reason for her indifference: my "magic trick." The freshly spawned, spherical anomaly hovered where the center of the mandala had been, resembling a stable yet miniaturized black hole. The light and colors around it warped inward, pulled toward some unknown destination. In total, it was hardly more than a few centimeters across.

"*That's* our gateway?" Rogaji asked, seemingly less impressed up close.

She lifted a finger toward it, but I batted it away. "Don't get careless. He could come through at any moment."

Rogaji just grinned. "No. He's waiting for us."

"How do you know?"

"Because it's his modus operandi. He would've come out by now if he wanted to."

I nodded grimly, acknowledging her point. "You think it's a trap?"

"Only one way to find out." Her eyes strayed from the portal, eventually settling on Akasha's lifeless face. "It may not mean much to you, Dak, but I'm sorry."

"She'll be all right."

"You, uh . . . sure about that?"

I smiled at her. "Trust me. I'll find her somehow, assuming we finish this."

"Find her?"

"Never mind." I gave a little shrug. "Besides, I've got you at the ready."

Rogaji's entire face soured. "Dak, you're a handsome man . . . so I don't mean any offense . . . but I'm not into men. Not at all."

"What?" I blurted out. "Oh, no. No. That wasn't what I meant."

"You're sure?"

"It was about the fight, okay?"

"Okay. I'll give you a pass on this one." She tossed me a light smirk. "So, is it time?"

"Yeah. Just . . . gimme a second, would you?"

"For what?"

I waved off her concerns and stepped a little distance away, making sure to avoid the worst of the floor gore. Then, with far more sobriety than I expected, I switched on my mental link with Modri.

"Hey, old friend."

Modri's heavy laugh came through. *"Old? Chief, we've known each other a few days."*

"Felt like longer in the Godmaker, though."

"Yeah. What a ride that was . . . "

"I'm . . . sorry for shutting you off for so long. All the time."

"And I'm . . . sorry for switchin' off on you," Modri said with more than a little discomfort, almost as though confessing his crimes before a firing squad.

"Thanks. I really felt that apology."

"Oh, c'mon. I gave it my all."

I sighed. "So you say. Got to hand it to you, though—you know how to call out the future bad ones."

"Had a few flukes in there."

"I'd give you a 60 percent hit rate," I said, wobbling my head in pseudo calculation. "Not too bad for a hunk of looping mental residue."

"Not too bad at all."

I paused, waiting for the inevitable . . . then growled. "Really? No snarky comments? Not even for old times' sake?"

"Nope," Modri said. *"You've done good, kid. So far, anyway. I'm gonna be clownin' on you every day in the afterlife if you bite it in there."*

"You heard the Wellspring. My mind's already spoken for."

"Hell sounds like fun. Maybe I'll join you if you kill this pissbaby. Although, between you and me . . . I think Ro's gonna take the crown."

I tossed Rogaji a glance, but she was too busy running her hands around the portal's exterior. "Yeah . . . about that. Not too sure I want *her* becoming the new host of the Glorious Game."

"Point taken," Modri said, chuckling. *"We'll have a beer when this all shakes out, Purifier. You and me."*

"I'd like that."

"We'll, uh, even raise one for your girl."

"She's not my girl. She's just—"

"Your crush?"

"No," I said, shaking my head. "She's a future Wayfarer. I know it."

"Whatever you say, buddy." Modri sighed. *"Listen. Not to rush our little smoochin' sesh, but I think Ro's itchin' to fight. Better get in there before she handles it herself."*

"Getting rid of me that quickly?"

"Love 'em and leave 'em."

I smiled. "See you on the other side, asshole."

"Back atcha, fucker."

And with that innocent farewell handled, I proceeded to my destiny.

25

So," Rogaji said, staring at the tiny, silvery hole in spacetime, "what do we do?"

I shifted my weight about, thinking. "I have no idea."

"Do we . . . poke it?"

"One way to find out."

After glancing her way and receiving an uncharacteristically nervous nod, I tried to poke it. I say *tried* because my finger never quite reached the surface. It just kept moving deeper and deeper, the portal itself just out of reach.

"This is taking too long," Rogaji said with a forced exhale.

Before I could figure out her intentions, much less stop her in any meaningful way, she hopped toward the portal. I stepped back, half expecting her to slam into something solid, half expecting her to be torn apart by gravitational flux. What actually happened was far stranger. Still midair, her body began . . . condensing, shrinking to impossible dimensions. The portal swallowed her entire form like a leaf washed down a high-pressure drainage circuit.

I looked about, suddenly alone apart from Akasha's body. "Fantastic." With one final look at the woman's peaceful, vacant eyes, I followed Rogaji in her mad leap.

Given my past experience with entering rifts in reality, I'd expected an overpowering surge of energy, followed by total loss of bodily sensations and consciousness itself. That didn't happen this time. Instead, I felt every molecule of my form being compacted, squeezed, folded into a subatomic shape no living thing was supposed to occupy. My visual field stretched around me like taffy, and sounds skittered out into long, whizzing tones.

Then I was inside the vortex, rocketing forward past streaks of black and red, trying to hold on to my fragile mind as it was once again pulled to the breaking point. I accelerated constantly, gaining speed I'd never envisioned. Every particle of my body thrummed and rebelled against the structure of my genetic code. The pain was unbearable. My lips flew open to loose an involuntary cry, but there was no air, only the void. I kept my gaze fixed ahead, using that small, impossible end of the tunnel as my guiding light. All I had to—

Without warning, my heels landed on solid ground. I registered Rogaji's presence at my side. Normal sensations flooded the body—my heartbeat, my breathing, my orientation in space—but what I saw was far from normal.

We stood inside a vast, rippling sphere, almost as though we'd somehow entered the cavity of a hollow planet. When I say *vast*, you might imagine something truly big and impressive . . . but not to this scale. We were nothing but ants. The walls were slick and crimson, oozing a variety of fluids that left the entire sphere striped.

Even the ground beneath our feet squelched, threatening to suck up our boots. When I looked down at it, I noted that it was nothing but cancer-riddled, chewed-up meat, *breathing* through small, gushing pores. In fact, I soon realized, the entire sphere was breathing. It moved in discordant cycles, bulging and flattening in different areas.

The crown jewel of this hellish new world, however, was the central stalk that seemed to support the structure. It ran from floor to ceiling, striated with tendons and bulging knobs and veins of dark, slurping fluid. All light was derived from this column of flesh. Specifically, from the glowing red lifeblood that swirled in rubbery sacs up and down its length.

The Source.

Rogaji whistled. "Well, that's one way to decorate a foyer."

I just stared her way, crinkling my nose at the omnipresent stink of disease. It smelled like the inside of a veterinarian's surgery bay.

"Sorry," she said, though she clearly wasn't. "So . . . this is it, huh?"

"I guess so."

"You *guess*?"

I shrugged and started moving ahead, hoping we might get answers from the glowing stalk. Was it really this easy? Did I just walk up, rip it open—with *love*, naturally—and claim it?

Rogaji caught up a moment later. "Get excited, Dak. This is our moment of victory."

"Don't celebrate prematurely."

"I'm not *celebrating* . . . I'm savoring the anticipation."

Somehow, I just couldn't share her excitement. It had nothing to do with Akasha—I'd made peace with that already—but I sensed that something was, indeed, wrong. I'd forgotten something. Overlooked it. The feeling was so thoroughly ominous that I nearly stopped short and asked Rogaji for her take on things. Nearly. Because the moment I did stop and glance at her, I figured out what it was.

You see, my subconscious spat out the name *Duplicitous Contender* when I looked at her. By this point, I knew Izamem had claimed that spot, so the Contender's identity wasn't the root of the problem. No, the *problem* was that the prophecy was off. I'm not talking about the exact methods through which those three minibosses were handled—whether Akasha or I had slain Izamem didn't matter much—but rather the mere existence of said minibosses. Even if the notion irked me, I couldn't dispute that the monks had been spot-on about much of my journey thus far. Hence why I needed to figure out this conundrum.

Izamem had been the first kill, serving as the Duplicitous Contender. Akasha, as much as I *hated* to admit it, had probably been the second, serving as the Mad Regent. That left just one more: the Sun Swallower.

Before I could voice this issue to Rogaji, the sphere constricted like a cell preparing to defend itself against invading microbes. Rivers of blood frothed through sphincters in the walls and gushed down toward the middle basin. Chaotic undulations raced through the floor.

"Oh, I hope we're not about to be drowned in bile," Rogaji whined.

"No," I said, staring at the ever-expanding, blood-raining hole in the ceiling, "I think it'll be much worse."

The *thing* that began squeezing its way into the sphere wasn't a serpent, as the monks' carvings had predicted. Then again, they'd also predicted Izamem to be a human and Akasha to be a man . . . but enough about that.

First to emerge were long, twitching feelers, followed by scores of milk-white eyes, a forest of teeth, scales, blood-crusted little hairs, the legs of a cockroach, tentacles, bony armor plates, more scales, a bulging egg sac reminiscent of a pregnant spider . . .

Rogaji and I exchanged a quick look, confirming both our mouths were hanging wide-open.

The creature *just . . . kept . . . coming.* Before long it was a slithering, chittering mass more than two hundred meters in length, with no end in sight. It just kept pouring itself down the ceiling, twisting into strange curls and spearing the walls with its bony legs, gibbering like a mammal whose mind was currently being devoured by the worst possible parasites.

"Dak," Rogaji said softly, "what is that?"

I pulled in a deep breath. "The Sun Swallower."

"The *what*?"

Three hundred meters . . . four hundred . . . it just wouldn't stop. Just as I was beginning to fear it would unfurl itself throughout the entire chamber, its entry hole widened to allow the exit of a thick, carapace-like tail that looked far too similar to a lobster's. The abomination loosed an ear-splitting screech, then dug its legs and pincers and tentacles and stingers into the wall so it hung perfectly horizontal.

"Think it sees us?" Rogaji whispered.

In reply, the Sun Swallower began madly dashing along the walls, raking open the structural flesh and feeding the pool of juices that had already reached my ankles. By the time I realized it was heading straight for *us*, it was too late. The thing came bearing down like a runaway train, its face a horrible mishmash of the 'verse's most despised creepers and crawlers. Fluid sprayed like an oncoming tidal wave, and the ground beneath my feet rumbled like never before.

Rogaji and I dived to opposite sides, hoping it would cut straight down the middle . . . but it didn't. It pivoted during its frenzied charge—straight toward Rogaji. Like a laser-guided missile, it slammed straight into her and drove her *through* the wall at her back.

I staggered to my feet, cringing at the amount of gunk all over me, and looked at the impact zone. The impressive, gory rut left by the Sun Swallower's charge ended in the newfound tunnel . . . where there was no sign of either it or Rogaji. Even as I stared at the hauntingly large opening, it began resealing, regenerating itself in strings of tendon and viscera.

I lunged for it, but there wasn't a chance in hell. The entire hole was gone by the time I got my hands on where it had once been.

"Rogaji!" I screamed, tempted but not foolish enough to try driving my hand into the living material.

The voice that answered me wasn't Rogaji's.

"You did it, Dak," the Unmade said coolly, his words drifting around me in a perennial echo. "You managed to come . . . *here*. Do you have any idea how proud I am?"

I turned to find the Unmade frighteningly close, levitating several meters above the blood-and-bile mix. Like on the mountaintop, they'd adopted their "human-adjacent" disguise. The red light of the central stalk played across his form, glinting off the myriad blades and torturous instruments driven into his skin. A stream of insects drained from his rotting mask.

"Where is she?" I asked, trying to keep my voice as calm as possible. If a Purifier several *hundred* ranks above me had just been catapulted out of existence, I had no chance in this domain.

The Unmade drifted around me in a lazy circle. "Preoccupied."

"Bring her back."

"Oh, I could, but I don't think I will. I wanted to give us this opportunity to speak."

I tracked the eldritch being as he floated about, maintaining a firm grip on the hammer. "About your ugly pet?"

"Beauty and ugliness are so . . . relative," the Unmade said. "You may not believe it, but the Sun Swallower was once a humanoid. Just like you. It's a shame they lost their mind . . . The least I could do was offer them a home here."

I thought back to some of the first words Akasha had shared with me. Specifically, the words about a shaman who had risen to prominence by accepting the first chok'tal into himself. It was probably the same being. One that had been born looking like Izamem, no less. I didn't even want to know how much defilement and power was required to warp a body that far.

More pressingly, it meant the Sun Swallower was also a Purifier with an unbelievably high rank. I prayed Rogaji wouldn't handle their fight with her usual levity, relying on her upgrades more as a source of entertainment than real weapons.

That was out of my hands, though. My fight was *here*.

"What's there to talk about?" I asked. "I came here to destroy you."

The Unmade cocked his head. "You aren't even interested in the *reason* behind the madness? After all you've done, all you've suffered through . . . don't you wish to know what it was all about?"

"Nah."

"Why is that, Dak? Do you fear what I might say?"

I sighed. "Let me tell you something. I've spent weeks slogging through miserable, hopeless conditions. I've had my body ripped apart so often I'd probably sleep through having my arm amputated. I haven't even been able to keep my feet planted in physical reality. But the worst—by *far*, the *worst*—part of this whole endeavor has been listening to monologues from assholes like you.

"I get it. Reality can be awful. Dreams can be crushed. But if you look around, you'll notice that 99 percent of people who get dealt a bad hand don't go on to become genocidal maniacs or egotistical torture aficionados. What happened to you and Chanzig and the seer and everyone else was tragic, and most certainly beyond your control, but everything beyond that has been your choice. You could've spent all these quadrillions of years perfecting meditation and becoming a guru to some alien species in the fifteenth dimension, but no . . . you *wanted* to destroy.

"So forgive me, a fellow survivor of cruel and terrible events, for not sympathizing enough to listen to your lecture on why you're justified in what you've done. I'll settle for ripping your goddamn head off and using it as a mug."

The Unmade studied me for a long, cold moment, seemingly taken aback for the first time in eternity. Then he laughed. "Dak, Dak, Dak. This is why—"

He didn't get a chance to continue. Shock and Awe converted my entire left hand into a scaled-down nuclear blast, temporarily washing out my vision and hearing. I staggered back, blinking and rubbing at my eyes, trying to see how much of the chamber I'd evaporated with the explosion. When vision trickled back in, I saw that I'd torn a vast, oozing crater into the walls, its inner surface scorched or outright blackened.

The Unmade was nowhere in sight. Turned to aerosolized carbon, maybe.

"Damn," I whispered to myself, watching my hand as the flesh regrew bit by bit.

Then a pocket of dead air replaced the humid breeze at my back. I spun around, instinctively bringing the hammer along for the swing, but the Sparkseed didn't connect with anything.

"So jumpy." The Unmade's voice, seemingly more amused now, drifted down from the same imprecise location. "All that tutelage from the monks, and then this? How crass."

I backed up with the hammer at my side, nodding at the dripping nooks and crannies of the sphere. "Come back out so you can see what else I've learned."

"No, I don't think I will. Not until you can restrain yourself."

"I guess you'll just have to kill me, then."

The Unmade's laugh crept along the walls behind me. "Let's meet in the middle."

Midstep, the ground beneath me quivered and hissed with a sudden spray. I leaped back, but not fast enough to avoid the gigantic, fingerlike spur of bone that tore through my back—and out through my stomach. I stared down at the makeshift hook, disbelieving and wide-eyed, not quite able to make sense of my impalement. When I finally did try to squirm off—with the aid of Soaring Death's wings, no less—the bony protrusion sprouted row upon row of serrated teeth. What this meant, in practice, was that any attempt to extricate myself would also rip my entire torso open.

I flopped back and breathed through the pain, simultaneously confirming that here, in this realm, there was no HUD. No Kill Points to be gained.

Right on cue, of course, the Unmade drifted down and into my field of view. He hung above me like an angel of agony, his posture so casual that even *I* knew I wasn't going anywhere.

"All right, asshole," I said, tasting blood, "you've got your captive audience. Now what?"

"*Now,*" he said, "we talk."

"Go ahead."

Again, he laughed. "You just continue to delight me, Dak. I can never quite predict what you're going to do."

"I've heard that a lot lately."

"Yes, well, they surely don't appreciate it as I do." He drifted closer. "We're *finally* on the same plane of existence. Everything is so . . . immediate."

"Yet you still drag things out."

He sighed. "There's no such thing as wasted time, Dak, when *everything* is fruitless. In a reality without meaning, everything is meaningful. Do you see the paradox?"

"I see the *irony* of you trying to give me philosophy lessons."

"It's not about philosophy," he said with sudden harshness. "It's not about dead words, dead ideas, dead minds. It's about *here. Now.* This very breath. Open your eyes and see the truth of it. Feel that vast, vast emptiness. Can you?"

I settled for giving him my most hateful stare.

"Very well," he said at last, floating back once more. "By the time we're done here, Dak, you'll see it. You'll beg me to make you unsee it."

"Oh, so that's the plan? Torture me? How original."

His eyes narrowed, and now I could see the rage bubbling just beneath the surface. The razor's edge of losing control.

"All I ask of you is one civil, honest conversation," he said quietly. "If you grant me that honor, I'll give you the fight you desire. I'll let the pieces fall as they will."

I considered it for a time, swinging between attitudes of total defiance and resignation. By this point, I didn't even know what I was fighting for.

Akasha was gone, Rogaji had been sucked into a nether dimension, the universe was aflame with dickwads, and I was bound for hell or a new career as the Unmade's replacement. Any way I sliced it, this was an unwinnable situation. Because of that, however, I came to a decision that seemed best for the both of us.

"Fine," I said through clenched jaws. "One conversation, no tricks, and then we settle the score."

"Excellent!"

"Yeah, excellent . . . Mind letting me off this thing?"

He ran his stare up and down my ravaged body. "Certainly." With a flick of his fingers, the bone retracted and lowered me to the gummy, blood-flooded ground.

I bit down a cry as I stumbled to my feet, the Anima already doing its miracle work of repairing my flesh—and thus consuming my limited stores of energy. Shock and Awe had already cost me a shitload of calories. I could only imagine what it would take to rebuild the gaping hole in my torso.

Upon looking up, I found that the Unmade had summoned—no joke—a table-and-chair set formed from the same gloopy tissue as the sphere itself. The furniture was connected to the floor, rising up like cancerous mounds before me.

"Nice touch," I said as I warily staggered over and slumped into one of the chairs. It squelched and sagged beneath me.

The Unmade, in his cordial facade, took the other seat. "That's better, isn't it?"

"Much."

"Unfortunately, I have nothing to offer by way of food or drink," he explained. "Nothing that would appeal to your human mind, anyway."

I crossed my arms. "You wanted to talk, so talk."

For several moments, the Unmade didn't. He just sat there, studying me, looking away, studying me again. It was apparent that he'd been waiting for this moment for a long, long time, and yet they still lacked the right words. Strangely human, given all I knew about his nature.

After far too long for my liking, he said, "What do you know of love, Dak?"

"Oh, for fuck's—"

"An honest conversation," the Unmade cut in. "What do you know of it?"

"Depends on the context."

He shrugged in acknowledgment. "I'm not speaking of romantic love or its fixations. *Love.* Universal love. Unconditional love."

"I know what it isn't," I said, gesturing to the grisly sphere around us.

"First impressions are often deceiving." The Unmade settled back, sighing contentedly. "Do you remember our last conversation?"

"Something about the Absolute being a monstrosity," I said. "How it gives birth and kills itself in various forms."

"Yes. Very good, Dak. Just so."

"What's your point?"

"I'd *hoped* you would reach my ultimate conclusion on your own, but I now see that I was too optimistic." He fixed me with those empty, maggot-riddled eyes. "When one is faced with the madness of reality, Dak, they have two choices. They can either lean into it . . . or be dragged by it across eternity."

"I know which one you chose."

"Do you?" he hissed. "For a long, long while, yes . . . I chose the latter. I raged against the unfairness of existence. I destroyed all that I came across. But eventually . . . *eventually* . . . I understood that I'd been unkind to reality. I'd been playing it wrong the whole time."

"What the hell do you mean?"

"Why do you think animals are willing to die for their young, Dak? Why do soldiers maim their brethren? Why, even, do dictators crush their people?"

"Survival, fear, power. I don't know. Everyone wants to live."

"You're thinking too abstractly. Why do *anything*, Dak? Why fight all this way to reach me?"

"What do you want me to say?"

The Unmade studied me for a time. "It's all *love*, Dak," he said at last. "We do what we do . . . for love."

"You've got a sick sense of that word."

"Perhaps, but what can one call it when a mother bird consumes half her offspring so the others may live?"

"That's just nature."

"Which . . . is . . . *love*," he growled. "Reality itself is love. It kills itself for love. It tortures itself for love. It *loves* to exist. It *loves* to amuse itself. This is all a vast game, Dak, and there is no prize . . . beyond love. Reality loves itself so much that it sees all things as worthy of sacrifice."

I studied him back, more convinced than ever he'd lost what little remained of his marbles inside this hell for one.

"You don't believe me," the Unmade said, smirking. "I understand. It took me eons to grasp even one word of this. But it's true. It's all true. Even the worst, most terrible thing you can imagine was done for love. Love of power . . . love of flesh . . . love of hatred. It's the very thing that animates this world and all the worlds beyond it. Love."

"Would you quit saying the same fucking word?"

"Now we come to why you're here," he went on. "As you might guess, it's because of love. I truly *grasped* it. I tasted it. Devoured it. For trillions upon trillions of years, I contemplated love . . . and all the ways in which I might share it with reality. There were endless games I could've made for the beings of the endless cosmos, but all of them ended too soon. The prizes were too limited. I dreamed of the most wonderful, most incredible, most amazing game of all time . . . a game that could *never* be beaten. It would stretch on and on, persisting as long as existence itself."

"You did *what*?"

"That's right," the Unmade said, nodding giddily. "With every other game, Dak, one can complete it and set it aside. They can forget its rules. Forget its prizes. Soon they're returned to normal, pointless reality, craving the excitement of games they cannot beat. From then on, they exist in a different game. The game of feeding themselves. Eating. Shitting. Fucking. A constant, useless game played for nobody."

"Survival isn't a game. It's just survival, asshole."

The Unmade cocked his head. "You say that, but as I've pointed out . . . how many humanoids love to bury themselves in danger, even if it's merely simulated? This is what you all want. A game in which one receives glory or destruction. A game with no room for mediocrity or boredom. A game with no ending."

"There's about to be an ending."

"Only if you want there to be." I looked at the Unmade in confusion, but he just kept on rambling. "You think this is the final level, Dak, but it isn't. This is merely the beginning. The end of a tutorial."

"*What?*"

"Please . . . do you *really* think I'd be so shortsighted as to build a game that ends so easily? No, of course not. You've just qualified to play the real game."

"Stop trying to mind-fuck me."

He laughed. "It's true. You've seen how many Purifiers attempted to reach me. They all played by the standard rules, slogging through my dimension . . . but none reached this place." He let out a crestfallen sigh. "I *wanted* them to reach this place, Dak . . . I truly did . . . but some laws are even beyond my control. You see, in making this place, I separated myself from everything else. I created a prison none but the truly determined could enter."

"What you mean to say is, you fucked with spacetime so badly you built an unwinnable game."

The Unmade wagged a finger, urging hesitancy. "Not quite. I knew that eventually one would love the game enough to find me. And you did. You came to me."

"Yeah . . . to end this."

"Perhaps, but you don't need to. This can be the beginning."

"Beginning of what?"

The Unmade leaned toward me. "Of a game for two."

"Spell it out."

"Don't you *see*, Dak?"

His eyes flashed, and suddenly the walls of the sphere puffed outward, their pores expanding to preposterous widths. Through the thousands of pores, I saw mirrorlike windows—peepholes into other worlds, other times, other modulations of reality.

"There's so much more of the game to play," he said, gesturing to the endless portals all around us. "Soon I'll break through to more. I'll send the chok'tal to new competitors. New aspirants."

"What is—"

"We're on the same plane of existence. We can share in the same power. Together, we can grow as gods, moving between the infinite worlds and devouring them. We can even keep score. You've proven that you can wield my powers, so—"

"Are you kidding me?" I asked, unable to stop my small bark of amusement. "You really thought I would come all this way, kill all these people, take all this pain . . . just to *join* you and help you conquer the multiverse?"

"Why not?"

"You made me into a fucking monster," I growled. "If not for you, I'd never have been born where I was. I'd never have gotten that slug inside me. You *made* me into this. Do you know how many people I killed? Do you have any idea?"

"Oh, plenty. It was a thrill to watch."

"You're unbelievable. You don't even see what's wrong with what you've done, do you?"

The Unmade meshed his fingers on the table. "Dak, why do you resent me so much? Every good story needs a villain. Without me, you'd just be . . . a clone. A nobody. I gave you the chance to excel, and you've done just that. You've set yourself apart from every mortal in your tired little universe."

"I did what I *had* to . . . to get here. Why would I possibly agree to another round?"

"A shared game is better than playing by oneself."

"Fuck your game."

The Unmade flinched, seemingly shocked for the first time in our exchanges. When they spoke, their voice was small and meek. "But . . . I built this for us, Dak. For one who was strong enough. And you are. You're just like me."

"I am *nothing* like you."

"Aren't you? You've slaughtered just like me. You've felt the indifference of a cold, uncaring world, and through it, you found power. We are the same. We're brothers."

I steadily rose from the chair and took my hammer in both hands. "I think our honest conversation is over. It's time for me to fucking erase you."

Without missing a beat, the Unmade drifted up from his chair and dispelled the entire furniture setup. "Would you like to summon a Geno-facturing Cube for you? How about a few guns? A sword? Just tell me, and I'll make them. No strings attached."

"Why the hell would you do that?"

"To even the odds. It would be *terribly* wasteful for you to have gained so much power . . . and then refuse to employ it during such a momentous encounter."

"I didn't gain that power because I wanted it," I said, staring into his dead eyes. "I gained it because I had no choice. Do you think I *like* guns? That I *like* crushing the life out of people who can't even fight back? There was no joy in what you made me do."

"I didn't make you do anything, Dak. You did it out of love . . . for your own survival."

I tightened my grip on the weapon.

"Even as we stand here, with all your posturing, it's clear you want to keep playing," the Unmade continued. "Just as I thought you would."

"This isn't going to go how you expect."

"Oh?"

"You think I'm going to stand here and trade blows for hours on end," I said, my words sounding cold and hollow in my own ears. "Maybe you think you'll get to transform into ten different final boss forms, each more hideous and larger than the last. Maybe a few battlefield shifts thrown in for flavor, right? Oh, or maybe you plan to torment me with visions of hopelessness . . . realms of nightmares . . . all the things that will force me to look deep inside myself." I stepped closer, dead-eyed. "This isn't about me at all. This is your own stupid, self-serving little pageant to show that you're a strong, powerful bad guy who knows how to put on a final encounter." I smiled at the way he began drifting back, shriveling in on himself in discomfort. "Well, fuck you. This isn't a boss battle, and it sure as hell isn't a game. This is where a self-obsessed, lonely *loser* dies."

For a few seconds, it seemed that my monologue had truly broken him. His mask slithered with insectoid movement, but that was it. The rest of him was utterly still, frozen in what I took to be shell shock. Not a huge surprise, really. He'd surely been hyping this moment up for trillions and trillions of years, itching for the release of a gigantic, bombastic fight to serve as the climax of his little combat sim.

Fuck that.

When he finally spoke, his voice was thin and wounded. "You know, Dak, from the right perspective . . . everything's a game."

He then snapped his fingers, and suddenly the entire sphere filled with long, interlocking filaments of flesh, much like a disordered spider's web. The muscle fibers and intestinal cords bound together, blocking off my view of the central stalk and stranding me in a small subchamber with the Unmade. All around me, I heard and felt the slithering of the flesh as it continued to solidify into a tunnel network.

At the same time, a fresh message appeared in my HUD:

Chok'tal Death Timer: 9:59

Shit.

Thinking fast, I sprouted the wings of Soaring Death and buffeted myself backward, intent on tracing a roughly direct path to the stalk. The Unmade zipped after me, but a fingertip-size blast of Shock and Awe was enough to evaporate his body—and a wide swath of tissue around it.

I knew it wouldn't be the end, though. I'd already vaporized him once, and from what I'd gleaned, his body wasn't *really* the core of his identity. That damned stalk was. It seemed likely that no matter how much

I harmed his physical avatar, he would continue regenerating himself, rejoining the fight.

This theory proved correct when, twenty or so meters down the twisting, enclosing passage, my wings collided with something. I spiraled off course and slammed into a wall, twisting around to find the Unmade hovering a few meters away.

"Where are you going?" he asked, more curious than taunting. "You seem to be in some kind of rush . . . "

Rather than answering in words, I used Overclock to spring myself off the wall and strike his head with a backswing. The mask and skull crumpled beneath my blow, but he was quick to float a short distance away and repair himself as though nothing had happened.

"All that wasteful energy use," the Unmade said in a patronizing tone, "and no way to regenerate it."

Much as I despised the bastard, he had a point here. I couldn't afford to keep using high-cost powers and duking it out in combat. My goal was the stalk. Nothing else mattered.

More to the point, I refused to take part in the Unmade's little drama. He wanted nothing more than an eternal, pointless war, and I had no doubts that if he succeeded in trapping me here, he'd keep me alive for that very reason . . . no matter how much I begged for death. In that sense, it was in his best interest to tire me out, distract me, and try to lure me into a direct confrontation, further wasting what little time he'd granted me. Conversely, that meant it was in *my* best interest to ignore his taunts and run like my head was on fire.

Nine oh two . . .

I whirled around and took off down the passage, doing my best to pump my wings despite the tunnel sealing on all sides. Even as I glided over the spongy, bleeding floor and scraped through tight sphincters, the flesh continued to constrict. Before long, I was narrowly dodging sets of teeth and bones that formed before my very eyes. A set of narrow, riblike slats forced me to spin to one side and tuck my wings at the last moment—and still managed to shear off the edges of one wing.

Eight thirty-four . . .

Gritting my teeth, I dispelled the wings and kept bolting toward the approximate center of the madness. It wasn't too hard, considering the presence of skull-splitting energy emanating from one direction in particular. What *was* hard, though, was navigating the increasingly twisty passages. I found myself scrambling up waterfalls of blood and crawling down fleshy throats packed with grasping tongues, calling on every upgrade in the book to keep me moving.

Seven twenty-eight . . .

My four arms ripped at the claws that came jutting from narrow canyons. Nocturnal guided my feet in lightless, growling stomachs. Shock and Awe carved black passages into sheets of solid keratin and marrow. Pestilence kept the hordes of mindless, howling abominations off my back.

Before long, I was dazed and shaky, sprinting through the collapsing nightmare with nothing but thoughts of *survival* pumping through my skull. Constant use of my upgrades had stripped the fat, muscle, and even connective tissue from my legs. My arms were little more than knots of dried meat. My organs cried out from the constant strain.

And worst of all, the timer was bleeding out.

Five forty-five . . .

All around me, the Unmade screeched and resisted. No matter how much I slashed through, climbed over, or blasted aside, more continued to come. Through my flickering vision, I noted the space's continual warping. Just like the poor fuckers who'd tried to storm the Unmade's citadel from outside, I felt I was continually receding from the goal, being forced back by onrushing tides of skin and guts.

"Give up on this quest, Dak," the Unmade said, his voice drifting through the yawning pores of the walls. "You've come all this way . . . I believe I deserve a proper challenge. The hero *must* confront the villain, after all. It's in every proper story, across all universes, all times . . . Stand and fight."

"Fuck off!" I screamed back.

"Stop running and just play the game. You will not escape."

I resented that notion, but second by second, it appeared more likely as the outcome of all this. Ahead of me was a wall of gnashing fangs and rippling bladders. No matter how much I whacked it or blasted it with Shock and Awe—which was now too expensive to use, given my lack of energy to regrow my body—it remained just as dense and impassable as before.

Four seventeen . . .

I eased back, breathing hard, staggering. Maybe this *was* the end of the road. The part of the story where I turned my back on everything I believed and accepted the Unmade's tainted mercy. It seemed appealing. Fated, even.

Just as I was beginning to seriously contemplate dropping my hammer and giving in to the whirling voices in my head, however, something far more convincing—and deafening—filled the passages.

I turned around just in time to see the Sun Swallower come barreling through a patch of flesh, all eyes and teeth and feelers, its maw stretched wide to swallow me whole. All I could do was stagger back as the gargantuan abomination bore down on me, coming closer, closer, ripping up the floor, spraying me with blood, shrieking . . .

Then stopping.

I stood there, totally aghast, as the Sun Swallower slid to a halt just five paces from me. It was so monstrous that I couldn't pinpoint where to look on its face, which was generally a mass of terrible things that had no business being sandwiched together. It was so large it had chewed through the ceiling of this chamber and into those above it.

I was even more stunned when a small, dark figure appeared atop the beast's head. They lifted a hand and . . . waved?

"Up here!" Rogaji called, whistling. "And make it snappy! I'm on a goddamn timer, and I'd bet my last bottle of champagne you are, too!"

26

Shocked as I was, I wasted no time sprouting those energy-inefficient wings, soaring up to her, and landing on quivering legs just behind an infected horn.

"The fuck is this?" I panted.

"I tamed it," she said with a proud smile, patting a random section of cracked chitin. "I think I'll name it when we get out of here."

"Rogaji, this is a goddamn corrupted shaman. You can't just—"

"Do we want to kill the Unmade or sit around on this thing's head and let the timer take us out?"

"Fair enough," I said, shrugging. "We need to breach the central stalk. Y'know, that thing that was glowing. It's the source of his power."

"*Ooh*, a final challenge for the final boss!"

"This isn't a game." Thinking back on the Unmade's thoroughly insane rant, however, I shook my head. "Fuck it. Take us there."

She smirked at me and settled in behind an ear, where she seemed to have gathered a pair of "reins"—also known as neural fibers she'd ripped out of its head. "Knew you'd come around, Dak. Now, settle in and hold on! We're going to the core!"

Given the thing's colossal size, I didn't think there was any need for that warning. I was wrong. The Sun Swallower rocketed forward as though trying to break the sound barrier, sending a finger-laden ceiling straight toward my head. I ducked into a crevice of fungus-infested plates at the last moment, and when the thing's enormous head raked the ceiling, every one of those bony fingers exploded in a spray of bone and blood—all over me.

Then we were racing through the Unmade's innards, the walls ripping and splitting above me, my clothes constantly spattered in deluges of fluids that came too fast for me to analyze. Probably for the best, all things considered. Rogaji's mad cries of adrenaline were the only things keeping me conscious. Despite the obvious excitement of it all, my mind was flitting in and out. My body was failing. I wished, against all logic, that I'd taken the cannibalism upgrade to restore my energy.

Three oh one . . .

Darkness clouded my vision, broken only when I heard Rogaji's wild shout.

Sitting up, I learned what she was so worked up over.

The Sun Swallower had somehow broken through the far side of the Unmade's world of flesh. On paper, that sounds good. Miraculous, even. In reality, however . . . not so much.

You see, the far side wasn't a nice, grass-laden patch of earth right in front of the stalk I needed to reach. Instead, it was a void. A swirling, dark void of such unbelievable cold my joints began to ache within seconds. It was as though we'd broken through the outer wall of a cliff, only to face the yawning valley below.

This being the case, we were currently plummeting downward, racing to the roiling darkness that filled the bottom of this new pit. Whipping air bit at my eyes and screamed in my ears, and it took every drop of my wherewithal to look up and spot the objective.

The central stalk hung in the very center of the void, no more than a hundred meters away. Its eerie red light painted the inner walls of the new sphere, exposing the ripples of frantic motion and cancerous growth. Now, however, I also spotted something new. There was a distinctive, blazing bulge about two-thirds of the way up the stalk. Some kind of center.

My target.

"Rogaji," I shouted through my hoarse, blood-drenched throat, "I'm heading in!"

She didn't seem to hear me. She was too busy pulling back on her bio-mechanical reins, hollering in what could've been fright or utter entertainment. In either case, there was no time to check in with our pilot . . . and certainly no time for *anything* else.

Two twenty-five . . .

I drew a deep breath, braced for the upcoming hit to my pain receptors, and triggered Soaring Death's wings once more.

Everything from my throat to my bowels burned, probably brought on by the severe cost of growing these new appendages—again. Whatever fat I had left was channeled into those wings as I launched myself off the Sun Swallower and into the great, looming darkness below. With a yelp of sheer torment, I angled the wings and sent myself ripping skyward. Or, well, what would've been the sky. Here, the only thing that faced me was a mass of scar tissue posing as a ceiling.

Before I could orient myself, and just as the frost began eating at the tips of the wings, I caught sight of a nightmare I'd hoped to forget. An enormous, mutant arachnid was lumbering over the walls, coiling its legs in preparation to—

It moved faster than I'd expected. With one heroic launch, the Unmade's spider form tore past me in a storm of legs and pincers and tendrils, catching the edge of my wing midspin. Pain tore through my shoulder, and it took all my determination to continue banking toward that luminous stalk. I couldn't afford to fight now. Couldn't afford to take my chances with that *thing*.

Glancing down, I saw Rogaji and the Sun Swallower tearing through the floor, vanishing into some new and festering layer of the abyss. The help had been welcome, but I couldn't rely on it again. Not if I wanted to bring an end to this here and now.

One forty-six . . .

I cut left as the Unmade leaped across the chasm once more, but this time I wasn't fast enough to avoid the barbs of its teeth ripping through my right foot. I cried out and spun, pulling my leg in just long enough to note that the fucker had, in fact, torn off everything below the knee.

This was a problem. Not because I needed intact legs right now, but because my stupid body would continue to regenerate so long as I was alive. Translation? It would keep sucking up Anima, regardless of how much I actually needed to use it.

Still, the central stalk was close now. *So* close. Just ten more meters, then five, then three, its mottled, slithering surface coming toward me . . .

Something sharp and serrated tore into my left leg. I screamed, lurching mid–wing pump, my arms helplessly straining toward the stalk's churning sacs. When I glanced back, I wished I hadn't.

The Unmade loomed like a mad god, his mutant, infantile face grinning with sick pleasure. Their pincers were firmly clasped around my thigh, ripping at the skin.

"Oh, fuck *off*," I grunted, swinging my hammer downward—and straight into my kneecap.

I screeched as the leg completely snapped, the remnants of my femur giving a subtle *pwop* as it slid from the stringy meat of my thigh. My lower half slid into the Unmade's teeth, and my upper half launched. Then I was free, leaking blood, madly beating my wings to clear the final distance.

One twenty-eight...

My hands collided with the wet, syrupy exterior of the stalk, quickly followed by my face, given the speed with which I impacted. A brief look downward showed me that the Unmade was climbing fast on my heels... and with my leg flopping from its teeth.

Shaking my head at the sheer stupidity of the plan, I turned around and swapped out the wings for my additional Tumorous Growth arms. My new, extra arms took hold of the stalk and began climbing toward the main bulge, fistful by fistful, while my original arms took hold of the Sparkseed hammer and angled it down as a weak show of defense.

It didn't mean much in the face of the Unmade, which was truly a hideous face to behold. The fur-laden legs and spines and tails lashed madly, morphing by the second as the Unmade drew from the stalk's overwhelming power. Even now, I could see the momentary threads of power that ran from its engorged egg sac to the stalk itself. The eyes set in its misshapen face were ablaze with glee.

"Come down, Dak," it called in broken tones. "Let's play the game, you and I..."

I didn't have long before the last of my strength left me, but at that moment, I felt the colossal accumulation of the stalk's center. That pushed me into desperation mode. Keeping the hammer between us, I sank one of my Tumorous Grasp arms into the stalk, then used the other to dig frantically into the pulpy knot. Handful by handful, I sensed the energy pouring forth. The defilement. The fear. The corruption that had spread for countless eons.

Fifty-seven...

The Unmade jabbed at me with legs and tendrils, but each assault was beaten back by the hammer. Still, they took their toll. My strength was weakening. My fingers were numb and frostbitten. Every fiber of my body was on the verge of catastrophic failure.

Just a few more handfuls...

The energy burned my extra arm, scalding it to the point of blisters, but I kept digging. It was close. Right *there.* Glancing up, I saw the light spilling out of its patchy surface. If I could just—

"All right, enough of this," the Unmade cooed.

Before I could look down, a forest of long, crablike tendrils rocketed upward and speared me through the torso. I cried out, but it made no difference. The Unmade lifted me away from the knot, dangling me over the void.

Forty-eight . . .

The Anima toll was immense. The flesh struggled to reform around my bounds, but there was no way. No hope. Consciousness faded in, faded out. My skin was a sheet of blood.

"There, there," the Unmade said, turning me around so I faced my failed objective. It hung on the stalk like an oversize predator, the glowing knot perched just above it and bleeding its precious energy. "You came quite a long way, Dak, but you've disappointed me."

Breathing around the tendril speared through my throat, I recalled the Tumorous Grasp arms and simply stared at the knot of energy. I really *had* come close. When I focused through the blood and thumping pain, I could see my exact target lurking inside its fleshy confines.

To be precise, I saw the body of a small child furled into the fetal position, almost as though the energy itself were its womb.

"There I am," the Unmade whispered, elongating its warped, juvenile face to stretch toward me. The haunting visage came within a meter of my own head, then stopped. The lips spread wide. "Did you *really* think you could escape from me? You're not the first to think you understand the darkness of the cosmos. But it's all right. I have eternity to reteach you. We'll be together."

A wet, choking laugh slipped out. "You don't even know who I am."

"A human. Just like all the others."

"No . . . before that."

A glimmer of unease passed through the Unmade's milky eyes. "And what *were* you?"

"A beja," I whispered, eyes tracking the motes of light that came streaming from the ruptured stalk. "I'm sorry . . . for what happened to you."

That unease was now replaced by darkness. By rage. "You're lying."

"I wish. You don't even know your own mother, do you?"

"You can't—"

I grinned, losing myself in the euphoria of pain. "Your mother gave . . . everything . . . to try to help you. Do you remember her? Her face?"

"Be *silent*."

"She sacrificed her own rebirth to find you . . . to help you," I choked, wincing as the Unmade redoubled the force of the tendrils driving through my guts. "And do you know her name? When she was reborn?"

"Shut up!"

"Her name . . . was Akasha," I sputtered, "and she was wonderful. You killed her. You and your mad . . . quest. Do you remember ripping her open? Torturing her?"

The Unmade's face, in spite of its arachnid design, began crinkling with fear. True, visceral fear. "It's . . . it's not true."

"Look at what you've made," I said, hacking out a wad of lung tissue. "She just wanted to love you. And you destroyed her. Isn't . . . that right, *Tarkal*?"

At that instant, something shifted—and not in the way I'd hoped. You see, throughout my little exchange, I'd been telekinetically guiding the hammer toward the stalk, carefully sliding through the rungs of flesh and nubs of flabby veins. Sure, I wanted to rub my knowledge in the Unmade's face, but I *mainly* wanted to distract him long enough to destroy the body within the stalk. That plan had been going swimmingly . . . until I took a half second peek at my progress.

The Unmade noticed.

Nine . . .

In a snap of motion and legs, the Unmade's tendrils exploded outward and seized the hammer. It was just three paces from the body.

"It doesn't matter who I am," he boomed, "or what you are, or what any of this is. We will *make* a new reality. I'll remake *you*, if I must."

Six . . .

Despite myself, a smile emerged. I stared directly into the Unmade's beady, wrath-clouded eyes, feeling the chaos, the sorrow, the long years of torment they'd endured in this hellish world.

What had they done to deserve such a fate? Nothing. Nothing but having the karma to be born into the Suharkayan Empire. From that instant on, they'd been thrown into the blender of fate, punished and abused and even butchered due to the whims of forces and minds beyond their own control. They'd been changed from a child to a monster.

From that angle, I realized it could've been anybody. Any being born in that particular slice of space and time would've been turned into *this*. It was simply the flow of cause and effect. The unfortunate end result of a chain of events that stretched so far into history there was no discernible cause. As much as I *wanted* to hate them, to resent them for everything they'd done and taken from me, it was impossible. At their core, they were still a child. A lost, lonely child who'd been forced to make his own games to avoid insanity.

Now, as I looked deeper into those grim eyes, I truly saw the boy he'd once been. The innocence that had resided there before it was beaten and stabbed out of him. I even saw his terror, his shared recognition of how absurd it was for everything to have turned out this way.

Like me, he was a being caught in an infinite machine of killing and defiling. He could no more change his nature than I could rip out the chok'tal.

And somehow . . . in a way I couldn't comprehend with any shred of my logical brain, which was shutting down by degrees . . . I *loved* them. I truly, deeply loved them. I loved the beauty in their tragedy. The endless, ceaseless web of changes that had created them out of the primal flux of existence. He and I were brothers in that process. Seeds growing according to our own nature.

One . . .

"It's been . . . a good game," I whispered, lending my final burst of conscious power to pushing the hammer toward the stalk.

The Unmade's eyes crinkled in confusion . . . and then there was only Shock and Awe.

I pushed the upgrade into every cell of my body. Every morsel of DNA, every nugget of tissue, every nook and cranny in every bone. For the briefest of instants, too fast to be tracked by any supercomputer, I felt a blossom of warmth in my core. Then I was gone. Scattered.

Sort of.

My consciousness resided in the vast, blinding light of the explosion, rippling out to the farthest reaches of spacetime, tasting the dark matter at the birth of creation, everywhere and nowhere in the same instant. I felt a sense of stretching, then tearing, and suddenly I viewed the world from ten trillion eyes, a kaleidoscopic whirl that would've puzzled my mind if indeed there *was* any mind present. But there wasn't. All was stillness. Radiance. Eternity.

There was no *me*, only witnessing. The déjà vu of the Wellspring encounter returned. I was nothing but a silent, empty watcher for the happenings of reality. I could feel the great wheel spinning, pulling me apart and reassembling me and dragging me toward the reaches of my fated hell.

Only . . . I didn't go anywhere. Vision condensed, localizing itself in the same sphere where I'd detonated my body. All I saw was the light. The long, infinite light of the Source, stretching up into unknown heavens and down into unseen hells. There, tucked within the safety of that light, was my hammer. What *had* been my hammer, anyway, back when there was a me to own it.

Now there was no me, no here, no there. I watched, thoughtless and void, as the hammer burned away the form of the child that had previously nested there. A new light pulsed out of the weapon. It seared away the Sparkseed, brightening that reddish glow and purging its influence from the entire structure. Soon there was only blinding, pure light, emerging in great torrents that deconstructed the sphere and erased every drop of its corruption.

Suddenly there was no confusion. Only joy. It didn't matter where I ended up. It didn't matter if I was tortured for ten quadrillion years. I held on to that joy, cherishing it, spreading it, willing it to flow to the ten directions and enlighten all beings in all worlds.

My work here was done.

Then, from the vast light of eternity, a voice emerged. "YOUR WORK HERE IS NOT DONE."

27

The instant I heard—or perhaps, merely cognized—these words, every-thing changed. *Everything.* It wasn't as though I was knocked uncon-scious, woken up elsewhere, and brought back up to speed. No, I was quite literally teleported to an entirely new situation before I had a moment's time to realize who or what I was.

I stood in a small, white room decorated with frilly golden trim. There was no furniture, and the only distinguishing feature was a door engraved with . . . a mandala? Looking closer, I noted that it was *my* mandala.

"Hello?" I called. My voice came out deeper, more resonant. Weird.

This led me to look down, at which point I realized I no longer had my old body. Every centimeter of me glowed with the vibrant, living texture of Sparkseed, very much reminiscent of the form I'd possessed when using Mind Cascade. The sight should've scared me, but it didn't. In fact, there wasn't a drop of fear in me.

I felt . . . free. Easygoing. The more I leaned into that whole-body feeling, the more it grew. Soon my whole body felt like a diffuse cloud of bliss, crackling and fizzling all over with pure euphoria. I had vague memories of the pain I'd felt during the fight, but they were suspiciously absent here. Deeper than even that, I sensed the loss of a primordial, vengeful energy that had been burning inside me from the moment I accepted the chok'tal. The background hum of its demands had subsided to a soft, pleasant hum.

Was I in heaven? It seemed likely, given the tangible existence of hell realms. A thrill went through me at the idea—not so much in regard to the notion of earning an afterlife in heaven, but more because it meant this was all over. I'd *won.* That last-minute, balls-to-the-wall gambit had actually paid off. The Unmade had been nullified through love, and all was right in the world.

But . . . that still left me with questions. What the hell was I supposed to *do* in heaven? Who was the head honcho? Would I get in trouble for ending my big fight with a nuclear cascade? Was Rogaji all right? What about Akasha?

Only one way to get my answers.

Pulling in the breath of a man who's dodged death one too many times, I went to the door and warily opened it. The light that spilled through the door frame was strong enough to nearly blind me. I eased it shut, but as I did so, I picked up on a faint, ethereal chime. Interesting. After a few muttered curses and a good squint, I opened it once again.

This time, the light was bearable. The sight itself was a bit more overwhelming.

Rather than a hallway or a stairwell or even a stoop, my door opened up to . . . empty space. This is because I was situated about three-quarters up the interior of the very same sphere I'd just invaded. Now, before you start yelling about this being a trick ending or some sort of implanted hallucination—no. This was very much real, but it was a far cry from the sphere's prior form.

The central column was, as I'd seen in my Wellspring vision, about as bright and strong as the twin beams of a pulsar. It saturated the entire space with motes and bridges and struts of golden light, its movements so plainly *alive* that they caught my breath in my throat.

On another note, I wasn't breathing. So there's that.

Anyway, back to this new heaven. It now resembled the interior of some vast gigacolony, much like the inner dwelling of a Dyson sphere. The inner walls, a jigsaw of shifting golden segments, flowed about and fluttered softly with warm currents. Scattered along and within those walls were hundreds of thousands of beings, many of them golden like me, but others as plain and human as anybody you'd find walking Halcium Beta.

Those of my nature had no need to walk; they drifted and lazed through the air, pirouetting among the fleshier inhabitants forced to use bridges and floating cubes of pure light for mobility.

Down at the bottom of the sphere, which I judged to be roughly ten kilometers below, there was a full-fledged city. Buildings of pure light rose among gleaming, diamond-frosted trees and vibrant gardens of every color, and even at this height I could see the bobbing forms of countless beings wandering the multitiered streets. Laughter and songs floated up to greet me.

The entire thing was *incredible*, but I still found my attention glued to that central column. Inside its brilliance, phantom hands and eyes materialized and dissolved, flowing through the structure like quantum interactions that persisted long enough for the naked eye.

"Hot damn," I whispered, leaning against the door frame. "That crazy Wellspring did it."

The instant I said this, I sensed a presence taking shape behind me. I was more perplexed than alarmed by this newfound detection ability.

"Yes?" I asked.

"Purifier," the arrival said, their voice androgynous and tender. I turned to find what I can only describe as an emanation of pure energy—a pulsing, diamond-shaped vortex of golden light. "We wish to speak with you regarding your new incarnation."

I smiled at it. "Are you the Wellspring?"

"Yes and no," it said. "We are the collective voice of those within the Wellspring."

"Oh. So, the Wellspring."

"You may think of us as a welcoming committee." It paused. "Did you appreciate this joke?"

"I certainly did." I stared back out at the sphere's shining expanse. "So, it worked? I destroyed the Unmade with love, and you were able to, uh . . . stabilize the dimension or whatever?"

"Your valiance was unmatched. Thanks to your efforts, we were able to reestablish our dominion over the Source energy. As a result, we have shaped this dimension to create a pure abode for all beings."

"Meaning?"

"You might consider this a form of training ground," the Wellspring explained. "Those with the requisite karmic seeds will be born here, allowing them to learn from our wisdom and cultivate pure minds without the dangers of physical reality."

"So . . . it's an interdimensional monastery."

"You may conceive of it that way, yes."

I nodded, rather impressed with myself. "What about my body?"

"As you may be aware, you underwent the death process in the course of your encounter."

"Yeah, I'm fairly aware."

Though it may have been my overactive, newly gained senses, I swore the Wellspring wasn't too pleased with my snark. "At the moment of death, your mind was spontaneously liberated by the ripening of your karma. Your act of pure compassion was sufficient to ground you in this dimension."

I nodded along but didn't feel as though I'd parsed most of that. "Can you dumb it down?"

The Wellspring flared with what I assume was a sigh. "You succeeded in pure killing, which prevented your mindstream from being devoured by the defiled realms. You stepped beyond karma. Beyond fate. We did not believe it would be possible, but you seem to have drawn from the Source directly. We provided this place for your rebirth, and you accepted it."

"I didn't accept anything!"

"You may not remember, but it was done. You should be proud of this form."

I glanced down at my golden flesh. "What exactly is it?"

"That of a Wayfarer."

"A *Wayfarer*?" I sputtered. "Me? You're sure you picked the right guy?"

"The Wellspring cannot create Wayfarers," it said. "It can merely guide Wayfarers toward their true home."

"Then that means . . . "

"You became a Wayfarer through your own merits," the Wellspring finished.

"Nice," I said, quite satisfied with that news. "So, can I manifest myself anywhere? Grow ten legs and sixty heads?"

The Wellspring's annoyance reached me loud and clear. "You are not yet a Radiant Wayfarer . . . only a Wayfarer. You have seen the laws of reality, but you are little more than a newborn in your current state. To actualize and employ the full power of the Absolute, you will need to train. To become what you cannot imagine."

I sighed. "All right, but that can start tomorrow. I need a day off." Looking out across the golden metropolis, I thought back to that frantic final confrontation. "Just, uh, to make sure—"

"The chok'tal is gone," the Wellspring said, giving me a sweet dose of relief. "In fact, all chok'tals have been rendered inert. We have starved them of energy."

"That's . . . good. What about the Unmade?"

"His mindstream has been purified."

"Meaning?"

"You lack the language to understand it."

Fair play, I supposed. "And . . . what about his victims?"

The Wellspring hovered around me, sensing my discomfort. "You are wondering what has become of the minds within the Unmade's clutches. Within his creations."

"Yeah. I, uh, had a good friend in there."

"Many were reborn in the hells, given their karmic seeds," the Wellspring said. "But we suspect you are inquiring about Jekra Modri."

"That's the one. Let me guess . . . worst of the worst dimension?" Fresh memories, fresh names, came spilling into my head. "What about the other Purifier, Rogaji? Or Akasha? Or—"

A brief sizzle of light, probably equating amusement, bled off the Wellspring. "We would like to show you what you seek, Purifier."

The Wellspring spent approximately twenty minutes trying to convince me that I could, in fact, fly. This didn't take the form of a rational discussion, but rather the Wellspring hovering over the enormous drop just outside my new front door, alternating between chastising and taunting me.

When I finally worked up the courage to take the plunge—maybe not the best term, all things considered—I found myself hovering in empty space, looking down on the city with unusual calmness. There was no vertigo, no sense of losing control. My body effortlessly hovered there in defiance of ordinary physics.

"There," the Wellspring said. "You've just learned to use your first gift."

I followed it down at breakneck speeds, marveling at the sheer ease of navigating a world without gravity. Well, okay, there *was* gravity—but it didn't apply to me. I sailed under bridges and over long, sapling-covered roads, feeling mighty privileged in comparison to the poor rubes who needed to use things like legs.

While flying was fun and all, it wasn't what I really wanted or needed at that moment. No amount of freewheeling aerial stunts could make up for the knowledge of what had happened to my friends, regardless of their actual fates. Even if the truth was terrible, I needed to know it.

This being the case, I let the Wellspring guide me lower, and lower, and lower, eventually skimming the busy streets that had once seemed like an ant colony. Much to my surprise, life was moving at a fairly normal clip. It wasn't a usual city, of course, full of hustling and bustling and bargaining. No, this city was more like opening day at a new amusement park. People milled about, inspecting the scenery, tugging each other this way and that. Most were human, or at least humanoid, though I did spot a few aliens in the mix.

The Wellspring took me down a few alleys, then to a small door at the bottom of a stairwell. In the physical world, such a spot would've seemed shady, if not downright criminal—but not here. Its underground appearance was offset by rows of vibrant flowers scaling the golden walls.

"What's this?" I asked, gesturing to the door. "Some kind of bar?"

"Yes," the Wellspring said, much to my surprise. "Some beings wish to consume beverages that alter their consciousness."

"Wait. You built a utopian dimension and people can *still* get loaded?"

"We are not a realm of subservience, but of choice. Even unskillful choices must be respected."

"Point taken. Are you buying drinks?"

The Wellspring really didn't care for my ongoing commentary. Without a word of reply, its energetic core turned and nudged the door open.

The clamor that spilled forth was enough to assure me that, true to the Wellspring's answer, there was rough-and-tumble enjoyment to be found in this new world. Mugs were clinking, people were singing, chairs were scraping over tiles.

When I stepped inside, a few of the patrons quieted. I initially thought they'd shut up due to the presence of the overseer—that is, the giant, floating tuft of pure power—but I was quickly disabused of that notion. All eyes were on *me*.

There had to be a hundred or more people crowded in that dingy space, though unlike most bars, the stench of hard drinking was covered by floral tones. They all sat on long benches or with feet dangling from the rafters, half with their stares glazed over from boozing. I didn't recognize most of them, but that didn't seem to matter. They sure knew me.

"King Purifier!" they all shouted in unison, raising their cups and bashing them together.

I just looked out on the sea of strange faces, completely bemused. Then I noticed the patrons' hard, corded muscles and scarred features. Soldiers—or, at least, people who'd been turned into soldiers. These had to be the remnants of the Unmade's victims. The ones who'd just spent immeasurable time locked up inside his mental universe.

I smiled back at the warm reception, even cheering when someone pressed a mug of cold *something* into my hands, but . . .

Where was Modri?

That question was answered no less than three seconds later, when a cloth partition leading to the back of the bar swung open and revealed two figures.

One was Rogaji, who emerged with no fewer than five cups gathered against her chest. She didn't seem to see me, as she was too busy grumbling and sipping chaotically at the drinks she couldn't keep from spilling.

The other was a tall, rugged man with a shaved head and scars all over. He wouldn't have looked out of place or even remarkable, given the bar's clientele, if not for a small twinkle in the back of my mind. He had a face I'd seen before. But where?

Then it hit me.

Jekra goddamn Modri.

The two of them stopped short about halfway into the room, eyes meeting mine in a scene that would have any cinema buff whooping with ecstasy. All three of us pulled on broad, shit-eating grins and rushed inward.

"Why the hell didn't anyone tell me he was here?" Rogaji shouted, fixing the crowd with a brief yet nasty look. Then her face dissolved into its usual self-satisfied mask, and she looked at me with warmth I hadn't expected. "You did it, huh? You really did it."

I patted my golden body down, smirking. "And all I got was this stupid body of light."

Modri, wasting no time, clapped a meaty hand on my shoulder. "Nice to meet you, kid. Name's Jekra Modri."

Shaking my head, I put my own, decidedly less meaty hand on Modri's shoulder. "Name's Dak Korasa."

Rogaji sipped the froth of her drink. "So, are you two dating?"

Modri and I faced her in tandem and barked, "Hell no!"

"Well, excuse *me*," she said, harrumphing. "You sure do look chummy."

I rolled my eyes. "So, what happened to you two?"

They exchanged a look that told me they'd already discussed the question. "We're not quite sure," Rogaji said. "One minute I was riding the Sun Swallower . . . and the next, *poof*. New body, new world. New beer."

"Yeah, she had it easy," Modri grumbled, plucking one of the mugs from Rogaji's tenuous grasp. "It was all dark, dark, dark . . . then no more dark. Just sort of, uh, woke up here. Not complainin' about that, of course."

"Not bad," I said, nodding. "Can you leave?"

"Leave what?"

"This universe. You sure your body isn't just to move around here? For all we know, you might turn to dust the second you step out into physical space."

"Aw, shit," Modri said. "Just when I thought I was all done with existential crises . . . "

I smiled warmly at them both. "It's good to see you. To know you made it."

"Made it?" Modri asked. "Purifier, you knocked this shit outta the park. Truth be told, nobody thought you'd, uh, actually do it. But it's nice to be surprised sometimes." He winked at me. "And from a goddamn useless civvy, no less."

I crossed my arms. "Thanks. It means the world . . . "

"I'm a tad disappointed you didn't let me cinch the kill," Rogaji said, slurping down her own drink, "but in fairness, I also didn't know that whoever had that honor might be subject to creating another nightmare world, trapped in their own sins. So, all in all, a net win." She shrugged. "The things you learn from interdimensional beings of light."

"So, what's next for you two?" I asked.

Modri groaned. "Figurin' out how to exist in interdimensional space, I guess."

Rogaji nodded in approval at that answer. "I, for one, would like to find out if I'm still capable of dividing my consciousness among two hundred bodies."

"Worthy goals," I said.

"It's not as though there's much else to do right now, given our lack of connection to the physical universe." Rogaji shrugged. "What about yourself, *King* Purifier?"

I grinned. "I've got someone I need to see."

The Wellspring took me to what seemed to be one edge of the pocket universe: a broad, flat plateau crisscrossed by streams that became waterfalls at the rise's edge. Below us was an infinite mist sparkling with golden light. Farther out, however, on what would've been the horizon in the physical universe, mist cascaded and coiled, hinting at what might lie beyond its shifting curtain.

"What's that?" I asked. "Some sort of in-development neighborhood you plan to add?"

"No," the Wellspring said. "This is a liminal boundary. Someday—someday soon, no less—it will serve as a branching point to another universe. Another layer of reality. Right now, however, it is sealed so we might regain our strength in solitude."

"Sort of like how the Unmade had portals to other worlds."

"The very same. This universe is not linked to space and time, yet it can be. It *will* be. Once, we were able to spread our wisdom to countless dimensions. We hope we will be able to resume this process."

"Very noble. But what does this have to do with what I'm looking for?"

The Wellspring emitted a thin beam of light, which it then used to denote the wall of mist before us. "It is not easy to locate neighboring worlds and establish links to them. Given your skills, however, we believe you might be well suited to such a task."

"Really using the name *Wayfarer* literally, huh?"

"It is the source of that title. A holy duty granted to those with pure vision."

"I thought you said I'm not ready to be a full-blown Wayfarer. A Radiant one or whatever."

The Wellspring retracted its beam and faced me. "You are not. However, this is an excellent time to hone your skills."

"All right, but it still doesn't explain—"

"We are reaching the point," the Wellspring interrupted. "You seek the Cobalt Seer. She has taken birth in one of the many worlds."

"Which one?" I practically shouted, more out of excitement than frustration.

"We do not know. What is clear, however, is that she seeks one who is also dear to her."

"Her daughter," I said, thinking back to the miscarriage I'd witnessed in the Godmaker. "How do you know that?"

"Because she has called out to us. Appealed for our aid."

"So . . . she's out of the hell dimensions?"

"We cannot say. But we have heard her, Purifier. Her voice is dim, yet it has been heard."

I nodded, trying to take it all in. "You really think I can locate her if I focus hard enough?"

"You are a Wayfarer. All things are possible."

"I'm still getting used to that."

"Yes, you are," the Wellspring said, its tone somewhat darker now. "For this reason, Purifier, we counsel you to remain here and continue your practice for a time. If you seek her out now, you risk falling back into defilement."

"But . . . if she's out there—"

"She may not possess the same form in which you knew her. She may be an animal, a demon, a creature beyond your comprehension."

"It doesn't matter."

The Wellspring shivered with something like uncertainty. "Purifier, we are telling you this for the benefit of your own mind, as well as the minds of all beings. You are urged to temporarily set aside this quest and continue on your path. There is a war you cannot perceive, and it still rages. This universe, as it so happens, is merely the newest front line. You are needed."

"Then you *definitely* need Akasha. She's stronger than me."

"Purifier—"

I shook my head. "I appreciate the advice, but I need to find her. She deserves to be here. To help you."

"Even if she resides in a world beyond your deepest fears?"

"Even if."

The Wellspring studied me for a long while, floating back and forth in indecision. "Very well. We cannot force you to remain. Do as your heart instructs, Purifier, but remember your merit. You may not be able to return here without the proper guidance."

Shortly thereafter, the Wellspring's avatar drifted off and left me standing on that misty precipice. I stared out at the veil, wishing I could part it here and now. That I could see Akasha, and hold her, and assure her that things would be all right. Still, there was an unshakable joy within me. A sense that, even if it took eternity, I would locate her. I would bring her back.

I knelt down on the golden stone and stared out at the mist, trying to join my mind with it as I'd done to other objects in the past. It was dense, almost impenetrable, but slowly I found and exploited the cracks. Ripples of energy spun off the mist and pushed through me. Whispers of dead worlds and dead places arose, and I faced them all with neutrality, with the even and cutting gaze of a Wayfarer.

All I needed was one wisp . . . one hint of her presence.

Hours passed, the universe's day-night cycle slipping toward its darkest point, and yet I persisted. Thousands of realms and dimensions drifted past by like flotsam in a river, each of them teeming with life, with minds and hearts crying out for deliverance.

I wanted to help them—I *would* help them—but at that moment, I was as focused as a quad-crystal laser. My mind swam in and out of the currents of consciousness, seeking, grasping, ever straining toward even the faintest indication of her. Still, there was nothing. Just the buzz of endless universes going about their days, blind to my own desires.

After a long, long while, when my knees ached and silence pervaded, I let out a breath and prepared to stand. Maybe tomorrow. Maybe the next day. Maybe even next century, if indeed Wayfarers lived that long.

At that very instant of rising, however, a whisper trickled out of the mist.

It landed softly at the forefront of my awareness, almost like a gift. A kiss across time and space.

I'm here, Dak.

ABOUT THE AUTHOR

Curator Omega is an interdimensional traveler, archivist, and occasional author from the deep reaches of the void. He is best known for curating tales from the Cutthroat Cosmos, including the Purifier series. In his free time, he enjoys sailing in the hearts of dead stars and studying cookie recipes from extinct empires. He resides in the quantum flux right behind you.

Podium
DISCOVER
STORIES UNBOUND
PodiumAudio.com